One Thousand Moons

Martin Hurcomb

Matador
9 Priory Business Park,
Wistow Road, Kibworth Beauchamp,
Leicestershire. LE8 0RX
Tel: 0116 279 2299
Email: books@troubador.co.uk
Web: www.troubador.co.uk/matador
Twitter: @matadorbooks

ISBN 978 1800463 134

British Library Cataloguing in Publication Data.
A catalogue record for this book is available from the British Library.

Printed and bound in the UK by TJ Books LTD, Padstow, Cornwall
Typeset in 11pt Adobe Garamond by Troubador Publishing Ltd, Leicester, UK

Matador is an imprint of Troubador Publishing Ltd

Contents

1	Goodbye Vaughan	1
2	After the Funeral	15
3	Jubilee Day	29
4	Death is a market place	47
5	Hillstone Hall	60
6	Code 085	74
7	'Stapleton's'	90
8	Tea for Two	107
9	A Confession	127
10	Empty chairs and empty tables	139
11	A hand on her shoulder	154
12	Piccadilly Circus	172
13	One Thousand Moons	190
14	Apples, sunglasses and flapjack	200
15	Battle lines	216
16	A tight squeeze	236
17	Role reversal	248
18	The Music Room	266
19	Close, so close	287
20	Bombers' Moon	305
21	Table 7	310
22	Marks in the floor	326
23	A negative ending	340
	Acknowledgements	367

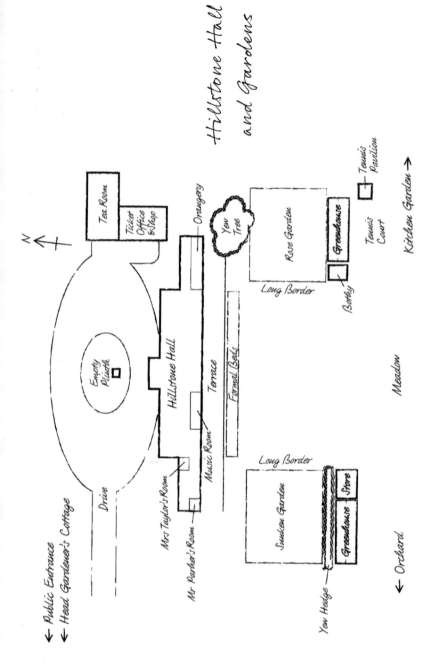

Hillstone Hall and Gardens

N

Public Entrance
Head Gardener's Cottage

Drive

Tea Room

Ticket Office & Shop

Empty Plinth

Hillstone Hall

Orangery

Mrs Taylor's Room

Mr Parker's Room

Music Room

Terrace

Formal Beds

Yew Tree

Rare Garden

Long Border

Bothy

Greenhouse

Tennis Court

Tennis Pavilion

Kitchen Garden →

Long Border

Sunken Garden

Yew Hedge

Greenhouse

Store

Meadow

Orchard →

CHAPTER 1

Goodbye Vaughan

It was not really the weather for a funeral, thought Alba. Funerals should take place on cold damp November days when the grey clouds and the moisture-laden air encouraged you to look down, to bury your chin into your black woollen scarf and when your fingers felt snug in their fleece-lined leather gloves. Days when the weather made going to church almost tolerable, days when it was dark before dinner time, days when everything seemed morose.

Today was not one of those days. "This is not a day to be inside," Alba said out loud to no-one, as she closed the sash window in her bedroom. The sun shone brightly this Thursday morning. The sky was blue, a real July blue, with just the odd wisp of cloud high up. She lowered the blind so as to protect the photograph on her dressing table from the sun, which would otherwise catch it later on, as the golden sunlight moved around her room. Although it was only a short walk to the church, from her little cottage, and the funeral would only be a quiet affair, she wouldn't want to rush away. There would be tea and cake and for all of Mrs Rowan's failings, she could bake, and Alba knew Mrs Rowan had agreed to make the cakes for after the service, but, most importantly, Alba needed time there to say 'goodbye' to Vaughan. She lowered the blind a little bit more.

Her mother would have told her to wear a hat to the service but her mother was a different generation and wearing a hat to a formal occasion just wasn't Alba – a sunhat, as she worked in her garden or as a volunteer gardener up at the Hall, naturally, of course she'd be under a hat then. But today, no, and the dear beloved Vaughan wouldn't want her to change her style for him. Black skirt, to just above the knees, black tights, a white long-sleeved blouse and a charcoal-grey silk scarf would be all that was needed on this summer's day. The scarf, with silvery threads woven in, wasn't really for show, as much as something to weave between her fingers if she got nervous or found herself alone after the service. As she passed her dressing table, she replaced the birthday card, which she had earlier been re-reading, in her jewellery box and closed the lid, having chosen to wear her grandmother's rings on her right hand.

As she walked down the stairs she suddenly felt conscious of no longer having a ring on the third finger of her left hand. Being both a gardener and left-handed she hadn't enjoyed wearing it, fearing it would fall off into the soil or that she would damage it. She hadn't regretted taking it off that final time but today, knowing what today would throw at her, she accepted to herself, as she walked down the last three stairs, that she felt, for the first time, just a little bit naked and just a little bit alone without it.

She stopped by her hall table to glance once more at the old faded photograph that her aged friend Vaughan had lent her on that fateful day. They had, on a previous occasion been chatting about whether people always looked like their brothers or sisters, and Vaughan had lent her an old photograph of his brother, Clive, in his RAF uniform with his squadron comrades standing in front of, and along both wings of, a Lancaster Bomber. He'd told her which Lincolnshire airfield it was taken at but today its name escaped her. Remembering that wasn't important, the challenge Vaughan had given her was to pick out his brother Clive – three attempts and, if successful, he had promised her two trusses of tomatoes from his greenhouse. He had assured her that was a tasty prize. Looking at the photograph today, everyone who was looking back at her seemed to be from a time way way before 1943, so much further back in time than the mere fifty-nine years that separated her from the time when all these young men, and a few women in their WAAF uniforms, had stood around that plane. A time she had never known herself, having been born in the seventies. Alba knew she had no way of being told whether she had guessed correctly. Vaughan was the last in his family and perhaps that was why she and the other volunteer gardeners had taken so warmly to him when he started volunteering with them. Somehow, Alba thought to herself, they all knew they were to be a surrogate family to him – and they were, they truly were. Even when he started as a volunteer, he was an elderly man, mid-seventies, and they accepted he always got given the light duties – not for him the cutting of the yew hedges in summer, the winter pruning in the orchard or the tedious back breaking work of collecting the fallen rose leaves from within the rose garden. Rather, Vaughan rode the little ride-on mower, propagated in the greenhouses or entertained the garden visitors with his garden tours – for his plant knowledge and his way of enthusing his love of plants and gardens into those little groups of visitors left all the other volunteers, and Mr Parker, the Head Gardener, in awe.

Vaughan just had a way with him, so natural and unassuming, with his weathered and worn gardening journal under his arm or in his pocket. Alba sensed Mr Parker both valued having him in the garden, for the comments cards the visitors left up at the shop and ticket office at the end of the day always praised the garden tours and that meant Mr Parker was praised by Lord Hartfield, the Hall's current incumbent Lord, but also that Mr Parker deeply resented having Vaughan around. That resentment was born out of Vaughan being so well liked and so willing to share his passion, qualities Mr

Parker wholeheartedly lacked. Of course Vaughan was always the last one back out to work after their lunch break, and often, if there was no garden talk to give, he could sleep until three in the afternoon in their little gardeners' hut but, Mr Parker aside, no-one minded, for they all loved him – and his stories that he'd tell over their breaks, or the home-made biscuits he always seemed to produce on days when they were sheltering from the autumn rains, or the wisdom he would offer up if you found yourself sharing a problem with him. All these things made him the person he was.

The photograph was a good foot wide, in its simple frame, and it didn't look right where it was, dominating the table and the two vases of cut flowers and the three figurines. It also threw the symmetry out – flowers, two figurines, picture, one figurine, flowers. It looked wrong. She repositioned one of the figurines to the other side of the photograph. "Arrgh, still no," she exasperated to the figure of the lady sitting in a chair with a cat curled up asleep on her lap, half expecting the cat to hear her, rouse itself, stand up, arch its back, turn a half circle and then settle down once more to go back to sleep on the lady's lap. "It looks wrong and it feels wrong," she lamented. The photograph should only have been there just a day or two, but here it still was several weeks on. It had nestled here, in the way that an elephant nestles in a china shop, for too long but she didn't know who to give it back to. Maybe today, at the funeral, she'd find someone who could advise on what to do with it. She picked it up once again, holding it with both hands letting her thumbs run along the glass from the centre outwards, along the span of the wings. "Where are you Clive? And how many more operations did you have before your last fateful one?" She put the photograph back down, stood the lady and her still sleeping cat behind the picture and, still irritated that that wasn't a solution either, walked into the kitchen.

She poured another half cup of tea from the still warm yellow teapot and then drained the leaves – to be scattered around the roses later once she was back and changed. She stood at her sink, glancing out into her garden, watching the birds at the feeder. 'Why is it that nuthatches always seem to be upside down?' she thought just as a magpie swooped in. Alba grabbed at a tea towel and swung it at the window, scaring not just the magpie but all the birds away.

There was a knock on her back door, as it opened.

"Mind if I come in?" said Helen.

"Not at all, I'm ready – if one can ever be ready for a funeral. But it's still a bit early to leave. New top? Cup of tea before we set off?"

"'Phase 8'. No thanks. I was hoping we could walk via the post office. I've got a card to send to one of our old university friends. He's still out in Uzbekistan you know. It's his birthday in six weeks. He'll be the last of our group to hit the big three zero; I saw from the road, Alba, that you've still got some of your 30th birthday cards up in your living room. Anyway, you remember Terry, don't you Alba?"

"Oh, yes. He ran away there didn't he?"

"Alba! You're being unfair. You know full well, he's a missionary out there. 'Called' he said, 'I've been called'. Amazing what he gave up. For a late August baby, he excelled, top of our year group. Won the Hawthorn prize. He had his pick of City firms, worked for one for about a year and then five weeks later he'd gone. Uzbekistan of all places! I ask you."

"Ran away."

"Alba! Shame on you. I seem to remember you went up to see him once or twice when he was working in the City."

"I saw him at an exhibition once, another time I bumped into him at Marble Arch and we went for a drink. He ran away."

*

St Mary's was fuller than Alba had expected. As she and Helen had walked to the church, she'd been surprised by all the extra parked cars in the lane. As she had walked under the lich-gate she had been

5

surprised at all the people milling around the church door and now, as she sat, she could hear the church filling up behind her.

Alba sat in the left hand side of the nave, second row from the front. Apparently, Vaughan, being a man of order and organisation but not premonition, had mentioned to the vicar how, when it was his, Vaughan's, funeral he wanted his 'gardening family', the team from the Hall, to be at the front. According to Helen, Vaughan had also said to Reverend Quinn, that he wanted his coffin carried in to Michael Jackson's 'Bad' but that Vaughan's chuckle that followed told those then present that that very much was a joke.

So here she sat. In front of her, Mr Parker and his wife. Sally was next to Mrs Parker. In her row, Alba had Helen to her right, then a gap and then David. It wasn't that Helen and David didn't get on, for they were good friends. Rather, it was a statement they had all agreed to make and even Mr Parker, when they had felt obliged to tell him their intention to do it, even he, the Head Gardener at Hillstone Hall, the remote, the sombre, the man who never brought in mince pies for his volunteers in the week before Christmas, known to everyone as 'Bic', well to everyone behind his back as 'Bic', even he had found it beyond himself to oppose the statement they had planned to make today. So here they sat, with a gap for Tom.

Tom wasn't running late, he wasn't going to be one of the bearers, with that grim task of helping to carry Vaughan in, to be rested on those wooden stilts just in front and to the right of her. Tom wasn't running the show up at the Hall, covering for them. He wasn't on holiday or visiting his ill mother. Tom wouldn't be here because he couldn't. Her Majesty had seen to that – or at least the local Magistrates. Being on remand for murder and attempted murder made it hard to get out, thought Alba wryly to herself, particularly when he'd been charged with the murder of the very person whose funeral it was. The Governor wasn't going to grant him a temporary licence so he could attend and the Police and the CPS weren't about to withdraw the Charge Sheet. So there he was, locked up in HMP South Down.

They would keep a seat for him, though. It was how they sat every break time in the gardener's hut. Mr Parker seldom joined them, so it was, in a kind of arc that Vaughan, Sally, David, Tom, Helen and herself, Alba, sat in the hut each break time. Poor Tom, newly appointed Deputy Head Gardener – he'd gone for the position encouraged by Vaughan, who told Tom he could see the potential in him. The position, his debt to Vaughan, his youthfulness didn't carry any weight to the Magistrates or the authorities. The evidence was there – and, to be fair, it was – and so they'd remanded him.

"He didn't do it though; he wouldn't have done. But of course, he could have done," Alba found herself saying very softly to herself. "He could have, both of them."

"What's that you're saying, Alba?" said Helen.

"Oh nothing, nothing," she said as she weaved her thin scarf between her fingers. "We were right to leave a seat for Tom, Helen, weren't we?"

"Yes."

The church continued to fill and on the front row, on the other side of the nave, sat Mr Edward Chapman, more formerly known as the 7th Lord Hartfield and owner of Hillstone Hall, and his wife, Jane. There was movement and a kerfuffle in the row behind Alba, as Mrs Rowan decided she needed to be on the end of a row so she could extract herself during the last hymn, in order that she could start laying out the cakes, heating the sausage rolls and quiches and checking on the coffee machine. Mrs Rowan regretted not sitting on the back row, to enable her to do a head count to help her in her preparations, but changing rows now, as well as position within this row, would be too embarrassing even for her – still, she could approximate the number when she half-watched the mourners when they gathered outside, through the kitchen window, as they formally lowered the casket in to the ground.

"Lord Hartfield's here!" Helen said in impressed tones. "Still, he's known for coming occasionally," she added. "Recognises his role within the community and that his privileged position brings responsibility. I heard he was at the village cricket match, supporting his team. What about you Alba, did you bump into him that day?"

"Well, yes, actually…"

However, before Alba could add anything further, Helen continued, dropping her voice as she did so, "I'm surprised to see his wife here. I wonder if she's trying to impress this new vicar?"

"I don't know, can't work the woman out – Lady Jane Hartfield, née Trerose. Part of the Brasted Society before she met Lord Hartfield I believe but that's all I know of her. I know her as well as you do, Helen, but I really can't fathom her. Anyway, she's worlds away from us."

"It's odd, isn't it?" replied Helen, "we've helped in her garden for years and we've never even met her and know precious little about her. You hear about so many Lady this or Duchess that, who take an active interest, often a leading role, in their gardens but Lady Hartfield is not like that, is she? Can't recall ever seeing her in the garden, where she's enjoying it as a garden. I imagine, using the 'space' as a backdrop to a garden party is fine for her but I don't think she can see it as you or I can, this thing of beauty that needs to be cared for and shaped. You and I can see it, all in a single moment, how it looks now, how it looked a century ago and how it could look a hundred years hence. We can grasp the masterpiece that is 'The Garden' at Hillstone Hall, whereas she, I rather fancy, prefers being at her London home."

The movement in the row behind had ceased and the church, as a whole, was beginning to quieten down.

"True. True," replied Alba and, not having anything to add to Helen's assessment of Lady Hartfield, continued on a different theme altogether. "There's a lot of history here," she said, "not the people, I mean the plaques and the memorials. Look at that one over there – it says:

'To the memory of John Grove, Organist of this Church for 32 years, 1949 – 1981'.

And that one:

'To the Glorious Memory of the late Lieutenant Arthur Crosby, 19th Regiment of Light Dragoons, who fell on 23rd September 1803, during the Battle of Assaye, India'."

"I know Alba, I know. I've read them all a hundred times. You seem to forget my parents brought me here as a child and this is where I still come. As a child, I found myself reading all these memorial stones and plaques, trying to pass the time. Would try to make stories to connect all these people – I think in one story I had the organist playing the bagpipes as he led the soldiers into the battle of Assaye. You know what, that story wasn't so far off the truth, there were Highland Regiments fighting alongside the Dragoons at Assaye. I know, I read up on the battle once when I was doing my A-Level History, simply because the name 'Assaye' has been seared into my very being. Another one of my stories had Lt Crosby using one of the organ pipes as his lance! And you don't want to know what Mr Grove the organist had to do, in one of my stories, with the 3rd Lord's wife, who's commemorated behind that pillar over there – I was a seventeen-year-old when I came up with that story and it's not for re-telling before the watershed!"

"They must have been fun services for you! Poor Helen! You know, it's almost 200 years since Lt Crosby died. The world has changed so much since then."

"The services couldn't have been so bad, my dear Alba, I still find myself here most Sundays and perhaps the history of this place made me feel part of something bigger than even what an individual congregation can offer. And, no I don't think the world has changed that much, at least not the people. Science, medicine, ways we travel and communicate, yes, but the people, no. You see, as we are doing today, when someone like Vaughan dies, we come here to give thanks for his life and to come together to help us in our grief – just as Mr and Mrs Crosby and their friends undoubtedly did. OK, perhaps, the memorial service for their son didn't start with a Michael Jackson song but otherwise we're still the same."

"Helen, I refuse to believe Vaughan would come in to that! A Sinatra song, a Matt Monro, perhaps even Eva Cassidy but the 'King of Pop', no!"

Alba re-adjusted her hair and was about to change topics completely and discuss the rose garden up at the Hall, when the organist, the current one, who had never been to India, played the bagpipes or ever owned a Michael Jackson record, started up, playing 'Abide with Me' and the congregation stood, as one and in silence.

By the time the instrumental of 'Abide with Me' had finished, the four men from 'Parks', the Funeral Directors, who had been led in by a female colleague in her black tail coat, carrying her polished and silver-topped walking cane and wearing her top hat, had placed the coffin on the wooden struts. They faced it, took a co-ordinated step back, bowed their heads, turned and moved to the back of the church – led by their female colleague, who, Alba thought, had, from what she could make out, the hair that should never be hidden under such a hat and kind of resented the fact that the lady undertaker had been compelled by custom to wear her hat into the church.

Once Alba had stopped focussing on the lady's auburn hair, she heard Helen whispering to her:

"Who are the two people who followed Vaughan's coffin in, the two who've just sat next to Lord Hartfield and his wife? Did you see that? They must know each other, for the bloke, as far as I could make out, just shook Lord Hartfield's hand?"

"As well as that," replied Alba "now that the undertakers have moved away, look at what's on the coffin itself. Look! That's odd."

But before Helen could answer, the Reverend Quinn, who during these few moments had glanced at his notes a final time, nodded at the couple who had followed the coffin in and undone and redone his watch strap at least twice, probably to exactly the same notch as before each time, decided to take his position and started to speak.

He offered everyone a warm welcome on this sad occasion,

mentioned that there would be tea and coffee after the service and something to eat, and that it would be an opportunity for him to get to know a few more people and then invited everyone to bow their heads for an opening prayer.

Years later, Alba would still admit there was something about that opening prayer that moved her. She had already realised why Helen was rather taken with this new vicar, who probably was a few years younger than themselves, refined in appearance rather than good looking and endearing because you could tell he was nervous, his mannerisms told you as much. And yet, it wasn't any of that, it was the prayer itself – the simplicity of it and the way it looked for peace in the trauma of Vaughan's murder.

There were then a couple of hymns, a reading from Joshua 24, verses 1 to 15, a few words from Mr Parker, about how nice Vaughan was, knowledgeable on his plants, conceded that Vaughan grew better tomatoes than himself – so it would have been a prize worthy of winning, thought Alba, as she momentarily saw the picture of Clive and his comrades in her mind's eye – and that Vaughan would be missed up at the Hall amongst the gardening team.

Why, thought Alba, as Helen, David and Sally undoubtedly did too, hadn't Mr Parker suggested one of them give the talk instead? Any of them could have brought Vaughan back to life, as it were, for a few moments at least – Mr Parker knew about Vaughan, you could say, but they, each of them, knew him, the man. They would have spoken of the man's warmth, the way he would put his arm around you, if you were sad, the strength in those arms despite his advancing years and the recipes he'd share with you. They'd have spoken of the home-made biscuits that appeared on wet days, that his favourite plant was Honesty, the way he'd dodge the question any time someone asked him about his time in the Army, serving in France and Germany in the final years of the war but the way he'd talk of Clive with such enthusiasm, always leaving you feeling that you also had waved Clive off on each operation too, standing at the edge of the runway waving to a fading dot in the sky and the fading sound of four Merlin engines. Alba, Helen, David or Sally – or Tom had he been here – would have spoken of the family they were and how they had each lost, in a true sense, one of their own.

However, Mr Parker had kept the talk to himself and the service was the poorer for it. Still, at least Helen had organised a recording of the service, ensuring that it would be put on to a cassette so Tom, at some stage, could hear it. Another hymn, in effect the 23rd Psalm, and then Reverend Quinn addressed the congregation.

"There is a small village in Belgium called Zillebeke," he said. "It lies just east of Ypres and just south of the Menin Road. In the Churchyard there, there is the grave of Lt Colonel Gordon Chesney Wilson, Royal Horse Guards and Member of the Royal Victorian Order. He died on 6th November 1914 during the 1st Battle of Ypres. Now, on Commonwealth War Grave headstones, relatives were allowed to add up to sixty-six characters for a personal message. On Lt Colonel Wilson's headstone, his family put:

'Life is a city of crooked streets,
Death the market place where all men meet.'"

Alba thought it an unusual start to a sermon but the Reverend went on to address, head on, that life the day Vaughan died, the day of the Queen's Golden Jubilee, the day of the charity cricket match between the Lords and the Commoners, the day the Battle of Britain Memorial Flight went over, that life on that day was very crooked, very crooked indeed. And that someone had an innocent man's blood on his or her hands. Yes God, he said, is in control of all things but that he has also granted the descendants of Adam and Eve the freedom to choose good or evil – and on this occasion someone chose evil.

'No elephants in the room for this minister', thought Alba, 'no beating about the bush'. 'Good', she continued to think, 'let's recognise Vaughan was brutally taken from us having remembered the man he was'.

Probably others too, in the congregation were surprised, that the Reverend Quinn didn't take the easy option of saying something about justice being promptly done and how good the police were to arrest someone so quickly. The Reverend Quinn didn't mention Tom, rather he went on to speak of the Vaughan he knew, from the chats he had had with him in their Home Group and, even more informally still, over the odd half of ale they had shared in 'The Sun and Moon', the local Vaughan had introduced him to since the Vicar's appointment to the parish. In his conclusion, he stressed that each person present was destined to die one day, that Vaughan's trust had been in the Lord but where or in whom had everyone else placed their trust.

"Good address," said Helen once the Reverend Quinn finished his talk and was looking in his notes for the title of the last hymn. "What did you think, Alba?"

"Different," she said reflectively as they stood as the organ started up.

Hymn over and everyone was expecting just the closing prayer but the Reverend Quinn had something else to add:

"Before a final prayer," he said, "I am sure everyone has noticed that there are five items on the coffin in front of us. Not for him a big floral display. Rather, five specific things Vaughan had wanted on his coffin, according to his written instructions, to remind us who he was. And things he wanted passed on to Sally, David, Helen, Alba and Tom."

In rather unsure tones, the Reverend added, "I am aware that Tom can't be here today."

Invited by the Reverend Quinn, the remaining four, gingerly and in a very self-conscious way, stood up – Alba leaving her scarf behind as it had slipped to the ground during the final hymn – and moved out to the front in absolute silence, much to Mrs Rowan's envy.

Being up by the coffin enabled Alba to really focus on the items that were there laid out in front of her and the others; a red rose, a sheet of A5 paper with writing on it, Vaughan's leather Aussie hat, his holstered secateurs and his battered old gardening journal.

"Five items," said Reverend Quinn, "that I guess don't wholly define the man but are very personal reminders. Now, I have no need for my notes for this bit as it is so unusual and quirky that I learnt it straight away. So, to Sally, being a Lancastrian, as Vaughan was, the red rose. Plus, for they couldn't have them on the coffin, the two shrub roses that are in pots on Vaughan's patio. To David, the old leather hat which, dare I say, is in need of a bit of boot polish. To Helen, this piece of paper, Vaughan's previously secret biscuit recipe. For Alba, the journal. And Tom is to have the secateurs. Interestingly, Vaughan had originally intended the items to be the other way round for Alba and Tom but his handwritten amendment to his typed notes very clearly swopped them over. I wonder why? Alba, can we entrust the secateurs to you until it is, err, appropriate to give them to Tom?"

Alba nodded an acceptance.

With each of them holding their items, the Reverend Quinn, in the way that all ministers do when they want people to sit back down in their pews, raised his arms to either side of himself, to about chest height, palms facing outwards and, in an almost invisible movement, made it clear they were to re-take their seats. 'Thinks he's shepherding his flock', thought Alba. Knowing they were right at the end of the service, the four of them didn't bother to resume their original seats and Alba ended up taking Sally's seat, with David, Sally and Helen behind. Alba held the journal incredibly tightly; 'Bic' Parker wasn't getting to see it, at least not for a good while.

Final prayer over, and with the organist trying his best to play 'Over the Rainbow' and making a mental note to himself about asking the Church Treasurer for an electric keyboard for such moments, the congregation stood up as Vaughan's coffin was carried out, for the final act, the burial. The mourners, save for two, followed; Mrs Rowan, who had somehow already got herself in to the church hall, and Alba.

Alba just sat where she was.

CHAPTER 2

After the Funeral

Slowly Alba roused herself after what to her seemed like an age but to anyone else were just a few minutes. Still clutching the journal and the holstered secateurs, she slowly walked into the church hall.

It wasn't that she didn't know what was going on outside. She had been in two minds about whether she would want to see the burial itself. She had considered it was the 'right' thing to do – whatever 'right' meant on occasions like this – to stand at the graveside, letting a handful of soil slip between her fingers. Not that it would in fact slip through her fingers at all, for the soil in the churchyard was heavy clay. She had learnt that from tending other graves up here, and it would just be a lump that would drop whole. Maybe the Church Warden had bought in a bag of top soil for the occasion; 'Is that what they do on occasions like this?' she found herself somewhat absently wondering. Equally, she had thought about avoiding that final act, not wanting to be left with the last grim image of looking down into a hole in the ground.

It was that, not wanting to look into the hole, combined with a sudden sense of weariness, stemming in part from the sudden and unexpected involvement in those final moments of the service itself, plus not wanting to misplace or drop either the journal or the secateurs – for she was aware she'd already lost her scarf since leaving home – which prompted Alba to opt out of the final act within today's service. Slowly and wearily, beguiling anyone who might have followed her, as to her age, not that anyone did, Alba made her way into the church hall.

She sat against one of the walls, at right angles to the now open serving hatch, from where she could hear Mrs Rowan beavering away and giving short but precise instructions to someone else in the kitchen; 'No, not there, over there with the others', 'that's it, stack them like I've done to the left, excellent', 'yes, dear, best we fill the other urn and get that on in a few minutes' and 'oh, it's so useful you got out of college early and could get the bus, so you could come and help, bless you my dear'.

Alba thought she was out of sight of the servery, and indeed she had sat intentionally out of sight as she hadn't felt in the mood for a conversation with Mrs Rowan, nor, somewhat selfishly had Alba wanted to get roped in to helping in the kitchen. So here she sat alone, feeling alone – especially so when she instinctively went to twist the ring that was no longer there on her left hand. She placed the secateurs on the chair to her left and was about to open Vaughan's gardening journal when footsteps alerted her to someone approaching.

"Brought you a cup of tea, my dear. By the look of you, you need it," said Mrs Rowan.

"What? Oh pardon, sorry," replied Alba as she looked up, having been caught off-guard.

"Tea, my young dear. Did you want sugar?"

"Sugar? No. I mean, no thank you. That's very kind of you. I didn't think you were ready to serve and I didn't want to put you to any trouble by loitering by the hatch," said Alba almost apologetically, as she sensed the warmth in Mrs Rowan's gesture.

"Second rule of catering," said Mrs Rowan.

"Second?"

"The second rule is, always get the small kettle on and make a pot of tea for yourself and any assistant you are lucky enough to have with you. Events like this are always hectic, I mean everyone's polite and courteous, but it's hectic from a catering perspective, and a good cup of tea inside me helps wonderfully. And there was enough in the pot for you as well – I heard you come in, heard the slow steps and thought it might help. The big urns are just coming to the boil now but the little kettle is invaluable. Always bring it with me to catering events like this. As for everyone else, my Sam can make the tea and check on the coffee. Still, I'd better get back – they're still outside but it won't be too long."

"Mrs Rowan, I am touched, truly I am. This tea is just my strength too."

As Mrs Rowan turned to go, Alba staring at her cup, suddenly and inquisitively said, "Second?"

Alba had really been speaking just to herself but Mrs Rowan turned back and replied, "Yes, second. And before you ask, there is a first. It's 'Always sit on the back row at funerals, so you can do a head count'. You see, the vicar and every vicar we've ever had here if the truth be told, is always way off when they come to me and ask me to do the catering and give me their estimate of numbers. I tell you, always well off, so much so they might as well pick a number out of a hat. But I've learnt, if you sit on the back row, you can do a head count easily, which helps with the drinks. Obviously, I have already guess-timated for the sandwiches, quiches and cakes but not all of it has to be put out at once, and if there are any spare cakes it's always nice to offer the relatives a whole cake to take home with them. But as for drinks, you see everyone wants a hot drink immediately they come in. So, first rule is 'Sit on the back row and do a head count'."

"But you didn't – you were right behind me."

"I know, I know, I don't know what I was thinking as I sat down in the pew. Think I was dwelling on something Mrs Lyle said the other day to me about her village shop and Vaughan. Now what was it? Oh, never mind, guess it wasn't important. Anyway, I was able to count through the kitchen window, so Sam and I are in control but jolly useful she got out of college early and was able to help. Bless her!"

As Mrs Rowan went back into the kitchen, Alba found herself revived by the cup of tea and warming to the person who had just brought it to her; the person whose voice she could now hear saying, 'Bowl for the dirty tea spoons and some more napkins and I think we're done. Well done Sam'.

Alba placed her cup next to the secateurs, ran her fingers along the aged leather holster that the red handled secateurs nestled within, and continued the motion with just two fingers along the red handles. They were seemingly identical to hers – you could tell that simply by the colour of the handles. She'd heard once that 'BP', the petroleum company, had sought a trademark for their shade of green and wondered whether 'Felco' had considered the same for the distinctive red of their handles. The holster, too, was identical – well, she thought, completely different, in that it was scuffed and worn in different places, and had the odd deeper scratch on it, which probably came, as the ones on her holster did, from that session they once had together cutting back the pyracantha around the side of the ticket office up at the Hall, but kind of equally identical because of its wear.

*

Alba opened Vaughan's journal at no particular place. It was clearly, even from this superficial look, not a journal in the sense of a diary, more a notebook, a place for jottings, ideas, thoughts, words of gardening wisdom and the odd non-horticultural thing shoved in too. She replaced a loose sheet of paper with Hilaire Belloc's "The South Country" poem written out in Vaughan's handwriting.

Alba noticed, as she flicked through the journal, that not all the jottings were in the same handwriting and some, especially towards the front, were really quite faded. The fact that not everything was in English made it even more personal – if that were possible – for there was Latin and German by the looks of things too. She closed it up, being conscious that she could sit there for the rest of the week reading it and learning from it; there was even something on lunar planting, with a list of things to plant in the first quarter of the lunar cycle. As she closed it, at the bottom of the notes on lunar planting, was boldly written, and circled around, the phrase '1,000 Moons'. But close the journal Alba did, not wanting to give the impression to the other mourners that she'd skipped the burial to study her prize or that she was covetously guarding it. To her it was indeed to be treasured but she recognised that to anyone else, it was a knocked about old notebook, decades old, dog eared and stained. It had been left out in the rain and dropped in the mud on more than one occasion; it was nothing special but treasure it she would. However, that wasn't the impression she wanted to give, especially today. So she closed it up and 'hid' it under her cup of tea. Of course, it was not hidden, in the literal sense, but Alba had a theory that if you put a cup of liquid on something in a social setting then no one else ever dared to touch it or try to move it – not wanting to run the risk of spilling the drink, especially when they were already holding their own cup and plate. So, there it would sit hidden, for the entire world to see, on a chair, underneath a part drunk cup of tea.

Other mourners started to enter the hall.

Ignoring the rugby scrum that was forming around the serving hatch, David made a bee line for Alba.

"You alright, Alba?"

"Better now, David, thank you. I just couldn't face that last act so I've just been sitting in here. Mrs Rowan kindly brought me a cup of tea and I'm beginning to feel a bit more alive. Oh, not the best thing to say today." Alba smiled wryly to David, as she stood up, straightening her skirt as she did so.

"Don't worry, I know what you mean and Vaughan would probably have smiled at your *faux pas*."

Helen joined them. "Sal's in the queue for the coffees and tea. She's cheekily going to ask for four drinks, so I'll go over to help her carry them when I see her at the front of the queue. Tried the hat on yet, David?"

"No, not yet, not today. Today it's still his hat but, maybe when I'm next back up at the Hall and it's late in the day and quiet, I'll try it on then. It should fit; Vaughan tried my cricket hat on once and said it was a perfect fit for him, so the reverse should be too. But the Rev's right, it needs a bit of polish to get it back to being good for rain as well as shine – a good wide brim, such as this, is good for keeping the rain as well as the sun off." He passed the hat to Alba for inspection and then said:

"Ooh, she's at the front of the queue, I'll go."

And off David went before Helen could say anything to the contrary.

Sally and David re-joined them, bringing a further cup of tea for Alba.

"So, Vaughan's five things are re-united," said Alba as she passed David the hat back and simultaneously pointed to the two things on the chair behind her.

"Err, not quite," replied Sally. "You see, what can you do with a single rose? I couldn't put it in my little shoulder bag for the rest of the morning, I wasn't for pinning it to this dress and I was definitely not walking around with it in hand – like you, Alba, I'm not looking for love at the moment. A lonely marriage I might have but I won't be the one to leave it. So, I put the rose back on the coffin just as they lowered it. I've obviously still got the two pots with the roses in. I've got to pop to the village shop on Saturday, so I'll possibly collect them then, given Vaughan's little cottage is next door to the shop. You know what Mrs Lyle is like if you're late paying your paper bill – she gets quite nasty. She has an unhealthy love of money, if you ask me."

"Oh, by the way and before I forget," said David "'Bic' said could you call in to see him when you're next up at the Hall, Alba. I think he was hoping to catch you in the churchyard but as you weren't there, he said could you pop in to see him. Don't know what it's about. Said he couldn't hang about for you as he had to do something about Mrs Taylor up at the Hall."

"Alright. I think I'm back there tomorrow – I'll check my diary when I get home. You sure he didn't say what it was about?"

"Sure. And you know he doesn't give anything away in his facial expressions. He's a cold one, that one. He must know a little bit more than we currently do about Mrs Taylor and whether she'll recover or not given he is a 'Head of Department', if you apply business speak to how the Hall is structured and run, and therefore he's equal to Mrs Taylor in that sense. So, he's likely to have been briefed by Lord Hartfield. But, as I say, 'Bic' doesn't give anything away. I wonder why he wants you Alba; I'd have thought he'd speak to us all together."

Neither Helen, Sally nor even Alba herself could offer an explanation. Instead the conversation turned to grape vines.

*

The food was up to Mrs Rowan's usual high standard and her cherry and almond flan was something quite exceptional. As Alba returned one of her cups and a plate to the kitchen, plus a couple of others she gathered on the way, she noticed the couple, who had followed the coffin in, talking to Reverend Quinn by the doors and then saying their goodbyes to him. The man was vaguely, very vaguely, familiar but Alba couldn't place him. She felt he ought to trigger a recent memory rather than something from decades ago but that was as far as she could get. She turned and placed the crockery at the serving hatch.

"Thank you," said Mrs Rowan. "It's Alba, isn't it?"

"Yes, how did you know?" replied Alba.

"Oh, don't worry, I haven't been spying on you or rifling through your recycling bin."

"No?" replied Alba somewhat inquisitorially, having always believed that things said supposedly in jest were usually true, and starting to regret the warming she had been experiencing towards Mrs Rowan over the last couple of hours.

"Of course not, dear. I've seen you around the village a few times and I saw you at the charity cricket match, on the day Vaughan died. You, or someone who looks very similar and with your colour hair, I saw walking around the boundary rope just as I'd finished setting out the lunch that day. But I was a bit flustered that day and not in the mood to talk to people – I hope that didn't come across to people that day but I fear it did. Plus, my Sam said to me she thought she recognised you from up at the Hall – she's just started working there one day a week and said she's spoken to you in the tea shop there, where's she working."

"That's possible," said Alba, "but I don't go in to the tea shop very often. If I did, I'd spend more on food and drink in there in a week than I get in expenses as a volunteer at the Hall for a whole year. Still, I love being up at the Hall helping and it gives me a lot of time to think about things. Oh, hold on, yes, there was a new girl up in the tea shop. I went in the other week as it was just me volunteering in the garden one day – I was expecting Tom to be around but he wasn't. You see, whilst normally we take our tea breaks in our bothy, our little gardeners' hut, if you are sitting in there by yourself it's not quite the same, so that day I walked round to the tea shop. If it was Sam I spoke to, then she probably saw my volunteer's card – it does get you a discount, a little one mind you! And, if it was Sam who served me, I can say she seemed to be completely at home there and very efficient. I'm beginning to see who she gets it from. She might see me again next week, possibly even tomorrow, thinking about it.

You see, one of Tom's tasks for next week was to prune the climbing hydrangea that grows around some of the walls of the tea shop. It's just past its best and now in need of some attention. Tom would have done it but, as he's on remand, I think I'll offer to tackle it. I'll pop my head round the door and say 'hello' to Sam if she's there – I've seen her through this serving hatch this afternoon so I know who to look out for. The hydrangea will take me several sessions, so there's a chance I'll catch her."

"Remand. Really? I'd heard the rumours in the village yesterday about that, especially when you're in the queue at 'Stapleton's' to pay your paper bill or buy some stamps. You know how people gossip," said Mrs Rowan.

It was a sad but predictable feature of village life, thought Alba, how rumours got around and frequently false rumours at that, although not on this occasion. Sensing that Mrs Rowan was part of this village's gossip mill, Alba was careful with how she replied – 'I'll offer up facts, not opinions', she thought.

"Yes, remand. He's being held at HMP South Down. He was arrested on Tuesday evening, shortly after Mrs Taylor was rushed into hospital. He appeared in Court yesterday morning and was remanded. I'm going to try and visit him next week but I don't know how to go about that at the moment."

"You don't think he's guilty then?" replied Mrs Rowan in surprise.

"I didn't say what I thought," said Alba tersely.

"Not in your words my dear, not in your words. But your actions – well they speak volumes. What's the saying 'By their fruit you will recognise them'. So, you can't think he's guilty – the group of you left a seat for him in the service and you wouldn't even talk about visiting him if you thought he was involved. So you see, your actions have told me what you think as to his guilt."

Alba didn't know how to respond, needing again to re-evaluate Mrs Rowan and wondering where her previous assessment of this woman had come from.

A couple of other people brought cups and plates back to the hatch, stacking them to the side, and then the Reverend Quinn added his cup also.

"An empty for you, Mrs Rowan. Lovely spread and the millionaire's shortbread was particularly fine – made by yourself I assume?"

"Yes, that always goes down well. Seldom do I get a bit of the millionaire's to take home for myself after an event like this."

Turning to Alba, the Reverend went on:

"We haven't met – well other than in the service. I mean we haven't spoken properly. An unusual finale to a funeral service, I'll say, wasn't it?"

"Thankfully I haven't been to too many funerals, I'll grant you, but you sprung that ending on me and Helen and the others. Done anything similar in other funerals you've taken?" replied Alba, unused to men of God talking to her.

"No, not all, not in either of my previous two parishes. It did remind me, though, of a sermon I heard when I was newly ordained about park benches. A sermon I wished I'd written myself but never could have. There we go, maybe one day I'll give a sermon someone will remember! But I won't trouble you about park benches and their relevance to funerals now. It's been an emotional morning for you, I can tell. Sorry, I forget myself, I'm the Reverend Quinn, I'm pleased to meet you but I don't know your name – I haven't seen you here before."

"Reverend, this is Alba, one of Vaughan's gardening colleagues from up at the Hall," interjected Mrs Rowan, keen to be involved in the conversation and a little bit too desperate to share what little she knew about Alba.

'Listens to gossip in 'Stapleton's' – instigator of it more like' thought Alba.

Without trying to sound too sarcastic, Alba said to Mrs Rowan, "I think he's worked out my connection to Vaughan given my having to stand up at the front at the end of the service." And turning to Reverend Quinn, went on, "Yes, I'm Alba and you're right, you haven't seen me here before. Helen keeps encouraging me to come with her but it's not for me."

"What, being here with Helen?" enquired the Reverend as he slightly tilted his head and almost imperceptibly raised an eyebrow. "Come by yourself then, you'd be very welcome."

"You know full well what I mean and I don't appreciate people twisting my words to make a silly little joke. Not today. So, if you'll excuse me," added Alba curtly, "I must go and collect another cup. You see I left a book under it and there are some secateurs I ought to pick up. I think it's time I took those items home and place them by an old photograph."

*

Walking home, having left the churchyard behind her, having looked for her scarf by the lich-gate without success, Alba held the journal in her right hand and the leather holstered secateurs in her left. She moved her left hand around to her back, to the base of her spine, and was about to instinctively clip the holster on, when she realised she wasn't in her gardening get-up and, relieved not to have got any oil on her clothes, took the secateurs in her right hand also. Using her now free hand she removed her hair clip and clipped it between two of her blouse buttons.

The sky remained blue, the earlier wisps of cloud having now disappeared, and, as she glanced down, the sunlight still caught her grandmother's rings – 'Gramps must have had good taste when he bought these for grandma' she thought. She hadn't expected to be at the service for quite as long as she had and her plan for the jobs she'd get done in her garden during the afternoon was now under threat. 'Still', she reasoned with herself, 'if I start on the wisteria around my front door, that'll be a good job done and then I can harvest a punnet or two of soft fruit. They're cropping really well this year and I'll pick some extra and take some round to Helen's tomorrow, given she had a rabbit in her garden which took most of her crop'.

She walked past 'The Sun and the Moon' public house. The hanging baskets were up to their usual high standard and, glancing over the low-cut hedge into the beer garden, the vases of flowers on the tables were full of fresh flowers but the pub should have been busier. There were only a handful of people to glance at; a couple of cyclists having a drink, whilst their bikes rested against a neighbouring empty table, the three roofers who were doing the loft conversion on the house two doors down from the pub and a small group of walkers. It was a lovely summer's day and the garden should have had more customers but, Alba reflected, a lot of the locals had been at the funeral.

Glancing up at the pub's sign, Alba's thoughts turned once again to the phrase Vaughan had circled in his journal. She was sure it was a phrase he'd used once, whilst they were chatting one break time in their little gardeners' hut, but she just couldn't remember anything else about it.

In time, her walk home took her past the village cricket ground. The ground's beating heart was the picturesque little wooden pavilion, which would have looked finer still had it not been for the uneven pot-holed gravel car park that surrounded it on three sides. Still, from its far side, with its wooden steps leading down towards the cricket outfield, and particularly when viewed from the far side of the ground, it still retained an old-worldly charm. That charm took on an even higher level, when you found yourself sitting by the boundary rope, on that far side of the ground, in your favourite camping chair, half watching a game of weekend cricket, over the top of your Saturday paper, in the shade of the three tall beech trees, at about 12.30pm just as you started to anticipate what would be for lunch in the pavilion – then, especially then, when all those factors combined as if they were planets aligning in the heavens, you would find yourself glancing up, looking between the wicket keeper and the slip catchers, at the pavilion and fully grasping the simple charm of it. It oozed innocence and you found yourself comforted by the thought that if you'd sat in the same place a hundred years earlier, you'd have had the same view and felt the same keenness to get around the boundary rope to get into the pavilion for lunch.

Alba had never really been into sports. She had never 'got' cross-country running whilst at school – leave earlier if you needed to get somewhere in a hurry was her philosophy to running. Neither was netball of interest, compounded by not being quite tall enough, nor rugby, where she lacked the build and the stamina. As for table tennis, well she had found herself nearly always scrambling around for the ball under a nearby mat that some other schoolgirl was about to somersault on to. At university she hadn't rowed, cycled or kicked a football. She trialled for the hockey team but that was only to get her tutor off her back, complaining as he had been about her not embracing university life enough, that time she'd gone to him about struggling to fit in that first term. Needless to say, she didn't make it through the hockey trials.

And yet, since coming to the village, she'd found herself drawn to the game of cricket – well, the watching of it. She thought again of the old-worldly charm of the setting and the innocence of it all and then, inevitably, how that innocence had been completely shattered – for it was in the pavilion that Vaughan had been murdered. No-one can be murdered in a 'nice' way, reflected Alba, but at least Vaughan had been asleep in the deckchair, at the back of the pavilion, when someone had stabbed him from behind. She hoped he wouldn't have really felt it and, when she discovered him, he didn't have a look of pain on his face, but that was only some small comfort to hold on to. The innocence was gone though. Vaughan himself was gone.

*

Brushing past the wisteria by her front door that had, over the years, entwined itself up and around her little tiled porch, Alba sighed, a relieved exhausted kind of sigh, as she unlocked her front door and let herself in. She picked up the post, placed it on her bottom step, and, having placed the journal and secateurs next to the photograph on the hall table, making the whole table ridiculously congested, headed to the kitchen to put the kettle on.

As the kettle boiled, she topped up the bird bath and, as the tea brewed, she went up and changed. Pleased to be out of the funeral attire, especially the tights, she felt she could breathe a little bit more freely as she clothed herself in scruffy trousers and an old gingham checked shirt. Her grandmother's rings were returned to the little box, the sash window slid open and the blind was re-adjusted.

Back downstairs, as she sat at her kitchen table, mug of tea in hand, her mind wandered back to that day, just a few weeks ago, the day of the cricket match – the day of Vaughan's murder.

CHAPTER 3

Jubilee Day

Thus, as she sat at her kitchen table, Alba thought back to the day of the cricket match – the match between Lord Hartfield's eleven and the village eleven.

*

She was satisfied with the little food hamper she had put together. Although lunch was being put on in the pavilion, paid for by the parish council, she was so used to, since she started volunteering up at the Hall, stopping for tea and cake at 10.30am and again mid-afternoon, that time for just a drink and biscuit, that she instinctively put a little hamper together.

Home-made fruit cake to go with the mid-morning cuppa and some all-butter shortbread for the afternoon. "Admittedly," Alba said quietly to herself, not that there was anyone to hear her on this occasion either, "these biscuits may well stay unopened, if Vaughan offers round his biscuit tin." Still, she continued to reason, Vaughan might not make the match at all. He had, after all, been very tired last week up at the Hall. They'd all noticed that as early as the Wednesday.

Then on the Thursday, although he made it in, they'd encouraged him to go home early, after they found him sleeping in the hut before the lunch break and he'd missed Friday altogether. Not that she or Helen or Sally or David or Tom had minded at all – poor old Vaughan, he'd said he'd been feeling his seventy-seven years and it was beginning to show over the past week or so. So, not wishing to assume he'd make it or, even if he did, that he'd be supplying his marvellous biscuits, Alba packed some she'd made herself.

The cricket match was not scheduled to start until 11am but she wanted to get there in good time, in order that she could get her usual spot in the shadow of the beech trees – well, she'd get the shadow in the afternoon and benefit from being out of the direct sun then. Plus, it would be nice to be settled before the coin toss and to have said hello to those around her before play got under way – so she'd be in need of her mid-morning tea before, probably, even the first ball had been bowled.

The match was between the village team and Lord Hartfield's invitational eleven. Alba had been impressed when she'd heard that Lord Hartfield had decided to close the Hall for the day of the Queen's Golden Jubilee, and forgo the profits he'd undoubtedly make from Bank Holiday visitors, to enable his volunteers and staff to be part of the village Jubilee events – particularly the cricket match and the unveiling of the new village sign. There was also the Battle of Britain Memorial Flight that, it was hoped, they'd all get to see; it was entirely co-incidental that the route took the Memorial Flight over their village but once the parish council had learnt of the route, they and Lord Hartfield were keen to ensure as many villagers and staff from the Hall had an opportunity to share in the spectacle. Finally, the parish council, once they realised that the new village sign was going to come in under budget, used their unexpected surplus to pay for the lunch that Mrs Rowan was to put on in the pavilion. One local 'scrooge', on the publication of the day's itinerary and how everything was paid for and within budget, had accused, in a letter to the local paper, Lord Hartfield and the Council of trying to create their own 'Bedford Falls', from Capra's 'It's a Wonderful Life', but by vast the majority of the villagers, Alba included, were appreciative of the generosity and planning that people had directed towards this golden day.

*

Up at the Hall the mood was far from golden that morning.

"Jane, you in here? Jerry Haltwhistle has just phoned," said Lord Hartfield as he strode into his wife's dressing room.

"Yes," replied Jane unnecessarily since her husband was already halfway across her room.

Lady Jane Hartfield, née Trerose, sitting at her dressing table, placed her hair brush down and picked up her favourite bottle of 'Chanel'. She knew a monologue was about to be forthcoming from her husband – they'd been married long enough that she knew what was about to unfold. She didn't bother to get up to greet her husband that morning or even to turn round to offer him a cheek for him to place a simple kiss, rather she sat and just watched him in her dressing table mirrors as he walked across the room and stopped at the one full length window in the room.

The window looked out on to the rose garden and at this time of year it was easy to see why, when the Hall had been remodelled by the 1st Lord, this window was put in. The roses were in their prime at the moment and, had either Edward or Jane Chapman – that is Lord or Lady Hartfield – been minded to open the window, the scent would have filled the room and stunned another of their senses. However, Lady Hartfield preferred the scent bottles on her table in front of her, the ones that travelled from Hillstone to the London house, to the place in France or to wherever she was, to the fragrances that she might get if she opened a window. As for his Lordship, he was too pre-occupied with the telephone call he'd just taken.

"Bloody Jerry!"

Lord Hartfield went silent for a moment and just stared out of the window into the middle distance, focusing for no particular reason on a mature yew tree.

"I mean, bloody Jerry. It's 9.30am and he's just phoned to say Tobias his son can't play now. Do you know how hard it has been to get this cricket team together? Where am I going to get a replacement from? I can't just phone my friends and ask them, we're all too old now, all of us. Ten years ago, perhaps I could have got someone at short notice, twenty easy, twenty-five definitely. If you remember, we did, when it was the Silver Jubilee and Peter stepped in when he only had 45 minutes notice. But now, I mean, Jerry has left me right in it! There was never even a twelfth man this time around; I only just got eleven together – sons of friends, sons of my old business partners, even my cousin's grandchild's boyfriend. I know it's the 'Lord's Invitational Eleven' but even I have to admit I've been stretching the definition this time around. Blow and bother, at this rate the blinking Tesco delivery driver, if he delivers here this morning, will be asked to be part of my 'Invitational Eleven'. Bloody Jerry!"

Lady Hartfield offered no reply. Undeterred, but after a slightly longer pause, Lord Hartfield continued:

"Says one of his horses is lame and, what with the 'meet' they've got on next weekend, they've got to get over to the stables to meet the vet. Why Tobias has to go as well, heaven only knows. And in any case, why couldn't Tobias call me himself? He's 51 years old – I mean it's hardly a difficult age to make a phone call. Blinking Jerry, blinking Tobias."

Lord Hartfield shoved his increasingly rheumatic hands as deep into his trouser pockets as he could and silence returned to the dressing room until her Ladyship spoke. It was a question for her husband but her eyes remained focused on her own reflection, in particular her neck line.

"Why do you bother, Edward? You involve yourself in the village too much."

"Oh Jane, that's your standard response to anything that goes wrong around here."

"Edward, half the villagers are indifferent to us and the other half would turn us out of the Hall as quickly as Tony Blair turned you out of the Lords. Despite all you've done for the village, they'd as quickly turn us into a golf course as help us out of the financial problems we currently find ourselves in."

"Jane, that's not as I see it."

"I think we both know we see a fair amount of things quite differently, Edward. As you know, I don't particularly care for the garden that you're staring at out of that window. Plant more roses, plant fewer sweet peas, re-plant the borders of the 'Long Walk', I don't care, really, I don't care! Leave that to Mr Parker. But I'd still wish to know there is a garden below my window. That it is there is what is important to me and if the Royal Horticultural Society or Country Life want to come and do an article on it, that's fine by me. Others can fuss over the details but what would be ghastly would be to see it turned into a golf course. I accept the village probably wouldn't want us to be turned in to a housing estate, as befell Cassiobury House – I remember an aunt telling me about the demise of that beautiful mansion and its grounds – but a golf course they'd accept if they could get shot of the Lord and Lady of the Manor. I mean, have you heard what's going on at Brocket?"

"Jane, that's not fair what you say about the villagers and you'd know it if only you involved yourself in village life a bit more. And I think people do want us here and do look to us in a positive way – for guidance and patronage. It's not me personally that appeals to them, I know that I'm just some aged bloke called Edward, but the title, the history, the stability that having a Lord and Lady around the village, that's what people buy into. That's what they want, especially on the occasions when the community does come together

– not some successful but non-descript local business person or a district councillor to open their fete, award the rosettes at the country show or organise a cricket match. They want the person who lives in Hillstone Hall because, in a weird way, it's their Hall too – the villagers have a stake in what goes on here. Deep down they neither want a golf course nor a housing estate and therefore we, I believe, have a responsibility to them in return, whether we're in a financial spot of bother or not. I know you weren't happy with my decision to shut the Hall to visitors today but let's not re-visit that disagreement now. In any case, I haven't come in to discuss our finances, the merits or otherwise of historic house ownership, the Blair Government or what that chap Charlie Brocket has done, I've come in to say I'm a man down for the match that starts in just over an hour's time. I need your help – is there anyone you can think of that I can ask?"

"Edward, how on earth do you expect me to help? I don't know the first thing about cricket!"

"Jane, your sporting knowledge is monumentally poor, I know, and thank goodness you don't try to bet on the horses to raise the funds we need, otherwise we really would have had to sell up pronto and see this place turned into a theme park or a golf course. But I don't need you to explain the lbw rule to me, rather I need you to suggest someone we can ask, someone who simply can stand in the out-field for a few hours without falling over and, if necessary, walk to the crease holding a cricket bat the right way round. If they drop every possible catch and are out for a golden duck, right now I don't give a damn. If they turn up with a bat, as opposed to a tennis racket or a billiard cue, then they're in. So Jane, please, any ideas?"

"Harry?"

"Already playing."

"Derek?"

"Ditto."

"Marco?"

"Yes, I thought of him too but his work has taken him to Japan, his secretary has just told me."

"Colin?"

"We know several Colins; Colin who?"

"Colin, err what's his name? Colin, err his name makes me think of chocolates – Colin Lane. That's it, Colin Lane."

"Contacted him originally but he said he's taking longer to recover from the operation than he originally anticipated. I don't think I should call him now and put him under pressure to play – he needs to recuperate properly, given it was such a major job he had done. I really haven't got time to ask but why on earth does Colin Lane remind you of chocolates?"

"Oh Edward, isn't it obvious?"

"No, it isn't, really it isn't."

"Colin Lane – don't you see? Lane, avenue, cul-de-sac, road, street. Street! 'Quality Street'. You see – chocolates!"

"Oh, for goodness sake! It always annoys me that they never put enough green triangles in but anyway, anyone else?"

"Scarlet's father, Mitch?"

"Playing."

"Oh, hold on a minute, hold on. At last week's auction up in town, when we were chatting to Simon the auctioneer beforehand, wasn't he talking about it being such a small world because his son had just moved to our village?"

"That's right, go on."

Lady Hartfield continued:

"Simon said their son had moved here before they, Simon and his wife Anne, had told their son about how much of Simon's business was due to us of late. Plus, Simon was telling us about how Anne already had a tenuous link to the village. Oh, what was the link?"

"Wasn't it something to do with her ex-husband?"

"That's it, Edward, you're right. Anne's ex-husband moved to our village a couple of years ago. What was his name?"

"Jane, his name isn't important, but whatever it is it probably reminds you of a packet of crisps or your favourite restaurant or…"

"Edward you are being facetious. It doesn't become you."

"Sorry my dearest. But his name isn't important. But Simon's son's is – if we can remember, then I can ask Barnes to try and get his number and get him on the phone. Simon was always pretty sporty so I'm hoping his son is too. Plus, if he hasn't been living here too long he probably hasn't been selected to represent the village but we'll only know that for sure if Barnes can get him on the phone."

"Justin. It's Justin. Not the ex-husband's name, rather Simon and Anne's son is Justin."

"Jane. You are a marvel – well done old girl. It's not guaranteed but I'm hopeful; now let's see if Barnes can get hold of him and then I can have a word."

And an elderly man turned away from the window, moved towards his wife and tenderly placed his lips upon her cheek, which she had turned towards him. She offered him her hand also, which he took for just a moment before replacing it upon her dressing table by her enamelled hair brush. Lord Hartfield left the room looking, if not ten years younger, then perhaps five years younger than when he had entered.

Through her door, that hadn't quite closed properly, for the hinges were worn, she could hear her husband in his study talking with Barnes, their butler of many years standing, and Lady Hartfield knew, success or not, Edward would update her on his way out as she breakfasted with Edward's brother, William Hartfield, who'd been back about six months now, in the dining room.

*

Alba replaced the lid of her thermos flask and, as the tea brewed in the cup by her feet, she turned to the man nearest to her on her left, who was just pitching his 'camp'.

"Morning Neale. You alright?"

"Yes, thanks. It's a glorious day isn't it? Good to have such fine weather on a Bank Holiday! I sense we're going to get a full day's play today. Flapjack?"

"Blow, you've only just sat down but I'm partial to a bit of flapjack. I'll trade you a bit for a bit of my fruitcake in return, if you want some later."

"No need to trade, although your cakes are lovely. The flapjack is offered freely and without any conditions attached. But it's not home-made, I'm afraid."

"Don't worry about that. You're busy writing – that must take up all your spare time. How's the book coming along?"

"Slowly. I'm up to chapter 12 but I do know where I'm going with it and the next three chapters are there in my head but, as you infer, it's finding the time to sit and write. So, the flapjack is bought, nice though isn't it?"

"It's very good. It can't be from 'Stapleton's'. I mean, Mrs Lyle is good for organising our newspapers, for milk, when I'm running low, and the odd hundred grammes of cinder toffee but I can't believe 'Stapleton's' have started stocking cakes of this quality."

"You'd make a good amateur detective!" said Neale as he stood up to brush some crumbs from his shorts. He offered a bit of flapjack to the elderly man on his left before turning back to Alba and continuing:

"Alba, yes, you're right. Not 'Stapleton's', though I will grant Mrs Lyle does stock my preferred brand of digestives and, to be fair to her, the reams of printer paper that she sells aren't too expensive and I am getting through paper quite a lot as I send some of my initial chapters off to different publishers. No, I got these from that new community café that's just opened up. Have you been in yet? It's really quite quirky – part charity shop, part tea room, part advice centre. I think Citizen's Advice or Christians Against Poverty are using the room above. So far I've just discovered the cakes. It will be interesting, well maybe not that interesting but you know what I mean, to compare their millionaire's shortbread to Mrs Rowan's. I hope she's made some for today's lunch."

"You and me both. So, when am I going to get a look at chapter 11? The first 10 chapters have been reading quite…"

But before Alba finished her sentence, a hand placed itself on her shoulder.

"Morning young Alba, in your usual spot I see."

In one movement, Alba turned her neck, lifted her chin and her eyes to look upon the speaker's face but the voice had already told her it was Vaughan.

"Vaughan!" she exclaimed as she instinctively got up and, narrowly missing her cup of tea, gave him a big hug. "How are you? Rested, I hope. You haven't got a chair with you but I'm not surprised, your one is pretty heavy. You should have said you were coming and I'd have brought my spare. Still, you're here now and, as the umpires have just come out, you take my seat and I'll sit on the grass." And Alba gestured her beloved Vaughan towards her stripy camping chair.

"You do like fussing over me don't you but I can't have you sitting on the grass in that pretty little white dress that you're in and anyway I don't think Neale would take kindly to me taking your seat. He hasn't 'just' sat next to you, you know, simply to share his cakes and talk field placements."

"Vaughan!" Alba said as sternly as she could to Vaughan, which wasn't stern at all, rather more of a resigned plea. "Don't be daft, Neale won't mind."

"Of course not," said Neale, as he too stood up and to Vaughan said, "Can I suggest, you take my chair instead? I'll happily sit on the grass."

"Neale you are just so adorable." She then turned to Vaughan. "But before you add two and two and make twenty-seven thousand, Neale met someone when he was last out in the Middle-East. He's shown me some photos and she looks lovely – such dark hair and a beautiful smile. He's going out to South Africa next month to meet her family, as that's where she is from. So please sit down. Oh rats, I've missed the coin toss – did you see who won?"

"From the gesturing," said Neale, "I think the village team are batting first. But more importantly, Vaughan, please take my chair."

"Thank you but no. I'm on my way to the pavilion, I thought I'd watch the morning's play from over there and the wooden benches aren't too bad if you liberate a cushion from the pavilion itself and then…"

At which point Vaughan half stumbled and, with one hand, grabbed the back of Alba's chair and, with the other, caught hold of Alba's arm.

"Oh Vaughan, are you alright?" asked a worried Alba.

"Yes, thank you. Yes, I'm fine," replied Vaughan.

"Really, Vaughan? I can walk you home if you like, Neale can look after my stuff, and we'll take it slowly."

"I'll come too, if that would help. Our stuff should be fine – the flapjack is good but the local master criminals probably have their eyes on other targets today."

"You two are very kind. It seems a shame to me that you've apparently met someone else, Neale. I thought you two might get together after all, now that Alba's by herself once more. But no, once I get over to the pavilion, I'll be fine and I can rest a while there."

"If you're sure," said Alba still in her worried tone. "If you're sure," she repeated, "then at least let me walk you round to the pavilion. Actually, I insist on it. Let me just take off my cardigan but grab my little bag." Then, turning to Neale, issued her orders. "Keep any roving dogs out of my hamper, don't let anyone grab my spot and, in return, we'll have a piece of my fruitcake when I get back."

"Orders received and understood, Captain," said Neale with a boyish grin on his face, as he stood and attempted a salute.

"Wrong hand, Neale, you used the wrong hand," said Vaughan sadly and he shook his head. "It should always be the right. Oh, you youngsters – boy, could I tell you some stories about army life and my time in France and Germany."

Yet Vaughan paused before continuing. A counsellor, familiar with post-traumatic stress, might have noticed the pain in Vaughan's voice and would have sensed that, even after so many years, Vaughan hadn't stopped because he didn't want to bore a younger generation with his wartime tales but rather that he stopped because to have continued would have been too distressing for the teller.

"But I won't," continued Vaughan. "Rather let me tell you about the last time I saluted my brother Clive. We were both on leave, it was..." However, Alba, having taken a sip of her stewing tea, took Vaughan's arm and said:

"Tell me on the way, tell me on the way. We ought to get you settled."

Neale watched them go. As they did, he could hear Vaughan saying to Alba something about having brought the photo he'd promised her and something about spotting Clive, tomatoes and *myosotis* but their voices were too far away by then for him to make sense of their conversation. Neale watched them as they slowly walked around the boundary rope; arm in arm and with Alba's head angled towards Vaughan's shoulder. Vaughan was in a checked shirt and gilet and had his usual leather hat that, Neale thought, could have done with a bit of boot polish being applied to it, and Alba in her white dress, with its little blue forget-me-not flowers embroidered around the end of its short sleeves. Neale fished out the tea bag from her cup, threw the tea bag under the laurel hedge behind him, and, with her cup in hand, watched as the game started.

On finishing Alba's drink, and having offered a passing 'hello' to Tom Wychfield who had walked past, Neale found himself counting the players. Twice, three times he counted ten for the fielding team and was about to ask the gentleman beside him about it when a further person descended the pavilion's wooden steps, still pulling on his white tank top and with laces trailing from one shoe.

*

"Amen," said the Reverend Quinn and, with one hand placed on his desk chair, came up off his knees. He brushed some fluff from his trousers and resumed his seat at his desk and endeavoured to continue to work on his sermon for the coming Sunday. The passage from Philippians was an obvious one for a confirmation service and yet, still he couldn't concentrate. He'd prayed for clearness of thought and spiritual guidance for his talk but the prayers had seemingly gone unanswered for his thoughts kept taking him to the conversation he had had in 'The Sun and the Moon' last night.

He shoved his pen into his 'desk tidy', closed his Bible and A4 pad, took off his dog collar, placing it on top of the Bible, picked up his keys and his jacket and left the vicarage.

*

Cushions made the wooden seat surprisingly comfortable. Alba decided she still preferred her usual spot by the beech trees but she conceded that from this side of the ground, by the pavilion, those same trees, with the reasonably well-maintained laurel hedge slightly further back, formed a wonderful backdrop for the game that was now well under way. Plus, seated here, you definitely felt part of the hustle and bustle of pavilion life. You noticed the comings and goings of people into the wooden structure itself. You also were much closer to the players on the batting team, who were padded up and waiting. Noticing that one of them was David, she took her leave of Vaughan for a moment to wish their fellow volunteer well.

On her return to Vaughan, Alba said "David's still chuffed to have been selected to play for the village team, given he had an uncle who actually played for the West Indies. David said he's asked lots of people to take his photo but he's hoping, in particular, Tom will make good his promise and take several shots of him whilst he's at the crease. Tom is a good amateur photographer after all, so it'll be good to see what images he can create."

"Let's hope both David and Tom create some good shots today," said Vaughan dryly as he poked, ever so gently, Alba in the ribs. "Right," continued Vaughan "before I forget, can I give you this photograph? I've put it in a clear bag so anyone walking around where you and Neale are sitting, will be able to see what it is and hopefully not tread on it. As I say, three guesses to pick out my brother."

"Vaughan, you shouldn't have brought it today. Another time would have been fine. There are so many people around today I'm worried it'll get damaged."

"If you rest it between the chairs you and Neale are sitting in, I'm sure it'll be fine. I'm more worried about what's in this other bag. Perhaps I shouldn't have brought these today but I didn't want to disappoint Tom as I did say he could have a look at them."

"Oh Vaughan, what on earth have you brought that's even more inappropriate today? And whatever it is, you've got it simply in a Tesco carrier bag! Vaughan you're not being your usual cautious self."

"Here Alba, take a look" said Vaughan as he handed Alba the plastic carrier bag.

"Oh my word!" exclaimed Alba as she looked inside. With hindsight, the little metallic clink that she heard as she was passed the bag had been a clue as to what was within. "They're your wartime medals! Vaughan why on earth have you brought them? I'm not taking them out to look at; someone might see and get ideas."

She scrunched up the bag and passed it back to Vaughan with an irritated look on her face, which momentarily jarred Vaughan from his complacency. He was silent for a moment. Yet there was something about Vaughan this week that meant, as he took the medals out from the bag, that the complacency re-asserted itself.

"They're not my medals as he held them out proudly, although I've got that one myself," as he pointed to the 1939-45 Star, "and that one," this time pointing to the British War Medal. "These are Clive's."

Being only too aware of all the people around her, especially she could feel one group very close behind herself and Vaughan, Alba's hands shot out and she forced her elderly friend's arms down onto his lap. She manoeuvred his hands until they were on top of the medals and then she let out a long-relieved breath. Only then did she continue.

"They must be priceless. Put them away now!" pleaded Alba, who could never be angry with him, and she hoped her assertiveness would jolt him into a degree of common sense.

"Oh, they're not worth that much – no gallantry medals. Just the '39-'45 Star, Air Crew Europe Star, with clasp, the Defence Medal and the War Medal." Forgetting himself once more, Vaughan held the medals out again. "But see that one?" said Vaughan pointing to one in particular, "the oak leaves on that ribbon means he was once mentioned in dispatches." As he held them out, the bronze and silver looking medals gleamed in the June sunshine.

Alba placed her hand on his forearm and slowly, with the application of a little bit of force, brought Vaughan's arms down once again to his lap.

"But Vaughan I'm not talking about pounds, shillings and pence. I mean they must be of some value, rather I'm talking about their worth to you – they're priceless. Why did Tom have to see them today of all days?"

"He'd been asking after them for a while. You know how he's into all this re-enactment stuff, and had kept asking to see them. He said, as he'd have his camera equipment with him today, could he see them and take a photo or two."

"But that's daft on his part. He could have popped in at yours on the way to the match today and photographed them there. After all he walks past 'Stapleton's' on his way here, now he's lodging with Mrs Taylor, and you're right next door to the village shop. Why would he pressurize you to bring them out here today?"

Not really listening to Alba's concerns or puzzlement, Vaughan parted his hands and pointed to the ribbons and said "The ribbons mean something too, you know. The three colours for this star, the '39-'45 one, represent the navy, army and air force and the ribbon for the air crew star, do you know what the colours in that represent?"

Relieved that at least this time Vaughan was keeping the items on his lap, she looked at the ribbon he was pointing to, which was coloured blue, black and yellow. "Blue for RAF, yellow for the eggs they had on their return and black for death?" offered up Alba before adding "I'm not trying to sound flippant about the eggs, I couldn't think of anything else yellow might represent and didn't they have bacon and eggs for breakfast after a night-time operation? And," smiling a warm smile at Vaughan as she continued, "I'm not trying to sound jokey about using the word flippant when talking about fried eggs."

"I know, that's not your style. But wrong shade of blue for the RAF. This is light blue, to signify the sky. The black represents the night time operations and yellow for the search-light beams. But I like your thinking about the eggs, although it reminds me there was one breakfast Clive didn't make it back for." For a while Vaughan was silent and then he continued, "I know it's true for all of us, ultimately as it were, that there's one breakfast each of us won't make. There's a poet, Pam Brown I think, now how did she put it? Oh yes, it was *'For every person who has ever lived there has come, at last, a spring he will never see'*."

"But don't forgot her next line," interjected Alba.

"*'Glory then in the springs that are yours'*, I know" replied Vaughan. "And I think Clive did glory in those days – not glorifying in the war but the camaraderie, the training, the excitement and I know, in a sense, he was more alive then than many people are today as they trudge round supermarkets, watch TV and complain about the price of diesel. But I miss him, even now, after all these years, you know, I wasn't ready to have to say goodbye. Not that I actually got to say goodbye, for his last leave happened when I was back with my unit. I'd heard he'd been to see our parents again and then he was back with his squadron. I got one further letter from him and then simply nothing – nothing until my parents got that telegram."

"I know," replied Alba as she placed one arm around his shoulders and with her spare hand clasped one of his. Time passed as they sat there in silence, time in which one no-ball was bowled, before the bowler was hit for four, two, a further four and finally a single. "Not his best over," Alba continued quietly, as she nodded towards the bowler, who was now collecting his jumper from one of the umpires.

"Never mind Mitch," cried out someone from the pavilion steps.

The moment broken, Alba said "But how interesting, I'd never thought of 'reading' a medal in that way before but please, dearest Vaughan, please put them out of sight now."

He reverently wrapped them back up in their carrier bag and looked at Alba through old, weary eyes. She caught the sadness in his eyes as she spoke:

"I know, I know, a carrier bag doesn't do them justice. I'll pop round tomorrow – I've got a spare smallish biscuit tin, it's got a picture of a stag on it but don't they all, and with some cotton wool inside to lay the medals on, they'll be just fine. We'll put in a photo too. Promise me, though, they stay out of sight for the rest of the day. Promise?"

"Promise."

"Good. Now you're settled, I'll get back to my seat at the next convenient break in play. If I'm fortunate and Neale notices me walking round, he'll have a cup of tea brewing for me: I read somewhere that *each cup of tea represents an imaginary voyage*. It caught my imagination that."

"That's quite good. You'll have to mention that quote to Neale. It might make it into his book. These two batsmen are looking quite settled."

The batsmen were, for a couple more overs at least, until ten players cried out in unison "Howzat!" as the second slip went down and took a catch.

"Right," said Alba, "that's my cue. Speak later."

Sadly, they never would.

*

Alba got up and turned to walk behind the bench. Not quite looking where she was going, as she re-slung her bag over her shoulder and concentrating on the photograph she was holding under her arm, she walked into the group that were standing right behind the bench.

"Oh, sorry, I wasn't looking where I was going" said Alba instinctively but, as soon as she said it, was very conscious of just how close the group had been standing to herself and Vaughan.

"No harm done, I think. You're alright aren't you William?" said Lord Hartfield as he turned to his brother. William Chapman nodded an agreement. "Are you alright yourself?" Lord Hartfield continued, as his attention turned back to Alba. "It's Alba White isn't it, you're one of my volunteers aren't you? Didn't I give you a 'two years' volunteering badge the other month? Sorry, too many questions but you are alright, aren't you?"

"Lord Hartfield! I'm so sorry to bump into one of your party." Alba then looked at William and mouthed a 'sorry'. "Yes, I'm OK, just a bit embarrassed," she continued, "and yes, you did present me with a badge. It was good of you to find me in person; I'd assumed Mr Parker was simply going to leave it for me in the gardener's hut one day. Please accept my apologies again" and with that she made her way away from them and headed back to her chair.

"You can take a few knocks can't you, you'll be fine," said Lord Hartfield jokingly to William. "Almost fifty years in South America and not a scratch on you, six months back in the UK and you're assaulted at the first village cricket match I bring you to and by one of my own volunteers to boot! You almost dropped your cigarette case as well." Turning to Simon and Anne, who were also with them but had been talking between themselves, Lord Hartfield continued, "Great catch Justin just took. So pleased he could play and how fortuitous that you could get along and watch too."

CHAPTER 4

Death is a market place

"Is he alright, you've been gone quite a while? I mean, I could see you sitting with him for a good while but then, right at the end, you seemed deep in conversation with that group that were right behind you," said Neale inquisitively on Alba's return.

Alba placed the photograph gently against her chair, took off her bag and let it drop to the ground, so she could manoeuvre it under her chair with her foot. She replied as she sat down:

"He's alright, kind of, I think, but I'm a bit worried about him. No, that's not right, I'm a lot worried about him. That's rubbish English I know – would give my mother a field day, correcting me on my word selection! – but he's not his usual self and," as Alba twisted round to take her cardigan off the back of her camping chair and started to put it on "is it just me or is there a chill in the air? I know the sun is out and golden rays are falling all around us but suddenly I feel that there's a silvery edge to the air?"

As Alba buttoned up her white cardigan, Neale offered his reply:

"It's just you, old thing. The sun's almost at its highest, we've yet to get the shade from the trees behind us and it's the month of June

– you should be putting suntan lotion on, not dressing for winter. You're worried about him, aren't you?"

"Yes. I wish he had let us take him home. It was kind of you to offer to come as well, given you don't know him as well as I do."

"I know him a little bit and I bump into him in 'The Sun and Moon' now and then and we chat about this and that."

"Don't mention bumping into people," commented Alba, as much to herself as to Neale.

"What's that old thing?"

"Something about bumping into people but never mind." With that Alba went quiet.

"Tell you what," offered Neale positively, but without trying to sound too 'Boys' Own Adventurey', "Let me make you a cup of tea, especially as I drank your last one, and then whilst you have that, I'll go for a wander around the ground and check in on Vaughan and then report back to you. If we still feel uneasy after that, hang our spot here and we'll go and pitch camp over with him – I wonder whether he wanted to be that side of the ground because of the way the Memorial Flight will come in from."

"I'd forgotten about the fly-past. There's going to be a pause in the match isn't there, when the planes are due overhead? Actually, it would be kind, if you go and surreptitiously check on him."

As Neale sorted the drinks, another couple of wickets fell; one to a dubious lbw decision, that the opening batsman would contest for years to come, and one when the new batsman, keen to get off the mark, edged it to the keeper. However, David remained at the crease and Alba gave him a thumbs up, when he looked in her direction as he waited for the village team's fifth batsman to join him out in the centre.

"Right, that's it, I'm off for my wander. I'll just take my bag with me so it's one less thing for you to keep an eye on. Enjoy your tea and try not to worry too much – by the look of it, someone's chatting to him at the moment." With that, Neale was off.

Looking across the pitch, Alba could make out that a woman was standing right in front of Vaughan. She seemed to be gesticulating quite a bit and, given she had her back to the match, clearly had no interest in the match or even in letting Vaughan watch it as they discussed something that, from a distance at least, was seemingly agitating the woman in question. Quite how Vaughan was interacting with her, Alba couldn't make out and, but for Neale already being on his way, Alba would have been up and heading over to the pair because it just didn't look right. Alba did the very top button of her cardigan up, cradled her cup of tea and did her best to watch the game.

*

"I return bearing gifts," stated Neale on his return, as he offered Alba a piece of Mrs Rowan's millionaire's shortbread.

Taking the piece offered, Alba offered up her opinion as to where it ranked in the hierarchy of biscuits. "Truly the Queen of biscuits," she said and took a not insignificant bite.

And, as can sometimes happen in life, moments can seemingly last for years as Alba and Neale both sat and ate, comfortable in each other's presence, neither with a desire to be anywhere else – be it, for her, in the garden or, for him, at his desk writing.

The shortbread finished, Alba said, "For all her faults, she can definitely bake biscuits. I didn't think they were serving stuff mid-morning – is that why you offered to go and check on Vaughan? Rather deceitful of you, if you did!"

Looking a tad embarrassed, Neale said, "Err, I've got a confession, old thing."

"What dastardly deed have you done and, probably more importantly, why do you keep calling me 'old thing' today? Have I aged that much since we last met up?"

"Sorry, on that last point. You post-decimal children can still call yourself young, I guess, but you have to concede, you were at least born in the same millennium as myself! And, no, you haven't aged since we last met. You have achieved that Mary Poppins quality of being ageless."

"Apology accepted. You almost pushed it too far with Ms Poppins though – I still think I've got a good few years on her. But what is this dastardly deed you have perpetrated?"

"Well, err, they err, how shall I put it?"

"For someone so good with the written word, you ought to be able to string a sentence together, so come on, out with it, man!"

"They weren't serving refreshments in the pavilion, I lifted them. There, I have confessed."

"Neale! And you've now made me party to your crime, for I've eaten one of the stolen items."

"Tasted good though, didn't they?"

"Neale!"

"Sorry old thing."

"Neale!"

"You know what they say, first it's penny sweets, then it's the sprinkles, hundreds and thousands and, finally, it's millionaire's shortbread. I've worked my way up the criminal's confectionery ladder, you know."

"Neale, I hope you're joking and I expect, at lunchtime, you'll go and apologise to Mrs Rowan."

"I'd prefer not to, she was somewhat irritable and flustered, from what I could make out. Something had got to her as it were and, as I don't think she noticed 'Fingers McNeale' lift the shortbread, it would be simpler to leave things be."

"Oh, how convenient!"

A further lbw appeal, which this time was declined by the umpire at the wicket, was quickly followed by the fifth batsman being bowled. Alba watched as the wicket keeper replaced the bails and as the other fielders went over to congratulate the bowler. Cries could be heard of 'well bowled Derek' coming from some of the spectators over towards the pavilion, where Lord Hartfield and his small group had located themselves, and, as David stood at the non-striker's end waiting for a further partner, Alba looked through the scene and noticed Vaughan wasn't to be seen.

"Neale?" she said.

"Yes, Judge White, have you determined my sentence? I've pleaded my guilt, offered my plea in mitigation, well I shared my loot with you, and so I await any fair sentence you care to impose. I'm sensing it might be a withholding of the fruit cake."

"No, shut up. Be serious for a minute – Vaughan's gone. Did you see him prior to your misdemeanours because you haven't actually reported in to me on how he was? There seemed to be a woman virtually arguing with him, or at least berating him, for he wouldn't argue with anyone, just as you left to go and check up on him."

"I didn't notice that. As you saw, I walked that way round" and he reiterated his point by raising his right arm and moving it in a general sweep off to the right, to the side of the ground where the practice nets were and the footpath that they would have used had they taken Vaughan home – as Alba was increasingly wishing they had.

"And?"

"And I bumped into the new couple who've recently joined the writing group that I go to. He writes sci-fi stuff. It's good if you like that genre but rather dark, a bit too dark if you ask me. His last piece was titled 'The day it didn't happen'. An intriguing title but his piece, on that occasion, didn't quite live up to the potential the title afforded. I don't know what she writes, she hasn't offered up anything yet. Odd couple – I might have to subtly put them into my next book, as it were. I think I could shape them into quite a memorable pair of characters. After a few minutes chatting with them, when he started talking about the new 'Star Wars' film, episode two apparently, and getting very excited about it, I said I was on my way to see someone and politely took my leave. I moved further on a bit and then stopped and watched David's two lads in the practice nets. Isn't that just typical of children? David's out there having a pretty solid innings – what's he on now?"

"Scoreboard says – 3rd Man, that's David, 42, 6th batsman, 2, extras 9," offered up Alba.

"As I say, a solid innings and yet his boys, Tommy and Arthur, are happier playing by themselves rather than watching their dad. I threw the ball back to them a couple of times after his younger lad mis-hit it but they've both got potential. Also asked them about a decent looking camera lying near their jumpers and rucksack; they said it was their dad's and he had asked them to take some pictures of him and also the planes. I suggested, with all the people about today, they at least put it out of sight under their stuff until they needed it. Thankfully, they saw the sense of that. That said, hope they now remember to use it. So, all in all, it took me a while to get round to the pavilion and by the time I got there, Vaughan was gone."

"Gone, gone where, do you think?" interjected a concerned Alba.

"Yeah, I was puzzled and a tad concerned too. I went and spoke with the St John's Ambulance people first" replied Neale, "in case they were treating him."

"Good idea. You've redeemed, well in part, your tarnished reputation, 'Fingers McNeale'. And?"

"Not with them and they hadn't had to help anyone by that stage. They were just by their vehicle watching the cricket – neither of them thought the opening batsman was lbw. After that, I went round to the back of the pavilion, is it the back or is it the front? Whatever, the road side of the building, that is, the side we can't see from here. Still nothing, so I went into the pavilion, through the door that side. As I went in, there was an elderly gentleman, but not Vaughan, leaving the gents toilets. He didn't see me as he headed out of the pavilion pitch-side. I popped my head into the gents – in case Vaughan had also been in there and had had a funny turn or collapsed in a cubicle but nothing – and then made my way into the main room in the pavilion."

"Yes."

"There he was, in the corner, in one of the pavilion's canvas chairs, talking with a youngish lad, probably mid-twenties. I'd said 'hello' to this lad earlier, as he walked close by me, but didn't get a response. He had a bit of photographic equipment with him. Anyway, Vaughan and this lad were looking at something quite small that Vaughan was showing him; they clinked a bit as they were being moved about and, from where I was standing, they looked like large coins and some rainbow ribbons – well, a rather dull rainbow, lots of blues and some black. I watched for a bit, I don't think anyone was expecting there to be someone in the doorway, where I was, as we all always go in and out of the pavilion from the pitch side, don't we? So, I just watched, as I promised you I would. Mrs Rowan, and a young girl she had with her, were beavering away, setting out the lunch but, again, I don't think either of them saw me. But back to the young lad, he was telling Vaughan, how excited he was to see these coins and how valuable they would be to buy at auction. A few other people, came in from the pitch side, whilst I was there – a couple of youngsters, who snaffled some cocktail sausages and a bowl of crisps but scarpered when Mrs Rowan spotted them and shouted at them, a couple from the batting team came and grabbed some pizza slices, who equally got an earful from Mrs Rowan, and finally that new vicar from St Mary's. But he, also, seemed to leave pretty pronto when he saw Vaughan and this other lad. Mrs Rowan was back in the kitchen area when he came in."

"I'm guessing the lad Vaughan was talking to was Tom. Sounds like he had caught up with Vaughan in the pavilion, although Tom had promised to be photographing David, I thought."

"Don't know about that but Vaughan put these coins away, albeit in a Tesco carrier bag by the look of it, so maybe they weren't valuable at all. This lad seemed to lose interest after that. He said something about photographing the planes and, sensing he was about to get up and turn around and possibly catch me eavesdropping, I took my leave – grabbing a couple of the millionaire's shortbread from the table that was temptingly within reach, before I turned and was out through the road door. To be blunt, having seen almost everyone else come in and nick food ahead of lunch time, including possibly an attempted raid by that new vicar, I admit I succumbed to the temptation that was placed before me."

The look of contrition on his face, as he finished, comforted Alba that Neale's baking misdemeanour was an aberration but this didn't stop her from repeating one of her mother's stock phrases:

"Neale, even if everyone else jumps in front of a bus, it doesn't make it the right thing to do. I trust you will make good to Mrs Rowan. As for Vaughan, if you've come away feeling he's OK, we'll leave him alone now until lunch. There are clearly lots of other people near him."

"Yeah, but, he still looked weary, even though he was sitting down. You could see him put his head back a couple of times and close his eyes, even when this lad, Tom you say, was chatting to him. I sense he went into the pavilion for some shut-eye and Tom followed him in."

*

Atop of the wooden pavilion was a little clock tower, with an 'Old Father Time' weather vane atop. As the clock approached 12.30pm, Lord Hartfield politely excused himself from his little group.

He went into the pavilion, to check on Mrs Rowan and the lunch. He glanced at Vaughan sleeping in the far corner and then, as a door swung, turned and caught sight of Mrs Rowan – who by now was out of the kitchen every time she heard the wooden steps creak, anticipating another food raid. Thankfully, being acclimatised to the relative darkness inside the pavilion, compared to the glorious sunny June day outside, she realised who it was, for she had been about to exhort him to 'bugger off' and to 'stop coming in and nicking everyone else's lunch, you thieving wretch'.

"All set for lunch, Mrs Rowan?"

"Yes, your Lordship. Thank you for asking. We'll ring the lunch bell at ten past one, just after the umpires have left the field."

Lord Hartfield checked his watch once more.

"Good. Right, we've still got seven minutes until the fly past is expected to reach the village. So, I'll quickly make use of the facilities."

"Oh, of course" and Mrs Rowan somewhat embarrassed excused herself and returned to the kitchen area – and as the plywood door swung shut behind her, she lifted her eyes to the heavens, put her hands together and said a prayer of thanks that for some inexplicable reason she had not told the 7th Lord Hartfield to 'bugger off out of the pavilion' and she committed herself to trying to be kinder to any waifs and strays that might appear early at similar functions in the future.

"You alright, mum, you look a bit pale all of a sudden?" said Sam.

"Yes, fine thank you. Now, let's get the carrot, pepper and celery sticks done – you've done the cucumbers already, haven't you?"

And mother and daughter continued working away in the kitchen.

A few minutes later, Lord Hartfield returned to the pavilion steps, checked his watch once, twice more, looked to the horizon where they would come in from, checked his watch a final time and decided the time was now.

He rang the bell. Slowly and consistently the bell rang out to suspend play. For those to whom it mattered, since Alba had relayed the scores to Neale, David had progressed on to 46, Andy, the sixth batsman, was on 7 and there'd been one further extra due to Mitch bowling another no-ball. The scorer didn't quite know what symbol to put on the card, to indicate play being suspended because of an incoming Lancaster bomber with fighter escort. He opted for a doodle of a man on a parachute as he wondered what advice the MCC – Marylebone Cricket Club – could give.

The players, batsmen and fielders alike, found themselves

congregating around the wickets, Mrs Rowan and her daughter Sam came out onto the pavilion steps and everyone else stood or sat where they were and had their eyes fixed on the sky. It was quite an exposed village cricket pitch – the groundsman didn't ever have to worry about the effect of shade anywhere on the outfield, meaning he could maintain a good healthy grass pitch – and so the villagers would see the flight come in, go overhead and then disappear over towards Hillstone Hall and then beyond to the Downs. Everyone watching would have, with such a clear blue sky above them, several minutes of being fixated with a world above them; watching from now, since Lord Hartfield had rung the bell, to three dots appearing in the sky, to those dots becoming bird-like in appearance, to those birds becoming majestic, elegant machines of flight, still watching when, in turn, those machines, as if they were receding back into the pages of a Basil Collier or a Paul Brickhill book, would grow smaller in the sky, resume, momentarily, their bird-like appearance and then become just three dots before fading altogether.

Everyone, eyes fixed, watched and waited – well, almost everyone. Two who didn't were David's boys. They continued in their own game in the practice nets, with their dad's camera, which he'd asked them to use, forgotten about under their tops. Forgotten about, that is, until the planes were overhead, with the growl of the engines filling their ears, when they suddenly remembered their dad's request to take some photos of the planes. Much to their relief, they were to get some, just, of the planes, above and then beyond the pavilion.

The people who watched were transfixed, as those echoes from the past, roared overhead; the power of the Avro Lancaster, the elegant outline of the Supermarine Spitfire and the squatter more hunch-backed Hawker Hurricane – machines that brought both defensive protection to the skies of southern England, in the Hurricane and Spitfire, and industrialised offensive destruction to so many parts of occupied Europe, in the Lancaster. They flew straight and true. The villagers knew it was fortuitous that they were under the route that the Memorial Flight was taking on the Queen's Jubilee and so probably soaked up the sight even more. Even when the planes had disappeared, further moments passed before people tilted their heads down, re-focused on the things and people around them and spoke to one another once more.

Lord Hartfield resumed his position on the top step and rang the bell, indicating that play would recommence.

*

A couple of uneventful maiden overs followed as the fielders and batsmen alike re-focused on their game, striving to forget the fraternity that they showed one another during the flypast.

"Right, I'm heading off to the pavilion," said Alba to Neale as the clock on the pavilion edged closer to one o'clock.

"Wanting to be first in the lunch queue – that's unlike you," quipped Neale.

"I concede that is how it looks but I want to check on Vaughan. Coming?"

"Err, I think I'll stay here for a bit longer – feel I should let other people have a crack at the food before me in light of my earlier deeds. I'll see you over there in a bit."

With that, her little bag over her shoulder, Alba made her way around the boundary rope. As she did so, David progressed on to 49 and Alba thought to herself that he would need to be careful and not make a silly stroke in a bid to get to his half-century before lunch.

As she approached the wooden steps, she paused and watched the penultimate ball of the over. David pushed it to short extra cover, cried 'yes' to Andy to indicate he wanted to take a single, and ran.

"Howzat" was the fielders' cry that went up after Harry, who was at short extra cover, had collected the ball and thrown it in a seamless action at the stumps David was running to. Despite David launching himself at the crease, he knew the ball had dislodged the bails before he had got there. A look at the umpire, whose finger was raised, confirmed what David knew and he walked, regretting his rashness, back to the pavilion.

Alba shook her head at David's decision-making and, not having seen Vaughan on the wooden bench, despite the cushions still being there, turned and went into the pavilion.

"You in here Vaughan?" she called out. "What did you think of the flypast? It must touch you in a way that I can't grasp. Vaughan, Vaughan" and as she looked into the far corner, remembering where Neale had said he'd seen him, there he was. "You resting again, you're very quiet," she said as she went over to rouse him.

David, heading for his kitbag and his drinks bottle, made his way into the pavilion – but stayed on the carpet because of his spiked cricket shoes. "Hi Alba, Vaughan" he said, a little dejectedly as he rummaged in his bag. Taking a swig of his drink he continued. "Rats, why did I think that the run was on? Too rash. Did you think it was makeable Alba? Alba? Alba, you alright? I said, did you think I should have taken it?"

But Alba wasn't listening. She was kneeling down by Vaughan and a look of concern was filling her face.

She turned, concern still showing on her face, and said "David, I can't rouse him" and, turning back, she continued to rub his arm and then ran the back of her hand along his forehead. "He's not responding. Come and see." Alba stood, turned once more to look at David and he could see that the look of concern had been replaced with panic.

"He's not responding!" she repeated.

David, not caring for the effect his spiked cricket shoes would have on the wooden floor where Alba and Vaughan were, made his way over. He took Vaughan's hand but it, and his arm, were limp. He also touched Vaughan's face, placing his palm against his friend's cheek. "You're right to be concerned," he said calmly. "He's unresponsive and cool to the touch. Here," he continued as he took his tank top off, "put this over his chest and I'll go and get the St John's Ambulance people."

As quickly as his spiked shoes would let him on a polished floor, he made his way out and down the steps. Alba put the jumper around her beloved Vaughan and tucked it about him, wedging it between his sides and the canvas chair he was on, but, as she withdrew her hands, her fingers were wet. Instinctively she touched her thumbs and forefingers together; they were not just wet but noticeably sticky and she looked at them.

As the St. John's Ambulance people ran in, Alba was still staring at her hands. They were stained red and flecks of blood had also made it onto the bottom of her white dress. She stood up, stared at Vaughan, stared at her bloodied hands and screamed.

CHAPTER 5

Hillstone Hall

Friday, the day after the funeral, saw Alba, as she had said to David in the church hall, back up at the Hall and looking for Mr Parker.

*

Hillstone Hall was a well-proportioned building, approached by a long drive, which came in from the west. The drive culminated in a surprisingly tight turning circle and, at the centre of the perfectly circular grass island that the drive curved around, was an empty square plinth. The figure that was meant to have stood there was still debated amongst the family and the House staff. Rumours, half-cocked theories from bored ticket office staff, lines that appeared in the grass circle during particularly dry summers, the 3rd Lord's ability to start a fire in the documents room, when he put his lit pipe down on his own correspondence, compounded by the fact that none of the last three House archivists could definitely give an answer, all combined to confuse anyone's attempt to establish what actually was meant to be there.

But this confusion enabled the very best room stewards to replace any visitor's initial sensation of 'something's already missing and I've paid a lot of money to bring my uninterested children here' with a sense of mystery and puzzlement. Liz, the *crème de la crème* of room stewards, could even have the odd teenage boy rubbing his chin in contemplation as to what might have been there and asking her the odd question in turn. The visitor would therefore leave the grand entrance hall intrigued, anticipating further mystery and, by the time he or she got to the shop and tea room an hour or so later, probably would have come up with their own theory as to what was meant to have stood there and why the plinth was empty.

The grand entrance hall, that lay beyond the covered porch, did exactly what it was meant to do; to make a grand statement to any visitor to Hillstone Hall. In centuries gone by, and up to just a few decades ago, it was to house guests, politicians and lesser royals that the statement was made. Whereas now, in the opening years of the twenty-first century, in an attempt to keep Hillstone Hall financially viable, it was to the paying public and, regrettably for Lord Hartfield, an insufficient number of private wedding parties. The entrance hall was adorned with a selection of swords, muskets and lances but, without any great military figures in the Chapman lineage, it was what Liz would call a reasonable selection as opposed to excessive militaristic overkill. There were also some pairs of antlers and three tapestries but not much more, for the 7th and incumbent Lord had years ago simplified what was on display in this room in order that visitors might see the architecture and grandeur of the room itself – the way the grand staircase took you up and out of this space, the magnificent fireplace and the way the doors that the servants once used were completely unobtrusive.

This Friday morning, Alba found herself walking up the drive with Liz. As the gravel scrunched beneath their feet, they chatted about coach parties but then, inevitably Vaughan. Liz was heading for the main entrance hall but Alba turned off the path sooner, in her quest to find 'Bic' in his Head Gardener's office, which was located in the right-hand wing of the property.

*

Mr Parker's office was on the ground floor, past Mrs Taylor the Housekeeper's room, at the end of a long corridor. By being at the end of this wing of the Hall, it was a double aspect room – with a window overlooking the drive that Alba had just walked up and another that looked to the sunken garden. It was an intimidating room to go into, as much from the layout of the room as from the occupant. The desk, being opposite the door and with 'Bic' sitting beyond the desk, meaning he faced you as you went in, always created a sense of confrontation and separation between the visitor to the room and Mr Parker – and intimidation was not far behind. Alba always wanted to suggest that he move the desk at right angles, push it a little bit out of the sight line that you had as you walked into the office and introduce a rug and a couple of more comfortable chairs. The width of the room would allow it all. However, a long time ago, she realised he would misinterpret her suggestions as outright criticisms of him and damage what was, at least, a formal working relationship.

For a while now, Mr Parker, the Head Gardener, had been known as 'Bic'. Never to his face and she never quite knew whether the House team had come up with the same nickname for him as the garden team had. The garden team had come up with it a year or so ago when bad weather had allowed them to shelter for a longer than usual tea break. Mr Parker, as was his habit, kept himself in his office – although to be fair to him, the role of Head Gardener was as much about budgets, 'heads of department' meetings and service contracts for the garden machinery, as being out in the garden with the team, 'mucking in' on the big re-planting jobs or simply taking groups round on tours of the garden; meaning he was in his office working a lot. And so, on that particular wet break time, when Alba had started telling the others about Neale and his then plans to start writing, the group of them had time to come up with the silliest, dullest and longest title for his inaugural book and then the pen name he should write under and on that Sally was quickest off the mark when she suggested 'Bic Parker'. Inevitably, compounded by his absence from the conversation, they transferred the idea of a pseudonym for Neale to a nickname for their boss. It was never meant maliciously but it definitely stuck and so 'Bic' Parker, as it were, was born – although never, ever, to his face.

"David said you wanted to see me when I was next here," said Alba, as she sat opposite Mr Parker. "Mr Barnes, who I saw on the drive, said you were in, so I thought I'd come and find you straight away before I get on with the climbing hydrangea – Tom was going to do it this week and, unless you tell me not to, I thought I'd tackle it on his behalf."

"Yes, thank you Alba. I was hoping to catch you yesterday after the funeral but I had to get back here. A number of us, you see, have had to pick up some of Mrs Taylor's responsibilities in her absence and…"

"Is she gravely ill? I've interrupted you, sorry, but Barnes said she's still in hospital and he had a very serious look on his face as he spoke."

"Well, since you have interrupted," replied an irritated Mr Parker – as Alba thought to herself 'anyone would have asked after the Housekeeper by now, I'm not really being rude'. "Since you have interrupted me" repeated Mr Parker just to make the point, "I think I am allowed to say 'yes' she is very very unwell. If she has actually been poisoned with what the police asked me to identify, she is seriously unwell. I fear not even the skill of the doctors and nurses in the intensive care unit that she is in, will be able to save her. I am not at liberty to say anything else, especially as the police probably will interview you at some stage."

"Oh, they have already, mostly about my movements on the day of the cricket match. Given I discovered Vaughan."

"No, Alba, not interview you about Vaughan's death but about Mrs Taylor's."

Alba sat bolt upright, a look of absolute surprise and bafflement shot across her face; "Mr Parker, you're speaking as if she's dead already!"

"Yes, I know. It might seem I am without a heart but she will die. Of that there can be no doubt" and Mr Parker, placing his pen down beside his notebook, looked at an uncomprehending woman sitting opposite him.

"There must be something they can do, there must be some hope, mustn't there? Isn't she now up at St. Thomas's – they've got arguably the best intensive care unit in the country."

"She is and they have but there will be nothing they can do beyond making her final moments as comfortable as possible." And as Alba stared at him wide-eyed and open-mouthed, Mr Parker continued. "Miss White, you may think I am a man without a heart or am a defeatist but I prefer to regard myself as a realist. The Reverend Quinn may talk about prayer, healing miracles and hope and I accept my agnostic standpoint can't quite rule that out – I'm not quite an atheist – but my head tells me that what has got in to Mrs Taylor's system will kill her."

"I guess if Helen were here," said Alba "she would say, 'well, you can still pray for her soul' and that Mrs Taylor can still be saved if not healed. I remember Helen once told me, that in the parable of the healing of the paralytic, the man was forgiven his sins before any physical healing took place. Helen said she learnt that in Sunday School twenty plus years ago but that it still puzzled and challenged her."

"Well, it sounds like it puzzles you too but we are not here to have a theological debate. And, as I have stated I am not currently at liberty to say anything more about Mrs Taylor."

"Sorry Mr Parker, I don't quite know where that last comment came from."

"Quite, yes. So, if you're quite finished, I'll get down to it. I wanted to see you as soon as I'd learnt Tom had been remanded into custody – I'd hoped to catch you yesterday at the funeral. As I think you know, Tom was arrested on Tuesday evening, following Mrs Taylor's admission to hospital."

"But I heard it was Tom who called the ambulance – he was cradling her as the crew turned up apparently."

"Miss White, how often does the perpetrator contact the emergency services himself or herself and be present as the medics turn up? It gives them an 'excuse', if you like, to be at the scene and thus, they hope, negate the significance of being forensically linked to the victim."

"Mr Parker, you are speaking as barrister for the prosecution! Tom didn't do it and, anyway, he lodges with Mrs Taylor so his fingerprints will be all over the place, literally."

"As I say, I am a realist. On the day of the cricket match he was with Vaughan in the pavilion, claims he left him sleeping and then walked up to the Hall all by himself. The property taken from Vaughan that day was found amongst Tom's equipment here up at the Hall. They've linked him to the knife that killed Vaughan and he was in Mrs Taylor's home as she was poisoned. But I am not trying to be judge and jury, I am simply stating the facts but the fundamental fact for me, and this is why I have asked you to come and see me, is that I am lacking a Deputy Head Gardener. I very much would prefer Tom not to be involved in this horrible business but the facts indicate that he is. But whether he is or isn't, I have a department to run here and I need, because Lord Hartfield needs, the garden and the grounds here to be maintained. He, and I now speak in the strictest confidence is that understood, in the strictest of confidence, Miss White?"

Alba nodded her consent.

"Good," continued Mr Parker. "As I say, Lord Hartfield cannot afford, financially, to see a drop in visitor numbers – which is what will happen if word gets around that the gardens aren't up to much. Visitors to the Hall are, our marketing man says, pretty constant year on year; coach companies book regular slots and, for some reason, one-off visits to Hillstone are pretty constant from one year to the next. But what can fluctuate year on year are return visitors, those, who generally live locally, who keep coming back to see the gardens through the seasons, even from month to month. And they're the type of visitor who wander round the grounds with their friends and then finish up in the tea room and shop. And that is where the money, at least the money that determines whether this Hall is self-financing as opposed to being propped up by Lord Hartfield's dwindling other revenue streams, comes from. So, the grounds and, specifically the formal gardens, need to be at their peak all year round. There are too many National Trust properties, let alone that property that the County Council have just passed on to English Heritage, near here that we will quickly haemorrhage those repeat visitors to, if we're not on the very top of our game."

"Oh, is that Horsham Grange? I was reading about that recently. It will be interesting how English Heritage open it up, as it were."

"Exactly, that is my point. We've a lot of competition around us, more so, if the Grange goes live as well, and whilst we are a slick and polished operation here, it's fine margins. Even that new tea shop come drop-in centre in the village, that has just opened, I, along with the other heads of department here, regard simply as further competition. Lord Hartfield's concerned, his accountants are hovering and Andrew, the heir, who rightly is taking over more responsibility from his grandfather, as the years go by, says he's desperate to keep the Hall financially afloat."

"Don't worry Mr Parker. I miss Vaughan terribly – it will be particularly so up here – but I'm still happy to volunteer and I'm sure we'll attract another volunteer gardener or two before too long."

"That is good of you to say that Alba but, and I'll cut to the chase as I have a meeting to be at in a few minutes, since I'm picking up a chunk of Mrs Taylor's work, particularly house staff and volunteer matters, and I've lost my Number Two, with Tom having been remanded, I need you to act up."

"Act up, I'm just a volunteer?" puzzled Alba.

"I've cleared it with Lord Hartfield and there's a temporary contract he's willing to offer. We need you to take on the position of Acting Deputy Head Gardener."

"But Tom's your deputy, it would feel like I'm betraying him. He didn't do it – I'm certain of that – and hopefully he'll be back soon. I couldn't take it."

"Alba, I've sat in enough meetings here to know that the finances are precarious. So precarious that there might not be a 'back' for Tom to come back to! We need to keep this ship afloat and I need a number two. In light of the time, please can I simply ask you to consider it. And, if you do take it on, the pressing tasks are tasking someone to do the beds around the tea shop – and I'm impressed you'd already thought about doing the hydrangea, that's why I've asked you, you see, – then there's the research in to whether we have any 'Verdun Oaks' within the grounds and liaising with the chef over what he wants from the kitchen garden over the winter months. Oh, one further little thing, photographs."

"Photographs?"

"Yes, as you know, in the Orangery there's a photograph of each of us. One of Andrew's ideas by the way, in case you didn't know. Apparently, the House volunteers said to him that the visitors occasionally asked, as they left the House, about the relationship between the Lord, the paid staff and the volunteers. So Andrew decided, about three months ago, that it would be a nice touch – 'make us feel like one large family' I think was his phrase, sickly-sweet, if you ask me – if, on a long table in the Orangery, there were photographs of everyone who lived, worked or volunteered here."

"Oh, yes, I remember being asked for a photo just after the Easter weekend but I'd sort of forgotten what it was for and it's been such a long time since I actually did a tour of the House myself. I didn't know it was in the Orangery that they were all on display."

"Yes, they're all there, mixed up, to create this 'family feel', so you or I could as likely be next to the Lord, Lady Hartfield or Andrew as to that new girl who works in the tea room or to Sally, David or Helen. Anyway, as callous as it might sound, it might be more discrete, probably less painful for the volunteers as it were, if you would be kind enough, sometime today, to go and remove Vaughan's photograph before visitors ghoulishly ask after him, for they may well know about him from the local papers and news coverage. But we must finish for the time being. I really must get along to this meeting I'm now due at."

Mr Parker stood, shut his desk drawer, having retrieved a burgundy coloured file from it, and offered his hand to Alba. He said "Please consider the position, there is no imminent rush to make a decision, I'm not that unrealistic, but by the middle of next week would be helpful."

Alba stood in response and was about to speak when Mr Parker's telephone rang.

"Yes, Parker here," said Mr Parker as he mouthed the word 'Barnes' to Alba. She was about to turn and take her leave when, to her surprise he held up his spare hand and, with thumb resting on his middle finger and index finger erect, indicated that he wished her to remain for a moment longer. She sat down and tried not to listen, trying instead, as she turned to look out into the sunken garden and allowing her eyes to follow the lines of the perfectly clipped box hedging, to focus on the discussion she had just had. That proved impossible as she couldn't help herself hearing Mr Parker's half of the conversation:

"What, St Thomas's?"

...

"And?"

...

"When?"

...

"Did they confirm from what?"

...

"So, their toxicology report confirms I was right. I assume his Lordship is fully aware?"

. . .

"And, any instructions from him?"

. . .

"As normal until informed otherwise, yes I understand. And the meeting I was just on my way to?"

. . .

"Two o'clock instead, same room, yes that's fine by me. By the way, I have Miss White here with me."

. . .

"Yes, it's Miss White we are asking to act up and she has kindly agreed to consider it. It is a big ask and she is understandably concerned for how Tom Wychfield may interpret any acceptance on her part. Still, given we have now asked her, I would like to share with her what it was the police asked me to identify, given the role we are asking her to take on."

. . .

"Yes, I'll hold."

. . .

"Yes, I'm still here."

. . .

"His Lordship has agreed, good. I will tell her what is relevant."

. . .

"Two o'clock, yes. Thank you, Mr Barnes, goodbye."

Mr Parker calmly and purposefully replaced the receiver. He turned and looked out of the window and his eyes followed the line of the drive as the first of the day's visitors made their way along from the car park. He adjusted the vertical blinds, angling them so people couldn't see in.

Turning back to Alba, he said "I would imagine you have worked out the salient points of what Mr Barnes has just told me."

"I would surmise that Mrs Taylor, Housekeeper at Hillstone Hall, has, as you said she would, died. I would further surmise that whatever poison it was that got into her system has indeed killed her. What I am unclear on, though, is that I didn't think we had spiders or scorpions or snakes in this country that could deliver such a lethal dose. I doubt she's been to a zoo recently where something has escaped, so unless she's been foraging for mushrooms, but I didn't think that was something she did, or her doctor wrote the wrong prescription out, then, no, wait. Oh, my word, that means they're going to do Tom for both murders, doesn't it? They're going to amend the charges, aren't they? Because it's no longer an 'attempted murder' is it – it's actual murder. But Tom didn't do it, I'm convinced, so Mrs Taylor must have been bitten by something accidentally. But why can't the police see that? Why can't they accept it must have been an accident? They're looking for a link. They've got one murder and now they want to see another but it's just a tragic co-incidence. Surely, it's just a tragic accident, whatever it was."

Pouring her some water from the glass bottle on his wooden filing cabinet, Mr Parker said, as he offered Alba the glass, "Alba, please have a sip. I can offer you something stronger if you would like but it is very early so I wouldn't really encourage it" and he gestured towards a quarter full decanter on the cabinet, next to the water. "Or I can make you a hot drink – I've got a kettle over there and some herbal tea bags hidden away somewhere," and he gestured to the top of a small bookcase.

"The water is fine, thank you," replied Alba.

He continued, "Alba, it wasn't snake, spider or scorpion venom, it wasn't a pharmaceutical mistake in her prescribed medication, it wasn't a mushroom that she should not have eaten, although in suggesting that, you were a step closer to what it was than perhaps you realise. Mrs Taylor was poisoned. It is possible she administered it to herself, either intentionally or through ignorance, but, in light of the current charges against Tom and, as you prophetically say, the probable amended charges against him, it would seem the police think someone else was involved. It was there in her salad."

"What was, Mr Parker?"

"*Aconitum*, Miss White."

"*Aconitum* – that's Wolfsbane isn't it?"

"Wolfsbane, monkshood, devil's helmet, queen of poisons – it has many common names but, fundamentally, whatever you might know it by, it is lethal if ingested. Perhaps if she had been found sooner by the paramedics, perhaps if the plant had been identified straightaway as the cause, then just maybe, she could have been saved. But by the time the police forensic team came to me to ask me to identify the plant it was too late to save Mrs Taylor. If anything, but please don't misinterpret me for I say this next point purely as a horticulturalist, I'm surprised she lasted as long as she did, 'til yesterday. That's almost forty-eight hours. I'm telling you, with his Lordship's consent and with the permission of the investigating police officer, in case the public need to be reassured as they explore our grounds."

"But we don't have a 'Toxic Garden' or the like," replied Alba.

"No, thank goodness. I know one or two stately homes that do go in for a poison garden, planted out with their wolfsbane, ragwort, rhubarb, yew, foxgloves, hellebores, spurges, nightshades, dog's mercury and the like. Not here thank goodness – the security, insurance and worry, all too too much."

"So why tell me what the poison was?"

"Well, you know the visitors we have, probably better than I do, as I don't have the opportunity to be in the garden as much as I'd like, what with all the paperwork and meetings I have to deal with" and Mr Parker slowly arched his arm over his desk, highlighting the mountains of work to be done. "They'll start to see wolfsbane everywhere, especially once the media are able to report it, so we need to reassure the visitors that it's not grown here. It's not but obviously we should do a sweep of the gardens, especially the beds around the tea room and shop, the car park and the kitchen garden, just to be doubly sure it hasn't self-seeded but I'm virtually certain it doesn't grow here."

"Of course."

"I've got several telephone calls I must now make, so I must get on with those. I am very grateful for your time. Perhaps, as we said a few moments ago, you could let me know when you can about the acting position. For now, if you could check around the tea room, shop and kitchen garden for the plant, that would be useful. I'll do the car park after the calls I must make – I could do with some air if nothing else. Oh, and if you want a drink from the tea room, whilst you're that side of the house, that's fine; we've both had an intense morning. Show them your volunteer's card and ask them to put it through on code 085 and they won't charge you. We use that code when we show dignitaries around and then take them for a drink. I think today, in light of what's just happened, you're OK to use it too and get them to call me if they object. Just today, mind you, Miss White, and the code is not for sharing with the other volunteers."

"Yes, Mr Parker, duly noted. And thank you for asking me about the acting position – I will need to think about it for a day or two but I will let you know as soon as I have decided and I will tell you first."

Mr Parker held the door open for Alba as she made her way out of his office. She smiled at him as she passed but it wasn't reciprocated. He simply said "Let me know as soon as you can," and with that, in a Mr Benn, of the children's cartoon, type moment, she found herself back in the corridor, momentarily unsure whether everything that had just happened in the office behind her was real, including the momentary glimpses she got of the person Mr Parker probably once was, before he became dour and remote, a person weighed down by the bureaucracy of his position. She also wondered whether she had dreamed about the cut-glass decanter, the till code, the telephone call from Barnes, the job offer and everything else that had just occurred, and that the only reality was what the corridor in front of her offered.

Alba ran her fingers through her hair, massaged the base of her skull for a moment, and, having gathered her thoughts following some deep breaths, each held for four seconds, decided what took place in Mr Parker's office was reality and that she should, whether she took the position of Acting Deputy Head Gardener or not, go on a wolf hunt.

CHAPTER 6

Code 085

"…and I'll just take off your volunteer's discount" said Sam.

"Actually" said Alba, as she put her volunteer's card, with its logoed lanyard back into her breast pocket, "Mr Parker said I could ask you to put it through on code 085."

"Really? Are you sure? I hadn't seen any notes about the garden people getting stuff for free in here."

"Quite sure but you're equally right, in that there haven't been any notices announcing changes to the perks we get. No, it's just today, just this one instance. I've kind of been running an unusual errand for him and I think it was his way of acknowledging that. Mr Parker said you could call him to confirm – I really don't mind if you do, I'm not going to be offended."

"No, that's alright. And you're sure that's all you want – you've only got a pot of tea for one! It's a free lunch, kind of, if we're putting it through on a code, you don't want a scone or a slice of carrot cake as well? Packet of crisps – the salt and vinegar are my favourite."

"Thank you but no. Mr Parker said I could have a drink, so I don't want him to think I'm abusing his generosity."

"Blow me, you're whiter than white!"

"White by name and…"

"Oh, why won't the till let me put this code through?" said Sam to herself, not listening to Alba's last comment. She then called to someone out in the kitchen. "Chloe, could you come and help for a mo, I've forgotten how to do something on the till" and, reverting to engaging with Alba, added "Miss, if you want to grab a table, I'll bring it over once Chloe's come and helped me with the till." Alba, wishing to avoid a modern day version of an 'Open All Hours' till moment, took her cue and went and found a table by the window, which overlooked the Hall's drive and the empty plinth.

Alba rearranged the condiments and, having smiled to herself at Ronnie Barker's comedic acting ability in that show, mentally, went over the route she had taken, first to the kitchen garden, then the beds around the shop and then finally the beds here, next to the shop, around the Hall's tea room, in her search for *Aconitum*, wolfsbane. There'd been no trace of the herbaceous perennial plant, with its rich green leaves and developing flower spikes that would produce deep purple hooded flowers. The shape of the flowers had seen it become commonly known as monkshood or devil's helmet, but, to Alba, she commonly called it wolfsbane, having read about how the plant was once used to kill animals of that name. She was, though, suddenly struck by the thought that she'd checked the flower beds around the buildings on this side of the Hall but hadn't actually looked at the trestle tables outside the shop that had all the plants for sale on them. 'Oh heck' she thought, as she jumped up, grabbed her purse, and almost collided with Sam, who was bringing her tray over, and with the Reverend Quinn, who was just to the side of Sam.

"Thirty seconds" she said to Sam, "give me thirty seconds, I'll be back for my drink, I just need to check something outside. Oh, sorry Reverend," she added with a puzzled look on her face, wondering what he was doing here.

*

Alba returned several minutes later relieved not to have found any wolfsbane amongst the plant sales but irritated to find the Reverend Quinn sitting at what had been her table. He was drinking a coffee and was halfway through a piece of cake. A further piece of cake lay untouched on the table alongside an empty tea cup and saucer. Unsure whether to join him or not, her decision was made for her when he looked up and beckoned her over.

"Please join me" he said. He stood as Alba approached.

"Join you? This was my table before you parked yourself at it. You heard me say to the waitress that I was returning."

"In that case, may I correct myself and ask whether I may join you?"

"Given that you're here I guess it would be rude to say no" and Alba unbuttoned her pocket and slung her lanyard and card down on the table, which caught itself around one of the cups.

As they both sat, Sam brought over a pot of tea.

"It's a fresh pot. Don't worry, no extra charge. I sensed something important called you away for a moment and didn't want you coming back to a stewed pot of tea. I gave the original pot to the lady in the corner, over there, who's sitting by herself, who had originally asked for just a glass of water and a mini packet of bourbon biscuits" and Sam nodded in the direction of where the lady was sitting. "Funny thing is," Sam continued, "like yesterday, today's a lovely sunny day and yet she came in wearing a fawn raincoat. What's that all about I wonder?"

Instinctively, Alba and the Reverend looked over to where the woman sat. Her fawn raincoat was now on the back of the chair, revealing a shortish sleeveless halter-neck dress, to, what Alba reckoned, would reach down to just above the knee in length, and with its neckline lost under a string of slightly too large wooden beads.

"She was a bit embarrassed and awkward at first, when I offered it to her, but she accepted it. Just a bit odd, all in all. Hey, ho."

Refocusing on Alba, Sam continued, "It's Alba isn't it? We spoke the other week in here didn't we? And mum was talking about you, I think it was, last night at home."

"Yes, we did. Sweet of you to remember me from last time I came in for a drink here. How are you? It was you helping your mum yesterday wasn't it, doing the refreshments at Vaughan's funeral? Must have been tiring for you both yesterday."

"Well, mum always says they're hectic but it was fine, really. If you remember the three rules of catering you can't go too far wrong. Not that I learnt them from my catering college, mind you. Mum and I have come up with them over the years."

"Three rules? Your mum only mentioned two yesterday," replied Alba, suddenly taken back to being in St Mary's church hall yesterday. "My, was it only yesterday? It somehow now feels like a lifetime ago."

"Oh yeah, mum told me that she'd been telling you about a couple of our rules. One about where you sit during the service and another about the kettle but she always forgets to tell anyone about the third and that's because she forgets it herself, bless her" and Sam chuckled to herself. "And because she forgets it, that is why she finds it so hectic."

"Pray tell child," chipped in Reverend Quinn.

"You what?"

"I think he's trying to say," Alba interjected, "What is the third rule of catering, à *la mode* of Mrs and Miss Rowan?"

"You what? No, just teasing, I did French GCSE so I got the pair of you that time. The third rule is simply 'assume no-one is the other side of the serving hatch'. I know, before you say anything, it kind of contradicts our first rule of where you sit, so you can do a head count. As I say, these are our rules not the college's but if, as you work away in the kitchen, you can tell yourself no-one is outside, be it in the church hall, at tables in a restaurant or outside at picnic tables, or wherever the punter is, if you like, then, by telling yourself it's just you working your kitchen by yourself, you don't get stressed.

Just you in your own space doing, hopefully, what you're good at. That way, you keep your stress levels down as you filter out people's expectations and demands, which will be met if you are doing your job properly. Anyway, I must get back to the till. Oh, the piece of cake, Alba, is on the house – you're too honest for your own good."

"Are you sure?"

"Course I'm sure. On that code, the till assumes a piece of cake or something similar is had as well. That's why I couldn't just put a cup of tea through on the code. Chloe reminded me I had to tell the till what else you were having. Enjoy!" and with that Sam headed back to help Chloe at the servery.

"Wise girl, well beyond her years" said Reverend Quinn.

"Yes, almost wasted at college one might say. Still, I guess she needs to learn the textbook approach to catering and hospitality and then create her own style. Her untapped genius aside, I'm not quite sure why she described us as 'a pair'. I mean you've sat at my table but that's it."

"I'll move if you want."

"No, don't bother, you're here now vicar. Anyway, with all due respect and stuff like that, why are you here?" At which point Alba started on her cherry and almond slice, adding "Not bad, cherries are not too sweet but the piece of Mrs Rowan's that I had yesterday was better." She looked at the man opposite her expectantly.

"I had a phone call from Lord Hartfield's office. Asked me to come up. One of my parishioners is poorly and there's a bit to discuss. I'm a bit early so thought I'd grab a drink here first – no harm being out and about in the community. The 'Tesco Test' a minister friend of mine called it. He reckoned there was no point driving to the next town and shopping in, say, 'Waitrose' if all your parishioners shop in the 'Tesco' where you live. A minister has to be seen in the community."

"Bit contrived that, isn't it? And, this, in case you hadn't noticed, isn't 'Tesco'!"

"Ah, that explains why Sam looked puzzled when I asked for washing powder, a pint of cream and some frozen peas."

Repressing a smile, Alba strived to maintain her suspicious tone. "Still, all a bit odd being summoned up here, don't you think? You don't come and chat to his Lordship every time someone who attends your church has a funny turn, surely?"

"No but this one is a bit different."

Alba raised a sceptical look. "So, you cherry pick" she said, tapping her fork on her near empty plate and highlighting one of the fruits that was still there, "eh, cherry pick which church members you get involved with, do you?"

"Not at all. Plus it's not a question of church attendance or membership. Those are your words. I've described her as one of my parishioners, for she lives in my parish, and I endeavour to minister to all, saint or sinner, church goer, agnostic or atheist. I'm here for all, yourself included Alba."

"Miss White, if you please."

"Sorry," said the Reverend, slightly taken aback by Alba's curtness. "Yourself included, Miss White."

Finishing her cup of tea and with the cake now completely gone, Alba rose, unconsciously re-positioned one of her bra straps and, speaking as she did so, said "I don't need any vicar ministering to me, thank you very much. You don't know anything about me or what I've been through recently. Let's keep it that way, shall we. And you could have just said you're here about Mrs Taylor. I'll let you clear the cups and plates, given you were so keen to sit at this table."

And lanyard in hand, Alba headed off to the gardeners' hut to belatedly sign-in, put her handbag in her little metal locker and to collect some trug buckets to put all the prunings in. She didn't look back, to see the now standing Reverend Quinn. The sadness in his face was clear for all to see, picked up even by the woman in the corner, who was also readying to leave and putting her raincoat back on.

"And Miss White, you don't know anything about me or what I've been through recently," the Reverend said to himself.

"What's that vicar?" said Sam as she came to clear the table. "All finished are we?"

"Nothing, just talking to myself. Thanks again for yesterday but don't worry yourself here Sam, I'll clear this table."

"If you're sure. I'll go and clear that table in the corner. Oh, before I do, Chloe said when you've met whoever you have come up here to see, could you pop back and see her. Something about Sunday she said," relayed Sam.

"Of course. I needed to catch up with her but didn't really want to disturb her at work but now she's suggested it – yes, always nicer chatting in person than on the phone. I was planning on calling her tonight but better this way."

"If you say so vicar. I'm sure she'll just delay her lunch break until you're back. Even if we're busy, I can cover for her, no problem."

'Wise girl, well beyond her years' thought the Reverend Quinn once more of Sam as she moved away to clear the corner table. As Sam cleared the other table, Reverend Quinn noticed that she bent down and picked something up that the lady in the raincoat had dropped under her chair.

*

By the mid-afternoon tea break, Alba had had her fill of climbing hydrangeas for one day, even though the task was far from finished. Back in the gardeners' hut, she and Sally chatted about Alba having been asked to 'act up' and cover for Tom.

Sally could sense from how Alba had talked about it that she probably wouldn't take the acting post; 'too much of a free spirit is that one', thought Sally to herself. Sally reminded herself of the time when Alba had first started volunteering here at the Hall and how she, Alba, had told them all how she had promised herself, when at university, that she would take a 'sabbatical' from work every seventh year in case ill-health in later life deprived her of a retirement. After her first six years in work, so Alba had continued to explain, she had indeed heeded her promise to herself and resigned from her then job. However, Sally continued to muse to herself, that was over two years ago and Alba hadn't quite, despite recently hitting thirty, got herself back into the world of paid employment – apparently a small inheritance from an aunt was tidying her over at present. Not that Sally wanted to see her friend go, as it were, it was just that she worried for her. Sally could volunteer for as long as she liked, her husband's high-flying high earning career, meant she didn't need to work, from a financial point of view. Yet her husband was hardly ever around and so, like Vaughan had and as the others too, each in their own way, she also needed this surrogate family, that the gardening team here at Hillstone Hall offered her. Sally knew that, though worried for Alba's situation, she would miss her terribly when Alba returned to the 'other world'.

"Quick top up?" said Alba as she got up from the comfortable but scruffy wooden-armed armchair that she'd been resting in.

"Please," replied Sally.

Instinctively twisting the electric kettle round, so she could lift it with her left hand, Alba checked the weight of the kettle, decided there was enough water in it already, returned it to its base and flipped the switch on.

As they finished their drinks, the pair of them then went through the chef's list of what fruit he wanted harvested that afternoon from the kitchen garden. First though, Alba said, she would go and retrieve Vaughan's portrait photograph from the Orangery.

*

If you stood by the empty plinth and faced Hillstone Hall, Mr Parker's office, the late Mrs Taylor's office and other assorted store rooms were in the wing off to the right of the main Hall itself. To the rear of the near-identical wing that was to the left was to be found the Orangery. It was in a rather warm Orangery that Alba found herself looking at the table with all the photographs on it. There were more than she'd expected and, she was encouraged to note, they weren't all centred around Lord and Lady Hartfield's two pictures. The table's arrangement did its best to present an eclectic mix of everyone who lived, worked or volunteered at the Hall.

She was able to pick out Sally's, where Sally was standing on the front at Morecambe in Lancashire, and David's, cricket bat in hand, quite quickly. Then there was Liz's, guidebook in hand standing on the front lawn, Mr Parker's, Sam's, a number of the room stewards that Alba didn't know by name, Helen's and Mrs Taylor's – Alba paused and looked into the eyes of Mrs Taylor's photo, knowing that this photo, too, was destined to be removed shortly but that it wasn't for Alba to do now. Then there were Chloe's, William Chapman's, the Lord's brother, as a slightly younger man standing in front of his ranch in Chile, that he'd recently sold up from, Andrew's, the Lord's grandson and heir, and Tom's. Tom's photograph was taken outside the gardeners' hut with his arms purposefully crossed and pair of red handled secateurs protruding from the holster on his right hip. Then there was Lady Hartfield, standing in the sunken garden, which, Alba thought was a tad misleading for, as she and Helen had discussed at Vaughan's funeral, they'd never seen her Ladyship in the garden. Next she saw Barnes's, Alba herself, Lord Hartfield's, where he was standing in his grand entrance hall, and then some further ones of the admin staff and the chef. No Vaughan, though.

Alba knew her task was to remove Vaughan's photograph but, suddenly sensing someone had already come and beaten her to it, cut her. Her beloved Vaughan was gone. It was tasked to her to retrieve it. It was, she had told herself during the day, her duty to take care of a further photograph that had once belonged to Vaughan. Subconsciously, she had already decided that she would ask to keep it and so be able to place it alongside the picture of Clive that she still had, even though she still didn't know which one Clive was in that Lancaster picture. Vaughan's photo was not here, though, and suddenly the tears welled up in her eyes. She dabbed at one eye, telling herself not to be so damned emotional, but the tears came nonetheless and they rolled down her cheeks.

The visitors around her didn't quite know what to make of this person, sunhat hanging from a chord around her neck, halfway down her back, holding the edge of the table with one hand, mopping at her tears desperately with the other and with holstered secateurs at the base of her spine. Her pink blouse was creased and had the odd dried-up little flower head from the hydrangea crushed onto one sleeve. None of the visitors thought to help. The best that anyone did, though doing nothing at all might have indicated a slightly higher level of compassion than what he in fact did, was what one father of three irritable children did, and that was to look annoyingly at the room steward, trying to indicate that somehow it was the room steward's responsibility to help this momentarily broken woman.

Perhaps she was grieving for another loss, too, but the proximity of the previous day's funeral and the now missing photograph of Vaughan, a person who had become a positive father-like figure to her, kept the tears coming.

Seeing Alba's lanyard, the room steward made her way over to Alba and reached her just as Andrew Chapman, fresh out of the rescheduled meeting that had involved Mr Parker, was making his own way through the Orangery. Coming upon the scene, he too stopped by Alba, just at the moment that the three children, by now beyond their father's control, started to run around the Italian carvings and push one another against the columns. They had even involved two other children, who had come in to the Orangery from the penultimate room of the house tour in advance of their grandparents.

"You go and intervene over there," said Andrew assertively

to the room steward. "And remember there is no such thing as a badly behaved child only badly behaved parents. So, if the father gets stroppy with you, I'll be right over but I'll help this one here," indicating Alba.

As the room steward made her way to the other end of the Orangery, Andrew spoke into his walkie-talkie, "Liz, if you can be spared from the entrance hall, could you come through to the Orangery and just help nip something in the bud? Thanks. Now, Miss," Andrew continued but now speaking to Alba, "can I help?"

"He's not here. I've looked but he's gone," said Alba, sniffing as she did so.

"Who?" replied Andrew, suddenly looking around him thinking he was now looking for another child, fearing not that he or she was playing hide and seek but that something far more sinister was unfolding. "Who are you looking for?"

"Vaughan, our Vaughan. His photograph's not here. Why would someone come and steal something like that?"

"Oh," said Andrew, who had now noticed her lanyard, and, despite being in the company of a woman still in a state of some distress, rightly or wrongly allowed himself to exhale a long slow breath in relief. "His photo you say?"

"Yes. Mr Parker has asked me to retrieve it before visitors see it and take some ghoulish interest in it. But it's already gone and 'Bic', I mean, Mr Parker asked me only this morning. Why would someone take it?" and she sniffed again and wiped at her eyes.

"I don't know. Come on, let's get you in the fresh air for a few moments" and he held his hand out towards her as Alba turned towards him. Liz walked past at that moment but didn't see the look of embarrassment and shock on Alba's face as Alba, having taken the proffered hand, recognised who it was who was now talking to her. "Oh bloody hell!" said Alba.

"None of your fancy French words on me, please, Miss" as they headed for the glass doors. "Come on, a few minutes outside will help. It's very warm in here." Glancing back, Andrew could see, with Liz's support and the fortuitous emergence of the set of grandparents from the previous room, that the children, particularly the original three, had been brought under control – much to the father's relief and embarrassment in equal measure. Andrew gave a nod of thanks to Liz as he led Alba out into the fresh air.

*

"We should have a portrait of her on the grand staircase," said Andrew. "We'll take down grandad's one and put up Liz's. I'm sure the Hall would just crumble about us but for her."

"Wouldn't the 7th Lord mind?" commented Alba, who, although her tears had now stopped, was finding the surrealness of the situation almost as unnerving as the emotions that had overcome her in the Orangery – for she now found herself walking along one of the long borders with Andrew Chapman, heir to Hillstone Hall. To anyone else, they were just a couple walking through the gardens, though the more romantic amongst them might go so far as to say, but for the redness in Alba's eyes and the relative scruffiness of her clothing compared to his, they were well suited together and that they reflected the beauty of the gardens themselves. They were indeed well matched, born just a year or so apart in the early 1970s, both educated and both entirely at home at Hillstone Hall – albeit one in the gardens and one in the Hall itself.

Alba not only had walked this part of the garden a thousand times before on her way to or from another part of the garden, but this border she had weeded, planted, mulched and sat and counted the butterflies that fed from it, to help Tom with a piece of research he had been doing for his Royal Horticultural Society qualification. She had picked slugs off, scattered broken egg shells and coffee grounds around the *hostas* and dead-headed the peonies. She had lived this bit of the garden in light rain and glorious shine, in the winter as the frost lingered on the dead flower heads of the *sedums* and in the summer as beads of sweat trickled down her back as she re-staked the *achilleas*. This was her territory she had always told herself but today, as she walked with Andrew at her side, it was as if she had never seen it before. She told herself to focus on the plants, the scent, the insects, the colours, to get back, as it were, into her comfort zone and not think too much about the man at her side. She couldn't though and the colours, aromas, wildlife, everything, all just seemed to recede into a grey nothingness and she could only experience Andrew.

Andrew walked along with his hands in his pockets and responded to Alba's comment about whether the 7th Lord would mind, "No, I don't think so, we're moving a few pictures and other bits and bobs out of the Hall, so I'll just tell him his portrait was another one that had to go." He smiled at Alba and put a hand on her shoulder and continued "Better now? It does get quite warm in there even on overcast days, let alone today. Or, thinking about it, we could leave his portrait up and have a statue of Liz installed on the empty plinth – what do you reckon?"

"Better – yes. I thought it was hot working in the garden today – you see I've been working on the climbing plants over by the tea shop today, and…"

"Yes, I can tell" interjected Andrew. "You've still got bits of it on yourself" and he brushed at the top of her sleeve and picked a couple of bits off her collar. "Hold on" he added, as he untangled a larger bit from her hair.

"Thanks. Yes it's a hot day to be working outside but I now take my hat off to the stewards on duty in the Orangery."

"We have to be careful, plenty of water and they rotate so no one steward is in there for more than forty-five minutes. Mrs Taylor's very, I mean Mrs Taylor was, err…" but Andrew's voice dropped and he became inaudible to Alba.

"Don't worry, I know," she said reassuringly. "I was with Mr Parker when he got the telephone call about her."

"Right. I was just going to say, she was very good at ensuring the stewards swopped as instructed. She'd often be in the Orangery herself, I noticed, checking on them. Some of our house stewards are a bit frail, one or two are older even than grandad and great-uncle William."

"I assume William is a younger brother to Edward, well he must be otherwise he'd be Lord Hartfield. Would you listen to me, calling them by their first names – I'm so sorry."

"Don't be. I only wish my great uncle had been back in the country about ten years ago, when 'Bill and Ted's Excellent Adventure' came out as a film, I'd have ribbed them both something rotten if ever I'd seen them together. I even had a poster of the film up on my bedroom door here at the Hall."

"Oh my word, that's a film from my past. Hold on, it was, it was Keanu Reeves and, and, oh, who was the other one?"

"Alex Winter?"

"That's right – takes me back to my teenage years."

"Me too. And yes, my great uncle is the younger by a year – the tenth plague would have taken grandad over great-uncle William. Odd thing birthright, especially so to a family like ours."

By now they had walked the length of one of the long borders, had crossed the lawn and were walking along the opposite border, heading back to the house. Andrew continued:

"But to finish what I was saying about Mrs Taylor, she was good at making sure no steward overdid it in the Orangery; she was often in there, as I say, checking on them. However, on balance I'm thinking of finishing the House tour somewhere else and keeping people out of the Orangery altogether."

"From the public's point of view that would be a shame if they never got to see it. Perhaps we could incorporate it into the garden tours instead; then it could be avoided all together on the hottest of days, like today."

"That's not a bad idea, I'll bear that in mind and perhaps speak to Mr Parker about it. Not today though for obvious reasons, in light of the news about Mrs Taylor. Funny thing is, given where I just found you, as it were, I think Mrs Taylor also had a thing about all our photographs on the table. She just couldn't abide them being knocked over or moved or hidden by the visitors, usually by our bored, younger visitors. She was always in there tidying the photographs up. Anyway, I'm sure Vaughan's will be there. From memory we should spot it easily."

"Why is that?" asked a curious Alba. "I haven't seen all the photos set out before – why would Vaughan's necessarily stick out? There's quite a few, as I now realise."

"It was a black and white one."

"But there are one or two other monotone pictures; one of the girls from the tea shop, Chloe's I think, is sepia. Why would Vaughan's particularly stand out?"

"Black and white, for one, and for another, it was him in uniform as a Sapper out in France or Germany towards the end of the Second World War."

"Really?"

"Yes, and I can tell you Mrs Taylor was not happy when Vaughan handed it in to be put on display in the Orangery. She came to me about it for she was of the opinion that it should be a recent photograph – which kind of was my original intention too. But Vaughan wouldn't back down and apparently said he didn't want people to think he'd only ever been an old man who pottered around the garden. Hearing that, I was happy to let it go, even if Mrs Taylor disagreed. If anything, it added something these last few months to our collection of photographs and gave it, dare I say, a bit of history. So there he stood, as it were, in his Sapper's uniform, somewhere in war-torn Europe, wearing his side cap and you could, I think from memory, just make out the shoulder flash of the Royal Engineers. I think, but I'd have to ask great-uncle William to be sure, that he was out in France too in '44 or '45 but I'm not sure which outfit he was with. Grandad was with the Intelligence Corps but I can't remember about great-uncle. Right, here we are" he continued, as they re-entered the Orangery. "Let's have a thorough look together, shall we?"

They did; on the table, underneath the table, behind the columns and in some of the larger ornamental pots. Alba asked the replacement room steward if he'd any ideas, Andrew spoke to Liz on the walkie-talkie about it and they both looked around the garden benches just outside the Orangery. However, Vaughan's photograph was not to be found. Someone had taken it.

CHAPTER 7

'Stapleton's'

When she'd first moved to the village, a neighbour had explained why the village shop was called 'Stapleton's' but, as the years rolled on by, Alba had forgotten. A combination of being too embarrassed to ask again and a sense that it really hadn't been that interesting in the first place, meant it stayed lost in the darkest reaches of her mind.

Mrs Lyle was the shop's current proprietor but, to the regret of most of the villagers, she lacked the warmth of her predecessor. Quite quickly, upon her taking over, people realised that they didn't go in for a friendly chat with her when they went in for the morning paper, bread and milk or one of those round tins of travel sweets – rather they would get what they wanted and be on their way, unless of course they bumped into one of their friends, as they queued to pay their paper bill, for then they could be in 'Stapleton's' for ages chatting amongst themselves about the wrongs in the world, rumours about life up at the Hall or even, more recently, how the loft conversion was progressing two doors down from the pub.

Yet what Mrs Lyle lacked in warmth she more than made up for in business acumen and she had turned what had been a failing little business into something that more than broke even. The villagers always knew when their paper bill was to be paid by and, by threatening to take a slow-paying customer to the local small claims court, Mrs Lyle had made it clear from her early days that a settlement of monies due was for her a fundamental, almost a matter of life and death, to the running of the business.

The warm July weather was still holding this Saturday morning and whilst 'Stapleton's' would never make the local charity calendar, for any given year, as one of the beauty spots of the village or surrounding area, it looked as good as it could this weekend morning. The shop formed part of a red brick semi-detached house. The ground floor was effectively given over to the shop itself, store-room and office. Mrs Lyle lived in the upstairs rooms. It would have had even more of a maisonette feel to Mrs Lyle save for two reasons. First, she lived in the knowledge that she had, when buying the business, also bought the freehold to the whole of that half of the property. Second, by it not being a maisonette, the rear garden of this half of the semi wasn't itself somewhat brutally further divided into two.

Although she owned the 'whole half' of the garden, Mrs Lyle wasn't a gardener at all. The grass got cut just about often enough but the main flower-bed, or what once upon a time was the main flower-bed, was now dominated by an overgrown evergreen shrub *Viburnum Tinus*. She didn't particularly like the *Viburnum* as it frequently seemed to be covered in a dull sooty mould, as if someone had thrown wood-ash over the plant on a damp morning. The other plant to dominate the bed was the leafy *Alchemilla mollis*, 'lady's mantle', but even that was beginning to get swamped by the *Viburnum*. In front of the wire fence at the bottom of the garden she had a leggy privet hedge. The odd and randomly located self-seeded young sycamore and elder trees added to the overall effect of a garden in decline.

The garden of the adjacent semi, to Mrs Lyle's right as you looked from the road, was similar in appearance but with the addition of a couple of children's bicycles, a sponge football and a badminton net, that had been used a couple of times one Bank Holiday weekend and then forgotten about. The sad state of both gardens, though, were in contrast to the garden of the property to the left of Mrs Lyle, which had been where Vaughan had lived since moving to the village a couple of years ago.

Vaughan's garden didn't offer perfection, nor had he lived there long enough to get it quite how he wanted it. Yet, the hedging had been brought under control and Vaughan had had a tree surgeon in to take out the dead wood and remove a couple of the lower branches from the mature oak tree in the back garden. The beds under the front windows were now weed free, the 'honesty', Vaughan's favourite plant, was present and the beds had benefitted from Vaughan's first batch of home-generated compost. The roses, that were also in the beds, had responded to his pruning and his discarded banana skins around their bases and they were beginning to assume that conical framework that he sought from them. His prize roses, however, had remained the two he had brought from his previous house, that were in the two Cumbrian slate pots on his rear patio. It had pained him, at the time, that he hadn't been able to find a supplier of garden pottery made from Lancastrian materials but he had consoled himself that the slate was possibly from the mountains he and Clive had looked out on, across Morecambe Bay, from their childhood home.

Vaughan's little detached cottage predated the semi-detached homes that had been added in the 1950s. His cottage wasn't quite centrally placed within its plot of land, with the result that between it and 'Stapleton's' there was, what to him was simply, his side-garden but to Mrs Lyle was a 'plot of land' that she had had her eye on for a number of years. She had visions, were she ever to acquire it, of simply getting it tarmacked so shoppers knew they had somewhere to park, for she sensed she was losing trade as people seemed not to stop if it meant parking more than three cars up or down from her shop. Furthermore, she reckoned she could then rent the space, on a Friday and Saturday evening, to a local wood-fired pizza van or the hog-roast van the butchers in the neighbouring village had. Alternatively, she had thought of extending the shop in the anticipation (secretly, she would have to admit to herself, the cruel hope) of the village post office closing down and her absorbing that business into her own.

When the previous owners of the cottage were selling, prior to Vaughan's purchase, they had offered Mrs Lyle the side plot. Unfortunately for her, she had not quite been able to raise the finances needed and so Vaughan was able to buy what, on solicitors' maps, was increasingly being treated as two plots. Even when Vaughan moved in, Mrs Lyle herself had not given up on acquiring the land – the land, that she increasingly told herself, the previous owners had promised her. Sometimes she would try to sweet-talk Vaughan and yet other times she was less than polite when she tried to convince him she had had a verbal contract with the previous owners, which had given her an 'option to purchase'. Each time, irrespective of her manner or how well rehearsed her arguments had been, Vaughan politely told her he was not selling. And each time, as if to re-enforce his stance, he would softly tell her about the variety of heritage apple-trees he had just planted in said strip of land and how he had always wanted an orchard area. It annoyed her immensely each time he told her about his 'Ashmead's Kernel' or 'Lord Derby' or any of the other heritage varieties he'd been thrilled to obtain. He would also try to tell her how he had planted oxeye daisy seeds in the grass, in order that they could grow up in the uncut sections of the grass in the orchard areas; but of course, she would always have walked away by this stage.

*

Alba was reading the notices in the window of 'Stapleton's' when Sally came out of the shop. The weather was due to turn in a day or two but for now, Alba's look spoke summer. She had large somewhat bulbous looking, chocolate brown sunglasses, with their silver motive on one arm, perched precisely on her head, holding back her hair. She was dressed in a light blue top, with its thin mesh segment running down the length of her back, white three-quarter length trousers and strappy brown sandals. Her little shoulder bag, that she'd had with her on the day of the cricket match, was over one shoulder.

"Morning Alba, seen the one about the Village Horticultural Society's day trip?" said Sally.

"Hello Sal. Yes, just seen that, it's been a while since I've been to Hastings. A day at the sea would be lovely but I don't quite feel old enough to be signing up to their day trips just yet."

"Please come. I've already signed up for two people but my husband is now refusing to come with me – stating he needs to book a business trip for that weekend." Sally paused for a moment before continuing, "You'd think he'd be willing to do the odd thing with me."

The dejection in Sally's voice almost persuaded Alba to say yes but Alba, deep down, didn't fancy a day of being told how long she had somewhere, when to be back at the coach or feeling compelled to eat her lunch with a bunch of people she didn't really know.

"I'll let you know. You'll probably have found someone else by the time I've checked if I'm free," and keen to change the subject added "Paper bill paid?"

"Yes, thanks," replied Sally before adding "strange the gossip you overhear in the queue as you wait in there. In front of me was Mr Morley, from the Post Office, and, as he was paying for something, he was telling Mrs Lyle how he'd had more than one envelope that had to be weighed recently so it could be posted off to Uzbekistan and what were the chances of that happening – two for Uzbekistan in the same week from our village. As I say, strange what one overhears in the queue here. Such random chit-chat makes for village life I suppose. Anyway, I'm rambling. If you're finished here, you could come next door with me if you like. I'm going to go and look at those two roses on Vaughan's patio, give them a water and decide which car boot they'll fit best in, if we come back on Monday."

"Sorry Sal but I'm busy Monday. I'll come with you now to look but can't do Monday."

As the pair of them turned and took the few strides to Vaughan's cottage, Sally said:

"No, it's me not making myself clear. Husband states he has a 'team-building' morning at the Surrey County course on Monday but I have told him that when he is back home, he is coming to help lift the pots with me then. How bacon rolls and a round of golf on a Monday morning makes them work better together, heaven only knows."

The gate to the side path wasn't locked. Whoever the Executor or Executors were for Vaughan's 'estate', they clearly had felt under no compulsion to make the premises more secure than they currently were. There was no padlock on this extra gate which, had there been, would have forced people to use the main gate which at least would have kept them on the path to the front door.

As Alba re-did the latch on the side-gate she momentarily wondered whether they should have asked permission from someone. Yet, as evidenced by the photograph that still remained on her hall table, she didn't know who was dealing with Vaughan's affairs and she didn't think Sally would either. Still, she reassured herself, they were only looking on this dry and sunny Saturday morning and there'd be no-one else about.

*

The Reverend Quinn had just put the finishing touches to the following day's sermon. It was the sermon he had been working on, on the day of Vaughan's murder, for a confirmation service. However, following the postponement of the confirmation bit of the service, at the confirmee's suggestion due to Vaughan's death, the Reverend Quinn had never finished it at the time. He was grateful for the extra preparation time and, by deciding to tie the passage in Philippians to the Book of Acts chapter 16, Lydia's conversion, he felt now it was usable. It would, he felt, speak to Chloe, who's confirmation service it was, much more than his original part-draft would have done.

Having finished the sermon, Reverend Quinn found himself wandering into the church office and offered to make both the church secretary and treasurer, who both happened to be there, a drink. The secretary declined as she was in the process of leaving but the treasurer, Richard, happily accepted.

"I've got another agenda item for our next church business meeting; the organist has put in a request for an electric keyboard. Says he'll look into some costings and submit some options, so the meeting can discuss them," said Richard.

"Oh my!" replied Reverend Quinn. "It was going to be a long meeting as it was but now we're going to have to talk keyboards as well."

"Says he's getting fed up trying to play all these modern songs at people's funerals on the organ."

"OK. Sugar in your coffee?"

"No thanks" replied Richard adding, "separately, one of the cleaners handed something in half an hour ago. Reckons one of the mourners dropped it on Thursday during Vaughan's funeral."

"Coffee," proffered the minister.

"Thanks. I think the cleaner was trying to impress on me how thorough she was doing her job. She said she found it as she swept under a pew. Apparently, it had fallen out of sight. There's nothing to indicate who it belongs to. Just wondered whether you had any ideas."

"I'm not really an expert on ladies' accessories and it doesn't ring any bells. I haven't really been here in the parish long enough to start to recognise parishioners' favourite clothing but, and I noticed this in my previous posting, people do have favourite jackets, tops, skirts, hats and the like that come out reasonably often. No ideas on this item, though, as I say. We need a clue as it were," added the minister, as he found himself wrapping it around one hand for no particular reason.

"Good coffee by the way – it's good when 'Fairtrade' stuff is as good as other makes, isn't it?" commented Richard. "Well, the only other thing the cleaner said was that she found it under the pew second from the front, left hand side. That doesn't help me, I was sitting near the back."

"Second from the front you say?"

"Well, I'm simply repeating what the cleaner said; I'm offering you hearsay. Obviously, you had a completely different view to me. Any ideas?"

"Left or right did you say?"

"Left, well left from the congregation's perspective but it would have been your right. Anything?" enquired Richard.

"A hunch, Richard, a hunch. Not one of our usual congregation, I think. Leave this with me" said Reverend Quinn, as he unwound the scarf from around his hand. "If it belongs to who I think it might belong to, I'll drop it in one day next week. It'll be good to have an excuse to pop by – I'll ask Helen for the address tomorrow after the morning service, for I'm sure she'll have it."

*

"I guess he got to see his beloved honesty plants in flower this May but he's missed the magic of their oval seed heads taking on their translucent form," reflected Alba, as she momentarily looked across Vaughan's front garden, as she and Sally made their way through Vaughan's orchard area.

"And he's been denied seeing how this orchard area is really coming on," added Sally.

This side plot was really beginning to reveal what Vaughan had wanted of it; a number of staked apple trees, patches of uncut grass defined by cut grass paths. The uncut squares of grass were never going to be a true wild flower meadow, for Vaughan had been feeding the grass a bit too much for that, but the oxeye daisies, meadow buttercups, common vetch and purple clover gave it a definite meadow feel.

"Looks like his grass cutter, Jim, is still coming in and cutting, even though he probably will never get paid for these last few weeks. These grass paths are too defined, they must have been cut recently. That's very good of him – I reckon he must have enjoyed working for Vaughan" continued Sally.

"Well, I hope Jim puts a note through the door each time he has come since the beginning of June, just in case whoever is managing Vaughan's estate chooses to reimburse him in due course. In a few years, as these trees start to crop properly, this will be a lovely part of the garden. Just needs a metal seat over there in my opinion, to complete it" mused Alba as she instinctively picked out a few distorted fruitlets from the 'Lord Derby' as she passed it. Sally, having seen Alba pointing, equally thought a seat would look good in the spot Alba had suggested.

As they rounded the corner of the cottage, Sally was the first to notice them. "Oh, I thought that might be the case" she said deflated. She was commenting on Vaughan's two potted roses. Not having been watered for over a month and a half they were both dying. Their soil was parched dry, so much so you could insert your fingers between the dried-out soil and the inside of the pots. The leaves had dropped and the flower buds had withered.

"You might be able to save them" said Alba trying to inject some hope into the situation.

"I'll try but I think we both know that they've had it. I just wish I'd kept that single red rose on Thursday now. If I'd treasured what he'd left me I could have, I should have, taken it home and dried it out or pressed it. I did neither, I just threw it away." As Sally spoke, she repeated her hand movement from Vaughan's burial, as if she were dropping a further invisible rose into a burial pit that only she could see.

Alba moved a step closer to Sally to be by her side and put an arm around her waist to console her. The pair of them looked at the two dying roses.

"They're going to die, aren't they?" mused Sally as the tears welled up in her eyes.

Alba's mind went back to yesterday and her time with Mr Parker in his office. She could hear him once again saying *'It might seem I am without a heart but she will die. Of that there can be no doubt'*. She held onto Sally now as much for her, Alba's, own benefit as for Sally's. Alba hadn't mentioned to Sally that she knew Mrs Taylor was dead. As much as she treasured her friendship with Sally, she had given Mr Parker her word that he was speaking in confidence and she didn't want to break her word. Alba wasn't exactly mourning Hillstone Hall's Housekeeper but the shock of a further death had affected her and the vision of Mrs Taylor's photograph on the Orangery's table filled Alba's mind.

Alba released her grip of her friend's waist and took her hand instead and spoke – "Yes, they will."

"I just threw it away" repeated Sally, "why did I do that? And now, now I've got nothing left from Vaughan."

"You didn't throw it away, Sal, you gave it back to him" and Alba squeezed her friend's hand to stress the point. "You've still got a lot from Vaughan; all the memories and I'm sure Helen will give each of us a copy of his biscuit recipe. The love is still there, too, don't forget that" and Alba, turning to her friend, tapped her on the chest, where her heart was.

Turning back to the garden, Alba added "And you've still got the two beautiful pots. If anything, the roses dying might be kind of a liberation for the pots themselves. If I'm being truthful, roses in pots never really work for me. Not that they're wrong but, for me, they're not right. You can have a beautiful pot and a beautiful rose but, together, they don't work and then my mind can't 'unsee' what I think looks, well as I say, not quite wrong but not quite right either.

To me, they are completely out of place. Roses in pots steal the scene, as it were, for the wrong reasons. Oh, how can I explain it better? It's like, like Father Christmas in CS Lewis' book 'The Lion, the Witch and the Wardrobe'. Not wrong and definitely not ugly but not quite right either; a scene stealer for not quite the right reasons. Do you get what I'm getting at?"

"I think so," considered Sally. "Like the David Shepherd painting 'Wise Old Elephant' hanging on the wall of the Trotter's flat in 'Only Fools and Horses'?"

"That's it, that's it exactly. Not wrong, not ugly but when you notice it, as it were, you can't 'unsee' it and you find your eyes drawn to it and you stop seeing what else is around."

They looked in silence for a few moments.

"*Agapanthus*?" offered Sally.

"Yes, that could work very well. I mean, you could keep the pots empty and treat them as a feature in their own right but *agapanthus* would work exceptionally well. Or what about, giving similar height…"

At that moment, though, a noise from the cottage behind them broke their conversation.

"That's odd" said Alba, "no-one that I know of should be in there."

"Sounded like the front door shutting. Come on Alba, let's go round to the front and see what's going on. Plus, we're kind of not meant to be here either, at least we haven't asked anyone's permission."

"No-one to ask, as far as I'm concerned, we were his family," stated Alba.

"True, although I still don't know who was sitting on the front row, next to Lord Hartfield and his wife at the funeral. Anyway, let's go and look because it seems odd, as you say."

*

As Alba and Sally got to the front garden, they could see two men beyond the front gate, back out on the pavement, walking the few steps to 'Stapleton's'. One was tall, thin and elderly. He had a gangly walk, as if his arms and legs were just a few inches too long for his torso, and his head angled forward, giving the impression his neck muscles were not quite up to the task allotted to them. Despite the warmth of the morning he had, from what Alba and Sally could make out above Vaughan's front hedge, a tweed jacket on. The other, and not just because he was a good forty years younger, had a far more elegant presence about himself. He simply had an open-necked, well-tailored shirt.

"Andrew!" Alba cried out.

Sally then recognised who the pair were but was stunned to silence that Alba had yelled out to Lord Hartfield's grandson and heir, the Honourable Andrew Chapman, simply 'Andrew'.

"Andrew," Alba called out again as Andrew, who had already stopped, was looking behind him and into the road itself to see where the cry had come from. It was only with Alba's second call that he looked over the hedge into Vaughan's front garden. His great-uncle, William Chapman, had also stopped by this point and he too now saw the two women in the front garden of the property that he and Andrew had just left.

"Andrew" said Alba a third time but this time much quieter and spoken out of relief of having got his attention. She was through the front gate in no time and suddenly found herself in front of the two Mr Chapmans.

"I thought it was you, I recognised you over the hedge. What are you doing here?" enquired an excited Alba. By now Sally had joined them too.

Demonstrating that same assertiveness, as he had shown in the Orangery yesterday, Andrew insisted the small group move along the pavement to be in front of 'Stapleton's' where the pavement was wider.

"That's better" he said. "Bit safer here. Hello you, it's Miss White isn't it?"

"Yes, yes, it is but please call me Alba."

"Alba it is. But I must immediately apologise" said Andrew.

"Must you?" queried Alba, fearing he was about to leave and get into the expensive looking BMW parked on the other side of the road.

"Yes, I must. You see, I forgot to ask you your name yesterday. I mean I knew your name, I read it off your lanyard when I first came upon you in the Orangery. However, it was remiss of me to not formally ask you. My apologies" and Andrew Chapman held out his hand to Alba.

Alba took it and, conscious of the firmness of his grip, gently shook his hand.

"So, Alba, you'll have recognised great-uncle William."

"Of course. Actually, we, err, met briefly at the cricket match," Alba replied to Andrew. She then turned her head to William Chapman and continued, but now in an awkward and embarrassed tone, "Good morning Mr Chapman."

"Hello, Miss White" he replied with a tone of voice that indicated absolutely he had no desire to make small talk with these two women, who in his opinion, were do-gooders who fussed around his brother's stately pile. If William had had his way, he'd have a garden maintenance company in to manage the gardens. It might cost a bit more initially, he reckoned, but after a year or two he further reckoned the maintenance company would be desperate not to lose such a prestigious contract and so he'd be able to renegotiate the contact to his favour. Plus, he could then dismiss the Head Gardener, whose position would be redundant. William Chapman didn't like Mr Parker; his dislike of Mr Parker, not that William Chapman realised it himself, was because Mr Parker reminded him of himself too much.

William Chapman then simply acknowledged Sally, with a nod

of the head, and, turning to Andrew, said "I'll just pop into the shop and get some matches and the 'Racing Post'. I want to see if Jerry Haltwhistle has got anything running this afternoon at Lingfield."

"OK great-unc, I'll see you in there in a few moments. As you know, I need to speak to Mrs Lyle about something" replied Andrew.

As his great-uncle took his leave, Andrew spoke to Alba and Sally, "He's never been one for small talk, even more so these past few months. Lost deep in thought at times, he is, but never lets slip as to what about. My guess, though, is that he's missing his life in South America. But enough of my family. Alba please introduce me to your friend and" turning to Sally added "your face is familiar but I am afraid I can't place you."

"This is Sally, Andrew. Another one of your garden volunteers."

Andrew again offered his hand, this time to Sally.

"What are you doing here, Andrew? I mean it's lovely to see you but I've never seen you in the village before" enquired Alba.

"Well, as you just heard me say, I need to speak to Mrs Lyle and I felt I ought to do it in person as it's not great news for her. Didn't seem right just to call her up and say the Hall is cancelling its daily newspaper order for the tea shop. We'll still get the two papers for the family but do you know how much it is costing the estate to get 'The Daily Mail', 'The Guardian' and 'The Times' each day just for people to read in the tea shop? Can't justify it any more but I know Mrs Lyle won't be happy about it. Apparently, Grandad tried to discuss it with her on the Golden Jubilee day, at the cricket match, when he saw her there shortly before err, shortly before errm…"

"Before Alba and David found poor old Vaughan," continued Sally, as she glanced at Alba and the pair of them, Sally and Alba, exchanged a look of sadness and loss.

"Yes, before that" said Andrew. However, not having known Vaughan, attended his funeral or even been at the cricket match when the trauma of that day unfolded, as first the St. John's Ambulance crew, then the NHS paramedics and then the Police turned up, there was a detachment to his words of *'before that'*. Had Andrew seen David's distress and monastic silence as he sat motionless on the pavilion steps or had he seen Alba wrapped in a St John's blanket, sat on those same steps, her bloodied dress protruding beneath it and her legs entwined around each other, as if she had to keep herself knotted together so she didn't shatter into a thousand silver pieces, perhaps Andrew would have spoken with greater empathy.

He hadn't seen, though, so he continued to speak, somewhat abstractly. "From another discussion I've had with Mrs Lyle, back at the beginning of May, about putting up posters to advertise the cricket match in her shop window, one thing I remember her saying was that she couldn't stand cricket. She was really quite contemptuous about it but surprisingly was willing to allow me to put a poster up. So, I'm surprised she was even there that day for grandad to come across her, near the pavilion so he said. Grandad tried to speak to her about the tea shop papers then but said she was far too cross about something else already so didn't pursue it. Said she had a real look of thunder about her. It fell off our to-do list for a few weeks. However, as great-unc was coming into the village, I thought I'd grab a lift and deal with it."

Two middle-aged women on horses, one horse a shade of brown that, Alba bizarrely thought matched her sunglasses, and the other an off-white, went past, holding up, for a moment at least due to the BMW parked opposite, a Range Rover with tinted rear windows.

"Why do horses need reflective ankle straps on a day like today?" interjected Sally in a rhetorical sort of way.

"Oh, is that his BMW parked the other side of the road?" queried Alba to Andrew.

"Oh no, way out of his price league. His is the dull purple Toyota Celica just up the road a bit and it stinks of cigarette smoke," replied Andrew. "Well, nice to see you Alba, Sally but I ought to speak to Mrs Lyle. I'll probably give her a week's grace, which will also enable us to have a notice in our tea shop to let customers know that papers will be stopping soon. See you around the Hall no doubt sometime soon."

About to say a reluctant goodbye in return, Alba was suddenly struck by the oddness of why she'd called out to Andrew in the first place. "It was you and your great-uncle who were in Vaughan's cottage just now, wasn't it?" she said inquisitively.

At that moment, William Chapman came out of the shop, copy of the 'Post' under his arm. "I'm done but you've still got to go and speak to her, haven't you? Do you want me to wait? I'll be in the car."

"No, it's alright thanks. It could be a bit of a lengthy discussion as she won't like losing any business. It'll take my best diplomatic skills to navigate through this one. You head off back up to the Hall. I can walk, it's a glorious day after all. The walk will be good for me," said Andrew.

"OK, see you later" said William Chapman and, without acknowledging either garden volunteer, retrieved his car key from his pocket and headed off down the road to his vehicle, lighting a cigarette as he did so from his metal cigarette case.

Alba re-positioned her sunglasses as Sally chipped in, equally curious, "It's not an estate cottage. I'm sure Vaughan told us he'd bought it."

Momentarily caught off guard by the two inquisitive people opposite him, Andrew found himself on the defensive as he said, "You're right" before adding to get himself back on parity with Alba and Sally, "None of us technically should have been there. You gave me a bit of a shock when I saw the pair of you through his lounge window, there on the patio, arm in arm. Not sure what shocked me most, the fact you were there or that you were staring at a couple of dead plants."

"You don't understand everything" snapped Sally to Andrew. "Heir to the Manor you might be but, sod it, staring at two women through a window is not right. Don't judge what you don't understand." Turning to Alba, Sally said "You know what, I'm going to go and give those plants a water anyway, I'll look again for any sign of life but probably the watering will be more of a ritual washing prior to burning as opposed to renewing life. Let me know what Mr Chapman says as to why he was poking around in Vaughan's home – given he seems to be on first name terms with you." With that, Sally was back through the side gate to Vaughan's orchard area without even the hint of a glance back.

Andrew stood shocked by the explosion from Sally, as both he and Alba could hear a further *'Sod it!'* and a *'Who does he think he is?'* coming from Vaughan's garden. He looked to Alba for something – something somewhere between support and explanation.

Detecting his prompt, Alba offered up "I won't say 'excuse my friend' because I think she had a point" and, suddenly emboldened, said "Actually, let's not stand here any longer. You can come back to speak to Mrs Lyle later, she's open all day on a Saturday. 'The Sun and Moon' won't be serving but we can sit in their beer garden, I don't want to be standing at the side of the road anymore and I think we'll be chatting for a bit."

CHAPTER 8

Tea for Two

The landlord, who'd been talking to the delivery driver from 'Theakston's', had said it was fine for them to sit in the garden. Andrew undid the buttons on his cuffs and folded each shirt sleeve up three defined turns, so the sleeves continued to just below his elbows.

"Seeing that delivery lorry from a Yorkshire brewery reminds me," Andrew said to Alba, "I was once in a pub in Chipperfield, a tiny little village. The 'Two Brewers', I think it was, and asked for a pint from their local brewery. They gave me a 'Doom Bar' – that's a Cornish ale! I was in Hertfordshire; how is that possible?"

"I've been down to Cornwall a few times," said Alba, as she looked at Andrew through her sunglasses. "Stayed at 'The Jupiter Hotel' a couple of times; Helston is its nearest town but the hotel itself is nice and remote and its grounds drop down onto the beach itself. As for a 'Doom Bar', that's Sharp's Brewery, isn't it?"

"Very good," offered up Andrew. "Yet, I was in Hertfordshire, I mean, come on, how can I be in a pub where I can hear the hum of traffic on the M25 and be served a 'local' ale from Cornwall? But that's not why we're here is it?"

"No. What I'm much more curious about is why you and your great-uncle were in Vaughan's cottage. And before you try and turn tables on me once again, Sally and I were there, for one, because we were the closest thing Vaughan had to any family and I know Vaughan wouldn't have minded, and that's not just me deluding myself for I know" said Alba, stressing most definitely the '*I know*'. She continued, "Sally, myself, Helen, David and poor Tom, we were effectively family to him. And, for another…"

"You didn't mention Mr Parker, as part of the gardening family Alba," threw in Andrew.

"No, I didn't. He's a capable head of department but I'm not here to give you insight into your employees. Where was I, yes, for another, had you been to Vaughan's funeral you would have learnt he bequeathed those two pots on his patio, and what were two roses, to Sally. She was allowed to be there for she's planning how and when to collect them. Seeing the dead plants, as I experienced yesterday in the Orangery looking for Vaughan's photograph, brought some tears to her eyes. Grief catches you out, even when you think you've started to accept your loss. You then, coming in a moment ago, telling Sally you were spying on her in that moment of grief, understandably generated the reaction you just got from her. Sal's got a lot on at the mo."

Andrew looked chastised. "Thank you for telling me the context. She did seem to explode for no reason but I understand now. Please convey my apologies to her but I'll speak to her myself when I next see her at the Hall. Would you know when she's back volunteering?"

"Where are we? Today's Saturday. As you know, none of us volunteer on a Sunday. Well, Vaughan used to do garden talks on a Sunday afternoon but none of us did any gardening. Sal's collecting the pots on Monday from Vaughan's, so probably Tuesday, Tuesday afternoon. She goes in and does a harvesting session in the kitchen garden for the restaurant and tea shop on a Tuesday afternoon. It would be good of you to go and find her in your kitchen garden on Tuesday afternoon and apologise."

"I will, Miss White."

"Please, it's Alba. We miss Vaughan terribly and I love Sally, she's a dear friend and I'll support her to the hilt, but don't go all formal on me, please, it's Alba."

"Alba it will only ever be" offered back Andrew. "Do you want me to see if they are serving drinks yet? What can I get you?"

To the now standing Andrew, Alba replied "Will you please sit down and if you evade answering once more, so help me the contents of that dog bowl over there that's half full of water will be down your fine cotton shirt before you know it. So please, why were you in Vaughan's home?"

Despite the threat, it was Alba's voice itself, as she asked the question once more of Andrew, that struck him. He sat down and spoke.

"It was great-uncle's suggestion. He'd have come by himself, I think. I cadged a lift off him so I could speak to Mrs Lyle. Once we were here, though, and I realised Vaughan's home was literally next door to 'Stapleton's', well, curiosity got the better of me and I followed great-uncle William in. And, before, you ask, no I'm not particularly proud of myself for doing it."

"You're absolutely right on that point, you should be ashamed of yourself. I doubt you'd have taken kindly to Vaughan, a couple of months ago, just innocuously wandering round your family rooms up at the Hall because 'curiosity had got the better of him'. You'd have not taken it too kindly and probably would have barred him from being a volunteer to boot – despite him being the best one you had. I'm disappointed in you, Andrew" stated Alba.

"Blow, they say a week is a long time in politics but a day is a long time in the company of Alba White – it's not even twenty-four hours since I chanced upon you in the Orangery. I am again chastised by your good self." He dipped his head in self-reproof. "I think," he continued a few moments later, "that was why I was looking out of the lounge window, watching you and Sally, it was more natural to watch the living than to glance over the possessions of the, err…"

"Of the dead. He's dead, just say it for goodness sake" and this time Alba stood. Not to offer to get the other a drink but out of an overwhelming sense of frustration with Andrew, loss for Vaughan, concerns for Sally, different concerns for Tom and her own personal thoughts. Everything was all so mixed up together that she suddenly felt the need to stand, as if that would help her thoughts and feelings settle. She put her sunglasses back up on her head and let her eyes bore into Andrew's as she continued. "He's dead. Just say it man! He's dead. Someone killed him. He or she callously stabbed an old man in the back whilst he slept in the cricket pavilion. I found him; it was my dress that was pin-pricked with his blood. I…" but Alba stopped herself. She paused before continuing in a fractionally calmer tone, "So, please, stop pussy-footing around the subject. He's dead. He shouldn't be, there were years and years in him. David and I had even started throwing out ideas for what to do for Vaughan's 80th birthday. But he's dead. And yes, Andrew, I can be angry and grief stricken at the same time." Despite her voice having taken that slightly calmer tone, her eyes still bored right into Andrew's.

Gingerly standing too, Andrew for an unknown reason held out his hand and spoke. This time it was his turn to speak quietly, "Sit down Alba. Let's sit down. There's a bit more to tell you about why my great-uncle was coming to Vaughan's property. Great-uncle meant well, if that's any consolation."

Inevitably, as if there were some invisible rule of the universe that means interruptions such as the one that was about to happen, happen, the landlord chose that exact moment to come over.

"Sir, Madam, the Bar is now open, if I can get you anything. But please, do not ask for *Six pints of bitter. And quickly please, the world's about to end*. Do you know how many times I have heard that line from the 'Hitch-Hiker's Guide to the Galaxy'? The late Douglas Adams has made the life of a publican as difficult as Ronnie Barker has made life for the owner of every hardware store in the country."

"Tea, for two, if that's an option" said Alba. "Nothing to eat but a pot of tea would be nice – and we'll let you keep the change from a fiver!"

"I asked for that, didn't I?" said the landlord. "Very good, I'm impressed – quoting Ford Prefect. Are Arsenal playing this afternoon? No, never mind on that one. Seriously, I'll get one of the girls to bring it out shortly" and with that the landlord headed back into 'The Sun and the Moon'.

"Tell me" said Alba to Andrew.

"Well," said Andrew, "Great-Uncle William, I think because of his selling up in Chile and so being used to sorting stuff out and getting rid of stuff, offered to clear out Vaughan's locker up at the Hall."

"Why would he do that?" asked a puzzled Alba.

"Oh, no reason, just trying to be helpful I guess. We were in a Heads of Department meeting and, well, not that great-uncle is a Head of Department but grandad lets him sit in on the meetings. Brothers after all, plus great-uncle was running his own estate out in Chile for years and years, so grandad values his input."

"But he's not Vaughan's executor is he, I mean, why would he be? Your great-uncle isn't a solicitor by profession, he and Vaughan weren't related or best friends or anything like that, they didn't even know each other. I assume you're not his executor either? I only ask because Vaughan lent me something, a photograph but not the one we were looking for yesterday, that I need to return to someone but I don't know who," commented Alba.

"No, no, nothing so formal as that. No idea who the executor is. I guess there might not even be one if Vaughan didn't make a will. No, just great-uncle trying to be helpful. Mr Parker was about to have a few days leave, I seem to remember, but wanted the locker emptied so great-uncle offered to help. As I say, I think he's so practised of late, of sorting through stuff, that he was happy to offer his services."

"But how does that place the pair of you in Vaughan's home

this morning?" said Alba, feeling she was still missing a couple of sandwiches from this particular picnic.

"Easy, really. In Vaughan's locker was a set of keys, highly probable they were a spare set for his home. Quite a clever place to keep a spare set, I thought. Well, having got rid of some tissues and some stale biscuits, that were in a not particularly air-tight tin, great-uncle offered to return the other items – spare shirt, some loose change, some pills, a couple of books on UK wildlife and some other bits and bobs. Actually, there was also a box half-full of spent shotgun cartridges but I'll come back to those. Great-uncle said he was happy to test the keys when he was next passing through the village and that Vaughan's property, save the cartridges, ought to be returned to his home. The spent shotgun cartridges are still at the Hall – we've informed the Police about them but they haven't rushed to collect them. My guess is they don't think they're relevant as Vaughan wasn't shot but it remains a mystery to me why he had spent ammunition in his locker. Anyway, as I think I've already said, I wasn't planning on going into Vaughan's home myself, I was just cadging a lift to 'Stapleton's' but curiosity got the better of me. To be fair to great-uncle, I think he'd have preferred to go into Vaughan's cottage alone, as he put the stuff back. I guess, as they were both of a similar age, he probably felt that was more respectful."

"But you must have been in there before Sally and I turned up and we were in the back garden a while" mused Alba.

"True. I'm not sure how long I was watching the pair of you from the lounge but great-uncle was taking his time in Vaughan's living-room come study so I just watched the pair of you until great-uncle said he was ready to go. Guess curiosity got to great-uncle too. As I've also already said, I found myself happier watching the living."

A Mediterranean looking girl, possibly northern Italian or Croatian thought Alba, brought their tea. They let it brew a while longer while Alba asked a question.

"But why didn't you come into the garden and say 'hello',

you knew we were there, and you were quite happy to talk to me yesterday. It was, err" and momentarily Alba was the one who found herself stuck for words.

As he waited, Andrew stirred the pot of tea.

"Err, nice. It was nice talking to you yesterday," she said. She was immediately disappointed in herself for using such a weak word as 'nice' and pictured her mother's face in her mind's eye, with an equally disappointed look and Alba could also hear her mother saying '*Is that the best word you could use when talking to Andrew Chapman, heir to Hillstone Hall. Did all those years at University teach you nothing better than the word 'nice'?*'

"Milk?" enquired Andrew and Alba nodded. Andrew added, as he poured, "I've heard it said that '*Each cup of tea represents an imaginary voyage*'. Catherine Douzel, apparently. Sorry that was really me just musing to myself. Tea" and he passed her one of the cups.

Taking her cup, Alba offered a quiet 'thank you' but just looked at him as he continued.

"Yes, I'd seen you around the Hall's garden a few times, so it was good to finally say 'hello'. I guess," he said as he looked at her as she put her cup to her lips and took a sip, "I wouldn't necessarily have chosen when you were crying as the first time to come and talk to you. Never mind, I'm pleased I was passing through the Orangery when I did. As for not coming to speak to you in Vaughan's garden just now, I think we, I mean great-uncle and I, were a bit too embarrassed and, definitely great-uncle was keen to leave quietly. Unfortunately, the front door was a bit harder to shut than I'd hoped – had to give it a bit of a slam and that, as they say, is where you, well you and Sally, come in."

They chatted for a bit longer about the pub itself and its summer menu. They spoke about the gardens at the Hall and Alba seized the opportunity to throw out her idea of cutting an arch through one of the long yew hedges, which would allow the gardeners to get around parts of the gardens quicker and easier, especially on the occasions they had barrow loads of mulch with them. They paid – jointly – for their drinks when Marie, the waitress, walked past and they headed back to 'Stapleton's'.

*

As Alba and Andrew stood outside Mrs Lyle's shop, the breeze was just beginning to get up and the day was beginning to cloud over.

"I think we have had the best part of the day" said Andrew. "They said the weather would be turning later this weekend and I think we're in for some bad weather on Monday. Still, it's been lovely for weeks so I guess, as you'd probably tell me, the gardens need some rain. Hope you're not volunteering on Monday; you'll get wet if you do."

"No, not Monday, I'm off to see someone. Well, hopefully."

"Hopefully, that's an odd word to use if you've planned meeting up with someone. Might they not be there?" asked Andrew.

"Oh, he'll be there alright. He's not going anywhere. It's just whether the paperwork has been cleared or whatever they have to do, to approve my visit."

"Now I'm really confused," admitted Andrew. "Are you a spy, by the way. Obviously, you won't tell me if you are, but are you?"

"Am I a what?" replied a completely bewildered Alba.

"A spy? Well, I assume it was a coded message the landlord gave you, when he took our drinks order."

"What are you on about, have you been in the sun too much this morning?" offered up a still bemused Alba.

"No, not too much sun. We're in July, you see."

Alba clearly didn't see and just looked back at Andrew hoping he'd explain.

"Yes, July. The football season is over – so why would Arsenal be playing later? And now, you're talking about VISA applications or something of that ilk."

"Oh, my goodness me" and Alba laughed. She tossed her head back and just smiled back at the man opposite her. She ran both her hands through her hair, laughed again and then said, still with both her hands upon her head, "No, I'm not a spy."

"I think you'd make a good one, or a detective; you have a way with you that puts people at their ease and they talk to you."

"No, not a spy or a detective" replied Alba. "The landlord's reference to Arsenal playing later was simply the next line in the 'Hitch-Hiker's' book – 'foregone conclusion, Arsenal without a chance' and all that."

"Just because it's the next line, doesn't mean it's not a coded message. Grandad once told me that the French Resistance were informed D-Day was coming via BBC radio broadcasts of a Paul Verlaine poem. Grandad said different lines were broadcast on different days to tell the Resistance how imminent the invasion was. *Wound my heart with a monotonous languor* was the line broadcast on 5th June, albeit in French. So, what I'm saying is, just because the line about Arsenal playing is following a script doesn't mean the landlord isn't sending you a coded message. If anything, it makes you both being spies more likely!"

"Andrew, I am not a spy" repeated Alba.

"As I say, that's what a spy would say."

"Oh, for goodness sake. I'm not. Look!" she added as she turned around to show him the mesh panel in the back of her top. "See, nothing." As Andrew studied her back, following the line of her spine down from the base of her neck to the top of her white trousers, Alba continued to speak, "I'm not mic-ed up, no weapons taped on and no wires. I think you must have heard one too many wartime stories from your grandad. He was in the Intelligence Corps you said?"

"Yes, intelligence, whereas great-uncle was more front line. Europe in the later stages of the war, I think. I really must ask him about it sometime – it's a topic you always put off to ask another day and then it's too late."

"You should. I wished I'd asked Vaughan more about his experiences, now. He would always talk about his brother, who was with Bomber Command, but avoided talking about his own experiences. I wish I'd pressed him a bit more on what he lived through. But let's be clear, shall we, I'm not a spy. It was just lines from a book. That's it, OK. You must have read the book or heard the radio play?"

"No, never," answered Andrew.

"Shame on you. I've got the radio plays on cassette somewhere. I'll lend you the first series. Have you got a towel with you? No, never mind – that one will be lost on you too! And as for VISA applications, no nothing so dramatic as that. No, I'm hoping to see Tom the day after tomorrow."

"But he's in prison, isn't he? He's been charged."

"Charged, yes. But he didn't do it," responded Alba.

"But the evidence…"

"Damn the evidence. Tom didn't do it. We all loved Vaughan, Tom included. As for Mrs Taylor, Tom had recently started lodging with her and seemed very settled – he had no reason to harm her."

"But the police think he did."

"Stuff what the police think or the magistrates. As I say, damn the evidence. Tom didn't do it, wouldn't have done it. Somehow I'll prove it," asserted Alba.

"Will you?" asked Andrew.

"Yes" replied Alba, emboldened for some reason that she couldn't quite determine why. "But I need to see Tom to start with. Hence the paperwork; I can't just walk in. I had to apply. I'm hoping it cleared in time, he was only remanded on Wednesday. I'll go, nonetheless, and find out when I get there as to whether they'll let me in. HMP South Down, apparently, unless they've already moved him."

With that, and with impulse getting the better of her, she gave Andrew a peck on his right cheek. She was about to head home when for some reason she grabbed his hand and said, "'Stapleton's' can wait a few moments longer for you, I'm going to show you something."

*

Alba White led Andrew Chapman back into Vaughan's garden. They ignored the honesty and roses in the front garden, they moved through the orchard area without stopping, went past the dead roses and made their way to Vaughan's small vegetable patch. They stood in front of Vaughan's bamboo frame that would have taken his runner beans.

"See?" said Alba.

"See what?" replied a non-plussed Andrew.

"The answer."

"The answer to what?" queried Andrew.

"Oh, I'm so tempted to say 'To Life, the Universe and Everything' but that will be equally lost on you – so I won't. No, the answer to your mystery; I might not be a spy but maybe Alba White should become a detective after all!"

"What are you on about, Alba? I think it's my turn to say you've been in the sun too long!" said a still baffled Andrew.

"No. Look. Look at the bamboo frame. Or, turn around and look at the canes that Vaughan had set out for his dahlias or sweet peas in the bed over there."

Andrew did look but it still meant nothing to him. "Bamboo canes made into a fairly sturdy frame; other canes set out in a nice row. But I don't get it. I mean yes, Vaughan clearly was safety conscious and put 'tops' on any cane that could have your eye out but, Alba, I really don't know what I'm meant to be seeing."

"Look at the cane toppers, Andrew. You don't notice at first, I didn't when I first got to know Vaughan and he showed me his garden. I just assumed I knew what I was looking at, so didn't see anything else. He did the same up at the Hall but no-one noticed until he pointed it out to people during his garden talks. Do you see?"

Andrew looked again, at what he had assumed were simply green rubber tops on the canes bought from the local garden centre, but this time he saw what Vaughan had actually used; spent shotgun cartridges. "He's used spent shotgun cartridges as his cane toppers. That's ingenious!" exclaimed Andrew.

"Re-using other people's rubbish, was how Vaughan described it. In his garden talks, he'd give your visitors other examples too – compost bays made out of wooden pallets from building sites, discarded plastic bottles filled with tap water to put around your pumpkins. You see, the water captures the warmth of the day and then acts as a radiator to the plant during the night. Vaughan was full of such ideas and your visitors loved the novelty of his talks. Financially, saved himself a tidy sum, too. But back to the point…"

However, before Alba could get to the point, Andrew stated it first. "So, the box of spent ammunition we found in his locker up at the Hall, was simply one of Vaughan's little ways of saving our gardening budget."

"Yes," confirmed Alba. "He'd pick them up when he came across them when out walking, I do too, now. Seriously, though, I think it might be worth giving the police a call and saying they really needn't bother coming to collect them and putting the ammunition through forensics – all that would do would be to lead them to one of the local farmers. So, as I say, I have solved your mystery."

"Well, blow me, you have. I'd never have spotted them. You look at something quickly, don't you, and you assume it's what you've already told yourself it will be. But you never really look properly. Or you tell yourself something is where you already assume it will be or left in a way you assume it would be left but you never bother to actually truly check do you? As I say, I'd never have noticed!"

He paused, then added:

"We all go through life, don't we, making too many assumptions and never slowing down often enough to check things out for ourselves. And, next time I'm out on a shoot, I'll get my loader to pick up the casings at the end of the day, so we can re-use them up at the Hall. Just ingenious!"

*

Standing back outside 'Stapleton's', Alba was just wishing Andrew well, as he prepared to go in and speak to Mrs Lyle, when a further 'Andrew' was shouted out by someone.

"Not me this time" stated Alba, "came from the other side of the road, didn't it?"

The two of them turned to the road to see the indicator lights on the BMW flash a couple of times as a woman opened a door and got in the passenger seat. The man, however, left his driver's door open as he came over the road, with his hand outstretched towards Andrew.

"Morning Andrew, I thought it was you" said Simon.

"Simon, good morning" replied Andrew. "Small world, Anne not wandering over, too?" added Andrew as he gave a nod towards the lady who had just got into the car.

"No, she's not feeling quite herself today. We were having a walk around the village to explore a bit, to get a feel for where Justin has moved to, but we've cut it short. I'm just going to drop her at Justin's now, whilst I head up to the Hall to see your grandfather. I need to discuss a couple of bits with him in advance of this week's auction – check a couple of reserve prices for starters."

"Sorry to hear about Anne. I didn't recognize the car, I thought you had a Volkswagen" stated Andrew.

"Oh, I did but business has been quite good this year and so thought I'd treat myself. Plus, I don't want to give Chancellor Brown any more than I need to" smirked Simon.

"You've only had a good year because of all the business we've given you, you vulture!" said Andrew to Simon, trying to sound jokey. Yet to Alba, simply listening to the exchanges, she had the feeling that Andrew wasn't completely joking. Alba felt that perhaps Andrew did regard the other with an element of mis-trust.

Alba was suddenly struck that this was the man she had seen at Vaughan's funeral, who'd been talking to the Reverend Quinn in the church hall whilst she had been returning cups and plates to the serving hatch. He was also the one who had sat on the front row during the service itself. This person, who she now knew to be called Simon, had sat alongside Lord and Lady Hartfield on the other side of the nave to where she, Alba, had been sitting next to Helen. Plus, Alba recalled, Simon and a woman had followed Vaughan's coffin in. Instinct suddenly kicked in and Alba looked into the BMW, through the open door, at the woman, who was now sitting in the passenger seat with her head back against the headrest and with her eyes closed. Alba was certain that that woman who had followed her beloved Vaughan's coffin in, was the same woman that she was looking at now. Yet Alba could not shake the feeling that she had had at the funeral, that she knew of this person from somewhere else too.

"Simon, can I introduce you to Miss White? She is one of the Hall's loyal gardening volunteers," said Andrew.

"Hello, Miss White. We've met before, kind of" commented Simon.

"Have we? I saw you at my friend Vaughan's funeral. You followed his coffin in, didn't you? You and the lady in your car unless I'm mistaken."

"My wife Anne, you mean? Yes, we did. I didn't really want to; in fact, I'd never even met Vaughan and felt very awkward having to follow him in. It was the Reverend Quinn's idea, I think, but you'd have to ask Anne exactly how it came about – along the lines of the minister feeling someone should follow the coffin in, that he belonged to someone as it were. As I say, you'd really have to ask Anne. But not now, as she's not feeling very well."

"But he belonged to us!" exhorted Alba. "He didn't have anyone else – us merry band of garden volunteers up at the Hall were his family. We should have been asked to walk behind him."

"But you weren't married to him, were you Miss White" stated Simon. "Whereas Anne was."

A look of incredulity spread itself across Alba's face. She looked to Andrew for an explanation, for support, for anything but all he offered was mild puzzlement on his face. She looked back to Simon, with an expression that spoke of 'you have to give me more than that'. She massaged her left temple as he simply added "Yes, Anne was married to Vaughan."

"But you just said Anne was your wife" said Alba in response.

"I'm also a bit confused now" chipped in Andrew. "You've been married to Anne for as long as the Chapman family have known you. Plus, it was your, as in you and Anne, son Justin, that grandad was able to call up at the last minute to make up his 'Invitational Eleven' for the cricket match on the day of the Golden Jubilee. The day Vaughan was murdered in cold blood."

As he finished saying that last sentence, he looked to Alba. She gave Andrew the faintest of nods and offered him the briefest of sad smiles, to 'thank him' for listening to her earlier, when she had pleaded with him to recognise what had happened to her dear friend.

Andrew then added, to Simon, "Grandad even said you and Anne were able to come and watch him in the match on that fateful day."

"That's where I've seen you before!" exclaimed Alba. "I was convinced I'd seen you somewhere before the funeral itself. It was at the cricket match, wasn't it? I remember now. You were with Lord and Lady Hartfield's group, weren't you? I'd been talking to Vaughan, where he'd been sitting near the pavilion. He'd been showing me something."

"His war medals, you mean? His campaign stars and war medals. He kept showing them to you, didn't he? A good auctioneer can spot war memorabilia – quite rare one of them" but Simon stopped himself from saying anything else about them. He simply added, needlessly, for it was implicit from what he had just said, "Yes, we were there, watching Justin. So that was Vaughan was it, who you were with?"

"Yes. They weren't his medals, by the way" stated Alba, to which Simon didn't respond. "But," she continued, "you saying that, reminds me just how close the whole group of you were standing to myself and Vaughan. Thinking about it now, any one of you could have heard our whole conversation. You were so close, I literally bumped into Andrew's great-uncle, when I got up and was focussing on not dropping the photograph Vaughan had lent me."

"So, you're the pretty woman grandad told me about" interjected Andrew to Alba. "Over breakfast the next day, he'd said to me someone had walked into his brother William, whilst his group had been watching Justin field – took a great catch in the slips by all accounts." Simon nodded to this last comment.

"You were so close" repeated Alba.

"There were lots of people watching the match that day," offered up Simon – to which Alba wasn't convinced was a sufficient explanation. Experience had sadly taught her to notice half-truths when they were offered up as explanations. She'd almost drowned in a sea of half-truths not so long ago and was now very attuned to them. She challenged Simon on the point.

"Yes, the match was well attended but that doesn't really explain why the group was so close."

"Oh, it was just how we stood, I think," said Simon. However, at that point a car horn sounded, as a passing car indicated its displeasure to the driver of a certain new BMW, who had left the car door open on the road side.

"Better go, I suppose" said Simon. "See you up at the Hall later, perhaps" he offered up to Andrew.

"But Vaughan wasn't married," repeated Alba.

"Not any more. Not for the last, let's think, err, not for the last fifty-two years. Anne had been his wartime bride. They'd married in 1945, during a period of Vaughan's leave, but it didn't work out and they divorced in 1950. They'd stayed on amicable terms even when she met me a few years later."

Alba cut into Simon's explanation, saying "I can believe that of Vaughan, being on good terms with someone."

"If you say so. Anyway, they'd stayed in contact – birthday cards, Christmas cards, that kind of thing. Guess Vaughan must have mentioned her to his minister at some stage and he contacted Anne about Vaughan's death."

"But surely she knew what happened to Vaughan. You were at the cricket match, near the pavilion in fact. In fact, you were standing right behind myself and Vaughan!" exhorted Alba.

"As I say, Miss, err, White, I didn't know it was Vaughan we were standing behind. Our group for some reason just seemed to creep closer to the boundary rope as the morning went on. We heard later in the morning that someone had been taken ill in the pavilion but we'd gone before any other news was available" replied Simon.

"Didn't Anne recognise Vaughan?" queried Andrew.

"No, I don't think so. You'd really have to ask her but she has one of her 'heads' so we can't disturb her. Fifty-two years is a long time, you know, and she probably only saw him from behind. He wasn't the only old man watching the game of cricket that morning – Vaughan, in one sense, could have been anyone. We knew he'd moved to this village and, it shows what a small world it sometimes is, when our son Justin moved here a few months ago" concluded Simon.

"A very small world," repeated Alba. "I take it you know it is Vaughan's house that's next to the village shop we're standing outside of," stated Alba, as she pointed to the detached house to the left of the shop.

"No," replied Simon. "Gosh, it's a really small world in that case. Perhaps…"

However, and as a Great Spotted Woodpecker swooped low across the road, another passing car offered up a sounding of its horn in annoyance, due to an open car door, cut Simon short. Instead, he succinctly said to Andrew:

"I really must go, see you later perhaps." Then to Alba, Simon added "Miss White, good morning, oh and here's my card. Get along to one of our auctions sometime – you never know what you might pick up."

With that, Simon was across the road and into his car and away – pulling out a little bit too quickly, Alba thought, to the frustration of the car coming up the road behind it.

*

"Strange," said Alba. The word was out of her mouth before she realised.

"What's strange?" queried Andrew.

"Surely they'd have parked at their son's house. That would have been logical. Even if he were not going to walk round the village with them, if they're coming to see him as well, they'd surely have started and finished their walk at his house. Pop in, say 'hello', use the loo, and all that and then have your walk. Why park here of all places? I mean, they were right opposite Vaughan's little cottage, weren't they?" puzzled Alba. "Bit of a co-incidence" she added.

"That was no co-incidence" replied Andrew.

"Go on" said Alba.

"Well, we both heard him say Anne had stayed in correspondence with Vaughan" stated Andrew.

"Agreed" offered up Alba. "Meaning Anne at least knew his address," she added.

"Exactly, so how likely is it that Simon also knew the address?"

"Pretty likely," speculated Alba.

"Pretty? 100% likely, I'd say – wife stays in contact with first husband, second husband will have made it his business to know where the former one lives. From what I know of Anne, she wouldn't have hidden Vaughan's address, it will have been there in her address book all these years. Simon will have 'accidentally' come across it no doubt."

"Is he a good auctioneer?" queried Alba, suddenly wanting to come at this from a different angle.

"Good? He's the best in the south-east. As I'm sure you've worked out from what Simon said just now, plus what Mr Parker will have had to tell you yesterday, in explaining why he's asked you to act up to cover for Tom, we're having to sell a number of items from the Hall to keep ourselves financially afloat."

"I'd surmised but…"

"But" interrupted Andrew, "I won't say any more on that now. Another time perhaps but not now. What I will say, is that Simon is the best auctioneer around. He's got us some very healthy prices for a lot of the stuff we've auctioned off, with the result that we've been able to hold on to two or three of the items that were scheduled to be sold – the Italian carvings in the Orangery in particular."

"And yet?" speculated Alba.

"And yet, and yet I'd trust him as far as I could throw him. He denied he knew that this was Vaughan's house. Also, he noticed those medals you said Vaughan was holding on the day he died, didn't he? Valuable too, he hinted. As I say, trust him as far as I could throw him. Always have to check the small print with him, has a way of 'adjusting' his commission rates if you don't keep a close eye on him. There's something else, too, about him but I've never been able to work out what. Leaves me a bit worried he's off to the Hall, chatting to grandad and I'm not there to keep an eye on things. It'll take a while to walk back and I haven't even spoken to Mrs Lyle!"

"I can drive you, if you like" offered Alba.

"Would you?"

"Of course. It's not far to my house. I can wait here whilst you talk to Mrs Lyle or go and get the car and meet you back here."

"Hang Mrs Lyle, so to speak. It'll wait another week. We could lose far more money if grandad doesn't notice any changes to the small print. Let's just head to yours – close is it?"

"Just a few minutes."

As they walked over the road, passing the spot where Simon had been parked, Andrew said to Alba "No co-incidence at all, they'd parked here. Simon was checking out Vaughan's home. No doubt before you, Sally, myself or great-uncle William had got here, Simon and possibly Anne had had a peer through his windows, to study the furniture, pictures on the wall, quantity of books and so on."

"You jokingly called him a 'vulture' when he first said 'hello' this morning," said Alba.

"Did I?" replied Andrew. "Well, he is. He and Anne were circling around Vaughan's home today, I'm sure of it."

"I wonder if Anne really was poorly," pondered Alba. She then added "Here we are," as she lifted the latch on her front gate.

"What a lovely home you have. I love the wisteria," said Andrew.

CHAPTER 9

A Confession

"I murdered Vaughan," stated Tom solemnly to Alba.

*

It was Monday morning and Alba, sitting on a red plastic chair, had just entered the visitors' hall at HMP South Down. She was damp from the walk across the courtyard in the pouring rain and still wishing, to herself, that she'd asked the name of the mum and little boy that she'd been escorted across with. Tom had offered an awkward 'hello', looking more at his feet than at Alba opposite him, as he did so. As Alba instinctively tried, without success, to reposition her chair, she was about to offer a 'hello' back when Tom added those three words – 'I murdered Vaughan'. It stunned Alba to silence and she was unable to offer any words in return. She sat there motionless, in a chair that itself was motionless, being bolted as it was to the floor.

Alba tried to stir, if not herself physically, then at least her mind. She tried to put to one side her experience of coming through prison security and process what Tom had just said. 'Had she heard it? Hadn't she? Then again perhaps she hadn't heard him correctly', she found herself wondering. She knew, though, that she had heard Tom correctly. Tom Wychfield, part of her gardening family and the newly appointed Deputy Head Gardener at Hillstone Hall, had just sat opposite her and confessed; confessed to the murder of Vaughan. Tom had just confessed to killing her beloved Vaughan – 'no, damn it,' she found herself mentally correcting herself, 'their beloved Vaughan, hadn't they all loved him, Tom included?'

Tom didn't rush her for a response. He knew what he had just said would take Alba time to digest. As he waited, he looked past Alba and studied the Prison Officer who was standing with his back to the dull blue double doors, through which Alba had come just a few moments earlier. Prison Officer Stevens was, in one way, a nondescript kind of person. Had you seen him, Tom thought to himself, at a bus stop on a dull day you wouldn't have given him a second glance – he would have been lost, even if he had been there alone, against the grey bus shelter, the vandalised glass panels and the back-lit adverts for some supposedly age-defying beauty product. He wouldn't have warranted a second look. There was no real presence about him. However, in here, Tom reflected, there was something unnerving about him. PO Stevens stood there in uniform, in his perfectly ironed white shirt, with his black clip-on tie and highly polished shoes. He stroked his key chain and repeatedly undid and did up the press-stud on his black leather key pouch that his thick black belt held in place by his right hip, as he stood and looked, through uncaring eyes, across the visitors' hall.

For a moment, Tom became fixated with the Officer's leather pouch. Tom found it mildly ironic that he, Tom, also routinely wore a leather accessory on his belt, that equally sat on his right hip, when he went to work. However, since last Tuesday evening, once the paramedics had attended Mrs Taylor's home and the paramedics themselves had asked for Police attendance after Tom had mentioned 'I think she's been poisoned', Tom hadn't been back at work and his holstered secateurs remained, not in his locker at work where he kept them, but in, he was told, a transparent plastic police evidence bag. As with all of his other locker items, the police had seized them once they had found the 'Tesco' carrier bag containing Clive's wartime medals, in Tom's work locker, that Tuesday evening.

Having been thinking about his work tools, Tom instinctively put his hand to his hip – as a gardener does subconsciously many times a day to check the holster hasn't unclipped itself and fallen off into a flower bed or a hedge. His hand, though, just felt his jogging bottoms, and that suddenly brought his train of thought back into the room.

Before he dwelt again on the prison officer, and why Officer Stevens made many inmates feel uncomfortable, Tom decided to add to the comment he had just made to Alba:

"Both of them actually. I killed both of them – Vaughan and Mrs Taylor." After a pause, and still in his quiet tone, he added:

"I'm sorry, Alba. I'm so sorry."

*

HMP South Down was one of those modern looking prisons. Built in the early 1990s, from a distance, and if you had never visited before, you might, just might, upon your first glance of it might have thought it had been made from Portland stone. It wasn't. Rather it was built from concrete blocks that offered up a dull yellow with just the faintest hint of a pale pink hue. The building, or at least the perimeter wall – for you couldn't really see the actual buildings that lay within the wall – was ugly and angular. At set points, the wall bent 15 degrees or 40 degrees inwards and any bird flying overhead, had it a thing for British coinage, would have compared the outline of the prison wall to that of a very badly cut twenty pence piece. Away from any avian take on the prison's design, Alba in her naivety, as she had woken up that Monday morning, had somehow assumed that the prison would be surrounded by a perfectly circular outer wall. However, as she had walked from the visitors' car park to the entrance, she had realised that modern prison design was not based on Cornwall's Restormel Castle, which indeed had a beautiful circular outline. 'I guess', thought Alba as she had waited to be searched by a young petite female prison officer, upon first entering the prison, 'that modern prisons shouldn't model thirteenth century west country castles'; yet she remained puzzled as to what actually had inspired the Whitehall mandarins to go with that design and the choice of building materials.

It was embarrassing to have a prison officer run her fingers around and underneath the roll neck of her jumper, down the length of each arm, around her shoulder blades and under her arms, down her front and then similarly her back. Thereafter she had felt those same hands work around the top of her jeans and down each leg. The hand-held scanner beeped as the officer waved it over Alba's jumper but Alba didn't think anything of the noise and the officer ignored it. Alba had already removed her raincoat, shoes and, had she worn a belt, that would have equally gone through the scanner on a grey plastic tray with the coat, shoes and a locker key – a tray that would not have looked out of place in the slots underneath a six-year-old's school desk where a child would keep his or her spelling book, selection of broken, blunt and chewed colouring pencils and that proverbial assortment of acorns, bits of 'Lego' and plastic beads from a broken bracelet. The key was to a locker in the first room that Alba had had to pass through, where she had been required to leave her handbag, passport, driving licence, money and car key.

Alba could sense, though, it was even more embarrassing for the young mum who went through before her, with a toddler at her side. Whilst the toddler seemed to enjoy showing another female officer that he could put his own shoes back on and do up the Velcro strips all by himself, Alba could tell the mother was not enjoying her experience at all – shorn, as she was, of her black leather boots, with her thread-bare socks on display. The mum was also minus her belt, earrings, three metal bracelets and a watch – which had all been placed in further identical grey trays and which were now beyond the scanner, the contents of which were waiting to be collected. Alba thought the watch face was a tad too large for the woman's wrist. The young mum, Alba noticed, had also triggered the hand scanner because she had left her locker key in her pocket along with some coins. The officer confiscated the coins, assured the woman that they could be collected from the desk in the first room they had been through, at the end of the visit, and pedantically placed the key in a further grey tray and sent it through the scanner all by itself.

They were the only two visitors this morning. The rain, a twenty-four-hour bus strike and, with the end of term just a few weeks away, meaning there were plenty of end of year school events for parents to be at, probably had discouraged any others from making the journey today.

"We were lucky today," the woman with the toddler said to Alba, as they were being escorted across the courtyard towards the visitors' hall.

"Lucky?"

"Yeah."

"In what way?" queried Alba.

"This is your first visit to this place?"

"Yes. You can tell, can you?"

"Oh, yes," replied the mum, as she resisted once again the toddler's attempt to pull away from her. "You were trying to talk to the guards, kind of, like, as an equal. You were smiling and saying thank-you and stuff."

"Was I? And is that wrong?"

"Oh, you were, missy, and it is. You'll learn soon enough, after a few more visits. You'll see. Don't engage with them, eyes down, say nothing."

"Really?"

"Yeah," said the mum but she then paused, as they passed

the officer who was waiting for them at an unlocked and opened gate. The officer beckoned them through, into the second half of the courtyard. The mum waited until the officer had re-locked and moved on ahead of them once again, before continuing with her advice to Alba. "I guess some of these screws are alright. This one, who's walking us to the hall today I think is OK. But some are right bitches. There's one, I tell you, right posh bitch, speaks with a real plum in her mouth, thinks she's in charge of the prison. I tell you, when she's on visits, she's a right cow and gets on a right power-trip. She wasn't on today, so we were lucky."

"What does she do that's different, for us to be lucky today?" asked Alba.

"Snide comments for one, especially towards those of us with children. Actually, now you ask, it's more a case of snide comments about our children, how scruffy they are, that their socks don't match, whether their shoes are too worn or too expensive, whether they pick their noses or the like. She'd never be brave enough to say anything to our faces, always to her colleagues or to herself as she rummages through our items as they go through the scanner but always loud enough for us to hear. But also, did you notice how the hand scanner beeped when they waved it over me?"

"Yes, you'd left the locker key in your pocket."

"That's right but didn't you hear it beep before that?"

"No," replied Alba.

"As I say, I could tell this is your first time. You probably were too busy looking at everything to hear or just thought it was meant to beep to start with. No, it beeped a first time because it picked up metal then too. The same happened when they scanned you but the officer let it go for each of us."

"Did it? Gosh, I didn't hear. Why did it do that? I'd put all my metallic stuff in the tray. But, equally, if it did, why let it go? Surely they'd have looked for something?"

"As I say, we were lucky. The posh bitch wouldn't have let the beeps go. She'd have taken great delight in taking us off, in turn, to the side room and forcing us to strip off our top halves. You must have wiring in your underwear today?"

"I'm not mic-ed up, if that's what you mean. I'm not an undercover reporter or a spy," offered back Alba – and in that moment she thought of Andrew and the conversation they had had on Saturday morning outside 'Stapleton's' just as the wind had started to pick up.

"No, not microphones or radio transmitters or stuff like that," said the mum. "I mean have you any wiring sown in? For me, I don't have any choice, I don't have much money for clothes."

"Oh, I see what you mean. I don't instantly recall as I got dressed in a hurry this morning. It was pouring this morning as I was getting ready, so I changed my mind on what I was going to wear. I can't recall what I've got on underneath these two tops. I guess I must have," offered up Alba.

"I know you have," replied the mum. "The scanner beeped, didn't it? Fact. And, as I say, there's this one screw that wouldn't let that go, and would use an under-wired bra as an excuse to make us strip and be further humiliated. I mean, it's bad enough what we have to go through to see our boyfriends and bring our little children along – it's an absolute effing nightmare – but it's so much worse when that one cow is on duty. As I say, we were lucky today."

"Not that lucky, we're getting sodden walking across this courtyard. Shame they won't allow us to bring our umbrellas with us," mused Alba out loud.

"Bloody hell, you really are new to this, aren't you," said the mum as they got to the double doors of the visitors' hall. "Lots of lovely little sharp pointy bits of metal in an umbrella; sure they'd trust us and our boyfriends with those. Anyone could have half a dozen metal struts off in no time and hidden down their trousers. This the first time your man's been remanded?"

But before Alba could answer, the prison officer had unlocked the doors and was ushering them through. Alba was about to try and offer up a kind of answer but, before she could, the toddler had finally escaped the grip of his mother's left hand and darted to the far side of the hall. The mum instinctively chased after him. As Alba stood where she was, trying to shake the rain from her jacket, she could hear a very young voice cry 'Daddy', quickly followed by a different voice and the words of 'Hi babe'.

The officer who had escorted them across the courtyard, having spoken to her colleague, Officer Stevens, let herself back out through the double doors. Alba could hear the key working the heavy-duty metal lock and then a fainter jingling of keys and chain as the officer, Alba correctly assumed, returned her bunch of keys to their leather pouch.

With only two visitors having got to the prison this Monday morning, there were only two prisoners sitting in the hall, waiting expectantly to see a happy face – or, at least, a face they knew. For, despite what the inmate might hope to see, their visitor's face would generally only offer up a look of weariness, stress, exposure to the weather and, but not this morning at least, embarrassment from the security procedures they had just gone through.

It was easy for Alba to see Tom. He was sitting virtually in the middle of the hall, looking at his feet, on a dark green plastic chair. Between his chair and, apart from their colour, the three identical chairs opposite him, there was a small, low, table. The table and the four chairs were all fixed to a black angular metal frame and the frame itself was screwed to the floor. Looking around at all the empty chairs in the hall, Alba could see that everything was screwed down – 'if there were to be a riot', thought Alba, 'whatever else happened, the chairs and tables weren't going to be part of it'.

*

Alba sat opposite Tom on one of the hard plastic red chairs. As Tom offered a mumbled 'hello', she instinctively tried to move the chair closer but, with it being screwed to the floor, couldn't. Tom's double confession, that immediately followed, stunned her. She sat there motionless, trying to process what Tom had just said.

As she sat there, trying to formulate a response, she could sense Tom was looking beyond her to something or someone by the doors she had just come through. Finally, Alba heard herself say:

"But Tom, you wouldn't have. I don't believe you."

"Alba you need to believe me. You must believe me!" He could see the confusion and the sadness in Alba's eyes and he knew the pain his words had caused her.

"You can't confess to something you didn't do," offered back Alba.

"But I have confessed, haven't I?" replied Tom, his voice heavy with resignation.

They both sat there in silence. Alba could feel the fire that had been burning within her start to die, a fire stoked by her belief in Tom's innocence. She'd convinced herself he was innocent; she'd tried to convince Mr Parker and Andrew. Furthermore, Mrs Rowan had detected Alba's belief in Tom's innocence. Sally, Helen and David each thought Tom was innocent – hadn't they all left a space for him at Vaughan's funeral last week? Yet now that fire was rapidly dying.

Tom quietly spoke once again, "Yes, you must believe me Alba. You must. I have confessed to you this morning. To you, Alba, no-one else, at least not yet. I had to speak to you first – and now I have. When I'm back on my wing, I will ask to see the prison officer who has been assigned to me, for welfare issues and the like, and ask him to contact my solicitor – he's the duty solicitor I got last Tuesday evening when I was arrested. I'll ask that solicitor to come and see me in order that I can formally confess. At the police station he advised me to say 'no comment' but, after my time here, I just want to get this thing over with. If I confess to this whole ghastly business it'll be so much simpler. It's just easier this way."

Suddenly Alba could sense the fire within her spark back to life.

"Tom," Alba exhorted. "You bloody young fool! Don't you dare, don't you bloody well dare!" Alba's right arm shot out and she pointed her index finger right at Tom's face.

Officer Stevens, hearing Alba's raised voice and gesticulations, took a number of steps forward and had his hand poised over his radio to call for assistance, in anticipation of things escalating further.

However, Alba quickly composed herself once more. She dropped her arm, gave Tom a half smile and, for some unknown reason, chose that moment to pick up her raincoat, refold it and place it over the red chair to the other side of her, to enable some more of her coat to air dry. Officer Stevens, detecting the heat of the moment had gone, allowed his hand to drop away from his radio and he moved back to his original position – but nonetheless keeping his focus on Tom and his female visitor, in preference to behaviour of the toddler on the far side of the hall.

"Sorry for swearing Tom but you are a young fool. Thank goodness you tested out your decision on me first and you haven't gone straight to your solicitor – oh, you're such a young, young fool. You just can't throw your life away like this."

"What do you mean, Alba? I know what I'm saying and what I'm going to do. It's easier this way." With that, Tom shut his eyes and dropped his head and, if one can give the impression of folding oneself away without actually moving, Tom did exactly that. As she watched Tom sit there, Alba thought it was as if he were trying to fold himself up and lose himself in this near empty visitors' hall.

"Tom," Alba said ever so quietly, placing a hand on his knee as she did so, "I know you didn't murder anyone. You wouldn't have done anything to Vaughan and, as for Mrs Taylor, well I didn't know her but you wouldn't have done anything to her either. You were happy lodging with her, you said so yourself. So, whatever has been going on – 'evil' the Reverend Quinn called it during Vaughan's funeral – you weren't involved. Of that I am sure."

Tom was still head down but Alba could tell his eyes were open once more and, she sensed, he was listening to her in a way he hadn't for the whole of her visit so far. She continued:

"So whatever ill-thought out plan you've got into your head, it ends right now. Do you hear me?" With her voice rising, she repeated herself. "It ends now, do you hear me! You are not going to ask to see your solicitor, at least not to confess."

She took her hand from his knee and sat there unmoving until Tom finally lifted his head and returned her gaze.

"But Alba there's so much evidence against me. Officer Stevens, who gave an introductory talk to all of us newly on remand, said that people – well, he said 'offenders' and he was just so smug when he called us that – get through their sentences with less hassle, and normally get released sooner, if they confess to their crimes. He said, if we can indicate that we can make better decisions next time around and convince the Parole Board of our remorse, it helps. I know it'll take me years and years but being here is a nightmare; being confined like this, is truly horrible. I mean, you know how much I love being outdoors – I still can't believe Lord Hartfield promoted me and pays me, well, was paying me, to do something I love. Being stuck in here is just awful. I just can't cope with the thought that I might be increasing the time I will have to serve by saying I didn't do it."

"But you didn't Tom," insisted Alba.

"But the evidence, Alba, the evidence says I did do it. There's just so much evidence against me," and Tom looked at Alba through eyes welling up with tears and with such a forlorn look about him. After rubbing a forearm across both eyes and then again across his running nose, Tom added, "I can't swim against such a tide, the police have so much evidence. You should have seen the look in the duty solicitor's eyes when he turned up at the police station and read through my file. He was there with me in the cell. He was just open-mouthed as he read."

"Tom," Alba said defiantly, "we are a family, you, me, Helen and David. As was Vaughan, as we both know. So, whatever your answer is to my next question, I will still regard you accordingly. It might change many things and it might be very painful but our little group will somehow stick together. So, ignore the look on your solicitor's face, ignore the 'advice' from that prison officer, dismiss, for a moment at least, the evidence that is stacked up against you, put out of your mind which path might seem easier and, if you can, ignore the fact that I'm asking you. Think of me as a mirror, if you like, as if you are asking the question of yourself. It's a simple question that requires a simple answer. All I ask of you is that you tell the truth. Once we've established the truth, we can move on and deal with whatever comes next. What will come next I've got no idea – I'm a volunteer gardener who's in between jobs and have been for a while. So, I've got no idea where we go from here but let's just establish the 'here' where we are at." Alba paused, straightened her back, took a deep breath, held it for a few seconds, and then asked her question.

CHAPTER 10

Empty chairs and empty tables

"Did you murder Vaughan, Tom?" asked Alba.

Tom composed himself as best he could, given his tear-stained eyes and that he was still sniffling. If not straightening his back, as Alba had just done, he at least maintained his head upright and he held Alba's gaze. He answered quietly but clearly.

"No."

With that single word answer, it was as if, if not the weight of the whole world then at least the weight of a sizeable continent, was lifted from Tom's shoulders. Alba sensed that a dam was about to burst and in that split second she could see in her mind's eye, even though Clive hadn't flown with the dam-busting Lancasters of 617 Squadron, the photograph of Clive on her hall table and also Vaughan showing her the war medals on the day of the cricket match.

The dam did indeed burst and Tom unleashed a torrent of dialogue.

"Of course I didn't! Vaughan was like my grandfather, the best grandfather anyone could ever have. I've cried for him. We all have, haven't we? But I've cried for him night after night. He saw something in me that no-one else ever has and he believed in me. He encouraged me to go for the promotion and he tutored me prior to my interview – helped me to prepare answers to 'Bic's' probable questions."

"I didn't know he'd tutored you," interjected Alba.

"Oh yeah. He came around to Mrs Taylor's a few times and we'd sit in her living room. She didn't mind if it was a night she was out. We'd think through answers to probable questions and examples I could give. Vaughan got me focussing on answering in a way that 'Bic' would want to hear – visitor numbers, health and safety, information boards, wear and tear on the grass paths. All that kind of stuff. If it hadn't been for Vaughan I'd have just talked of pruning the step-over apple trees in the kitchen garden and replanting beds in the sunken garden. Vaughan, though, got me seeing things through 'Bic's' eyes – one idea Vaughan suggested, as an example of tempting our regular garden visitors to come back yet again and possibly even pay for a talk and guided tour around the estate, was 'Verdun Oaks'. Mr Parker really liked that idea and said, when I was offered the position of Deputy, that type of idea showed I was thinking the right way for a modern country house. I was about to start researching whether we had any of them when I got arrested."

"Oh, the oaks," but Alba cut herself short, not wanting to let slip that Mr Parker had asked her to act up into Tom's position and do that piece of research into whether the estate had any oak trees grown as memorials to First World War soldiers – trees grown from acorns collected from the Verdun battlefield in northern France.

Alba was thankful Tom, being in full flow, didn't pick up on her awkwardness.

"Yeah, oak trees. I was really looking forward to researching them – horticulture and military history, my two passions, coming together like that. It would be really special if the estate had some. So, yeah, Vaughan was so kind to me and he was so excited when I told him I'd got the promotion – he gave me such a hug. When he gave you a hug, you got a hug alright, didn't you?"

"Real bear hug," offered back Alba.

"So, I wouldn't have murdered him, would I? I miss him so much, you know."

"I know, Tom, I know," Alba said reassuringly.

"Him in his leather hat, his battered old journal in his pocket and always in a checked country shirt. Dear old Vaughan. I wouldn't have harmed him ever. And Mrs Taylor, to save you asking," continued Tom, "I didn't kill her either. I was happy there – well, happy enough. She had a few rough edges, as it were, and always insisted I paid my rent on time. I think, but I couldn't quite say why I always thought this, she must have had some money issues – I mean, why take me in as a lodger otherwise. Still, rest her soul and all that. But, as for staying there, I had a lovely room, that overlooked the woods beyond her garden. The rent was a bit more than I'd ideally have liked to have paid but I wanted to be somewhere in the village and, as she had two bathrooms, I had quite a lot of privacy given I was really only renting my bedroom."

Tom paused, just for a moment as he watched another prison officer come and replace Officer Stevens, and then resumed his full flow. "Do you know, Alba, of all the random little things I think about from the day of Vaughan's murder, I keep thinking of that 'Tesco's' carrier bag. I was very humbled that Vaughan was willing to show me his brother's medals. I hadn't asked to see them that day specifically, well not at the cricket match – if anything, it was a silly day to have them out of the house. Thinking back, I thought I might have popped in at Vaughan's later in the day and had a look at them then. You see, I had all my camera equipment ready for that day, what with the fly-past and David being in the cricket team – lens polished, flash gun charged, you know, that kind of stuff. It was odd, I remember thinking beforehand, that he insisted on bringing them out with him."

"That's what I thought too," offered back Alba. "Said as much to him, as he and I sat on that wooden seat by the pavilion. Kept holding them out, talking me through them and their ribbons. You having just mentioned Verdun oaks, reminds me one of the medals had an oak leaf emblem on that Vaughan was very proud of but I can't remember what it signified."

"Mentioned in Dispatches," Tom enthusiastically replied. "It meant Clive had performed an act of bravery which had been formally mentioned in a report sent to HQ by a senior Officer. It's sort of a step down from a gallantry medal."

"The Victoria Cross, you mean?" offered back Alba, as she trawled her limited military knowledge.

"Well, that's the highest but there's also the Military Medal or Military Cross, Distinguished Flying Medal or Distinguished Flying Cross; all depending on branch of the armed forces you were with and rank. And that's just four of them. There are several different medals for bravery and the differences between them can be very subtle at times. But a 'Mention in Dispatches' is still a very special thing – Vaughan was right to be proud of his brother."

"But I still don't understand why he brought them out that day. He just wasn't quite himself that day," said Alba.

"It intrigued me at the time and I did ask him directly, when we were in the pavilion itself and it was just him and me."

"Did you?" asked Alba somewhat nervously as she found herself unable to not think about finding Vaughan; she saw once again his blood on her hands and her white dress.

"I did," said Tom. "Vaughan said it was because of the fly-past. You see one of the planes was a Lancaster bomber; it's what Clive flew in. Well, not that particular plane, but you know what I mean. The Lancaster was what Clive flew in and died in. Vaughan said he somehow felt called to bring the medals out that day, so the medals, especially the one that air crew received, could kind of be reunited with their heritage. I think I understood what Vaughan was getting at – as if he was hoping the midday sun would reflect off one and onto the other or that the shadow of the planes might, just might, fall across the medals. Maybe, to use modern speak, he thought it might give him a bit of closure."

"I guess," offered back Alba and they were both silent for a moment before Alba continued.

"We will never grasp what it was to live through, will we? The war I mean, and how it still affects people to this day; how it affected Vaughan on his very last day. He never got over Clive, did he?"

"No, I don't think he did. But I'm pleased I asked him why he had the medals with him that day – otherwise I'd have been puzzling over that as well as that infernal carrier bag. I mean, why keep them in that, of all things? But that's not important. What is, is that after he showed me the medals, he put them back in that plastic bag and put them under his chair. He was tired that day, I could tell, so having got a couple of poor photos of them – the lighting in the hut was rubbish you see – I left him so he could rest. I thought, if he rested, when Lord Hartfield rang the bell, Vaughan would be more with it and get out to see the fly-past. And what you want me to say Alba, is that when I left Vaughan he was alive; resting in the chair but very much alive. I didn't stab him in the back, I didn't accidentally push him onto a knife and I didn't steal the medals."

"But," said Alba with a degree of certainty in her voice, "there wasn't anything under his chair when I was there – tucking David's jumper around Vaughan. I wasn't looking for anything, obviously, but I'm sure nothing was around or underneath where Vaughan was sitting."

"They weren't missing for too many weeks, were they Alba?" threw back Tom. "The police found them easily enough in my locker last Tuesday."

"We'll come back to that in a minute Tom. Let's just, as I said, establish our starting point, and that is that you didn't murder Vaughan? Correct?"

"Correct."

"Right. Good," said Alba, so matter of factly, that she kind of caught herself off-guard with her response. "I knew you hadn't, I just knew. But your stupid confession this morning almost had me doubting myself and you. I was starting to believe you, for a few moments at least, and then I worked out what you were up to. It wasn't a confession I was hearing it was a surrender, wasn't it?"

"I guess so; over this weekend, being here, locked up, mentally I just gave up. When I was told they had allowed your visit – I'm still amazed the paperwork got processed, bloody miracle that – I decided to sit on my decision until I'd seen you. So, what did I say that allowed you to see through what I was saying?"

"It was when you said it was easier – you said 'It's just easier this way'. That's not a confession – that's a statement of resignation. You were waving a white flag, if you like. It's as if you saw a narrow and a wide path ahead of you and, in your time here, you were only being allowed to see the easy-to-get-onto wide path; a path that would take you years and years to walk. But you were just so keen to start walking, that you'd walk anywhere – especially in light of the 'advice' from, if you ask my opinion, that moronic Officer Stevens and your lame sorry excuse of a solicitor. They'd have happily both let you walk in the wrong direction and ruin your life because it would make their working lives momentarily easier. They allowed you to take your eyes off the narrow path, so to speak; a path where truth matters and innocence is to be sought after. Oh, it does annoy me so, these so-called professionals, with their comfortable salaries and attractive pension pots, failing to look out for the vulnerable and the confused and those who, like you Tom, have just been completely overwhelmed by everything that's befallen you these last few weeks."

Tom offered nothing back. There was nothing to say, for Alba was reading the situation perfectly.

"I mean, imagine, just imagine, if the police officers who first arrested you, the prison officer, or the solicitor, had said 'tell us the truth, that's what we seek here, don't tell us what you think we'd like to hear, or what's easier to say, we want the truth and we'll do all we can to ensure there's no miscarriage of justice'. As I say, just imagine.

But it doesn't happen that way, does it? It's why there are so many miscarriages of justice I guess."

With that Alba paused, thinking back to a case she'd read about as a student. It flashed back into her mind and she continued, "People like Stefen Kiszko. A bit before your time, I reckon Tom. Sixteen years he served before the courts finally accepted he was innocent beyond a shadow of a doubt – gosh, it must be about ten years since the Court of Appeal ordered his immediate release. The poor, poor man. If only one professional around him at the time of his arrest in 1975 had sought out the truth, rather than accept the timid confession of someone completely overwhelmed by the system who just wanted to go home – if only they'd endeavoured to seek out the truth. But that's what we're going to do Tom. As I say, I'm not quite sure how but if we seek the truth, then maybe we'll get somewhere. We'll go with what we know, look into what we don't and be ready to go off at a tangent if something comes up. The truth will out – there's a new moon rising. You with me Tom?"

"Yes, Alba. But where on earth do we start? There's just so much evidence against me; that's why I thought it would be easier just to go with the tide and say I did it and be done with it."

"Tom," Alba said, reverting to her stern voice. "Yes, there's evidence against you but, hey, there's evidence against me. I was there in the pavilion, all by myself with Vaughan, I had access to any of those knives too and I could have planted the medals in your locker up at the Hall. So, we've got to look beyond what is incriminating and look to what we have in your favour."

"Like?" said Tom despairingly.

"Like," continued Alba, "you haven't confessed, unlike poor Stefan did all those years ago. Like, even if the medals were found in your locker and the knife amongst your gardening tools, there won't be your fingerprints on them because you didn't take them or use the knife. Anyone could have planted them amongst your stuff."

"But my prints should be on the medals, shouldn't they? I've never denied being in the pavilion with Vaughan and looking at the medals with him – there are pictures I took of them on my camera, thinking about it. So, my prints should be all over them – well, maybe not all over them as I handled them carefully – but there should be a half print or two shouldn't there? Yours should be on the medals too. But thinking about it, police forensics have already stated I wiped the medals clean of prints to avoid detection. But…"

"But," continued Alba "why wipe them clean but still hide them in your own locker? That's just daft."

"And," added Tom, suddenly enlivened by the realisation, "why wipe them clean but leave the photographs of them on my camera? They're valuable – priceless to Vaughan – but to a collector, still worth several hundred pounds, possibly over a thousand with associated bits of memorabilia. So, a collector would be interested."

"Or an auctioneer," offered back Alba.

"Oh, yeah. I'm sure an auctioneer would love to get his or her hands on them, they'd make a nice little commission on selling them no doubt and be quite a prestigious lot to sell, so it would bring kudos to any auction house. So, they're valuable all right and a thousand pounds would be quite a nice sum to have all of a sudden but if I murdered Vaughan for them and wiped them clean why not delete the photographs too and hide them somewhere less obvious and less incriminating than my own locker, where someone could find them?"

"Exactly. Exactly," said Alba as she concurred with everything Tom had just said. "Someone planted them in your locker and left the knife amongst your tools too, to incriminate you."

"So, all we've now got to do is work out who, when and why – reckon we can have this done by lunch time, don't you?" and, for the first time for a long time, Tom smiled.

"Good to have you back, as it were," replied Alba, "but, as we both know, this isn't going to be easy. There were lots of people at the cricket match and many others from the village or from further afield could have sneaked in and out of the pavilion virtually unnoticed if they went in via the road side. Actually, that's what my friend Neale did. He'd gone to check on Vaughan as we were worried about him and Neale found the pair of you in the pavilion. He'd gone in via the road side and left the same way once he'd heard you say to Vaughan you were going off to get ready to photograph the fly-past."

"Never did photo the planes, actually. The police and magistrates held that against me too. I accept I told the police that that was why I left Vaughan. But I'm not that good a photographer really. I mean, I love my history and the re-enactment stuff that I do and I take lots of pictures but it's always stuff close up, like the medals, or re-enactors posing. But seldom big stuff that's moving – wouldn't really know how to deal with the lighting or the speed of the object. I was sort of thinking I should photograph them, and that's what I did say to Vaughan, but when I heard the sound of the engines, you know what, I had this sudden inclination to just watch them. Not to 'see' them through a camera lens, just wanted to see them for 'real' as it were. Do you understand what I'm getting at?"

"I guess so," offered back Alba. "Unfortunately it means your reason for leaving the pavilion is a bit weak."

"I know. The police and probably my solicitor think I was making my escape, having stabbed Vaughan in the back, and heading back to the Hall to get rid of the knife and hide what I'd murdered him for."

"But you didn't and somehow we'll prove it," said Alba defiantly. "We'll…" but her voice was swamped by a shout from someone else in the visitors' hall.

"Visitors," shouted the officer at the double doors behind Alba, "you have ten minutes left. Ten minutes."

Alba continued, "So, we've got to find who put the medals in your locker and…"

"And who placed the knife amongst my gardening tools," interjected Tom.

"Likely to be the same person," threw back Alba "but we can't be sure on that. We don't know how many people we're looking for. Also, since you didn't murder Vaughan, we've got to prove someone else went into the pavilion after you but before me."

"Then there's Mrs Taylor," said Tom – and this time it was him, rather than Alba thinking back to being with a dying person. "Connected?" pondered Tom out loud.

"Certainly. I don't like co-incidences. Connected for sure but in what way?"

"What do you mean 'in what way'?" asked Tom.

"Well, was she killed because she saw who murdered Vaughan? At least that would be the logical reason why."

"But she wasn't at the cricket match, as far as I'm aware and I'm sure she'd have mentioned it to me if she had been, given I was lodging with her, in the weeks between Vaughan's death and hers."

"OK – so it may not be an obvious connection. For example, maybe she was killed because someone wants the police to look in the wrong direction; she might have been killed purely to lay a 'red herring' as it were."

"How do you mean?"

"How does that theory go? Kill person 'X', then 'Y' and then 'Z' and the police assume there's a link between all of them but 'X' and 'Z' have been killed purely to give the impression there's a link, whereas in reality the murderer was callously 'hiding' one death amongst several in the belief he'd be more likely to get away with it. Put simply, maybe Mrs Taylor was killed as a smoke screen so we stop looking where we really should be looking."

"Flipping heck, Alba, you're wasted as a gardener; you should be a detective!"

"I don't think so – and I've still got so much to learn about gardening. For example, why do beech hedges hold onto their leaves in winter but beech trees don't. I haven't quite worked that one out. Or, why, given all the apples that fall from the average apple tree, do you not get a thousand apple tree saplings growing up in the vicinity in the way that you do with a sycamore or ash tree. Or, no wait, being completely serious for a minute, what if Mrs Taylor wasn't the intended victim of the poisoning – what if you were."

"Me?" said Tom.

"Yes, you Tom. We've all assumed Mrs Taylor was the target but you were living there as well. You shared the kitchen. Maybe whoever is behind all this meant to put the aconite leaves in your salad not hers. The police have assumed, haven't they, that because you survived and Mrs Taylor didn't that that was the 'correct' way around, so to speak. But just possibly, it was intended that you were meant to die and Mrs Taylor was meant to be incriminated."

"Perhaps," said Tom "but Tuesdays is my night when I go down to 'The Sun and Moon' pub. As you know, Tuesdays are pie night – a pie and a pint for £8, not bad. So, I never ate at Mrs Taylor's on a Tuesday. If it isn't a completely random psychopath doing all this, it's probable that they knew I wouldn't be eating at home on a Tuesday meaning Mrs Taylor was the target."

"Good point – and with the possible bonus of getting you further implicated and so linked to both deaths," contributed Alba.

"Two minutes, visitors, two minutes to wrap up your conversations," bellowed the prison officer.

"Two minutes. We've got to decide what our next steps are," stated Alba.

"I don't know – what can we do? I left Vaughan alive. Whatever happened, it wasn't me," stated Tom. This time Alba could detect a determination in his voice. Tom continued, "I hope he got to see the fly-past but I wonder whether he did. And, as for Mrs Taylor, it was me who called the ambulance and cared for her until the medics arrived – if, I'd wanted her dead, why call 999 and risk them saving her. I'd have just stayed in the pub for longer. But none of this is really tangible, is it? Nothing really outweighs what the police have against me."

"No. So, as I say, we really need to work out what our next steps are going to be. You know, it's a shame you didn't take more photos that day. Some extra pictures might have just helped us. If you'd some of the fly-past, that would perhaps have placed you at a particular location whilst Vaughan was known to be alive. Or, if you'd taken a few more of David playing cricket, that might have placed someone else where we wouldn't have necessarily have expected them to be. As I say, shame there's nothing more tangible. But just because we haven't got an obvious next step, don't, I mean don't, give up the moment I walk out of here. Don't speak to your solicitor – unless, of course, it's something for him to investigate."

"Of course not."

"I guess," continued Alba, "I could go and look round your room in Mrs Taylor's house but I'm not sure what I'd be looking for."

"It's just full of gardening magazines, Royal Horticultural and Gardeners' World ones, work clothes and my re-enactment stuff. And I reckon whoever is behind all this planted enough evidence amongst my stuff up at the Hall, meaning I'd be surprised if they 'overcooked it', as it were, and put stuff in my room as well. I sense they're trying to make the police feel they, the police, have caught me – as opposed to offering me up to the police on such an obvious platter that even the police suspect I'm being set up. Anyway, you couldn't get in – the police have my key. Plus, it's not truly Mrs Taylor's home for you to be poking around in. It's an estate property, so it sort of belongs to Lord Hartfield. Don't you go risking your good name and position up at the Hall by being caught breaking a window to get in. A good gardener you might be up at the Hall but you can't just go up to the Lord or his heir and ask to borrow a key, can you?"

And not for the first time that day, the interruption from a prison officer kept Alba from answering a slightly awkward question.

"Time," bellowed the officer.

Alba carefully constructed her response in her head before speaking it to Tom.

"Tom I'll investigate and, hopefully between us, we'll prove your innocence – leave getting into your room to me. Obviously, contact me if there's anything else you remember of significance. In the meantime, tell you what, you research the oaks up at the Hall so you can run with that project when we get you out. I'll post some literature in to you and the prison library must have some resources for you."

"But it's not a lot for you to be investigating, is it? Poking around my room, assuming you can even get in. It's kind of the last place the real killer would have incriminated him or herself."

"No, I agree. We really haven't got anything definite to focus on. Lots of agreement between us that someone has framed you and a shared belief that your actions don't fit what you'd have done were you in fact the real killer. But we've nothing really specific to look into have we?"

Clutching at straws, Alba, thinking back to Tom's description of Vaughan, which mirrored her own recollection, of him in his leather hat with his battered old journal in his pocket, asked Tom a question. "Does the phrase '1,000 Moons' mean anything to you?"

"No. Should it?" replied Tom.

"No. Just a random thought," offered back Alba. "I'll explain another time as we're out of time and we need to come up with something. I'm rather out of any other ideas – for I agree with you that I probably wouldn't find anything of use in your room."

Alba suddenly felt compelled to share with Tom at least a hint as to how she might gain access to his room. "It's interesting you mentioning asking Lord Hartfield or his heir for a key, for I haven't told you who I bumped into outside 'Stapleton's' on Saturday, you just won't believe me. It was…"

Yet Tom was no longer listening. "Tom, Tom," repeated Alba without response. She paused, frustrated at Tom for having chosen that moment to turn his head to the side, seemingly to study the empty chairs and empty tables in the next row.

"Tom," she said a third time but then cut herself off from saying anything else, sensing the young man she was trying to talk with was actually deep in thought, trying, she felt, to retrieve something from his memory, something that perhaps would determine her next move. She waited, sitting still but sensing the approaching prison officer about to tap her on the shoulder and, in no uncertain terms, tell her to vacate the visitors' hall. But still she waited, hoping Tom would pluck the thing he was searching for from the recesses of his memory in time.

She sat waiting, hoping.

The tap on the shoulder came, followed by the officer's voice – "Miss, I haven't seen you here before, nor the person you're talking to – who seems to have lost interest in you, I might add. So, I'll put it down to you both being inexperienced with how we run the prison here but 'time' means 'time'. Visits are over and you must now leave. Please collect your coat and follow me."

Alba mumbled an apology, stood up, picking her coat up and refolding it as slowly as plausibility would allow. As she moved away from the three red chairs on her side of the low table, she could hear a 'bye babe, bye son, see you next week I hope', followed by 'and babe, get Jimmy to come and see me'. Alba was five yards away from Tom. She stopped and, playing for a few more seconds, needlessly redid the laces on one of her shoes. She turned one final time, hoping against hope that Tom could offer her something.

"Miss, please. Before I get nasty," said the officer.

"Anything?" she mouthed quietly to her friend who was still sitting, unmoved, on the green plastic chair, still looking, as he was, at the empty furniture in the next row.

In that moment, as if he had heard her, even though he hadn't, he suddenly turned to where she now was and met her gaze. They both ignored the toddler running past her, back to his dad for a further final last brief hug. Speaking loud enough for her to hear, Tom said:

"Actually, she was at the cricket match."

"Who?" asked Alba.

"Vaughan said she was arguing with him as he sat on the bench outside the pavilion. He said that was why he went into the pavilion; told her he needed the toilet but that was simply a ruse to get away from her. She was there at the match and arguing with Vaughan."

"Who?"

"Mrs Lyle."

CHAPTER 11

A hand on her shoulder

It was not the table Alba would have chosen, being on the thoroughfare between the kitchen and the main restaurant area of the pub. However, not being a regular at 'The Sun and Moon' meant she didn't feel empowered to ask for another one, plus it was only her, by herself – as it now was these days. Inevitably the regulars got the tables by the windows or in the more secluded parts of the dining area – 'fair enough' she thought. Yet, being on this slightly 'exposed' table, with its collection of bent and torn beer mats under three of its four legs – and still, annoyingly, failing to address the slight wobble the table had – and being there alone, somehow reinforced the general sense of disillusionment the day had brought her. She didn't even have the distraction of being able to study anyone at the only other table in this 'corridor' part of the pub, given it remained empty.

As she sipped at her pineapple juice, regretting not stopping the barmaid from putting far too much ice in the glass, she studied the menu. There was the standard array of pub food to choose from – bangers and mash, beer-battered fish and chips, salmon fillet, scampi and chips, pan fried duck breast – but nothing really took her fancy. As for the special's menu, given it was a Tuesday night, it was populated with pie dishes; steak and ale, chicken and mushroom, ham and leek, game, and, but Alba thought it a bit of a cheat given no pastry was involved whatsoever, fish pie and shepherd's pie.

"Are we ready to order?" said Sam, who had appeared noiselessly at Alba's side and with notebook in hand. Sam continued, "And yes, the fish and shepherd's pies are not pie pies so I wouldn't have them on principle, even though they're good. The duck's not local and the chicken in the chicken and mushroom is not free-range, let alone organic; our poultry supplier has let us down this week. However, the ale in the steak and ale is a 'Theakston's' and the beef is sourced locally from 'Cawcutt's the Butchers'. So, if you're going for a pie tonight, that's the one I'd recommend. Evening Alba," and Sam gave her a wink.

"Sam," enthused Alba. "It's lovely to see you. I needed to see a friendly face after the day I've had."

"Ah, that's sweet of you. I'm sorry to hear you've had a rubbish day."

"I won't bore you with why as I wouldn't want your boss telling you off for taking too long in taking my order. I didn't know you worked here and I didn't see you as I came in."

"Started about a month ago. Just a couple of evenings a week but one of them is always Tuesdays as it's pie night. As the tea shop up at the Hall isn't pushing me enough, Mum suggested I got some extra paid catering experience sorted out for the summer before term finishes – get in before all the other students in the village realise summer holidays are quite boring after the first couple of weeks and start looking for part-time work. As for not seeing me, I was probably serving drinks to the big group we've got over in the restaurant area, that's why. I see they've given you the second worst table in the pub – second only to the empty one you're looking at. I can move you if you want."

"Oh, it's fine, really."

"Sure?"

"Sure."

"OK. Well, next time, I'll make sure you're not on one of these overflow tables. So, what will it be?"

"I'm afraid I'm not really sure. I'd promised myself, when I decided to come in for a meal, I'd have a pie on principle; you see, I met up with a friend yesterday, who was in here last week and had a pie, and it was sort of to honour him. Bit cryptic what I'm saying, I know, but it makes sense to me. Where were we? Nothing quite takes my fancy – sorry I'm proving to be a difficult customer."

"If you're undecided I can come back in a few minutes but, without pushing you, I'd recommend you place your order now as I'm going back to that large group next to take their food orders. If they get in before you, you'll have quite a wait. You could always double up one of the starters and treat it as your mains. Actually, let me just go and check something with the chef. It wasn't listed on the specials but I think we have just one thing left that might appeal to you. Bear with."

With that Sam nipped back into the kitchen, leaving Alba once again to reflect on a young girl who was 'wise beyond her years', as the Reverend Quinn had described her in the tea room up at Hillstone Hall.

Sam was back before Alba had really studied the starters menu from that different angle. Sam continued:

"Yes, we have one left – vegetarian wellington. Mushrooms, nuts and cranberries. Rather good I might add and, importantly, qualifies as a pie so you'll be able to honour your friend, whatever that means. Comes with chips, mash or new potatoes. I'd recommend the chips."

"Sounds perfect. The wellington it will be but with mash please."

"One wellington, mash. I'll assume vegetables over salad. Anything else to drink?"

"No thank you, Sam."

"OK. Probably it'll be about fifteen minutes. I'll bring you a roll and butter whilst you wait. That's a scruffy book you're reading there but must get on." With that Sam removed the two wine glasses from the table and disappeared back into the kitchen.

As Alba waited, she reflected on the day that she'd just had. She conceded to herself that no actual disaster had befallen her – no diagnosis of ill-health, no car accident, she hadn't been the victim of an assault or suffered a fire at home. Still, it hadn't worked out as she'd hoped.

*

The morning had promised so much. The wet weather of yesterday had passed and the day, as on the day of Vaughan's funeral, had been a glorious summer's day. She'd woken early, still excited by having seen Tom the day before and in one sense 'saved' him from the path he was about to embark upon. The sense of excitement that she'd woken with, mixed with, she had to concede to herself, just a little hint of adventure, started to dissipate as she sat at her dressing table after breakfast. She had found herself talking to the person in the photograph in front of her:

"Have I 'saved' Tom? Not really, at least not yet. I've talked him out of making a false confession but he's not really any closer to being released or found innocent. I've offered him nothing of substance. I'll try and get a key off Andrew, I guess, but how on earth do I really broach that with the heir to the Manor?" She wondered if the following might work:

Excuse me mate, can I borrow a key to one of your properties so I can poke around a dead person's home and the alleged murderer's bedroom? Yeah, I know I'm just one of your volunteer gardeners who, to my complete embarrassment still, gave you a peck on the cheek at the weekend. Why did I do that by the way? Where were we? Oh yes, key please, course you can trust me not to remove anything that might incriminate me, Alba White, who could easily be the real murderess. So, key please.'

"That's not going to work, is it?" Alba had said, still to the photograph. "And, actually, what have I given Tom? Hope, I guess, but that can be a dangerous thing, especially for someone in his situation. Might it not be better for him to accept the bad hand life has just dealt him? No, Alba, no! It's that mindset I've just saved Tom from. And yet… and yet…I've got to give him something more tangible than 'I hope this disaster sorts itself out, hope to have you back in the gardens soon'. But I can't just go in to 'Stapleton's', buy a pint of milk and some bananas and say 'oh, as I'm here, Mrs Lyle, why were you arguing with Vaughan shortly before he was killed and was it you? I'd like it to be you because then it wouldn't be Tom and I could give him some good news'."

Alba paused. She had studied the person in the photograph staring back at her and then had studied herself in her mirror. She accepted she was being a tad unkind on Mrs Lyle – Alba didn't particularly want it to be Mrs Lyle or anyone else in the village. Alba didn't have a particular soft spot for the owner of 'Stapleton's' but that was no reason to wish her to be a double murderess. Still, Alba did wish it to be someone other than Tom and if Mrs Lyle had been arguing with Vaughan moments before he was murdered that must be worth investigating.

Once again, speaking out loud, Alba had said, "But how? Oh, it seemed so easy yesterday, as I walked out of the prison, even as I woke up this morning. It seemed that all I had to do, as it were, was move a couple of pieces around the chess board or shake the jigsaw box a little bit harder and it would all be sorted and Tom would be home before the bread was out of the oven." She had allowed herself a half smile as she thought back to Tom's comment from yesterday of 'all we've got to do is work out who, when and where; we'll have this done by lunchtime'.

Perhaps the half smile allowed her to relax a little bit, perhaps someone was thinking kind thoughts towards her, perhaps she just focussed a little bit more and saw a task that needed to be broken down into smaller steps. 'Lunchtime' she thought, 'what can I have done by lunchtime?'

So, Alba had decided that her best chance of getting the key from Andrew would be that afternoon, when he would be, at Alba's suggestion, looking for Sally in the kitchen garden to apologise for his behaviour on Saturday. Before lunch, then, Alba could undertake what little was in her control and get to the library and photocopy some information on Hillstone Hall for Tom and then get it posted in to him at HMP South Down. At least that would make Tom feel she was keeping her word and keep him believing that it might turn out all right. Naturally, she could also call in at 'Stapleton's' on the way back from the Post Office and see whether she could engage Mrs Lyle in conversation but, Alba accepted, it might take a few visits to get the proprietor of the village shop to offer her something in conversation that would allow Alba to ask her about her argument with Vaughan. Perhaps if she went in, she thought, and bought some of Neale's favourite biscuits, tell Mrs Lyle she last saw Neale at the cricket match and see where that 'line of attack' took her. "Perhaps," she had said out loud, once again, but the person in the photograph remained silent, offering no response.

*

As she waited for her vegetarian wellington, picking at her brown bread roll, she told herself once more that she'd done her best today but, in reality, all she'd achieved was posting some information to Tom – although it did include some maps of the estate from late Victorian times, a 1919 article from the parish magazine about the new Head Gardener at Hillstone Hall, something on the history of the Commonwealth War Graves Commission and an obituary of a local nurseryman that would give Tom a few leads.

However, unfortunately, she hadn't happened across Andrew in the kitchen garden, hadn't found a way to start up a conversation with Mrs Lyle, despite buying three packets of Neale's preferred digestives, and hadn't thought of any other way to access Tom's room. It had not proved to be the Tuesday that she had hoped for when she woke up. Alba opened Vaughan's journal once more.

"Blow, I said it was scruffy," said Sam as she returned with the wellington. "The page you're on is barely legible – it's so faded."

"Oh, that was quicker than I expected," replied Alba. She was about to fold the journal up but decided not to, rather moving it to the side to allow Sam to place the food before her. Sam was about to turn away, when Alba said:

"Just before you go, Sam, could I just show you something in this book? I promise it will only take a moment." Alba gestured with her hand for Sam to sit opposite her.

"Course you can but I'll just half perch, if you don't mind, I don't want the boss to catch me looking too relaxed. Is it one of the great works of literature or is it signed by the author to 'Alba White, with best wishes from so and so'?"

"No, nothing like that. It's Vaughan's gardening journal."

"Ooooooohh," said Sam slowly. "Vaughan's you say? Oooohh. Yes, I remember mum telling me about the weird end to his funeral service and how some of you got 'keepsakes' from on top of the coffin. Bit creepy if you ask me."

"Poignant, yes, but somehow not creepy," offered back Alba. "Anyway, could you just have a look at these couple of pages? They're right at the beginning but the pencil handwriting is just so faded and I'm not a linguist – I'm not many things but definitely not a linguist. I'm asking you as in the tea shop, up at the Hall, last Friday when we were chatting with that blessed vicar – I still can't believe he was sitting at my table but hey ho. But back to the point, I'm not great at languages and as you said last Friday that you'd done GCSE French, could you help me just confirm what language I'm looking at?"

Alba placed the journal in front of Sam, opened on one of the pages with the faded writing.

"Course. Actually, I did a couple of years of German too but the school made me drop that as I couldn't do two languages as well as

Food Technology – Home Economics to your generation," added Sam innocently.

"Thanks for that," replied Alba – who suddenly felt her thirty years. "I'm guessing it is German albeit with some Latin words in the mix, all in the same faded pencil handwriting, but it would be of help to have your opinion."

"Yeah, no probs," and Sam studied the pages for a few moments. "Definitely a lot in German. No French in the bits I can make out and the odd words here and there that I can't make out I guess are the Latin. What does this line say? Something plants I can eat – what's 'hecken'? And this one? Something I can cook and drink. Yeah, Alba, you're right. Mostly German. Definitely no French that I can make out. Is that OK? I must get back to work otherwise I'll get it in the neck."

"That's great. Really good to have an expert confirm it for me. Food looks good, thanks again Sam."

"Tastes even better. I'll bring you some tap water once I've cleared a couple of tables. Enjoy your food. Expert – my foot – but pleased I could be of service."

*

Alba did enjoy her mains as well as the Eton mess she had to follow and she was minded to order a pot of tea to finish with. Sam returned to clear Alba's pudding bowl and glasses. As she did so, Alba looked at the empty table opposite her. These two tables were along the walkway the staff took between the kitchen and the main restaurant area. Behind Alba there was a stout, dark, aged, solid oak pillar and behind the second table there was a similar pillar. The inevitable consequence of the symmetrical layout of this section of the pub was that anyone sitting at the other table, if they were on their own, would sit with their back to the other pillar – as Alba had done at her table – and look inwards. Subconsciously, Alba thought how lovely it would be if Neale had come and sat there, but he was in South Africa until the weekend, or Andrew.

At least she was minded to ask Sam for a pot of tea until a certain someone was shown to the worst table that 'The Sun and Moon' had to offer. Just as Sam asked if Alba wanted anything else another waitress showed the Reverend Quinn to the adjacent table.

"Oh, why him? Of all people," Alba said silently to herself, before saying to Sam "No thank you, other than the bill, please."

"OK. I'll go and print it now, don't want you sitting here needlessly."

Alba was grateful that it seemed she wouldn't have too long to wait in the minister's company. As Sam moved away, inevitably the Reverend lifted his eyes from his menu and looked at Alba. Having finished finding the correct money in her handbag, to be ready for Sam's return, Alba chose that moment to look up and met his look.

"Evening Miss White. I hope you are well."

"Good evening, errr, Reverend Quinn."

"No, please, that's much too formal. Even if I were wearing my dog collar, it always sounds so formal and somehow sets me apart in a way I'm not comfortable with. So please, no need to call me that."

"What would you like me to call you then?" replied Alba somewhat sarcastically, as she desperately wished for the bill to arrive.

"Well, so long as you can refrain from calling me 'Harley' or 'tea sensual' I don't really mind but…"

"Ditto, for me," interrupted Alba "with regards to associations with 'Cluedo' or Tarantino's 'Reservoir Dogs' film. I've heard them all before and none of them are funny."

"Oh, I hear you," replied the Reverend Quinn but Alba's coldness was not lost on him. "My Christian name is Matthew. However, in light of our last meeting, if Matthew is too informal, just 'Rev' will be fine. But you might find that too informal also. Your call."

"To be honest," replied Alba "I'm not sure. I don't know you,

we're not friends and, apart from the fact that our paths keep crossing
– which is a bit weird as I don't believe in coincidences…"

This time it was the Reverend Quinn's turn to interrupt. "Nor do
I. God incidences yes but coincidences, no. Sorry, you were saying?"

"Oh, don't you ever take an evening off from theology? For
goodness sake! What I was saying before you interrupted me –" but
suddenly Alba paused. In that moment she was struck to the core,
for she could hear 'Bic' in not only her words but, more scarily, in
her tone and her attitude. She would describe that moment later as
if a hand had placed itself on her shoulder and a voice had quietly,
ever so ever so quietly, whispered into her ear, 'this doesn't have to be
you'. She instinctively put her right hand on her left shoulder, to feel
for the 'hand' that was there, but naturally there was nothing and she
only felt her shoulder blade and collar bone through her thin top.

The pause continued, as she could feel a tear welling up. At the
same time she was also aware of a sense of bitterness, one that had
been slowly building up and enveloping her these past few months,
try to strengthen its hold of her.

The Reverend Quinn could sense something was troubling her.
Experience had taught him that on some occasions it was better not
to rush in and start gibbering away, desperate to say anything, when
in fact silence was the best thing he could offer; he thought of Job's
three friends and arguably the best thing that they said to Job, in
chapter two of that book, which was nothing.

Alba sat and stared at the table in front of her, wishing on one
level that Sam hadn't been so efficient and removed even her near
empty glass of tap water. She thought of Tom and what he was going
through. She thought of Sally and the plight of Sally's marriage and
how desperate Sally had been to have a friend with her on a simple
day-trip to the seaside and how Alba wouldn't even support her in
that. She thought of Helen and how she, Alba, hadn't even trusted
her best friend with the innocent fact that she had got back in touch
with Terry a year or so ago and had herself also sent him a birthday

card – why had she chosen instead to rubbish Terry's name to Helen? She thought of David, who she'd made no effort to see socially since Vaughan's death, despite their shared experience from that fateful day. She thought of the poor man of God sitting opposite her who had only ever offered her a warm smile and a pleasant greeting and yet each time she had only offered him coldness and sarcasm in return. And she thought too of 'Bic', the remote and sombre man that he had become. She thought of how he made her feel last Friday morning, when he snapped back at her for interrupting him. Alba realised she was scared – scared not as to what she was becoming but what she had in fact already become, another Mr Parker. She dabbed at her eyes with her hanky, not really aware that Matthew had vacated his seat. She thought back to her failed relationship, of rings no longer being on her finger, but that hadn't been her fault. She thought of Vaughan and she thought of how sad and lonely so many people around her were – including this vicar, who seemed to have gone for the moment. As a matter of fact, she further thought, what was he doing in a pub eating all by himself and at the worst table the pub had to offer? Yet all she had offered in return, Alba reflected, was distance, coldness and a self-centredness. Her conduct repulsed her and she was cut to the core. She dabbed at her eyes again. Maybe she was being a little bit hard on herself, at least with regards to Tom, but to everyone else, she knew she was spot on and it scared her. 'Was it too late to save her from herself?' she thought.

"Water, Miss White?" offered the Reverend Quinn on his return. "Just tap water but I sensed you might need a sip or two of something. I thought if I bought you something you'd tell me it was wrong whereas I thought water might be acceptable." He placed it down in front of Alba and retook his seat at the other table and tried to focus on the menu.

"Thank you," replied Alba.

Looking up, the Reverend Quinn felt compelled to try once more with the woman opposite him. "You alright?" he enquired, knowing full well that she wasn't but only too aware that he didn't want to push her. He wanted to give her 'an out' straight away, in that she could say she was fine and that would be that. He waited for a reply.

"Er, I'm not really sure, to be honest." She paused before adding, "Thanks again for the water, that was kind of you."

"To be clear, I'm quite happy to buy you a drink if you'd like."

"No, thank you. The water is fine, really."

"OK. Would you like to talk? I'm a good listener."

"I don't think so. I don't even know you."

"That's fine but not knowing me could be an advantage if there's stuff you want to talk through with someone who's detached from what you're going through. But in any case, would it be such a bad thing if we did get to know each other just a little bit? I accept we're not friends – you've made that very clear over the weeks if I may be so blunt – but please, and I'm going to plagiarise Benjamin Disraeli here, whilst we are not friends, we are not enemies, or at least shouldn't be. I have hitherto been a blank in your thoughts, as you have been a cipher in mine, and so, perhaps, an emerging friendship between us might produce that something which your destiny requires. It's sort of from 'Coningsby'."

"I'll take your word for it." Alba took a deep breath and then added, "You're right, no need to be enemies. I'm sorry for my abruptness tonight and on previous occasions, I've had a lot on, what with Vaughan and Tom." Then, for the first time in her contact with the minister, she felt willing to offer him something, to keep the conversation going. "Actually, I went to see him yesterday."

"Tom?"

"Yes, Tom."

"How is he?"

"So so. I think he benefited from seeing a friendly face. I didn't know you knew him."

"I've met him a few times. Helen's invited him along to services once or twice. Further, but if you view what I'm about to say as gossip, I apologise, for I don't want you to view it in that way. I hope you'll appreciate me saying something nice about your friend given his present incarceration and the general consensus within the village as to his guilt."

"But he's not guilty," implored Alba as she tucked her feet right back under her chair, looping them around a wooden strut, to enable her to lean towards the Reverend Quinn as much as she could.

"I thought that's what you thought," replied the minister. "Good on you. Despite any *prima facie* case he's innocent until proven otherwise – that's what I always say."

"Oh, I am so pleased to hear someone say that at last. I was beginning to think it was just me. So, what were you going to add that wasn't gossip?" and she gave the Reverend Quinn a wink.

"I stress I don't think it's gossip. I think it's just a nice thing to say and it's kind of a statement as to his character or mindset at the time the police are holding him out to be a serial killer, going round the village murdering people."

"So, what is it?"

"I think he had a bit of a soft spot for one of my flock."

Alba looked puzzled and was about to ask for a little more detail when Sam reappeared.

"Chloe, you mean?" Sam said to the Reverend Quinn. Then turning said "Sorry for the delay Alba, that wretched large group are just a nightmare; I'm sure two of them at least are trying to scam the pub. Here's your bill. And you develop good hearing working in a pub – you have to. So, yeah," and Sam looked at Matthew and Alba in turn, before continuing "Chloe was telling me a few weeks back that she wondered whether a bloke called Tom was going to ask her out. He'd been popping by the tea shop up at the Hall a few too many times for Chloe not to start to suspect something. For example, he was asking about the feasibility of doing some themed food or events, such as marking the anniversary of the end of the war in Europe, and what were our views on that. But that was a discussion he should have been having with the chef, in first instance, so it was a ruse of his to chat to Chloe. That said, and although Tom is a few years older than her, I thought they'd get on quite well together if you want my opinion."

Alba looked to the Reverend for confirmation.

"Yes, Chloe. As I say, not gossip, rather a character reference I would dare to suggest," confirmed the minister.

"Meaning – " mused Alba and the Reverend Quinn nodded in encouragement for her to develop her thought. "Meaning," Alba continued "meaning that's another reason why he wouldn't have done it, if he had a girl pulling at his heart-strings. He wouldn't murder Vaughan, rather he'd want Vaughan to pop into the tea room at some stage as well to give Tom his 'grandfatherly' advice as to a possible *belle* he wanted to ask out."

"Another?" queried the Reverend Quinn.

Alba filled them both in on her visit to the prison yesterday, about Tom's love of Vaughan, the incriminating evidence but the puzzling lack of fingerprints and that someone was arguing with Vaughan shortly before he was murdered. She held back Mrs Lyle's name, not out of coldness or distrust of the two she was talking to, rather out of respect towards Mrs Lyle. Alba wanted to have a little bit more information first before 'naming names'.

"I'm so pleased he had a friendly face there with him yesterday," said the Reverend Quinn. "Since I heard he had been remanded I had been praying, amongst other things, that someone, a friend, would get to see him."

"Odd," said Alba out loud, though more to herself than the other two, as she thought back to a comment from Tom yesterday.

"Odd, what's odd?" queried the minister – which echoed Sam's thought perfectly.

"Oh, just odd but it's nothing. Nothing to it obviously but I was just reminded, for some reason, of something Tom said to me yesterday – that it was a 'bloody miracle' the paperwork had got processed, which allowed my visit."

The Reverend Quinn nodded just ever so slightly to himself and allowed himself the faintest of faint smiles in the knowledge of a service well done; Alba, who had turned to Sam, didn't notice.

"Sam," said Alba. "I know we're keeping you but if your boss tells you off later, let me know and I'll come and take the rap tomorrow and apologise."

"Ditto," said the Reverend Quinn.

"So, Sam," continued Alba. "Just a little question but thinking about it, it's a question I can't not ask. In asking it, though, it feels as if I'm beginning to move the chess pieces around – and if I can arrange them in such a way, I might be able to establish Tom's innocence. It's not the best illustration I know but…"

"And proving you're not an actual chess player," quipped the Reverend Quinn, hoping he'd judged Alba's slightly more relaxed mood correctly.

"Yeah, OK, I accept I'm not a chess player but you get my meaning. So, Sam, you were working here last Tuesday, right?"

"Yes – contract requires me to work on pie night."

"Good," offered back Alba. "Was Tom here last Tuesday, having a meal?"

"Yes."

"Sure on that?"

"Absolutely. I remember chatting to him – it was such a glorious summer's evening and I was winding him up as to why he was asking to eat inside and not at one of our picnic tables in the beer garden. He said he'd had enough sun for one day, given his job, and was quite happy at the table he had. Table 7, where Tom was and as you may know, has the best window view we have. Then he was asking me, ever so slightly like, something about the tea shop but I think he was hoping I'd start talking about Chloe. Then I teased him about not having a proper pie – he'd gone for shepherd's pie. He didn't stay too long I seem to remember; said he had another full-on day the next day so needed an early night."

"Good," replied Alba. "Not as to the pie choice but as to you being his alibi for last Tuesday. Good."

"Sam," interjected the Reverend Quinn. "I don't wish to be alarmist but given the seriousness of Tom's situation, once you're off shift could you write that down, that you served Tom here last Tuesday. Add in what he ate and what you chatted about, not because it's relevant – at least I don't think so – but because it's always the insignificant little facts that give any statement or record of events that air of authenticity. It's one reason why I believe the Gospels are true records – because they contain so many seemingly irrelevant facts, facts that would only have been noticed by genuine eye-witnesses. But back to Tom, Sam, if you could write your account down and sign and date it and give it to Alba then that would be a key piece aligned in this bizarre game of chess that Alba is involved in."

"Of course. Happy to do that. I'll run two copies off, once I've typed something up, so I can keep a copy for myself as well."

"Oh, naturally," replied Alba.

"I really must get back to serving other customers, unless you have any other questions? Oh, actually, before I go," said Sam directly to the Reverend Quinn "are you ready to order your food or would you like a few minutes longer?"

"Quite ready, Sam, thank you. I know it is pie night but may I have the scampi and chips, please? And half a pint of 'Theakston's' – or do I get that myself from the bar?"

"No, it's fine. I'll bring it over with your roll and butter. With your scampi do you want veg or salad?"

"Salad please but – "

"Yes?" replied Sam in a somewhat slow drawn-out way, knowing full well a begging request was coming from yet another customer.

"If allowed, could I have some extra sachets of tartare sauce? I do like my tartare sauce."

"I'll look some extra ones out for you. Food will be about twenty minutes but I'll bring the bread and your drink over in a couple of minutes." Turning to Alba, Sam added "Men and their sauce, I don't know! Do they ever taste the actual food I wonder or is it always just whatever sauce they smear all over it? Right, must get on. I'll leave the pair of you chatting but I don't quite know why you're sitting on separate tables."

Sam then added a 'thank you' to Alba as she noticed the tip that was being left.

The Reverend Quinn said, once Sam had moved away "Wise girl – "

"Well beyond her years. Yes – that's how you described her last Friday too. But you're spot on with her," offered back Alba.

"So?" replied the Reverend Quinn.

"So, so what?" retaliated Alba.

"So, would you like to talk? As you may have worked out, I'm not doing a lot for the next twenty minutes with my life. I'm happy to be a sounding board."

"Oh, I don't know. Seems to me you have an awful lot on. You've got a bread roll to butter, ale to savour and the puddings menu to ponder. That sounds plenty," and for the first time in a long time Alba smiled, not out of relief or nervousness or awkwardness but out of a sense of peace, something which had come over her this last half an hour or so.

"I'll eat it unbuttered, the ale can sit there untouched and I already know what I'm having for pudding, so we can chat if you'd like. But it's your call."

"Maybe a chat would be good. Maybe – but it's late and this is a pub after all. I tend not to open up in pubs. Another time perhaps," replied Alba.

"Another time sounds good," he agreed. As Alba got up, put her cardigan on and put her handbag strap over her head and one shoulder, the Reverend Quinn continued. "By the way, I think I have something of yours. Not on me, I might add. It was handed in to the church office by one of our cleaners, a couple of days after Vaughan's funeral but we hadn't used the building since then. But I won't turn this into a game show and make you guess and, in any case, you've said it is late. A grey scarf – a grey scarf was handed in. It was found roughly where I seem to recall you were sitting in the church.

"Oh, my silk scarf!"

"Yes. The church office is open tomorrow and Friday or I could pop round with it if you like. I was going to pop round with it in any case – rightly or wrongly I asked Helen for your address on Sunday, for I was certain it's yours."

Unsure which was worse, having a man of God on her doorstep or having to voluntarily walk in to a church office, in her new found spirit of goodwill, Alba suddenly found herself saying, "Pop round if you like." In the split second that followed, Alba replayed in her head the choice the man opposite her had given her as to how she could address him but none quite felt right. Then inspiration struck:

"Yes, pop round if you like, Reverend Matthew." As she said it, she felt she'd pitched it just right – formal but friendly with it. She then added, "Good night. Enjoy your scampi."

"Good night, Miss White. Safe walk home."

CHAPTER 12

Piccadilly Circus

A week had passed and Alba had got nowhere.

Admittedly Tom should have received his bundle of documents from her and she had contacted the prison to request a further visit but this time, it seemed, the admin office at HMP South Down were sitting on her request. More personally, she had been up at the Hall and done a couple of days of volunteering – mostly re-staking plants in the Long Borders and overseeing the cut flowers that ornamented both the private rooms of the Hall and the tables in the tea shop. Although she had failed to see Andrew on either of those days, on one of them she had at least, on a personal note, found time to speak to 'Bic' and inform him that she was not ready to take on the role of Acting Deputy Head Gardener. She'd explained to him that her sense of loyalty to Tom prevented her from accepting – although in reality, she conceded to herself, she just didn't want the responsibility. She had recommended he should ask Sally instead. Predictably, 'Bic' had made it clear in response that he didn't appreciate such recommendations from someone who had just shied away from 'stepping up to the mark'. As she had left his office, relief was her overwhelming sensation and she promised herself to have as little to do with the Head Gardener as possible from now on.

So, here sat Alba, at her kitchen table, watching the birds at the feeder. Suddenly all the tits flew away as a large jay swooped in and, clinging precariously to one of the suspended feeders, started to peck at a fat ball. Alba studied this normally elegant bird as it and the feeder swung from side to side, prompting the jay to keep flapping its wings and repositioning its claws in an attempt to hang on. After a further couple of hefty pecks at the fat ball, the bird gave up its awkward mid-air dance and dropped to the ground, out of sight of Alba, to gather as much as it could from what had fallen. Alba saw the jay fly off and knew, even though she could not see, with its departure, the dunnocks would reappear and start pecking the ground to glean the morsels that the jay had left behind.

Watching the long-tailed tits return to the feeder *en masse*, Alba wrapped her fingers around her mug of tea and tried to think, in the way one does when trying to solve that final difficult crossword clue, to look at things from as many different angles as possible. But she kept coming back to the same stumbling blocks – she couldn't think of a plausible way to get into Mrs Taylor's home and, despite the numerous conversations she had had with Mrs Lyle this past week, had whole-heartedly failed to get the owner of 'Stapleton's' to open up.

*

"Hello, are you in?" called out Sally as she came in through the kitchen door, in the way Helen had done on the day of Vaughan's funeral.

"Hi, morning Sal. Drink?"

"No thanks, not stopping long. I need to be up at the Hall soon. Glorious day isn't it?"

"It is and a complete contrast to last Monday morning when I was getting soaked walking across the prison courtyard."

"That's right," recollected Sally. "Last Monday was a complete washout. My dear husband," continued Sally but Alba could hear the sarcasm in her friend's voice. "He made such a song and dance about getting the boot of his car wet, as we loaded Vaughan's pots in. Strange, he'd been playing golf all morning so his bag and trolley must have been sodden but I bet he didn't moan about putting them in his car. I'm used to his attitude I guess but it does get me down. One day –" but Sally's words died in her throat before she said them.

"Oh, poor you," offered back Alba. Then, thinking back to her time in 'The Sun and Moon' last week, Alba continued, "Any joy persuading him to join you on the day trip to Hastings?"

Sally turned her face away from her friend and watched a couple of blue tits through the window. Without turning back, Sally replied "Have a guess, no don't bother, you already know, as I did before I asked him again, that it was a 'no'. Business trip, big project on at work, the story changed each time I asked but the message was the same, didn't want to come with me. I like the coast so I'm going come what may; I guess it'll be me by myself. It's just a shame the other ticket will get wasted – I suppose I could ask the Horticultural Society if they want it back."

"I'll go with you," volunteered Alba, to her friend's back.

"Really?" replied Sally, turning.

"Sure."

"I mean, really Alba, you'll come with me? I know I asked you the other weekend but you were so non-committal I admit I gave up on you coming."

"Yes, I'll come. Sorry for being a bit vague about it outside 'Stapleton's'. Talking of 'Stapleton's' and not giving up on people…" and Alba, not having seen Sally since they had spoken outside the village shop, for they'd missed each other up at the Hall last Tuesday, filled her friend in with the prison visit. Alba, having had already boiled the kettle, lifted the lid of the teapot with her right hand and poured the hot water onto the tea leaves with her other.

"Oh, alright," answered Sally to the question that the other hadn't even asked. "Go on then, just a quick cup of tea but I have to be up at the Hall by eleven."

Alba, who instinctively had already put two scoops of tea leaves in the pot, continued bringing Sally up to speed with her plans, or perhaps more accurately her hopes, for helping Tom.

"Why don't you ask Mrs Lyle outright? Stop fudging the issue, Alba" suggested Sally.

"I can't do that. She'll just cut me off – and probably cancel my newspaper delivery to boot!"

"I guess so. Probably not my most helpful suggestion. There are so many frank exchanges and accusations at home these days I suppose I'm getting conditioned to being too blunt at times."

"I think so too, I'm afraid – so I'll put that suggestion on the back burner. That said, I've got to come up with something. It's sort of why I turned down the Acting position that 'Bic' offered me. I feel I need time to work on helping Tom."

"Oh, that's why I popped by actually. To tell you 'Bic' has asked me to cover for Tom."

"Did he say that I recommended you?" quizzed Alba, as she passed a mug of hot tea to her friend.

"That was sweet of you to put my name forward. But no, of course not. He wouldn't want to give the impression he listens to advice. He was relieved I accepted, though. Seems he's got to take some annual leave soon, in a week or two, I think. Nice cup of tea, by the way."

"Pleasure. Cake? It's coffee and walnut."

"I'm tempted but no. No thank you."

"Well, you can leave researching the Verdun Oaks to Tom. As I said, that was what I posted into him. He'll need a project like that to distract himself at times."

They chatted some more over their hot drinks, discussing what Sally hoped to bring to her temporary position and what paperwork

'Bic' would trust her with in his absence. They spoke of wolfsbane and Sally's plans for Vaughan's two slate pots. Sally then took her leave so she could meet Mr Parker at the agreed time, leaving Alba to head into her own garden to harvest some of the last of her gooseberries whilst pondering what her next step should be.

*

Alba had just returned to her kitchen with a good half bowlful of gooseberries, when she heard a knock at her front door.

She opened it to see the Reverend Quinn standing there, out of 'uniform' in jeans and a polo shirt, with its 'Maine' logo, denoting, in all probability, the 'Debenhams' department store. Had she not known his occupation, Alba found herself relieved to think that, in his appearance at least, he didn't come across as a man of the cloth.

"Good morning, Miss White."

"Reverend Matthew, it's nice to see you. Off duty I see – how are you?"

"Oh, fine thank you. Just out delivering the parish magazine once again. May I leave you a copy?"

Alba nodded, allowing the Reverend to place a copy on the ledge in Alba's porch.

"These magazines aside," continued the minister, "then yes, Monday is my day off this week. I normally deliver them on a Tuesday but since I was running a few errands in the village today I thought I'd distribute a few whilst I was out and about. It's good to have a day in the week off, mind you, given I find myself working most Sundays for some reason."

Alba smiled before adding, "Now there's a surprise! So, to what do I owe this visit? It can't just be the magazine."

"Your scarf, I believe," replied the minister as he held out Alba's grey scarf. "It is yours, isn't it?"

"Yes, thank you, it is. I was beginning to think I'd have to call in to the church office to collect it. Sorry, that wasn't meant to sound sarcastic, I thought you may have tried last week to drop it off but if it was one of my volunteering days you would undoubtedly have missed me."

"I tried a couple of times, in fact. Was beginning to think I'd have to entrust it to Helen to return to you – but thought I'd drop by once more."

"You could have just left it here in my porch, you know, with your parish magazine. We're a pretty honest bunch in this village."

"Oh, I'm sure everyone is. That said, I wanted to hand it over in person. Guess I'm just a bit old-fashioned."

"Still living in the last millennium, are we vicar?"

"Last millennium? Reckon some of my parishioners believe I'm living in the one before that, in the dark ages in fact! The organist definitely thinks so, as I haven't signed off his request for an electric keyboard yet."

"Electric keyboard! Oh my, you'll have drums and a bass guitar next! You be careful."

"I'll try to be. It's nice to have caught you in at last."

"Sorry, I should invite you in but I've got some important paperwork that I need to sit down and work through. Another time?"

"Another time would be good," replied Reverend Quinn, hoping the disappointment he felt didn't come across in his voice. "Yes, another time. Just before I head back to the vicarage, however, I'd like to tell you I've contacted the prison."

Alba looked surprised. Reverend Quinn continued:

"Yes, you see, you inspired me."

"Me? How?"

"Well, you telling me you'd already been to see Tom, humbled me. He's been locked up for several weeks and I've done nothing. This young man, whom everyone thinks is guilty…"

"Ahem," coughed Alba.

"Sorry, almost everyone. Whether he's guilty or not – but as I say he's innocent until proven otherwise – he comes from my parish and, more than that, he's sat in my church building and listened to me preach. He's in prison and I'm called to visit him; Matthew 25: 36 says 'I was in prison and you came to visit me'."

"I'll take your word for it."

"You shouldn't, you know."

"Shouldn't? Shouldn't what?"

"Take my word for it. I mean it does say that but you don't know that until you confirm it for yourself. I always encourage my flock to question, challenge and correct me. Yes, I'm appointed to minister to them and I wouldn't misrepresent the Word of God but they need to always check it out for themselves. I've got a spare Bible in the car, if you'd like one? But where was I? Oh yes, don't take a vicar's word for it, for you see the next vicar they have might not be so – how can I put it?"

Before he could find a diplomatic way of putting that some ministers were power-tripped self-servers who put themselves where God should be in the Church, Alba found herself, to her surprise, asking, with a hint of sadness:

"Oh, are you moving on then?"

"No, no, I'm afraid the village have got me for a while yet. My calling brought me here and I sense I'll be around for a while. Nonetheless, it's still good for people to hold their ministers to account."

"I'll try to do that – starting now in fact. So, I expect you to get in to see Tom. I don't want to hear it was too much hassle to get in or that you were turned away by security – I'm now holding you to it, to see Tom and to support him. He's one of your flock so, to use your terminology, you need to be there as his shepherd. So, I'm now expecting you to deliver."

"I will do all within my earthly and spiritual powers to do as you ask. May I just point out, though…"

"Yes?" cut in Alba, sensing the minister was about to instantly backtrack. He didn't – well, not quite.

"There's a saying that goes *'A shepherd is working hardest when leaning on a gate, chewing straw'*. I'll leave that thought with you to reflect on. Good day, Miss White. Enjoy your paperwork. Another time, perhaps."

"Bye Reverend Matthew," offered back Alba, who was caught slightly off guard. "Thank you again for my scarf. Another time."

With that, the Reverend Quinn took his leave, leaving Alba weaving her returned garment between her fingers.

*

A mid-afternoon knock at the front door disturbed Alba from her scrutiny of her bank statements and latest credit card bills. "It's like flipping Piccadilly Circus here today," she said out loud to herself. She got up from her living room table, having turned each of the statements over in order that the information was hidden. She paused at her hall table, drawn to the rectangular black and white photograph on her hall table once more and became fixated with just how flat the countryside was in the background of the image. A further knock at the door broke the picture's hold over her.

An 'afternoon Alba' greeted her as she opened the door.

"Hello Neale, you're back. It's lovely to see you," offered back Alba, who had yet to see the woman standing behind him.

"Back Saturday lunchtime. Can't believe my time out there has already come to an end – those weeks have just flown by. Long flight, though, which gave me a lot of thinking time, which allowed me to reach a decision which I'm about to act upon."

"I'm intrigued and, possibly, excited for you. But I forget myself in the thrill of seeing you, please come in. Cup of tea? Coffee?"

"Tea would be good. I've brought a friend, can she come in too?"

"Course she can," replied Alba, who had already turned away, grateful she'd tidied her lunch things away. Alba assumed the friend would be the woman Neale went out to South Africa to meet up with

179

again, the lady he'd met in the Middle-East but who originated from the southern tip of the African continent. Alba was thrilled Neale had brought her to see her so soon after their return. Alba continued talking to the people behind her, "Kettle's almost on. I made a sponge yesterday, so we can have a bit of that. You like my coffee and walnut cake don't you, Neale? I'll get some plates out and we can sit in the garden. Funny, you popping round today. I was going to come and see you tomorrow. You see I've been picking gooseberries today and I know you're partial to my gooseberry pie so I was going to make you one. Oh, I'm so sorry, I've forgotten your friend's name, Isla was it?"

"Ilse," corrected Neale. "But…"

However, before Neale could finish and explain an important detail, Alba turned around, speaking as she did so, "Just lovely to meet you, err," and Alba was stunned to silence. She recovered herself sufficiently to be able to eventually add, "Mrs Rowan, it's lovely to see you. Err, what brings you here?"

"My doing," chipped in Neale.

"I hope you don't mind," added Mrs Rowan. "I feel a bit awkward being in your beautiful home – you've trained that wisteria so well around your porch, I might add. In my defence, Neale here said you wouldn't mind. I said I didn't believe him but he said I had to come anyway, as he needed to present me with something in your presence. I have to admit I'm completely baffled but I was free this afternoon, especially as Sam said she'd do dinner when she got home from college. Plus, in any case, Sam has been so full of meeting you on and off these past few weeks I thought I'd use the opportunity to thank you for being so enthusiastic towards her."

"I'm surprised, I'll admit. Baffled, definitely. Neale, well, I'll be having words with him in due course," and she shot Neale a look. "But I don't mind, really, just a bit caught out and now a bit embarrassed by the cake I'm about to offer up. If I'd known you, Mrs Rowan, were coming, I'd have put a lot more effort into my baking."

"Alba, don't put yourself down like that," offered up Neale. "Your cakes are lovely, just as they are. And, yes, that is a compliment. Mrs Rowan's are wonderful, I won't deny, but, if it's still on offer, a slice of your coffee and walnut cake will be a joy."

"Neale, springing this on me, well, you'll be lucky to get even a walnut off the top!" Alba stated. However, very much to his relief, he watched Alba place three small plates, a knife and some cake forks, as well as some napkins, on a tray. She then added, "Right, Neale, make yourself useful. Take this out to the patio. I'll bring the cake, the teapot and mugs on my other tray."

Neale placed something wrapped in brown paper on the tray before heading through the back door. As he went, Alba, giving the tea a final stir, spoke to Mrs Rowan, "I'm not sure what you mean about me being enthusiastic towards Sam, I mean I am, don't get me wrong, but it's Sam who's full of enthusiasm. Plus, she's an absolute natural at what she does. It was a real joy to have her serve me in the pub last week, for I needed a friendly face. Your daughter is just a delight and a real credit to you – and she's wise beyond her years, I can tell you."

"That's how the Reverend Quinn describes her, too," offered back Mrs Rowan. "I really don't have to stay. I know one or other of us, or even both, have kind of been set up by our local writer but I accept I am now kind of intrigued as to what he's got planned."

"Me too," replied Alba. "So, stay. It'll be nice to get to know you a little bit better. And, in any case, I've done a head count, twice in fact, and I make it that I'm catering for three. I've used my little kettle first, so I've got a drink and, if I kid myself I'm having my afternoon tea by myself, I'll manage my stress levels." She offered Mrs Rowan a warm smile, who returned it with an equally warm one.

"Sam's three rules – I'm impressed you've remembered them," replied Mrs Rowan.

Alba picked up the second tray and gestured, with a nod of her head, for Mrs Rowan to follow Neale into the garden. Alba added, "And, tea and cake will be a treat for a Monday afternoon."

"Maybe he wants to act out an idea for his next book?" speculated Mrs Rowan.

"Maybe. He's one for the dramatics, it would seem. Well, whatever awaits us, let's go and find out." With that, Alba also stepped out through her back door.

*

The table parasol offered welcome shade from the July sun but with the result that they were all sitting on the same side of the table looking into the garden.

"Tea, Mrs Rowan? Milk, sugar?" enquired Alba.

"Please. Milk yes and sugar, well just half a teaspoon please."

"There we go," said Alba offering Mrs Rowan a cup. "So, how is Sam getting on at college? What's the syllabus focusing on at the moment?" asked Alba.

Knowing how Neale took his tea, Alba just poured his and sliced the cake as Mrs Rowan replied.

"Really well, thank you for asking. She's just thriving there. She could have gone on to do more conventional A-Levels I guess, she's pretty good at French, but catering is her passion."

"Oh, I can tell," volunteered Alba.

"I think we all can. She's a natural," continued her mum. "She needs to push herself a little bit more on the savoury side and the sourcing of one's ingredients. Knowing where the stuff is coming from is key and knowing your suppliers is really important. I think working in 'The Sun and Moon' will be a useful step in that direction. As for her current college work…"

As Mrs Rowan spoke, Alba distributed three slices of cake. Neale was relieved to have been given a bit, arguably the smallest of the three, but grateful for any, given the surprise he had wrought upon Alba this afternoon. He consoled himself that he might be offered a slither more upon revealing why he had brought Alba and Mrs

Rowan together. Mrs Rowan continued:

"Lovely cake, Alba. Real butter cream in the middle – that says a lot about the baker. Where was I? Oh yes, college work. So, this term it's French cuisine – all building up to Bastille Day I suspect. Sam is just excelling. What with her language skills she's been using original French recipes much to her lecturer's consternation. Got an old French cookery book in that new charity shop come community café that opened the other month. Only 50p they wanted. Bless her, Sam said she gave them £2 for it as she was so thrilled to find something like that. Have you been in there yet?"

"A few times," said Alba. "Actually, the plate the cake is on came from there. 50p they wanted for it too. I like having a few random odd plates and dishes, it means if I give someone something I've baked I'm not pestering them for the crockery to be returned. Most of it comes back anyway but losing the odd plate is no longer the irritation it once was."

"That's a good idea. May I steal it from you as it were?" asked Mrs Rowan.

"Course you can."

"Talking of stealing stuff," interjected Neale. Alba was puzzled by the awkwardness in her friend's voice and watched him as he moved the brown paper package that he had brought with him into the centre of the table.

"Alba, your cake was amazing, as always," he continued.

"Another slice?" offered Alba warmly.

"Oh, yes please but in a couple of minutes as before that I must, sleuth like, reveal why I have brought you both here today." He repositioned the package slightly, ensuring it would remain in the shade of the moving sun as he spoke.

Two puzzled faces returned his last comment.

"Yes, I have brought you here," his voice now heavy with denouement, "to make good and to, hopefully as a result, be allowed to retake my place in Alba's affections."

"What are you talking about? You've never stopped being my dear dear friend. Is jet-lag making you all confused?"

"No, there's not too much jet-lag travelling back from South Africa. You see, you're travelling south to north not east to west. It is a tiring journey, because of the length, but it's not quite the same as being jet-lagged. But anyway, as I say, with time on the plane to think, I realised I still had a debt to pay off, or more accurately a wrong to right."

With that Neale unwrapped the package and laid out two pieces of millionaire's shortbread on one of Alba's trays.

Mrs Rowan's face continued to show puzzlement but Alba's broke into a warm smile, directed first towards Neale and then to Mrs Rowan. Alba then spoke, first to Neale then to the still confused lady sitting between them:

"Oh, Neale, you have, you really have. That's so sweet of you. What with everything going on, I'd almost forgotten but not quite. I'm so pleased. Well done, you! Mrs Rowan you have every right to be confused, baffled and bewildered but Neale will explain but it starts with a beautiful summer's day, like today, and two people were watching a cricket match – it sounds idyllic but it was the day Vaughan was killed. But, as I say, Neale will explain."

Neale did.

*

As Neale concluded his account, a look of understanding filled Mrs Rowan's face. She studied Alba's garden for a few minutes, envious of the variety of fuchsia flowers on display around the birdbath.

Alba stayed silent, curious as to how Mrs Rowan would react and happy to study both her and Neale. Neale, meanwhile, burden lifted, was willing to wait for her response, however stern it might be.

"Alba, would you be kind enough to pop these," Mrs Rowan asked, indicating the millionaire's shortbread, "in your fridge? As you can see, they're melting rapidly and we're not going to eat them now after your delicious cake that we've just had."

"Happy to," replied Alba. "But you're not going to berate Neale the moment I step indoors are you?"

"No, of course not. I'll just enjoy your garden a moment longer."

"OK," said Alba. "Neale, you're safe a moment or two more."

Alba took longer than the other two expected. Several minutes passed before she returned.

"As I didn't hear any screaming, I thought I would seize the opportunity to make a fresh pot," said Alba as she placed a further teapot on the table.

Alba and especially Neale waited for Mrs Rowan's response.

"Alba, you more than anyone know it's virtually impossible to talk about that day without that horrible horrible thing that happened to Vaughan. But, given why Neale has got us here together and the light-heartedness of it…"

"Light-heartedness?" quipped Neale. "As I sat on the plane planning my confession, one air stewardess having seen my facial expressions thought I was suffering from flight sickness, an air steward twice came up to me to say the toilet was free if I needed it and a fellow passenger offered to pray for me, believing I had a fear of flying. So, light-hearted, I think not!"

Mrs Rowan and Alba chuckled at his flight experience before Mrs Rowan continued:

"Nonetheless Neale, I think we all know there's an innocence to this drama that we're playing out here. So, if I may, I'll try and reply without refence to Vaughan. I didn't really know him but I don't think we'll be dishonouring him by thinking back to the innocence of that morning, before the Memorial Flight came over and what you, Alba, discovered shortly afterwards."

Alba nodded her consent – allowing Mrs Rowan to proceed:

"Innocence, yes, but it was jolly hard work. At least for Sam and myself – bless her. I don't think I could do such a large event any more but for her help. Catering for approximately seventy-five people is a lot of work." She looked at the other two for agreement, which she kind of got in the form of two unknowing nods.

"A lot of work, I can tell you. The kitchenette area in the pavilion is hardly my ideal work place and was definitely not up to Sam's hygiene standards; we spent the first half an hour there wiping down surfaces and cleaning the sink. And I have to accept I was getting quite irritated that morning; we were behind schedule, due to all the cleaning we had to do first, and then there was all that pilfering going on."

Alba caught Neale looking slightly redder in the cheeks following this comment from Mrs Rowan.

"And that was before your theft Neale, I might add," said Mrs Rowan. "But don't worry yourself over it and I'm enjoying the innocence of it now and, if I may say, I'm enjoying my tea and cake with you both this afternoon. You see, I fear my rather stern countenance has put people off me over the years but I am trying to lighten up."

As she said this, Mrs Rowan thought back to how close she had come, on the day of the cricket match, to telling the 7th Lord Hartfield to clear off. Alba, too, was thinking back to her time in the pub just the previous week and her renewed desire to rediscover her own sense of joy.

"Where was I? Oh yes," continued Mrs Rowan. "Maybe I was just more sensitive that morning or maybe there was more food being taken before time. Either way I remember being so wound up by it all and for several days afterwards I could still list all the people I'd caught. Plus, of course, I had to give a statement to the police, which listed every person I'd seen enter the building."

"Really?" enquired Alba.

"Oh yes, absolutely. I can now sort of add Neale to my personal list although as I didn't see him or catch him, I guess there's no need to get back in touch with the police and formally amend my statement. So, your misdemeanours will stay between just us three Neale – you're free."

"Thanks. Just having Alba knowing was embarrassing enough," offered back Neale.

"As for who I did see, well, there were a couple of young lads who definitely made off with at least a bowl of crisps."

"Tommy and Arthur, David's boys, do you think?" suggested Alba.

"No, it wasn't them. Remember, Alba, I passed them as I walked round the pitch; they were in the practice nets," said Neale.

"Yes, I remember now."

Mrs Rowan resumed her list, "Then an elderly man came in, don't know who, never seen him before at anything I've catered for, but he reminded me of someone but I still can't work out who. Then some of the batting team came and started on the pizzas and then Lord Hartfield, who I thought was just someone else on a food raid, but thankfully wasn't. It was a full-on and hectic morning without seeing food go before it was meant to. Why can't people just be patient? Why can't people understand there's also something in the presentation as well? It's so annoying when crisps are on the floor, half the sausage rolls have gone and the popular cakes are down in numbers before the lunch bell has even sounded."

Contrition fell over Neale's face, allowing Alba, who sensed Mrs Rowan had come to the end of her list, to add:

"Neale, I thought your list of food thieves was even longer. Remember, you were relaying it to me when you came back to our spot on the boundary rope, once you'd checked on Vaughan."

Mrs Rowan looked keenly at Neale as he took up the baton.

"Slightly longer. Yes. Obviously, myself."

"I hadn't thought people were sneaking food in and out of the door to the car park, as well as the pitch side doors. My, my, I'm surprised any food was left at all," mused Mrs Rowan.

"And then there was the new vicar."

"Reverend Quinn!" exclaimed Mrs Rowan.

"Well, to be fair, I didn't see him take any food but he definitely came into the pavilion via the steps, I thought to grab a sandwich or something, but he left empty handed when he saw Tom talking to Vaughan.

"The Reverend," repeated Mrs Rowan. "That's unlike him."

"He wasn't flustered or anything like that," added Neale. "He just came in, as if he were looking for something, saw Vaughan and Tom and simply decided to leave. Maybe he wasn't after food but he didn't come in for the toilets otherwise my cover would have been blown. So, I don't know what he was up to."

"I'll have to ask him the next time I see him," said Mrs Rowan.

"I should have asked him this morning," said Alba. "He came to deliver my silk scarf. I'd left it in the church on the day of the funeral – fallen under my pew apparently."

"I was flustered that day too," conceded Mrs Rowan. "Maybe I need to step back from big catering events."

"Please don't," Neale and Alba said in unison.

"Your spreads are just wonderful but what got to you on the day of the funeral? It couldn't have been my fault as I wasn't there," continued Neale.

"I can't rightly remember."

"It's why," said Alba, "you were sitting in the wrong pew. You were telling me about it as you brought me a cup of tea in the hall afterwards – something somebody had said, I think."

"Oh, I recall now," Mrs Rowan said with confidence. "It was Mrs Lyle. Nothing to do with food, catering or light fingers. A few days before the funeral, I'd gone into her shop as I had run out of icing sugar for a cake I was making. She was telling me about her plans to try and buy the piece of land next to her shop, you know, Vaughan's side-garden. She was asking whether I knew who the executor was so she could approach them before the property went onto the market. I thought it was wholly inappropriate. The poor man had only been dead a few weeks and we hadn't even had his funeral. It all came back to me that Thursday, the day of his funeral, and I forgot to sit on the back row of the pews, as I normally do when I'm catering afterwards. I was dwelling on what she said and it got me all flustered. She had even been complaining that Vaughan's gardener was still turning up and looking after the garden. She said, she was hoping the garden would be left alone, so it would look unkempt, enabling her to offer less for it."

"That's a bit calculating of her," suggested Neale.

The others concurred. Whilst Alba served Neale another, larger, slice of cake, and topped up Mrs Rowan's tea cup, Alba thought to herself – 'I really must speak to that woman properly, if I'm to help Tom'.

CHAPTER 13

One Thousand Moons

The following morning, having forgotten to pass them on to him yesterday, Alba had delivered three packets of his preferred brand of digestive biscuits to Neale. She hadn't stopped as he was stuck in a plot twist in chapter sixteen which meant he was having to adjust several of the earlier chapters to ensure continuity. He was grateful for the biscuits, even more so for a small gooseberry pie.

She chose to walk home via 'Stapleton's', hoping to find a way to this time engage Mrs Lyle in conversation about Vaughan. Yet, having got to the shop she just couldn't face going in to buy yet more boring digestive biscuits. How anyone can have a favourite brand of such a biscuit was beyond Alba, 'a digestive is a digestive is a digestive' she thought. She had already paid her paper bill, a week early to the owner's delight, and had more than enough groceries at home to prevent her from buying any more – 'enough is as good as a feast' thought Alba, echoing PL Travers' famous nanny. Alba had stood reading the notices in the window but felt any creative powers that morning were flowing through Neale's mind in preference to her own.

Alba moved away from the shop frontage but, rather than walking home, moved a few yards the other way and went and leant against the gate to Vaughan's side garden, the area that he termed his orchard. It was probably the sound of someone trying to start a lawn mower that caught her attention initially. It was a sturdy gate, weathered enough now to blend in colour wise, and to have been *in situ* long enough to allow the hedge, on each side, to encroach around the upright posts just enough to give a sense of continuity.

"Morning, Jim," called out Alba. "Playing up, is it?"

"Oh, hi Alba. Yeah, it's playing right silly buggers with me this week."

"Have you checked the…?"

"Yes, spark plug is clean, exhaust isn't blocked, it has fuel, the correct fuel and there's nothing blocking it underneath. The air filter is good and, yes, I am holding the 'kill handle' as I pull. Think it's going to need to be taken in."

"Guess you must know someone," offered back Alba.

"Absolutely. Graham is the best. Just hope he'll have time to look at it this week. It's just a bit frustrating – I've finished my morning job much quicker than I'd dared hope so I thought I'd come and give the grass here a quick going over before heading home. I was meant to be finishing off a design project this afternoon but I sense that'll depend on my call to Graham."

"It's good of you to still be cutting his grass. You know it's probably only you and me, oh, Sally too no doubt, that notice it's being cut."

"I'd like to say," offered back Jim "that it's simply my way of honouring him and an overriding love of horticulture as to why I'm doing it. Not that both aren't true but, if truth be told, Vaughan paid me in advance. I charge a fair rate, of course, even to Vaughan. Have to. As you can imagine, financially there are small margins to play with, in a job like this, so I can't be charitable to people, even to Vaughan, otherwise I'd be out of business pronto. So, given he's paid me, I'm honour bound to do the work."

"That's very decent of you, Jim."

"Well, he's looking down on us, isn't he? So, I have to fulfil my side of the contract, don't I?"

She was suddenly struck by the financial oddity of what her friend Jim had just implied to her. "But he's been dead for weeks now – must be getting on for two months in fact. He can't have paid you that much in advance, surely?"

"You're right to think it a bit odd, that I must have really mis-counted my weeks or that all these power tools have dulled my brain. But I haven't mis-counted and my brain is pretty good, I mean I do all my own business accounts and submit my own tax papers – can even list, in order I might add, all the British Prime Minister's since Lord Liverpool, actually from Spencer Perceval, given Lord Liverpool became Premier upon the other's assassination in the lobby of the House of Commons. But odd, yes definitely a bit odd."

"So, if I'm allowed to ask," asked a somewhat puzzled Alba, "How much in advance did he pay you? But you don't have to answer, you know that don't you?"

"Sure Alba. With some people I might decline to answer that kind of question but not you, not Miss White. Whatever has prompted you to ask is fine by me."

"I'm trying to help Tom, actually," said Alba. "He didn't kill Vaughan or his landlady, I'm certain of it. I'm just trying to find something to give the police a different lead to pursue so, hopefully, they'll stop assuming Tom did it. Unfortunately, I haven't got anything to offer them yet. So, how much in advance did he…"

"Let me think. Reckon it was Easter time when he gave me a lump sum. Yeah, I remember now, first cut after the Easter weekend."

"Easter?"

"Yup, Easter. Paid me six months in advance."

"Six months, you've got to be kidding?" said Alba. "No one pays their gardener six months up front!"

"No, I'm not. Six months in advance. I told him not to be so daft. I also told him he didn't need to buy my loyalty, said even if someone offered me more money per hour, his slot in my working week was secure. You see, Alba," continued Jim as he instinctively tapped his belt to check for his secateurs, "I was still learning from Vaughan. So many horticultural tips came my way from him, couldn't buy that kind of knowledge and experience. So, even if someone offered me a pound or two more per hour, Vaughan's slot was secure. So many little gems of wisdom."

"Like?"

"Like, let me see but you might well know tips like these already. There was, cut your hedges such that a cross-section of them resembles a capital letter 'A' not the letter 'V'; discarded wooden pallets make great free compost bays, but you need at least three of them."

"Oh, I do that – I got a couple from the roofers, who were working down the road from the pub the other month. I needed one to repair one of my bays but I got both whilst they were on offer. Roofers said they were destined for a skip otherwise."

"You got them, did you?" said Jim. "I had my eye on them one morning but couldn't stop and then they'd gone by the time I was driving back through the village in the evening. Still, good on you for making use of them."

"As I say, I needed one but the other is spare. Pop round and collect it, if you can make use of it. I'm not greedy, I just didn't want it going in a skip when I knew it still had a value to people like you or me. You have it."

"Thanks, Alba. That's kind. I don't need it for my compost bays but I wanted to add another layer to my insect hotel but couldn't afford going and buying some new timber for it. Vaughan said it was the sign, not just of a gardener but of an 'allotmenteer', if you looked into a skip and saw something that led you to think 'I can make use of that in the garden'."

"I hadn't heard that phrase before," offered back Alba.

"As I say, that was Vaughan for you, then there was what he did with used shotgun cartridges – using them as cane toppers."

"He showed me that trick as well," said Alba.

"How about his suggestion to put your banana skins around your roses?"

"I put tea leaves around my roses, Jim, but why banana skins?"

"Not just the nutrients for the roots but, according to Vaughan, the skins still give off a gas that acts as a fungicide which prevents rust and black spot."

"How ingenious. Vaughan's roses did always look so healthy, didn't they? I'll be doing that from now on, too."

"I'm sure you will. I do. I can't give you the exact science of it, nor could Vaughan, but it seemed to work. So, as I say, I was learning so much from him. Made me a better, more imaginative gardener, than I could ever have been without him. Such a wise man. Still, as he said to me recently, 'that's what comes from having had your one thousand moons'."

Jim's last comment stunned Alba to silence.

"You alright Alba? You look like you've seen a ghost."

"What did you just say Jim?"

"You look like you've seen a ghost."

"No, before that."

"That Vaughan was a wise man."

"No, no, no, after that but before ghosts."

"Oh, that Vaughan said that is what comes from having had your one thousand moons. Do you mean that?"

"Yes," replied a still stunned Alba. A moment passed before she added, "He'd written that phrase in his journal but I didn't know what it was connected to or even what it meant."

"Oh, have you got his journal then? I was wondering where it had gone and hoping it hadn't gone into a bin or just got lost. Hoping also, that if someone had it, they would know what a treasure it is. Must be full of gems – of wisdom and gardening lore. I'd quite like to have a look at it myself, if allowed."

"Course you can. I mean I don't have it with me at present but, from dipping into it, it is definitely full of gems and tit-bits. Has the odd poem too; one by Hilaire Belloc for example. There's also one by Lord Byron, in memory of his dog, 'Boatswain'. How does that one finish? Oh yes – *'I never knew but one and here he lies'.* Same could be said at Vaughan's graveside, I guess," said Alba being suddenly melancholy. Her mood instantly lightened, though, as she realised she wanted to talk about Vaughan in life, not in death. "The journal has more besides but I haven't really been able to study it in any depth as yet. I have come across a note Vaughan made in it to say he found the journal in a field in France, which would at least explain the staining on the cover. I keep opening it but then the doorbell goes or the waitress brings me my food or Mrs Rowan appears or..."

"Ah, Mrs Rowan," said Jim, raising his eyebrows as he did so.

"Oh, she's not too bad once you get to know her a little bit and her daughter Sam is lovely."

Alba then explained to Jim, who had not been able to make the funeral as he had been in Oxfordshire, visiting an ailing aunt in Woodstock, how she, Alba, had been given the journal at Vaughan's funeral. She told him how, with Sam's help, she'd established that it started off in faded handwriting, which was in German, and seemed to be about foraging and within the journal she'd come across the phrase 'one thousand moons' and was intrigued by its significance.

"So, what does it mean? I assume or, at least I hope, you know," asked Alba, with the faint hope that it might assist somehow, however obscurely, in her promise to help Tom.

"Want to have a guess? You don't have to but, just to reassure you, I couldn't guess it. Vaughan had to tell me," conceded Jim.

Jim took a swig of water from his bottle, which had been lying on its side by his kneeling mat, hand fork and trowel and keys to his van, as Alba considered whether the answer to this small mystery lay within her after all.

"He was a godly man, so unlikely to have been anything to do with horoscopes," offered back Alba, which gained a nod of assent from the man she was talking to. "Name of his favourite pub? But if so, doesn't seem to bear any relevance to anything else in the journal." Jim's silence told Alba that it did not relate to 'amber nectar'. "Oh, hold on," said an excited Alba, prompting Jim to look expectantly back, having slung his water bottle back down to be by his keys.

"Was it," continued Alba, who was convinced she had got it, "the name of Clive's wartime plane? You know, how the crews would name their planes, like 'City of Lincoln', 'Admiral Prune' or 'Memphis Belle'. Was Clive's plane called '1,000 Moons'? I mean, didn't Vaughan say most British bombing raids were done at night-time?"

"Alba," said Jim in neutral tones. He was conscious she was looking back expectantly, assured as she was, she had cracked it. However, his slow shake of the head that followed, left Alba crestfallen, so sure had she been.

"Alba, great guessing but I'm sorry to say you haven't got it. Much better than my attempts by far, I'll give you that. And, if ever I open my own pub, I promise I will call it 'One Thousand Moons'. As for Clive's plane, I don't categorically know but, if it had been called that, Vaughan would have said. It would have been called something else, I'm sure. Nice idea though. Wonder what his final plane was actually called."

"So, what does it mean?"

"Well, you know Vaughan was into his lunar planting?" asked Jim. Alba nodded, allowing Jim to continue. "'One thousand moons' is of a similar vein; it's part horticultural, part astronomy, part gardening folk-lore. It's how Vaughan measured how old he was or, more specifically, that he finally had to accept that he was old."

Alba's puzzled look told Jim he needed to expand his explanation.

"Vaughan thought as much in lunar cycles as solar ones. You and I live in yearly cycles. You're however many years old, if I may ask?"

"Thirty," offered back Alba.

"Really," said Jim. "I'd never have thought. Gosh, a few more than, but enough of that. So, thirty. That's based on how many times the earth has gone around the sun, right? For Vaughan, though, thinking in lunar cycles as he could do, he may have thought of you as being just shy of four hundred in age."

"Four hundred, now you really are flattering me!"

"Anyway, for Vaughan, he was really struck when he realised he had reached his one thousandth moon. It's about seventy-seven years old. I remember him telling me about it at the time and about the old gardeners he knew when he was a boy, shortly after the Great Depression, who he remembered celebrating their one thousandth moon. They would have been people born in the 1850s or 1860s, perhaps when Viscount Palmerston or the Earl of Derby were Prime Minister. To them it was always more than a bit of kudos to reach your thousandth, it was survival against the odds. In a time when there was no national health service as there is now, to reach your thousandth, warranted recognition."

"So, writing it in his journal was just…"

"Just Vaughan's way of marking to himself that he, too, had reached that milestone; the Elysian Fields for a horticulturalist. I've got a long way to go, you even further Alba, but if I get there, I think I will mark it too. I'll raise half a glass of something to the moon and another half to our old friend Vaughan – God rest his soul."

As Alba leant on the side gate to Vaughan's garden, she found herself looking beyond the orchard area to one of the flower beds and she found herself studying the seed pods of Vaughan's favourite plant.

"Do you know what Vaughan's favourite plant was, Jim?"

"Of course, as you do. It was Honesty."

"I understand why now – given the translucent seed pods look like the moon."

"Hence its Latin name, as you know, of 'Lunaria'. It's beautiful, isn't it?"

"I do miss him," said Alba.

"We all do," replied Jim. "And I'm not going to give up on getting his grass cut today. One more try of starting my mower."

"Just before you do, Jim, it's been lovely talking about Vaughan. I feel, for a few moments at least, we've kind of brought him back to life. It was especially fascinating to learn about his thousandth moon."

"Yeah, he was a wise, experienced man. He'd seen a lot of the world, seen a lot of types of people, especially so from his wartime days I reckon, and still had so much to offer those who were willing to listen."

"But, just before I leave you in peace..."

"Peace? With this machine?" said Jim, pointing to his mower.

"You haven't said why Vaughan was insistent on paying you six months in advance. I mean that's unheard of."

"Absolutely unprecedented. Many of my clients pay me a month after I've done the work for them. I mean, I quite like being paid after I've done the work, being paid in advance is a bit de-motivating in fact, much prefer getting my cheque as I pack my tools away as opposed to when I'm unpacking them. Vaughan paying me months in advance kind of exacerbated that sensation. Know what I did to 'manage' that situation? Opened another bank account and set up a standing order, moving a week's money over at a time."

"But why pay so much in advance?"

"Don't really know. As I say, he was adamant. I think he may have said he didn't want to leave me short if anything happened to him."

"If anything happened to him?" repeated Alba.

"That's what I remember him saying – 'if anything happened to him'. Thinking back, I challenged him on that, said he was in good health for a thousand moon man. He said, he felt fine but that things change. Then he said something that I thought was a bit eerie, he said 'but sometimes people don't change'. I asked him what he meant but he wouldn't be drawn and in his way, that we all know he had when he wanted to change the subject, he started talking about his garden, how he was rotating his vegetables and that he had ordered some heritage seed varieties he was keen to grow this year. Sadly most of this year's veg crop have now died. I mean I can come and cut the grass and weed the front beds to keep the place looking lived in but I didn't have the time, still haven't got the time, to come and water his veg plots every other day. The potatoes should be ok, the garlic and rhubarb are looking after themselves but everything else has failed through lack of water."

"Don't beat yourself up, Jim. It's good of you to do what you're doing as it is, whether he's paid you or not. And the cottage does look the better for it; to the stranger passing, the garden still looks cared for. But I wonder what he meant by it all – what could he have meant by 'sometimes people don't change'?"

"He never said," replied Jim as he tried to start the mower one final time. Catching both of them by complete surprise, the machine, with a puff of smoke from its exhaust, burst into life.

"Sorry, Alba," continued Jim but now in a much louder voice. "I'm not letting this opportunity go, it might not start again. I've got to cut as much as I can whilst it's going."

"That's fine, you crack on," she replied, equally voluminously, as she watched him depress the lever to engage the power drive. The mower took Jim off to the back garden.

Alba continued leaning against the gate, mulling over the chat they had just had. She found herself content to just listen to the sound of the mower going and having the scent of freshly cut grass wafting past her. All too quickly, though, she found herself pondering how she would make any progress with Mrs Lyle, in her attempt to find out why the owner of 'Stapleton's', the village shop behind her, had been arguing with Vaughan on the day of the cricket match, shortly before her dear friend was killed.

Yet, Alba needn't have worried. She wouldn't need to do anything at all, for Mrs Lyle was about to come to her.

CHAPTER 14

Apples, sunglasses and flapjack

"Is that blasted gardener at it again?" said Mrs Lyle, as she came out of her shop.

Mrs Lyle was at Alba's side before Alba could reply. The lady from the village store continued her monologue. "I can hear a petrol mower going. The people the other side of me have an electric mower, not that they use it much, less often than I use mine in fact. So, if it's a noisy petrol thing, it must be coming from here." With that, Mrs Lyle leant into the garden, over the gate, in an attempt to see if she was correct.

Alba took a half step to her right to give the older lady some additional room to allow her to arch her elbows out so she had better balance.

"I can't see him. I'm sure it's him, though," Mrs Lyle added, with her head and upper body well into the airspace of Vaughan's side garden.

Alba wondered whether she should move away and leave the other woman well alone and try and speak to her on another occasion, sensing she was already sufficiently wound up to prevent anyone from having a sensible conversation with her. However, Alba found herself suddenly possessive of the gate that, until a moment ago, she had been resting against, smelling and listening to the sound of a cared for garden in the summer time. She therefore decided not to surrender her spot and her sensations to this other person without offering someone back, albeit however subtly.

"Very observant of you to pick out the type of lawn mower you can hear," Alba said in as non-committal a way as possible.

"You develop excellent hearing, working in a shop. School kids thinking they can steal bags of crisps and magazines when they are out of sight forget I can hear their rucksacks being unzipped and done up again. Young mums, having dropped their little darlings off at pre-school, forget I can hear them adjusting the plastic rain covers to their buggies on fine days like today. But businessmen, passing through the village, are the worst. They stop for some cigarettes or a can of drink and think I don't hear them lift a bunch of flowers from one of the buckets outside as they head back to the car. They're the worst as they can afford to pay but still the temptation to steal takes over. Men! A bunch of thieving scoundrels, if you ask me; if only their girlfriends or wives, or, I suspect, both for many of the blokes I've caught, knew what they are really like."

"Do you let them get away with it?" enquired Alba innocently.

"Course not!" came the reply, as she continued arching into Vaughan's garden, angling her head in an attempt to spot the gardener. "The businessmen, well I tell them their car registration has been caught on my CCTV and unless they put the flowers back but pay double for them nonetheless, I'll be on to the police before they've driven out of the village. Thankfully most pay as, even if the police did prosecute, having to shut the shop for a day, even half a day, to enable me to appear in Court as a witness, would cost me significantly more money than a single bunch of flowers. As for the school kids and mums, as they're from the village I don't won't to lose their custom for ever, or, with regards to the kids, to antagonise their parents. I just ask them to pay up and I've learnt, in the time I've been here now, who I need to keep most of an eye on. Miss White, you're OK however – you've even started to pay your bills ahead of time now."

Alba elected not to tell Mrs Lyle why she was keen to get into the shopkeeper's good books of late. Sensing that Jim would be caught before too long in any case, Alba elected to 'sacrifice' Jim. If she, Alba, told Mrs Lyle it was that 'blasted gardener', she hoped it would keep the conversation going and further endear her to the other.

"It is your gardener, I think. He's cutting the back lawn, I guess." Then, going for broke, Alba added, "It's good of him to be looking after what was Vaughan's garden. You must appreciate someone maintaining it – it's looking rather nice, don't you think? This side garden in particular, is coming on a treat."

Alba hoped she hadn't 'overcooked' it. The noise of a solitary horse and its rider, going along the road, in addition to the general drone of the lawn mower, prevented Alba from hearing Mrs Lyle's opening words describing what she thought of the gardener. Alba sensed the lost words were not kindly ones. Alba equally sensed, correctly, that her pitch had been spot on: Mrs Lyle had taken the bait.

"…so who does he think he is, this gardener? It's not his property, he won't be being paid for doing it, so what's he after?"

Alba remained silent, hoping the other wasn't finished. Mrs Lyle wasn't.

"What's his angle, then? They say possession is nine tenths of the law, maybe he's wanting to be seen to be gardening in there. Maybe he's photographing himself out of sight of us, to try and convince a court that he's in occupation. Maybe I should do something similar?" Mrs Lyle said, turning to Alba.

Alba returned a puzzled look, prompting Mrs Lyle to continue.

"If I move some of my shop signs in, or some of the bags of kindling, and take some pictures, I'll be able to convince a court or a solicitor that I have a right to store stuff there. If I could establish a right to enter or a right of way over the garden, especially this side bit, that would be useful." Not knowing Alba's connection and loyalty to Vaughan, Mrs Lyle continued unbridled.

"Yes, if I could convince some legal people that Vaughan had granted me access to his garden, months before he died, that would be a bonus. This side garden was meant to be mine, in any case. Maybe later, or tomorrow, I'll move stuff in and take some photos. I'm not having this wretched grass cutter have a claim over this plot of land ahead of me. This was always meant to be coming my way in any case, even before that old man Vaughan moved in."

Shocked by the callousness of what she'd just heard, but keen to sound neutral to the person who Alba needed to keep in conversation, Alba offered back what she hoped would be viewed as a helpful comment.

"Mrs Lyle, we all worry about boundary issues with our neighbours. However, you can't take photographs and claim they show an arrangement that's been in place since the spring."

"Why can't I? I've got his signature on a letter he sent me, telling me he wasn't willing to sell his 'orchard' as he called it. But we won't tell the court about that. I reckon I could copy his signature on to the back of some photographs I'll take."

Desperate to not call the other person out as a thief or a fraudster, Alba nonetheless endeavoured to quell the other's scam.

"But you can't do that, Mrs Lyle."

"Can't I? I bet that's what the grass cutter is doing. You going to stop him, too?"

"Mrs Lyle, you can't. The photographs will give yourself away. You wouldn't want to convict yourself, would you?"

"Err, no. But how would I? For I'd date the back of the photographs, say some random date in March?"

"All the plants would be in the wrong season, wouldn't they? Roses in bloom, the honesty gone to seed, the trees in full leaf, you name it, the whole garden, without uttering a word, would give it away that it wasn't March. In March, you should be seeing daffodils, magnolia blossom and bare branches."

"Oh, hadn't thought of that. I think you've saved me a bit of embarrassment, Miss White."

Knowing she had Mrs Lyle on the back foot, Alba decided to push her new found advantage. "You'd like to have this plot of land, would you? Would you sell the apples at your shop each autumn?"

'Come on, come on' thought Alba, sensing a piece of the jigsaw, or a piece on this imaginary chess board, might move into place and so maybe, just maybe, help her to fulfil her promise to Tom.

"Apples! I'm not interested in the apples. If I tried selling loose fruit outside my shop, half would get thrown around by school kids and the other half would be eaten by dogs left outside by their owners. Hang the apples! The trees would be down pronto. If I could only get the land."

With that Mrs Lyle fell into silence, as she once again started coveting Vaughan's side garden. The silence was enhanced as Alba heard Jim's lawn mower cut out. Alba hoped he'd stay out of sight a while longer, trying to get it going again, or by finding a shrub to prune for a few minutes, to allow Mrs Lyle to continue revealing herself to Alba.

"Yes, if I could get the land. It's what the owners prior to Vaughan promised me. They promised to sell it to me. I could have extended my shop, I could simply have provided proper parking spaces for my customers, could have had a fish and chip van renting the space on a Friday night, could have had a whole load of different things going on with it. But that bloke Vaughan kyboshed all of my plans."

"Surely you spoke to him about it?"

"Course I did. Numerous times. Got me absolutely nowhere. He just wouldn't listen to reason."

Alba pondered whether Mrs Lyle had ever offered Vaughan any reason at all. Beyond wanting the plot, to which she had no legal right, there seemed to be no corroborating evidence for a verbal contract she had with an earlier owner and Vaughan was under no obligation to sell what he had therefore legally bought. Alba sensed, in all of Mrs Lyle's 'discussions' with Vaughan the only 'reason' would have come from Vaughan himself.

Mrs Lyle added, "I offered him a good price. You see, business had been good last year so I was able to make an offer for the plot. But he just wouldn't listen. Kept telling me about Lord Derby instead, whoever the heck he is. Could have offered him even more but someone owed me a fair sum of money. Strangely, she repaid what she owed, very recently. So, I could have offered Vaughan even more for the plot now. Quite a lot more, in fact."

After a pause, Mrs Lyle added:

"I was lucky she repaid when she did."

"Why was that?" queried Alba.

"She's since died."

"What?"

"Yeah, week or so ago. Poisoned apparently – or so I've heard from a couple of customers."

"Someone from the village?" enquired Alba as innocuously as possible but knowing, if Mrs Lyle mentioned anyone by name, she was about to say the words 'Mrs Taylor'.

"Course from the village; Mrs Taylor. You know, the other person that gardener from up at the Hall murdered. Miss White, you should get out more; seems like you don't know anything that's going on around these parts."

Knowing that she knew more than Mrs Lyle realised about Mrs Taylor, which she wanted to keep to herself, Alba changed the subject of the conversation back to the plot of land. Thinking back of Tom's claim that Mrs Lyle had been arguing with Vaughan at the cricket match, Alba enquired:

"I imagine the conversations with Vaughan must have got a bit tense at times, even with you being so reasonable."

"Tense yes but we never argued."

"Really? That was good of you."

"Yes, but that was because the blasted man wouldn't engage me in a proper debate. He kept trying to change the subject, talk about his plants, helping up at the Hall or cricket. I can't stand fancy gardens or country houses and I especially can't stand cricket! I think he changed the subject just to annoy me. I think, if we'd had a proper argument it might have helped. He'd have seen my reasoning and logic but he kept just closing me down. It got me so annoyed. Yet I was promised the plot before he bought the house. He wouldn't sell the side plot even though, as I say, the previous owners promised it to me. They promised it, I tell you. Bloody Vaughan! He knew I wanted it, wouldn't discuss it, more so than ever that last time, and he refused to sell. Well, look where it got him!"

Alba wasn't sure whether Mrs Lyle had intended to say that last comment out loud. She didn't have the faintest idea how to challenge her about it; in part Alba didn't want to challenge her because she didn't want Mrs Lyle to backtrack from what she had clearly just said. Alba opted to change tack once more and 'fish' one further time and, in deliberate contradiction to both what Mrs Lyle had just said and what Andrew had said to Alba about Mrs Lyle's dislike of the sport, said:

"Oh, I thought you loved cricket."

"Where did you get that idea from? Hate the game. Only good thing about it is that when there's a game here in the village, it brings extra business my way. So, I keep an eye on the fixture list and allow posters to go up to advertise one-off matches, as I need to order in extra weekend newspapers, ice-creams, sun block and the like."

"Especially so for the match on the day of the Queen's Jubilee, I imagine? You must have been in your shop all day long then?" said Alba, despite Tom's recollection, in those final moments of her prison visit, coupled with Andrew having also told her that his grandfather had tried to discuss the Hall's newspaper order with Mrs Lyle at the cricket match.

Mrs Lyle did not respond at first. When she spoke, it seemed evident to Alba that the other was deliberately not answering the question, for all Mrs Lyle initially offered up was 'I'm sure the grass cutter is here; I can hear someone pushing something'. However, with the sound of the shop door going, Mrs Lyle said no more, beyond a 'you'll have to excuse me', as she returned to her shop, preventing Alba from pursuing her line of inquiry.

*

Alba resumed her solitary position at the gate, waiting for Jim's reappearance.

"It's completely dead now," he said, as he came into view. "It's not even thinking about starting up. Thankfully I got the back done before it died on me. Usefully, as you can imagine, I've got my strimmer in the van, so I can do these grass paths with that. But you might want to move away though. I'll be wearing proper safety goggles; whereas I doubt your sunglasses are up to the same British Standard. If I catch a loose stone or even a fallen branch, a shard or a splinter could easily come your way."

"Course Jim. I ought to be heading home; I suddenly feel I've got a lot to think about. It's been lovely to chat about Vaughan."

As she turned to go, she added, "Oh, you were lucky. Mrs Lyle was on the warpath, you just missed her."

"Luck?" offered back Jim. "No chance. Luck had nothing to do with it. Once my mower died, after I'd checked there was still fuel in it, I could hear who you were talking to. I thought if I came for my strimmer whilst she was here, she'd be arguing and berating me for the next forty minutes. I went and retied some of the pallets that make up Vaughan's compost bays; a couple were loose you see."

"Good thinking," and with that Alba turned to head home – the first few strides taking her back past 'Stapleton's'.

*

She heard the shop door go before she could break stride and Andrew Chapman, who himself seemed pre-occupied, had clattered into her, or she into him, before either could do anything about it.

"Oh, Alba!" exclaimed Andrew. "I'm so sorry. I wasn't looking where I was going. You OK?"

She retrieved her chocolate brown sunglasses from the ground.

"I'll replace them, if they're broken," offered an apologetic Andrew.

"Not broken, no," replied Alba, playing with the arms. "Probably another scratch or two but don't worry since they're not my best pair."

Since seeing him in this very spot over a week ago, which had led to them having a pot of tea in the beer garden of 'The Sun and Moon' and then Alba driving the heir to Hillstone Hall back to the Hall so he could keep tabs on Simon the auctioneer, Alba, despite several attempts, had failed to 'bump' into Andrew. Now she literally had. 'Good fortune', she thought, 'seemed to be playing her a better hand this morning than all of her contrived attempts of the last week'.

"Don't tell me you're buying the 'Racing Post' as well now," joked Alba.

"No, not quite my thing. I mean riding a horse, that's quite something, across the estate; you should come with me one day. As for the racing side, no, that's not me. Plus, I think great-uncle William has the latest one already. No, I finally plucked up the courage to come and speak to Mrs Lyle about the newspapers up at the Hall."

"Did you? How did that go?" she asked but in the knowledge that Mrs Lyle had already wound herself up about Jim.

"So-so. She was hardly the calmest of people when the conversation started. Thankfully I had a back-up plan, a compromise if you like, which she agreed to. I could have just cancelled the whole order but that's not how grandad has taught me to engage with local businesses or our neighbours in the village. So, we've agreed to reduce the order to just two newspapers per week day and no weekend papers. I suspect most visitors get their own weekend paper in any case, if only for the TV guide. We'll see how this new arrangement goes – it'll save us a bit in the short-term but Mrs Lyle can still regard Lord Hartfield as one of her customers. Hopefully, win-win."

"Good. I'm pleased you've got that sorted out."

"Fancy a walk?" suggested Andrew suddenly. "If we follow the bridleway, loop round the small-holdings and come back via that newish community café, I can buy you a coffee if you like."

Alba nodded.

As they started off, Alba spoke:

"It's funny, I've been trying to catch up with you this last week without success and then I come across you exactly where you were last time we spoke."

"Any reason why you've been after me? Have I done something else wrong?"

"No, no, nothing you've done. It's a bit awkward, actually. I'm not quite sure how to put it."

"Try me."

"It's to do with Tom," stated Alba.

As they walked, she relayed her experiences of visiting him in prison and how he was just about coping. As with Neale and Mrs Rowan, she kept her suspicions about Mrs Lyle to herself; even though Andrew's grandfather had placed Mrs Lyle at the scene shortly before Vaughan was stabbed, Alba still felt she needed something more before airing her suspicions to other people.

"So, you still think Tom is innocent, do you?"

"Absolutely, one hundred per cent."

"I sense, though, a 'but' coming," said Andrew.

"Unfortunately, yes. There are things that don't quite fit but nothing tangible to offer the police."

"So, where do I come in?"

Alba found herself unable to ask for access to Tom's room, fearing her walking companion would be shocked and suspicious of her motives to poke around what, in effect, remained a crime scene. She stayed silent.

The path widened as they walked past the paddocks, containing their smattering of horses, old cast-iron metal bath tubs that were acting as drinking troughs and bundles of straw tied to gate posts. Andrew broke the silence:

"Look Alba, just ask. Clearly something is bothering you, something that you think I can help with."

He stopped and turned to look at Alba. He took both her hands and gently held them in his and looked directly at her, or more specifically at her sunglasses.

"Ask. The worst that will happen is I'll say 'no'. I have no doubt that you mean well by it, so try me. And, even if I say 'no' to whatever it is, I won't bar you from the gardens up at the Hall, I won't remove your volunteers' discount and I won't refuse to buy you a coffee when we get to the café. I reserve the right to say 'no' but you need to ask me whatever it is that has been burdening you this past week." He squeezed her hands ever so gently to encourage her to try him.

"I want," said Alba but she stopped herself, drew back her hands and continued to walk.

The path was dry and, after a further wooden gate, with its heavy sprung release catch, they were beyond the paddocks and walking in the shadow of a long high red brick wall. The bricks, in the century or so since their laying, were weathered and, since the council had cleared most of the ivy from it, the wall hosted an array of ferns, stonecrops and, somewhat precariously near the top, a smattering of buddleias. It was not until they were past this and about to get out onto the road that led to the café, that Alba stopped. Andrew, fiddling with his jacket's spare buttons that resided, as they always do, in a small plastic sachet in one of the jacket's outer pockets, hoped she would say something, anything, before they got to the café –

since he didn't really want to sit there in awkward silence for the next hour. Thankfully, Alba spoke.

"I ask, not because I am a nosey person nor because I want to retrieve something that incriminates myself, but because I want to help Tom." She paused before adding, "You do understand that don't you?"

"Yes," offered back Andrew. "Tom was our employee, I might point out. If only from a business point of view, I would rather it wasn't him. Could rather do with him being back, if truth be told. Mr Parker has asked to take another chunk of leave, which really doesn't help. I mean, he's allowed to but with Mrs Taylor's death, the result is we'll be without half of our department heads just as the summer holidays start. I was really hoping he'd delay asking for more leave until the autumn. So, I'm quite keen to do what I can to help Tom as well in fact. Obviously, up until this point, I've assumed the police know what they are doing and that they've got the right person. However, Alba, if you think there's something they've missed, I'm happy to help if I can. Plus, it will make a change from talking about budget cuts at Hillstone, what family heirlooms are next for the auction house or what items can be put to one side to be offered to the Treasury, under their 'acceptance in lieu' scheme. That scheme, if you don't know, allows reductions to the inheritance tax bill the estate will be faced with when grandad sadly dies. Not that I'm expecting that any time soon, I might add."

"That's what I thought about Vaughan, Andrew. So be careful, don't take your time with your grandad for granted."

"Thank you Alba, that's a good point – heartfelt too, I know." As he waited for her to speak, he found himself wondering what was on the end of her silver necklace, since the cut of her olive green top, which was drawn to a bow on her left-hand side, was too high in the neck for him to see the pendant or whatever it was.

"It's to help Tom," she repeated. To which Andrew nodded an understanding. He placed both his hands in his trouser pockets and waited.

"As I say, Tom didn't commit either murder; I'm certain of it. However, as of yet I have no proof or even grounds for reasonable doubt. I mean, I have my doubts but nothing I could take to the police. What I do believe is that someone, not Tom, was arguing with Vaughan shortly before he died. I was the other side of the cricket pitch at the time but, thinking about it now, I think I may have seen it. I can't be certain who it was but I have my suspicions. I feel I should keep that card close to my chest for now as I feel I need more evidence before casting aspersions. Nor do I want to, by bandying his or her name around, start convincing myself that I know who it was that I simply might have seen; I don't want to replace one innocent person in prison with another."

"That says a lot for your integrity, Alba," interjected Andrew.

Alba smiled before continuing. "I also believe, from a conversation I've just had this morning, Vaughan was worried about something or, perhaps, someone and had been for several months. Something, or someone, had unsettled him. My guess is it would have been back in the spring but it might have been earlier still. Also, I believe someone planted evidence in Tom's locker up at the Hall and poisoned Mrs Taylor when he or she, or they, knew Tom would be in 'The Sun and the Moon' that Tuesday evening."

"That's more of a list than you think," reflected Andrew. "But you don't think it's good enough for the police?"

"No," insisted Alba. "For it would go something like this. Police, *'Who did you see arguing with the deceased?'* Me, *'Can't be sure'.* Police, *'But you suspect someone. Have you confronted the person?'.* Me, *'Yes, I suspect someone. Yes, I've spoken to them but nothing specific back'.* Police, *'So what unsettled Vaughan?'* Me, *'No idea'.* Police, *'Who planted the medals in Tom's locker?'* Me, *'No idea'.* Police, *'How did they know Tom would be in the pub when they wanted to poison Mrs Taylor?'* Me, *'No idea'.* You see, Andrew, it's not compelling enough. To be frank, it's not compelling at all. I'm out of leads to investigate, almost."

"Almost?"

"Almost. But I need your help with both of them, otherwise I am truly out. I want," and Alba paused, took a deep breath and then said, "to be allowed to have a look at Tom's room."

"But he didn't have an office up at the Hall. Mr Parker does, Mrs Taylor did, but not Tom."

"No," replied Alba. "Where he lived. He was lodging with Mrs Taylor. It's an estate property, I understand. Basically, I need you to let me in. I don't know what I'm looking for – when I discussed it with Tom, he didn't think I'd find anything of significance but he said it was fine for me to look if I could get in."

"Oh."

"Guess I shouldn't have asked. Sorry." She was about to resume walking, out on to the pavement, when Andrew stopped her.

"No need to be sorry. Logical question to ask – Mrs Taylor tragically can't let you in, Tom can't for different reasons. You're hardly the type of person to smash a window, so all you can do is ask the 'overlord'."

"Obviously, that's your grandfather but I don't know him to speak to, like I do you now. Well?" enquired Alba in part dread and part hope.

"I'll have to run it past grandad but the police have told us they have finished with the property from a forensic point of view and they're happy for us to let tradespeople in if there's a water leak, the fire alarms go off, a roof tile needs replacing, you know, that kind of thing."

"And you'll let me in?"

"As I say, I'll ask grandad but, when I explain it to him, he'll be fine – I mean you're hardly going to be going in to lounge on the sofa and watch a film, steal the kettle from the kitchen or run yourself a bath, are you! Grandad or I will have to accompany you, I feel. But, don't think that's because I personally don't trust you, I just sense that would be more tactful towards the neighbours."

"Of course, of course," said a thrilled Alba. "I really don't know what I'm looking for but feel I should look nonetheless."

"When do you want to go? Just to say, though, I'm tied up with a lot for the rest of the week."

"The weekend, then?"

"Sounds good, when?"

"Sunday – how about midday?" suggested Alba.

"Perfect, that's a date. There was something else, as well, you said."

"Yes. As I say, something or someone unnerved Vaughan several months back. Apparently, Vaughan said, to the person who's recently relayed it to me, something along the lines of 'leopards don't change their spots'. It might be nothing but…"

"Yes?" Andrew said encouragingly.

"I assume you remember bumping in to Simon and Anne with me the weekend before last, well didn't Simon say his son Justin had recently moved to the village."

"You know, you're right!" said an excited Andrew. "A few months back, didn't he say?"

"Exactly!" said Alba. "Exactly. You wouldn't know this but Vaughan started paying his gardener months in advance, sensing something wasn't right. From Easter time, the gardener said. And Easter was…"

"A few months back," continued Andrew. "So, how can I help on this score?"

"Can you discretely find out from Simon, his dad, when Justin did move to the village, whether he knew about his mum's ex-husband, where he lived before and anything else that might be relevant."

"Leave that with me. You knew Justin was playing in the jubilee cricket match, did you?"

"Yes. So, there's one further thing about Justin I'd like you to find out."

"Yes?"

"The scorer on the day of the cricket match –"

"Liz's husband, Philip, you mean? He's also one of our room

stewards as you may know. Not up to Liz's ability, but then no room steward is. However, so I'm told, the best scorer ever to grace the game of cricket. Did it at County level for a while, so I'm told."

"So, he's unlikely to have made a mistake?"

"Would bet the estate on it, if I were a betting man, which I'm not."

"Could you get a copy of the score card from him?"

"Shouldn't be a problem. Why?"

"I just wonder whether there'd be any record whether the twelfth man was on the field at any stage, for one of the fielders; you know how fielders nip off the field from time to time, to change a bandage, their shoes, do some stretching exercises, toilet break, whatever, and the 'sub' comes on for a spell. Well, the Lord's eleven were fielding, meaning one of them could have nipped off the pitch for a while and..."

"One of them, you mean Justin, don't you?"

"Yes. I mean I know at village level there's often no spare players in a team, meaning a fielder might well, if they're down at third man, chance it and nip off to the toilet, even if their team is down a player for a few minutes. Alternatively, if there was a twelfth man on the day Vaughan was killed, I just wonder whether he was on the field at any time and whether Philip noticed it and recorded it. Equally, Justin may have been the twelfth man and so had a lot of spare time around the pavilion."

"On that last point, from memory, I think grandad was really struggling to put an eleven together. Someone dropped out at the last minute, Tobias Haltwhistle I think it was, meaning I don't think there was a twelfth man for grandad's side. As for whether any fielder nipped off for a few minutes, well, if Philip noticed it, he would certainly have recorded it. So, I'll ask him and we can have a look at the card together, OK?"

"OK," replied Alba as they reached the café. It was reasonably quiet this Tuesday. "I'm buying," insisted Alba as she led Andrew in. "I can recommend their flapjacks," she added.

CHAPTER 15

Battle lines

Mrs Taylor's estate cottage was in the village – just. It was located on the outskirts, with vehicular access being via a farmer's track, which, if you stayed on the track, would ultimately take you to Hurst Farm. The cottage faced farmland and backed on to woodland and, if one were to attribute it to any architectural period, it had more than a hint of the Edwardian style about it.

*

Noon, on this particular Sunday, saw Alba and Andrew Chapman standing on the track, looking at the cottage. The shutters, to the windows, were painted the 'estate colour' of dark green and the tiled roof was somewhat dominated by, what everyone thought was, a slightly too large central chimney stack. However, the wooden framed porch generated a 'welcoming air' to the property for anyone visiting.

"It's very similar to Mr Parker's cottage," observed Alba.

"Yes, the 5th Lord commissioned several extra estate cottages at the same time of a re-building of the Head Gardener's cottage. They're not identical but all in a similar style. Obviously, Mr Parker's cottage is within the grounds up at the Hall but the others are scattered further afield. Did you know, one year an enthusiastic history teacher, from a comprehensive school in East Grinstead, asked for permission to take her class to each of them to tie in with a project she was doing with the children. Or was she a geography teacher? Blow, I forget now. Either way, she moved schools a couple of years later and we didn't hear from her again. Anyway, grandad's fine with me letting you in. He said 'good for you' for wanting to have a look and hoped you'd find something to make the visit worthwhile."

"Please tell him I'm very grateful for being allowed in to have a look. It's rather timely, as I heard from the prison in the week. I've been granted another visitor's slot for tomorrow – meaning I'll be able to update Tom on anything I come across. I have to say, though, I'm not overly hopeful. The police will have gone over everything and neither Tom nor myself can think of anything I should be looking for."

"Never mind," offered back Andrew. "We're here now. So, take your time and satisfy yourself that you've had a proper look. I'm in no rush, well, not today."

"Busy week?" enquired Alba.

"Absolutely manic," replied Andrew. "You will keep my confidence, I know. Further meetings with the Auction House for starters."

"Simon, you mean?"

"Yes."

"Oh dear, poor you."

"They were on top of an all-dayer with our accountants."

"Gosh, you must be drained. You sure you've got the time to be here today? We can leave it and try and fit it in another day, if you'd prefer?"

"No, today's good. It's nice to get away from things – if going round the home of a poisoned woman and her lodger, who is the prime suspect in not one but two murders, is 'getting away from things'. I'm not making light of the tragedy of it all," insisted Andrew, hoping to pre-empt any stern rebuke from Alba for his moment of flippancy. "It's just strange how our human brains compartmentalise things at times, isn't it?"

"Yes," replied Alba, as she undid the latch on the gate. "Sure you've got time? I don't really know how long I'll be."

"Sure. I suggest we look around each room briefly together but then I'll leave you to delve a bit deeper if you want whilst I sort through any post that's relevant to grandad as landlord – personal stuff I'll obviously leave alone."

"As I say, I'm grateful you're letting me in and it'll be good to know you're around if I come across anything."

"Actually," replied Andrew, "knowing how busy my week has been, great-uncle William offered to come in my place today and let you in. He's bored, you see. He's so used to running his own show in Chile, he's desperate to keep himself busy. I think he was keen to come today, in fact. He and Mrs Taylor were getting on, kind of; I'd find them chatting up at the Hall on occasions and I think he offered to stop by here once or twice, to check on work our contractors had to come and do; the electrics, most recently I think. He must have viewed her a bit like a niece, I reckon, for the age gap was much too much for there to have been any romantic connotations to their conversations. I think she too had travelled a bit in her youth, so maybe they shared a 'wanderlust'. Nonetheless, I declined his offer, for today I wanted to come to let you in."

"Am I allowed to say it's much nicer to have you?" Once again Alba wished she could have come up with a better word than 'nice'.

"Front or back door?" queried Andrew as he jangled the keys.

"Strange you should ask. I mean, it doesn't matter does it? Yet, I was mulling it over this morning as I was in the shower, which way we should go in. I reflected, as we would be here to do a job, it would feel appropriate to enter via the back door."

"Back door it is," said Andrew.

The pair of them veered left from the path to the front door. They glanced right, as they passed it, at a vase of dead flowers on the windowsill of the bay window and made their way around to the back door. Andrew unlocked and, knowing the property wasn't alarmed, pushed the door open and then stepped back to let Alba enter first.

*

It was not a big kitchen Alba entered but, with an archway leading into a separate utility room off to her right, it did not feel cramped. A small table, big enough for two people to sit at but no more, was positioned under the window which looked out into the compact garden. The woods, the garden backed onto, however, meant, as Alba looked out, the rear garden was predominately in shade, despite it being just after midday in July. 'Still', thought Alba to herself, 'better than looking at a brick wall or the back end of a supermarket'. As with the view from her own kitchen window, a complex array of bird feeders was visible. These ones, inevitably, were now empty apart from a couple which each had a layer of mouldy seeds – seeds that had proved to be just beyond the reach of even the most agile of birds. Alba was tempted to go and bang out the mouldy contents and top up the other clean ones and instinct told her the bird feed would be somewhere obvious in the utility room. However, she resisted the temptation, thinking it kinder to the birds, who over the last few weeks would have got used to foraging for their own food, to leave them be. 'Tom will look after you when he gets back,' she said to a robin which had landed on an arch of one of the feeding stations – perhaps because it had heard the back door go.

"Mrs Taylor had permission to replace the kitchen, had she wanted, but, as with most occupants of our estate cottages, people make do until units are literally falling off the wall and then call our maintenance team in to fix them," said Andrew, as he cast his eyes over Mrs Taylor's kitchen.

"Oh, it's not too bad, Andrew," replied Alba. "There's a homely feel to it. And it's tidy, too. I doubt the police send people in to tidy up, so Mrs Taylor must have been a fairly orderly person."

"Her office, up at the Hall, was very neat and tidy too," offered back Andrew.

"Very tidy," mused Alba out loud as she cast her eye over the kitchen work tops. The main work top, which was to her left, ran along the wall opposite the arch to the utility room. The sink and draining board were set into the left-hand end, allowing the waste pipe as short a run as possible to the outside drain. Then to the right of the sink was a small section of laminated work top, with a terracotta utensils pot and a bread bin. Then there was a gas hob and then a further, slightly longer, section of worktop. This section of worktop, due to the presence of a double plug socket set into the white tiled wall, was where the kettle, teapot, jar of coffee, sugar bowl and tea caddy were. Five things, which suited Alba's mindset and reminded her of her own hall table, with its two flower vases and three figurines – 'well, that's how my hall table did look until Clive's foot wide faded photograph was added', she thought.

"As I say, very tidy," continued Alba, "look even the kettle and teapot point in the same direction, towards the living room."

The living room was the room they had passed as they made their way around the outside of the cottage to the back door, which had the dead flowers in the vase on the bay windowsill.

"I'll go and remove those dead flowers," offered Andrew.

"Sling them under the front hedge, that'll be fine. They can rot down," suggested Alba to Andrew as he went into the front room. "I'll wedge the back door open, so if you go out the front door, we can let some fresh air blow through for a few minutes. Actually, whilst you do that, I bet the teapot needs emptying. Someone, perhaps a police family liaison officer, has washed up some plates, bowls and a couple of cups, so it's not a health hazard, but I bet they've forgotten to empty the teapot. The tea leaves or bag will be going mouldy by now no doubt."

Being left-handed, Alba didn't even need to swivel it around as she lifted it to take it out into the back garden to empty under a forsythia bush. The tea bags had gone mouldy so she left the pot on the wooden garden bench, intending to wash it out properly before they went.

As she re-entered the kitchen, Andrew was waiting for her, his task complete. "Anything here?" he enquired.

"No, nothing here. I mean, it's really Tom's room I'm keen to look at. I wasn't expecting to find anything here – no bowl of wilted wolfsbane with a note in it saying 'Best wishes Mrs Taylor, from Justin'. Nor am I trying to find," at which point she randomly opened a cupboard door, "a fake baked bean can containing a centuries old document that proves she was the rightful heiress to Hillstone Hall."

"She's welcome to it," said Andrew. "Don't get me wrong, I love the place but…" yet Andrew's voice tailed off. He rubbed the back of his neck and took himself off into the living room.

Alba followed him. She watched him, as he stood between the sofa and the bay window, running his hand along the back of the velvet sofa. A couple of times he stopped the movement, lifted his head, looked completely through Alba and was evidently completely lost in his own thoughts.

Alba had time to take the room in. A velvet sofa, with two matching armchairs, all of which were wearing a bit thin on the arms. A coffee table, with a neat pile of 'Woman's Weekly' magazines, the July edition of the parish magazine and a 'Stately Homes of Britain' book published by 'The National Trust'.

"Bet Hillstone Hall isn't in that book," said Alba deciding to break the silence. "I mean I'm not a betting woman but, if I were, I bet they've only listed their own properties."

She was relieved to see her comment had generated a rueful smile from Andrew.

"As safe a bet if ever there was one. It's odd though, isn't it?"

"What's odd?" asked Alba.

"How a lot of the public do seem to have this mistaken belief that any and every stately home in the country is owned by The National Trust outright or in some other way has accepted their oversight. Still…" at which point Andrew's voice dropped once more.

"Still, still what?" pressed Alba. "You can open up to me, if you'd like. You know I'll keep your confidence – there's no-one else here and there's no-one back at my home whom I'm suddenly going to off-load to the moment I get in, apart from a rather resourceful, if somewhat inelegant at times, jay as he hacks at the fat balls I put out for the tits. You don't have to but I'm a good listener," and with that Alba sat herself in one of the armchairs. Her right-hand found a TV remote wedged down that side and she placed it on the coffee table.

Andrew walked round the sofa and sat on the end nearest Alba.

"Still," he repeated, paused but then added, "we too might have to respectfully submit to them before very long; assuming they'll want to get involved with us – our finances are precarious."

"If you're about to sit there and say 'it'll be easier that way', so help me, I'll lean over and give you a slap. All Tom got, when he said something similar was a stern rebuke and some finger pointing. However, I was in a prison at the time, with a scary prison officer in close proximity, but that's not the case here. So, there's nothing from stopping me from giving you a hefty slap in the face to bring you back to your senses."

Andrew was somewhat taken aback from the directness of his female acquaintance.

"But we'll be broke in about three months. We've lost our housekeeper, we've lost our deputy head gardener, we're lacking volunteers, especially in the gardens as you know. The only profitable part of things is our café but I'll be damned if I have to re-package the whole estate to be a swanky restaurant and an exclusive wedding venue. Plus, although Simon has been having a field day at our expense, we're running out of, quite literally, the family silver to sell. It's getting desperate and desperate times are driving people to desperate measures up at the Hall but they didn't work out as planned," and with that Andrew stood up, shoved his hands into his trouser pockets and headed to the front door. "You have a mooch around," he said to the woman still seated behind him. "I'll be kicking some stones along the track as I need some air and time to think. Give me a shout when you're done and I'll come and lock up." With that, and ignoring the post on the hall mat, Andrew headed out into the front garden.

Alba looked to the heavens and said out loud to an empty room, "As if one crisis isn't enough, suddenly someone wants me to manage two – aarrgh!" She ran both her hands through her hair, sat there a moment longer before deciding to resume her look around Mrs Taylor's home. Encouraged by having found the TV remote, she lifted each of the cushions from the armchairs and the sofa in case she found anything else, wondering whether the police had searched the property at all. Her haul, though, was meagre; a copy of the job description for the position of deputy head gardener, eleven pence in loose change, three coloured paperclips, two purple and one yellow, and a February edition of the 'Radio Times'. 'Not even all the brains in Scotland Yard could make anything from these finds', conceded Alba to herself.

She replaced the cushions, straightened herself up and looked out the window. She watched Andrew pacing up and down, sometimes stopping for no apparent reason, sometimes throwing branches from the track, he had picked up, over the hedge on the other side of the lane. "Tom's my priority, leave Andrew to stew," she said to the still empty room. "You're talking to yourself again Alba!"

'Oh well,' she thought, 'didn't Rowan Atkinson's character 'Blackadder' do the same?' She paused, smiled as she remembered happier times, watching repeats of the comedy with her former fiancé, curled up together on the settee as her open fire kept the winter chill at bay. However, Alba knew she needed Andrew's input and interest if she was to get anywhere in actually helping Tom. With that Alba slung the final throw cushion down into one of the armchairs and, equally ignoring the post, headed out the front door.

Not for the first time in just a matter of a short few weeks, Alba found herself shouting over a hedge to get the attention of the heir to Hillstone Hall. This time it was not with some giddy excitement, rather her shout was confident and assertive. He heard her the first time and walked over.

"Done already? Or is there a problem that will require me to get someone in?"

"No, not finished, not by a long chalk. Equally, no water leak or the like. Look, as private as this lane seems to be, can we go in and talk?"

Andrew nodded and followed her in. This time they headed into the other reception room, the other side of the hall. They sat at a dining table but they both realised the room was never used for such culinary purposes for it was just too far from the kitchen. The book shelves, with their box files and stacked notebooks, and a locked bureau indicated to the pair of them that this was effectively Mrs Taylor's home office. A somewhat dated 'Amstrad' computer on a separate smaller table, against one wall, confirmed, if confirmation was still needed, that view.

"Look," said Alba, "I don't know how bad your finances are and I'm not a business woman who's about to tell you exactly how to turn the profitability of the Hall around. And, whatever desperate measures you or your grandfather have tried I'm not…"

"Grandad's scheme, it involved…" interjected Andrew but he got no further, for Alba was not about to yield the floor.

"As I say, I'm not interested in. Well, not today. I've already said I'm seeing Tom tomorrow, so my focus today is the here and now and what, if anything, I can do to help him. I might add, arguably the best thing you can do for the Hall right now, is to help me to help your deputy head gardener."

Andrew said nothing, knowing Alba was not finished.

"I might further add, though, you might want to offer your volunteers more than 10% off in your café and shop; I know it sounds counter-intuitive, if you're trying to make money, but I'm sure your break-even point is noticeably lower than 90% of the marked price. If you gave your volunteers, who, I might point out, all give so freely of their time, a slightly larger discount I reckon they'd spend quite a bit more. It's like telling the government to cut taxes to raise tax revenues. Plus, your shop should be selling more locally produced preserves – as good as the stuff from Essex is, visitors to stately homes want local jams, marmalades and chutneys. To that end, you should also get in touch with local jewellers, artists and authors. I could go on but…"

"But not today," continued Andrew. "Yes, I get it." He had realised, as he'd listened, that Alba, despite dismissing herself, had probably quite an astute business head on her elegant neck. "OK, Alba, you've got me. If someone is in prison who shouldn't be, then he should be my priority too. I would, however, like there to be a Hall, and therefore a job, for Tom to come back to."

"Meaning?"

"I will be picking your brains some more about business up at the Hall – but not today nor tomorrow but sometime. Deal?"

"Deal," agreed Alba. She took a deep, relieved breath. Her eyes were drawn to movement outside, as a flock of crows, taking fright at something, launched themselves into the air from the oak trees they had been resting in. Once they had flown out of her line of sight, she turned to Andrew and said:

"Right, I'm doing Tom's room next, then Mrs Taylor's bedroom. You look in here and, if you're willing, the loft. We'll do a bathroom each, which will allow us to turn the taps on for a bit to run some water through the pipes. Sound like a plan?"

"Sounds like a plan, boss." With that, Andrew stood up and reached for the nearest box file from the shelf behind where Alba sat, catching just a hint of her 'Lancôme Poême' perfume as he did so.

*

Tom's bedroom, as he had described to Alba, overlooked the woods to the rear of the property. The wardrobe and main, tall, bookcase, were against an internal wall, given the slope of the roof around the dormer window. The bookshelves had three shelves given over to gardening books – Alba read the spines of books by Gay Search, Geoff Hamilton and Alan Titchmarsh, as well as the 'official' Royal Horticultural Society books. On the shelf above were books by Christopher Lloyd and Stefan Buczacki. As she read, that last name reminded her of the miscarriage of justice case she'd spoken to Tom about, Stefen Kiszko, and it renewed her desire, if that were at all possible, to find something that might just help Tom.

On the next shelf up there were piles of gardening magazines. Alba picked up the top one from one pile. It had pieces of paper protruding as bookmarks, with keywords written on them, such as climbing roses, Japanese wine berries or composting. She flicked through it but nothing fell out, apart from the paper bookmarks – which she dutifully replaced in their rightful places. She did the same, but without losing the bookmarks, for the next six magazines in the pile but there was nothing of note. She turned the remainder of the pile around to see, away from the bulging stapled side of each, whether anything had been shoved between them. It hadn't, nor had anything in the next pile, nor between the history magazines on the higher shelves. Lyn MacDonald, Airey Neave, Martin Middlebrook and Richard Holmes were some of the authors for books on the top shelf. Nothing seemed out of place – the history books were on their shelf and the horticultural ones, theirs. Alba lifted six books off at a time but nothing was wedged or hidden behind them, any of them. She even stood at right angles to the bookcase itself and, with one eye shut, looked behind the unit – but nothing was there either.

The wardrobe offered nothing, there was nothing under the rug on the floor and Tom's dressing gown, hanging on a hook on the back of his bedroom door, wasn't covering anything either. Equally, the holdalls under the bed, with his re-enactment gear in, offered up nothing of significance, beyond the clothes themselves, a key ring with a solitary key and some black and white photographs in envelopes of, Alba assumed, Tom's friends in the re-enactment society – she did note that in the top photograph, of a pair of wartime soldiers, one was holding a can of coke and the other had a mobile phone sticking out of a pocket. The bedside chest of drawers equally offered up nothing besides spare toiletries, underwear and some compact discs – the inevitable randomly numbered 'Now, that's what I call music' CD plus albums by Madonna, Lisa Stansfield and Roxette. Alba picked out Madonna's 'Ray of Light' album, opened the case but there was nothing, beyond the CD in question.

The bedside unit had two photo frames on it; one of Tom in his Second World War get up and one of Chloe. Alba picked up the one of Chloe, having realised that it was one Tom must have cut out from the latest quarterly volunteers' newsletter, which the Hall produced, for Alba had seen the same picture in her copy. She turned it over and instinctively folded out the arm on the back so the photo no longer had to lean against the bedside lamp to stay upright. However, having placed it back down, she realised why the photograph had been leaning against the lamp, for the backing panel was the wrong way around for the picture. She folded the arm back in and placed the frame as she had found it. The small occasional 'tub' chair, in the recess to the window, revealed no secrets – even less than the chairs in Mrs Taylor's living room. She felt in the linings of the curtains, ran her hands under the mattress and ran her fingers underneath the radiator, all without yielding anything apart from cobwebs, the seven of clubs from a pack of playing cards and one sock.

Alba sat on the corner of Tom's bed and looked over the room but no inspiration came to her. Hearing Andrew come down from the loft, she called out, "Anything?"

She didn't hear a response, due to the noise of the loft ladder being concertinaed back up, so asked again as he joined her in Tom's room.

"Anything?" she enquired.

"No, sadly not. It's an interesting task we have before us, isn't it? Obviously, we're not looking for forensic clues, are we? A speck of blood here, some human hair there. Further, the police will have gone over this whole place already, so we're not going to find something big and obvious, such as the murder weapon."

"No, that's already been found amongst Tom's gardening tools up at the Hall," stated Alba.

"Yes, I know. I'm just saying that type of 'clue', if you like, the police would have surely found themselves. So, we're looking for something else. I read an autobiography once, by a police officer, a Superintendent I think he was. I remember him writing about looking for things that are just very fractionally out of place. Or, for he put it another way too, looking for something that's hidden in broad daylight. Something that's not obvious, at least not until you really hone in on it – they do say that the best place to hide a book is in a library."

"I know, I know," said a disconsolate Alba. "I've tried that approach, though. For example," and she gestured to Tom's bookcase, "the gardening books are with the gardening books and the history books, every single one of them, are with the history books. Blow, even the ones by someone called Lyn MacDonald are in chronological order – 1914, 1915, Somme and 1918, for even I know the battle of the Somme started on the 1st July 1916. So, I've tried that approach but nothing, I was kind of hoping someone had put a book back on the wrong shelf when they heard Tom or Mrs Taylor returning home."

"Me too," replied Andrew. "The receipts in the box files downstairs are in the right boxes, given their labels, the 'Amstrad' computer, despite its age, works but nothing is sellotaped to the underneath of the keyboard and there are dusty boxes in the loft but no non-dusty boxes."

"Hold on," cried Alba. "The picture frame!"

As she reached for Tom's bed-side unit, a puzzled Andrew said: "Picture frame, what picture frame?"

"Chloe's. Tom's got a picture of her right here. Had a crush on her it would seem. Sam thought they were well suited but that's not relevant right now."

"Sam?"

"Mrs. Rowan's daughter."

"Of course, that Sam. They work together in our café, potential in both of them, especially Sam. So, he's got a picture of Chloe. Sweet but I'm not following."

"Exactly, it's sweet. And yet he couldn't be bothered to put the back on properly so it could stand up by itself? See?" With that Alba demonstrated how the frame had to be balanced against something else to stay upright. "See, it can't stand up by itself. Someone's been tampering with this frame; because if you're going to the effort of cutting out a picture of your 'fancy' and getting a frame to fit, quite a nice frame too, if you want my opinion, surely you'd put the back on correctly, at least at the second attempt."

"He didn't put the back on, did he? At least, not the last time. Someone else has had that back off," stated Andrew unnecessarily for they both already knew that was what had happened.

Alba moved the framed picture over to the bed and placed it face down on the quilt. They both stood over it. Gingerly, one by one, in an almost ritualistic way, Alba turned the tiny brass retaining teeth. Having turned the sixth, she removed the velvet backing, then lifted off a piece of thin corrugated cardboard, then the original piece of paper that told the consumer the size of photographs the frame would take. As she removed that piece of paper, they were down to the reverse side of the magazine article that had Chloe's picture on it.

"What, is that it?" said Andrew on behalf of both of them.

"You saw me do it, nothing. There's nothing else."

"Check everything again."

Alba did. Together they turned each component over, they looked for something written by hand, very faintly, they looked for a set of tiny numbers to indicate a bank account, credit card or telephone number and they looked for indentations on each part to see if something had been written on a now missing part of the whole. Nothing.

"Shall we look again?" asked Andrew somewhat pointlessly after the third scrutiny.

"No, absolutely no point, as we both know. I'll reassemble it and put it back."

Alba did, adding as she placed the picture frame back on the bed-side unit, "Nothing. Yet, someone, I'm sure of it, was looking for a hiding place for something. Maybe they did hide it in there, originally, and then found a better place or opened the frame, realised it wouldn't fit and it's somewhere else."

"Shame," offered back Andrew, "I thought you'd cracked it."

"Me too. We've got to take it as an encouragement, though. Something was here and, if it's still here somewhere in this cottage, we've got to find it. Right, we keep going."

Alba did Mrs Taylor's room. Andrew, with renewed creativity, turned over every coaster on the coffee table in the living room, rummaged in each plastic container of breakfast cereal, which were in the kitchen unit above the bread bin, and stuck his hand in the bucket of wild bird food that was indeed in the utility room. Yet both Alba and Andrew had fruitless searches and it was a disappointed pair who found themselves locking up, rear and then front doors. As they stood by the now locked front door, Alba asked about the single key she found amongst Tom's re-enactment costumes. Once she described it to him, Andrew expressed a certainty that it was for an otherwise spare gun locker up at the Hall, that his grandad had allowed Tom to use, for his re-enactor's weaponry.

A disconsolate pair found themselves walking back into the village along the lane. Alba allowed herself a half smile as she slowly shook her head.

Andrew, sensing her frustrations and increasingly attuned to her emotions, spoke:

"Close, we were close. I know it. Be it in time or space, we were close."

"Close doesn't help Tom but, yes, we were close."

Silence ensued, which lasted until they got to the red telephone box. Then Andrew said:

"Strangely, though, we still don't know what we were looking for, do we? I mean, what would you hide in the back of a picture frame? Money?"

"Tom said he thought Mrs Taylor had money worries," said Alba.

"Yet, if she had money worries, surely she wouldn't hide money in the back of a picture frame in her lodger's room."

"No," conceded Alba.

"A letter, a confession, a suicide note?" suggested Andrew.

"Perhaps. Suicide note seems unlikely; if you're intent on taking your life, by poisoning yourself with aconite, you'd probably leave the note to be found."

"However, if someone wanted a suicide to look like murder, they'd have to hide the note – couldn't risk being found with the note in your pocket. Fact is, I'm sorry to say," said Andrew, "Tom found her. That could suggest he hid the note, in his own room, as he wanted it to look like murder. He tried the picture frame, decided it wouldn't fit or thought of somewhere better, but in his haste didn't put the back on correctly."

"That's possible, I guess. But why?" puzzled Alba. "He knew he'd been interviewed for Vaughan's murder. Why want to make a subsequent suicide look like a murder, if anything he should have made the second murder look like suicide. Plus, as he said to me during the prison visit, why come home from the pub as early as he did and call 999 if he wanted her dead?"

"Aaarrghh," exclaimed Andrew. "My head is spinning. Let's drop the suicide note idea for fear of our brains exploding."

"Yes, let's," agreed Alba. "Tom didn't do it; I just know it."

"So, what would you hide in a picture frame?"

Alba stopped in her stride, toying with her pendant necklace as she did so, touching the miniature Fabergé egg to her lips. She let it drop and, as Andrew watched it bounce against her chest a couple of times, she said:

"Another picture! Didn't you say the best place to hide a book is in a library? So, then, the best place to hide a picture is, or at least was, in the back of a picture frame behind another picture. If someone knew…"

"Someone being Mrs Taylor?" suggested Andrew.

"Perhaps. Someone, possibly Mrs Taylor, knew Tom only had one photo of the girl; he wasn't actually going out with her, was he? Why would he have lots of pictures of her? He's a good lad, he wasn't stalking her, he just had the one picture of her. So, if he only had one photo of her, he wasn't ever going to open the frame up to replace it any time soon. So, her hiding place would be a safe bet. Tom, in his innocence, would have probably told Mrs Taylor if he'd asked Chloe out or invited her around. So, the frame was a safe hiding place for a while."

They were back at the community café and, as they continued to explore their trains of thought, instinctively went in and sat down.

"A safe bet until she thought of somewhere even better," recapped Alba.

After they had ordered a pot of tea and some fruit scones, Andrew spoke for both of them:

"Yes, but where better than a picture frame to, as you perceptively have said, hide a picture? Plus, trying to be objective – although maybe my sugar levels are just dropping – an hour ago we weren't looking for a picture, were we? Something yes but we must be careful that we haven't gone off at a tangent. After all, we're trying to help Tom not look for a missing photograph. No photograph is missing, after all, is it?"

"Isn't it? Vaughan's photo is missing," stated Alba.

"Bloody hell, you're right!" exclaimed Andrew, to the disgust of a pair of elderly sisters at the next table. Their 'tuts' prompted an apology from Andrew, after which he spoke again to Alba:

"So, where would be better to hide his photo – especially as I reckon it would have fitted that frame? There weren't loads of photograph albums in Tom's room nor around the house, were there? I opened up every box file in the dining room come study."

This time it was Alba who offended the elderly women:

"Bloody hell, you bloody fool Alba, you absolute bloody fool. We've got to go."

She jumped up, grabbed her little bag and added, "I've been an idiot. We've got to go back to the cottage, the photo's there, I know it's there." She collided with a bemused waitress, who was in the act of bringing their order over, and headed out the door. Andrew followed as quickly as he could, having apologised to the elderly women once more, and put a £10 note on the waitress' tray.

*

Neither of them were wearing the clothes, let alone the footwear, for running but run they did, away from the café towards Mrs Taylor's. They were past the telephone box when Alba had to drop to a fast walk. Having caught her breath she said to Andrew, who had caught her up:

"There were other photographs in the house, lots of them, I saw them. There were lots of them in Tom's room. In one of the holdalls under his bed, the one with the key to the gun locker, there were bundles of pictures he'd taken of his re-enactment friends. Lots of photographs!" she exclaimed. "I doubt she was hiding it from Tom as such but hiding it from someone else who wanted it; a bloody clever place to hide it. Bloody clever – better even than the photo frame, that's why she switched it."

"I'm confused. Surely a picture of Vaughan would stand out amongst photos of Tom's friends?"

"No, it wouldn't. That's why she was so bloody clever. It will still be there. Whoever she was hiding it from would never have found it – they would have been searching all over the house, in snatched moments, either when distracting Mrs Taylor with pleasantries or when her back was turned for a few minutes. Furthermore, maybe they were still looking for it once they'd poisoned her but Tom's early return from the pub scuppered their final, desperate, attempt. We had plenty of time today, both of us together and we still almost missed it. But it was there – since it was taken from the Orangery it's always been there. First in the frame and then in Tom's holdall amongst his other photographs of his friends in their re-enactment gear."

"But a photo of an old man would have stood out a mile?"

"It wasn't, though, was it? You told me yourself," and the excitement was rising in her voice as she spoke. They made their way back into Mrs Taylor's front garden, Alba continued:

"Front door this time, we've earnt the right to go in through the flipping front door."

Andrew unlocked the door they had so dejectedly shut less than an hour ago. Sweating from the run, she could feel droplets of sweat running down the small of her back. She tucked some hair behind one ear and, with her eyes wide open in anticipation and as certain as she had ever been of anything in her life, Alba stepped in first. She hadn't seen the photograph, not 'seen' seen, but she knew it was there. Maybe, she somewhat bizarrely thought to herself as she ascended the stairs, as Helen came into her mind, that is what her friend's faith was based upon – knowing without having to see.

Just before she entered Tom's room, she turned to Andrew, who was right at her back, and spoke out loud what he had just remembered for himself about Vaughan's photograph, that was missing from the table in the Orangery at Hillstone Hall. He said nothing, letting Alba have her moment:

"Andrew, you told me yourself about Vaughan's photograph. Where it's hidden, it would never stick out to anyone else looking and I bet Tom wouldn't have looked at them that often, they were in a holdall under his bed after all. Plus, he didn't do re-enactment that often, once or twice a year: he was working too hard at the Hall. Furthermore, his eyes were now on a girl in your tea shop. If anything, he would have found Vaughan's photograph sooner, I guess and probably Mrs Taylor guessed too, had she left it in the photo frame by his bed. You told me yourself," and having planted a tiny kiss on his cheek, added "Didn't you? You told me yourself – 'it's black and white for one and it was him in his Sapper's uniform'. Where else would you hide, effectively in plain sight, a black and white picture of a young man in army uniform but amongst black and white photos of young men in army uniforms?"

"Like hiding a book in a library. Let's retrieve it then," replied Andrew.

And they did.

CHAPTER 16

A tight squeeze

It was a much busier visitors' hall this Monday morning, compared to a fortnight previously. Getting through the initial booking-in process, followed by the security checks and the physical searches of both person and belongings had each proved a more time-consuming exercise than on Alba's initial visit. Groups of about five or six adults, plus varying numbers of accompanying young children, were processed at a time and Alba was grateful she had first 'encountered' the prison on an exceptionally quiet day, due to the rain and transport disruptions that had kept, Alba sadly thought to herself, other, financially poorer, people away.

Had this been her first experience, with the standing around, a plethora of noisy bored children, buggies catching the back of her heels on more than one occasion and, worst of all, having to watch solicitors and probation officers jump the queue and be fast tracked through, Alba may well have turned round and walked out, desperate for some fresh air and the calming effect of looking at the sky or a tree or a patch of green grass. Not that she could have done that, even had she wanted to. This was because a pair of large, sliding, probably bullet-proof, glass doors prevented her. The doors were operated in a way to ensure that you were penned in as you came into the prison proper – as if in an air-lock trying to get onto a space station. For, one door had to close prior to the other opening, so any desire by a visitor to simply leave, on their own terms, was now impossible. Unfairly, Alba thought to herself, there must be a prison officer, sitting at a desk with two buttons on it, one labelled 'Door 1', the other 'Door 2', with the sole task, every day, of pressing one and then the other and so on and so on. It was perhaps an unfair thought but the delays, the unpleasant smells, the added pain in one of her heels as she took another whack from, this time, a double buggy, the personal intrusion as she underwent the physical search, all contributed to that sense of 'us' and 'them'; the 'them' being the prison staff – or the 'effing screws', as one woman, another visitor, with the straightest, most bleached hair Alba thought she had ever seen, described them.

Everything about the admission process engendered that sense of division, between staff and visitors, and everyone, well save for those 'professionals' who got fast-tracked, Alba reflected, seemed the poorer for it. She wondered, as she was led across the courtyard, whether the Reverend Quinn had been to visit and what his experience had been.

"You're back then, I see," said the young mum Alba had met two weeks previously at the prison. "I looked out for you last Monday but didn't see you; thought it might have all been too much for you that first time and you'd vowed never to return."

"It was uncomfortable and very intrusive but you adjust, don't you? I wasn't here last Monday simply because the prison didn't seem to process my request as quickly as they did the first time. It was sweet of you to think of me last week, though." Suddenly realising the young woman she was talking to was not this time being dragged along by a young child, forever yanking on his mum's left hand, Alba asked after the child's whereabouts.

"He had a bit of a temperature," replied the woman. "Got my mum to come over to my flat and look after him. He's not too ill, really, but a bit demanding when he's feeling groggy so I didn't think it was fair to bring him today. Think mum was happy to get out of her own house for a few hours, away from that drunken excuse of a boyfriend she's now got."

"Sorry to hear your son…"

"Cory," offered up the mum.

"Cory, that's a nice name, sorry to hear he's poorly," said Alba.

"Oh, he'll be fine. And mum will enjoy fussing over him and watching 'CBeebies' or a 'Disney' video with him – he must have watched 'Peter Pan' every day for a month now."

The conversation stopped, as they made their way through the metal gate that allowed them through one half of the courtyard into the other. Had either of them thought about it, they would have wondered why the courtyard was seemingly so unnecessarily divided into two by an eight-foot-high mesh fence, topped with razor wire, and with a solitary door connecting one half of the courtyard to the other. Unbeknown to them, it was a number of prisoners, escaping from high security prisons in Cambridgeshire and on the Isle of Wight, several years earlier, that had prompted the additional security feature.

Once through, and out of ear shot of the prison officer, Alba spoke once more to her confidant:

"We were lucky today again."

"Yes, but not last Monday; you missed that humiliation. You know, I bet they don't get solicitors to strip."

"No, probably not," offered back Alba before adding, "I wonder whether women vicars are treated like them or like us?"

"Now, there's a thought."

Just as they were approaching the double doors, Alba asked:

"I feel you've taken me under your wing. I'm very grateful for that but it feels awkward for I don't even know your name."

"Jackie, Jacs is fine. Short for Jacqueline – mum had a thing for Kennedy's wife."

"Well, Jackie, as I say, it's been good of you to look out for me; I'm Alba by the way. I'll catch you on the way out, perhaps?"

"Perhaps. But they might let us out in two groups, there's quite a number of us after all, so we'll see. Enjoy your visit with your fellow."

With that Jacqueline was off, to play the role of a loyal girlfriend to her once again incarcerated partner – with the result that, as before, Alba was unable to explain Tom was not 'her fellow' but simply a dear friend who, as things stood, was facing a grave miscarriage of justice. 'As things stood' mused Alba, but this time there were developments to discuss.

*

It was harder to pick Tom out this visit. The hall was much busier this time and he wasn't at the same table – this time being over in one of the far corners. Nonetheless, it was still a green plastic one that he was on and facing three empty red plastic chairs – empty at least until Alba took the middle one and placed her thin white cardigan over the one to her right. She stood up, tried to force her tight jeans down her legs a fraction, in order to lower their waistline, and then sat down once more.

"Jeepers, these are tight," said Alba.

"Don't think I've ever seen you in such a tight pair before, if I'm allowed to say that. I mean, they suit you but didn't think this was really your style."

"Flipping tight, was a minor battle to get them on this morning, I can tell you. My ex bought them, you know, or maybe you don't, in a way a bloke does when he wants his partner to dress in a way that appeals to them, rather than in a way we feel we can express our beauty but without feeling uncomfortable. Should have given them away to a charity shop before now but they're serving a purpose today. That said, they're really cutting in to me. Thank goodness you're sitting in a corner and I'm facing a wall, cause you're going to have to excuse me as I undo the top button at least."

Tom looked away as Alba placed a hand under her navy blue

'Monsoon' top, with its quarter length puffed sleeves, and undid the top button to her jeans.

"Better, but only just," said Alba.

"Why, may I ask?" said Tom, wondering why on earth she'd gone for such a pair of jeans.

Alba dipped her head very fractionally and lowered her voice as she answered:

"I've smuggled something in for you. It has no financial value and, maybe, I could have posted it in to you and it would have got through but I think the thrill of trying to sneak it in appealed to me. It will be a bit creased but I think it'll do until you get home and have your own one to look at again."

Tom didn't need to put any effort into the confused look he was offering back.

"Any 'screws' nearby or watching?" asked Alba, playing into her role with more aplomb and enthusiasm than she would ever have given herself credit for that morning, as she had come up with the idea over her breakfast cereal.

As Tom slowly shook his head, Alba moved a hand to one of her back jeans pockets and surreptitiously removed a folded piece of paper. Keeping her hand above it, she placed it on her leg with her hand still hiding it.

"Don't take it, not yet. They won't keep a camera on us indefinitely, there's too many other things going on behind me I suspect that they'll have to start watching someone else before too long."

"What is it? I thought you were coming for just a friendly visit and, hopefully, update me on anything, not smuggle in contraband. I'm not sentenced yet but it won't look good on my prison record, if I'm already getting caught smuggling money or pre-paid currency cards. I really don't need any extra money, there's hardly a 'Woolworths' tucked away behind the prison library for me to spend it in. I wasn't expecting this of you, Alba."

"Oh, Tom. I wouldn't do anything so daft and risk what few

liberties you have in here or mine. And, I did say it had no financial value, didn't I? Don't worry, even if the grumpiest guard in the prison came over and caught me, I really don't think we'd get into trouble. Might get a ticking off but it's just a tiny little bit exciting, don't you think?"

"No, to be blunt. Being remanded in a high security prison offers me enough 'excitement', if one can call it that. Don't forget I'm being held here as a double murderer – every guard who's read my file and every other inmate who's worth his salt, knows me as the man who stabbed an old man in the back for his valuables and poisoned his landlady because she suspected me. Furthermore, I might add, my risk assessment comes out as very high, both for probability of re-offending and for the level of harm I would cause if I were to commit a further offence."

"Surely not," insisted Alba.

"But yes, most certainly yes. That is my reality in here. Let me summarise what the prison-based probation officer has taken into account when determining my risk levels. I had access to weapons and, although they were kept under lock and key up at the Hall, I had the key. Next, I have had several different addresses in the last three years, then there's my financial situation, which is poor. I have a poor academic record with less than five GCSEs and I have a previous conviction."

"Really?"

"Really. I was done for shoplifting as a twelve-year-old boy; a packet of cheese 'Quavers', a can of coke and a pork pie. All from a corner shop near my secondary school."

Alba, being unsure of what to say in reply, allowed Tom, unprompted to offer an explanation:

"The circumstances were that mum had sent me to school once again with no lunch and I was hungry. It was the first time I'd ever succumbed to the temptation, you know. For weeks, since I'd started at that school, after we'd moved towns after my dad left my mum, I'd resisted the temptation each time I'd been sent to school with no food and no money. But that day, I'd foolishly followed my classmates into the shop and they were buying their lunches and I was envious and very hungry. So, I thought once, just once, I'd chance it. As I say, I was so hungry, it was a cold January day, we'd done cross-country in the morning and I was starving. Cold, starving and having to watch the others buy all they wanted, knowing they'd throw half of it away uneaten or just throw it at one another on the walk back to school. And, as is the way, but everyone in here will say the same, but for me I know it's true, I got caught the very first time I stole. I'm not proud and every month, since I got my first job at seventeen, I've given the value of what I stole to charity, to 'Shelter', 'cause the people they care for could have been me in a different life. Separately, I also got cautioned as a fifteen-year-old for being in a stolen car my friend was driving. I might add, I didn't know it was stolen, I trusted my then friend, but it was easier to accept a caution than to try and argue the case. Finally, we come to my current outstanding charges, which involve two pre-meditated murders, use of weapons and poisons, theft or robbery of high value items and being forensically aware. So, all in all, everything about me says 'high risk'."

"Oh Tom! I'm sorry. I'm not trying to turn this into a game; I'm really not."

"I hope not. There are others on my wing here who are scared of me, or at least of my reputation. Of me! If only they knew how scared I am on the inside or could read the thoughts that go through my head every time I shut my eyes. This is not a game, Alba! It's real and very scary."

"I'm sorry," said Alba once more. "But I've got a fair bit to tell you and I guess I just got a bit carried away with things this morning. I'll take the piece of paper away with me if you'd like but can I show it to you first?"

"OK," said Tom reluctantly. "No guard seems to be heading this way. Be quick then."

"As I say, it's come in in my back pocket. I reckoned a single, folded, piece of paper in these jeans would never get felt during my pat-down in security, it couldn't rustle as everything is so tight, nor does it bulge the pocket, so it can't be seen. The jeans are serving a purpose, I wouldn't wear them otherwise, trust me, and they'll be in the village charity shop, come community café, this time tomorrow."

With that, Alba lifted her hand and slowly unfolded the item and placed it on the table between them.

Tom found himself looking at a picture of Chloe. It was the same picture, in fact, as he had in a frame on his bed-side unit.

"Don't worry," said Alba. "It's not the one from your room. I've torn this one out from my volunteers' newsletter. It's for you, if you want to have it in here with you."

"You could have posted it in, I'm sure of it, even to a high-risk offender like myself," said Tom. "Me, high risk! Can you believe that? The only risks I present are to David's seedlings when he plants them out and I don't see them." Tom paused and studied the face of the girl in the picture once more, before continuing:

"I think she's beautiful. I really should ask you to take the picture away with you, Alba, 'cause I feel I should protect her name or image or whatever you want to call it from the sordid reality of life in here. But I can't. I need something to look at that speaks 'life' to me. Yes, yes, I know," added Tom anticipating a comment from Alba, "I haven't even asked her out yet. I would like to keep it, though."

Tom's head suddenly dropped and he burst into tears.

Through his sobs, his voice heavy with grief, he spoke to the floor but audible enough, just, for Alba to hear:

"Ask her out, I never even spoke to her apart from the odd 'hello'. Ask her out, that's a bit rich given I'm being held in a high security prison. What would she see in me now? What can I offer her, the role of a gangster's doll? Even if, being the good woman that she is, she liked me, would she wait the best part of twenty years to go out with me? Just forget about her, you idiot, and hope she's already forgotten about you."

"Tom," said Alba tentatively. "Tom."

He raised his head slowly and looked at the person sitting opposite him.

"Write to her," suggested Alba.

"Write?"

"Yes, the worst that can happen is that she won't write back. Don't go all 'gushy' in your first letter and don't go and declare your undying love for her but just write to her as a new friend. Tell her about your work up at the Hall, tell her about life in here, ask her about her work in the Hall's tea shop, whatever, just write a nice innocent letter. Then, whatever happens, you can at least tell yourself you've properly spoken to her. And, if you haven't got her address, write to her care of the Vicarage. I reckon you could entrust the safe delivery of any letter to the Reverend Quinn."

"Write, you say?"

"Yes," reiterated Alba. "Care of the Vicarage."

"I could, I suppose."

Tom had just about stopped crying by now. He blew his nose and then rubbed the palms of his hands into his eyes to try and stem the last of the tears. Alba sat and waited. She still had so much to tell Tom but felt she had to wait until he had composed himself a little bit more. She tried to look for a pattern in the magnolia painted breeze-blocks in the wall behind Tom but they offered nothing back. She tried to hone in on the conversation at the next set of chairs along from where she and Tom sat but that seemed to be about the possibility of getting referred to a hostel and a reluctant agreement to sign up to an anger-management course whilst on licence.

Still Alba waited. Finally, Tom said:

"He came to visit me a few days ago, the Reverend that is."

"Really? Good. He promised he would, I'm pleased he kept his promise."

"He was allowed to give me a Bible. Though there's a funny story to that," said Tom.

"Go on," replied Alba, relieved Tom's spirits were lifting.

"Not laugh-out-loud funny but you've got to admire the man for what he did."

"Why, what happened?"

"They wouldn't let him bring a Bible in to start with. When I say 'they', I actually mean one particular guard on the security detail. The Rev said she has a really posh voice."

Alba nodded, then added, "Haven't seen her myself but I've heard about her."

"So, the Rev is forbidden to bring in a Bible for me. Guard alleges he might have sellotaped money into it or hidden something between the hard cover and the first page and re-glued them together or underlined certain words or numbers to send in a coded message or something else or something else. So, she wouldn't let him bring it in." With that, Tom paused for effect.

"And?"

"'And?' you ask. What does the Rev do? He gives her the Bible and leaves the prison, well leaves the prison once they finally let him out the big sliding glass doors that I'm told they have; I came in, in the inside of a prison van, I might point out. Anyway, once out, the Rev goes back to his car and gets another Bible. Same thing happens – she refuses to allow him to bring it in. Same thing happens. He gives it to her and goes back to his car and gets another one. This goes on all morning; it takes time to book yourself out of a visit and then get back in, even once you're through the doors, even if you're an ordained vicar. The Rev even stopped and had a sandwich and a cup of tea in his car at one stage, he was that hungry, but determined to persevere. Apparently, so I've heard from other guards subsequently, by the afternoon, the other guards were taking bets amongst themselves as to how many Bibles they'd get to before one or the other would give up. She kept refusing, as I say, claiming money was glued in or drugs were infused into the pages or whatever and he kept saying she could have whatever money or maps or whatever she found within them so long as she also kept the book itself. Rev said she confiscated twelve before she gave up and allowed him to bring the thirteenth one in."

"Thirteen!" exclaimed Alba.

"Odd thing is," said Tom, "the one he brought me has hand-written notes all over it, between the columns, inside the front cover and has several loose inserts from different church services but that one got through. I don't think the prison officer even bothered to look at it that final time. It's like he's given me his own personal Bible. When he actually got into the hall here to see me, and told me what had been going on, I could tell he was thrilled to deliver it to me in person."

With that Tom, leant towards the table and picked up the picture, folded it back up and put it in his track-suit trouser pocket. "I'll keep this in the inside cover of my Bible. Then she won't be on 'display', if you like, but I'll have the picture out each time I write to her; that was a good idea of yours to write. And, I'll show this piece of paper to the guard on my way back to my wing, so she knows I'm not smuggling anything out of the visitors' hall. Seeing, who's on duty over by the doors I'll be going out through, to get back to my wing, she'll let me keep it. Yes, I'll write to Chloe," said Tom again. "It's a good idea but could you have a word with Sam first?"

"Sam?" enquired Alba.

"Could you ask Sam to tell Chloe she might get a letter from me?" replied Tom. "It'll be less of a shock for her then when she does get it; I reckon she'll benefit from a 'heads-up'."

"Course I will. And I'll tell Reverend to look out for a letter he's to pass on."

"Thanks," replied Tom.

"Right, can I tell you of my progress since I was last here?"

"Yes. Thanks for the stuff about possible Verdun oaks, that's given me something to occupy myself with when I'm allowed in the library. As for your progress, well, I guess there must be some, for you know I had this picture of Chloe by my bed so somehow, but I don't know how you did it, you've got into Mrs Taylor's home. Tell me."

"Well, it sort of started off with apples, sunglasses and then some flapjack."

CHAPTER 17

Role reversal

"So, there it was, in your holdall under your bed in the room you rented from Mrs Taylor," concluded Alba.

"I'm so impressed you've found something. That's brilliant and you're amazing. I hadn't dared hope for anything but, I mean, wow."

Alba allowed herself just a moment to bask in Tom's praise but, being conscious of the time remaining on her visit, was keen to both press on and to keep Tom's feet firmly on the ground – more accurately, the poor-quality carpet tiles beneath his feet. As she looked at the tiles once more, she still couldn't make her mind up as to what 'colour' blue they were – somewhere between 'yucky' blue and 'institutionalised' blue was the closest she could get.

"It must help us, or more accurately you, but…" at that moment, however, Tom cut her short.

"But we don't know in what way. Yes, I understand, Alba. Don't worry, I'm not getting ahead of myself. I'm not going anywhere fast but it must help, mustn't it? It just must!"

"It's got to," offered back Alba. "Got to. A missing picture of a dead man is hidden in the room, cleverly hidden, hats off to Mrs Taylor for that at least, of the leading suspect." Catching Tom's look,

Alba decided to clarify that last comment. "Well, Tom, on paper you are the leading suspect, I'm afraid. So, hidden in the room of the leading suspect by, in almost all probability, the next victim. Therefore, finding it has got to be of significance – we just need to work out the 'why'."

"Why it was hidden there or why it was taken?" queried Tom.

"Why it was taken in the first place and who she was hiding it from. We know why it was hidden there, for it was so perfectly camouflaged. As I say, Andrew and I so nearly missed it."

Tom smiled back at Alba a smile she couldn't quite make out. She raised an eyebrow in search of an explanation.

"Sorry, Alba, just amuses me how you're so informally calling him Andrew. In effect my boss's boss; I have to 'doff my cap' and call him 'Sir' or address him as 'the Honourable Mr Chapman', as you did up until a few weeks ago. Somehow, since then, you have progressed on to calling him simply Andrew. It amuses me, that's all, and I wonder how it'll work when we're all back up at the Hall, in our bothy having our mid-morning tea break and in he comes to ask someone a question. It could be a bit awkward, amusing or embarrassing, not sure which – hence my odd smile. There's something else as well behind my smile, about him, but I can't quite put it into words at the moment but it'll come to me."

"Well, obviously let me know if it comes back to you. Thankfully, you remembered about Mrs Lyle at the very end of my last visit."

"Useful she came and spoke to you," reflected Tom. "And very interesting what she said to you about Mrs Taylor repaying some money to her."

"Not just 'some' money, I think it was quite a bit. She described it as 'quite a lot' and also said, had she had the money earlier, she could have offered Vaughan more for his side garden – not that he'd have sold it to her. He wasn't interested in the money; the garden was his passion."

"Oh, absolutely. And he knew he was really planting it, especially the orchard area, for the next generation. Those fruit trees, he knew, will really only come into their own for the next owner. I wonder who that'll be, since he didn't have any children. Nonetheless, I always sensed he was creating a garden as much for the next incumbent as for himself," said Tom.

"Yes, I had that sensation, too. So, as I say, whatever money Mrs Lyle might have offered, he wouldn't have sold."

"Strange how Vaughan's hopes for his garden will now come to nothing. Guess the executors will put it on the market once they've obtained probate and sell to the highest offer. Do you think," Tom posed to Alba, "that's what Mrs Lyle has planned? She could get the side garden after all, that way? She's got the money now and Vaughan is no longer in her way to stop her."

"It's possible, alright. She definitely has a motive and she did, when talking about how he wouldn't discuss selling it, say something like 'well, look where it got him'. Couldn't quite make out if she realised she'd said that comment out loud or deliberately said it as a boast, almost a confession – said out of a brashness that comes from someone who thinks they've got away with something; that risk-taking behaviour that they've already demonstrated in their murderous acts. Both murders were pre-meditated but, in another sense, they were both highly opportunistic too. Whoever went into the pavilion to kill Vaughan seized an opportunity when they realised no-one else would be in there."

"Because of the fly-past," stated Tom.

"Exactly. He or she intended to kill Vaughan at some stage but, realising everyone was looking up into the sky, for several minutes, realised they had an opportunity there and then. It was a beautifully clear blue sky and we could see them coming in from a long way out. I was next to Neale…"

"Is he that author friend of yours?"

"Yes. Almost finished his book now and he's finally revealed to me the title – 'The Inorganic'. A gooseberry pie loosened his tongue on that front. From what I've read, it's good; there are several themes running through his book, so I think you'll like it too. I'll ask him if he'd be willing to send a draft in for you to read. So, as I say, I was next to Neale as the planes went overhead. But, more accurately, I was next to Neale as Lord Hartfield rang the bell to suspend play and as we stood up to look for the aircraft. However, I couldn't tell you, and I reckon the police, in their investigations into Vaughan's murder, have missed a beat here, who was actually next to me in those moments as I watched the planes come in, roar overhead and then fade back into the sky beyond the pavilion. In those moments I was mesmerised by what I expected to see, what I then could see and what I'd just seen – hoping one of the little planes…"

"You mean the Hurricane or the Spit?"

"Yes, one of those would loop round again or do a roll or something else, to make the fly-past last that little bit longer. So mesmerised was I, as we all were that day, that Neale could have moved away or taken something out of my handbag in that time. Or someone else could have come and stood right next to me on the other side, or someone could have come up behind me and put a knife to my back and I wouldn't have seen anything. What I'm saying is, everyone was where they were when the fly-past started and everyone was where they were when it finished. Where they were in the intervening time, I couldn't say."

"So," added Tom, "someone realised they had a window in which to act. They had wanted Vaughan dead and, in those moments, realised they had an opportunity."

"You almost have to admire their audacity, don't you? It was some sharp thinking. They suddenly realised everyone was looking up, everyone was fixated with something happening in the sky. It was as if time was standing still for them. That person, whoever it was, was so quick-witted, almost trained, to act on what had been in their heart to do, probably, for some time. 'Almost admire', I might stress – for what we're really talking about is some cold calculating heartless person who murdered our beloved Vaughan. I'm looking forward to seeing them in the dock in a courtroom."

This time it was Tom trying to stop the other from getting too far ahead of themselves:

"But Alba, this isn't evidence we're talking about, just speculation."

"Well, yes, I suppose. But it does allow us to cast our net into a smaller patch of the sea, so to speak. For example, Neale was next to me at the beginning and the end of the fly-past. What he did during the fly-past I can surmise, guess and speculate but I can never know. Ditto for the old man, who was sitting on Neale's left. He was there, next to Neale, as the fly-past started and, once it was all over, and I looked around as I sat down, he was there as before. What he did whilst the planes were overhead, I couldn't say."

"Unless, someone had taken a photograph perhaps," speculated Tom.

"Well, yes, that would help enormously. Pity, as we said last time, that you didn't take any of the planes yourself as that would have allowed an expert witness to place you somewhere geographically other than in or near the pavilion. So, without photographic evidence I can never know what the people around me did in that brief period of time. But, and this is a key 'but', I do know what they didn't do."

"How so?"

"Surely we can rule out what's impossible?"

"Oh, I get you," replied Tom.

"Good. So, whether I saw them or not, neither Neale nor the old man could have murdered Vaughan because they could never have got around the pitch and back in time, even if they'd run. Not even Linford Christie could have covered the ground in time. So, our speculation, our discussion around our murderer's opportunism, does allow us to rule many people out of consideration. So, what Neale did during the fly-past, I couldn't say, though he probably watched the planes as I did, but I can say with certainty what he didn't do. So, we can cast our net over a smaller sea, you see?"

"Anyone around the half of the pitch closest to the pavilion, you reckon?"

"I reckon a smaller area than that. Don't forget, as well as getting to and from the pavilion, they had to access it from the road side, stay long enough to ensure Vaughan was dead, stash the medals somewhere on their person or hide them in the pavilion to be retrieved later to be hidden in your locker subsequently and, finally, ensure they hadn't left anything to incriminate themselves. And all done silently. It was someone already close by."

"One of the players, even, following your logic?"

"Possibly," answered Alba. "I had thought of that already. From our reasoning, neither of the batsmen, which now rules David out as well – not that he'd have done it."

"And the 6th batsman, a guy called Andy according to some of the papers my solicitor has sent through to me," volunteered Tom.

"But one of the fielders, perhaps. And because that's a possibility, I've spoken to Andrew about that and he's going to check something out for me. It's…" but Alba stopped talking because of the look on Tom's face. She then added, "Tom, you've got that look again."

"Have I? Sorry, you were saying?" replied Tom.

I've spoken to Andrew about the cricketers. He's going to have a word with the scorer."

"Philip, you mean?"

"Yes, Liz's husband," said Alba. "Apparently, he wouldn't have missed anything with regards to the game, so if one of the fielders, having seen Vaughan go into the pavilion, left the field, so they were in there too at the time of the fly-past, Philip is likely to have recorded it. Andrew's going to get a copy of the scorecard: that might tell us something. You see, I've got my suspicions about one of the cricketers."

"Suspicions? Anything tangible, anything we can take to the police?" asked, almost pleaded, Tom.

"Not yet, not yet," replied Alba almost apologetically. "But we'll see. Let's see whether this scorecard reveals anything and what Andrew finds out from the player's father or mother."

"Are you referring to this bloke Justin, who you were telling me about? He's the son of the auctioneer, isn't he?" queried Tom, which prompted a nod of agreement from Alba and which allowed Tom to continue with his train of thought:

"So, as you said earlier, this bloke Justin moved to the village recently, just so happened to take someone else's place in the match at the last minute, just maybe was fielding near the pavilion – maybe even asked for a particular field placement, I mean, would the captain of the Lord's Eleven really care who stood where, given the team seemed to be a bit of a 'cut and paste' job. Surely, though, it's just co-incidence. Unless…"

"Unless what?" enquired Alba.

"Unless, Justin orchestrated someone having to drop out. Do we know what happened for that someone else to drop out?"

"Andrew said someone had to drop out because a horse of theirs went lame. I guess it is possible Justin got to the horse, as a way of 'getting' to one of the players. Possible but very very unlikely – after all, what odds would you get for such a sequence of events to work out exactly as you need them to, to enable you to play in a cricket match at the last minute? Very very unlikely."

"Not impossible, though," stressed Tom.

"No," agreed Alba. "Not impossible. Plus, such high-risk stakes would seem to fit the character of the murderer. Which keeps Justin in the frame, in my opinion. Especially because of what Jim was telling me about Vaughan paying his gardening wages six months upfront. So, if that time frame fits in with when Justin moved to the village, Justin becomes a real candidate. It's all conjecture at the moment but that's what I've asked Andrew to look into for us."

"So," summarised Tom. "We have Mrs Lyle and now Justin, the auctioneer's son – the auctioneer who's married to Vaughan's ex-wife. We have motive for one, possibly the other, depending on what the

Honourable Mr Chapman comes back to you with. But something is still not fitting there but I still can't work out what it is that's troubling me – odd thing is, I keep thinking of Christmas mince pies each time you mention the name 'Andrew'. I think that's why I'm smiling but, for the life of me, I don't know why one is making me think of the other. Still, Mrs Lyle and Justin, motive? Yes and maybe. As for opportunity? Yes, for both. Furthermore, both could have placed the medals in my locker on a subsequent day – Mrs Lyle obviously comes up to the Hall most days to deliver the papers to the café and I'm sure Justin could have accompanied his father on a visit. Then there's Mrs Taylor and how she links to either."

"Obviously, we can link Mrs Taylor to Mrs Lyle due to money." At which point Alba paused, and entwined the slack of her necklace around one finger. As she let the necklace go, she reflectively said, "You know, I almost hope the motive for all this isn't something so base as money. To think Vaughan's life might have been stubbed out simply for cash, to me feels an extra insult. So crude; for me, I wouldn't murder anyone just for money, it would be a real act of the heart for me."

"Careful Alba, please be careful with what you say."

"Sorry Tom. So, sticking with money, Mrs Taylor had borrowed money from Mrs Lyle. We can probably surmise that it was not for completely legitimate purposes, otherwise she'd have gone to her bank. She then, between Vaughan's death and her own, was able to repay Mrs Lyle in full. I guess, if she murdered Vaughan for something of even greater financial value than Clive's medals, it allowed her to repay her debt and then, out of guilt, committed suicide. But that doesn't feel quite right, even though because neither you nor I saw her at the cricket match doesn't mean she wasn't there. But, if it was suicide, surely she'd have left a note. Plus, would someone intent on leaving this earthly world be so intent on doing the washing up before they collapsed?"

"I doubt she'd have done the washing up. That was her least

favourite chore, normally she left it to the morning. So, I doubt that would have been her priority in her last moments."

"Meaning," said Alba, "we're back to our forensically aware murderer – the person who wiped the prints from the medals before placing them in your locker."

"Could Mrs Lyle and Mrs Taylor have been in it together?" suggested Tom. "If Mrs Lyle was desperate to get her money back and keen to get Vaughan out of the way, and clearly had a hold over Mrs Taylor, she could have enlisted Mrs Taylor to help and then poisoned her to keep her silent."

"Could be. But my hunch is still on Justin. Something happened or changed earlier this year, which put Vaughan on edge, made him uneasy, and that may fit with Justin's arrival to the village. Whereas, Mrs Lyle has been around a few years now. I really need Andrew to get back to me," concluded Alba.

"Ah yes, Andrew. Andrew," repeated Tom. "You've made a lot of progress with him. It's been a good job he's been around."

There was something in Tom's voice that put Alba on edge. There was a discrepancy between what Tom said and his tone, between what he said with his mouth and what his eyes said, between what Tom said and what he made Alba feel.

"Andrew," said Tom once more. "I've remembered why each time you've mentioned him today I've thought of mince pies. Have you ever heard of 'Operation Mincemeat'?"

Alba shook her head, allowing Tom to continue:

"It's a somewhat innocent name for what was an ingenious Second World War operation by British military intelligence to convince the Germans that the Allies were not intent on invading Sicily, even though they were and did in July 1943. What MI5 did, in April 1943, was to put a dead body in the sea near the Spanish coast, dressed as an officer with the Royal Marines and with a brief case attached to him, full of papers about Greece being the target not Sicily. Via Spanish contacts, the Germans, as the British hoped, got their hands on everything. However, unbeknown to the Germans, the officer, his personal effects and, most importantly, the papers were all fake. The deception worked – worked to such a degree that the Germans actually moved troops away from Sicily. You're looking at me blankly Alba, which I understand, as I haven't explained the relevance yet. The relevance is in the act of deception – the convincing of another that what they are seeing is real when in fact it is fake. It is kind of an art form when it is done so expertly, so seamlessly, so naturally that the other party never knew, never suspected they'd been 'played'. That hasn't helped, by the look on your face," conceded Tom.

"Not really," admitted Alba.

"What I'm saying is," pursued Tom, "whether you get what I'm saying or not, and irrespective of whether or not you've read Ewen Montagu's book, you've kept telling me how much progress you've made recently."

"Well, I have," insisted Alba, feeling slightly unsettled.

"Yes, but it seems to be because you've happened to bump into Andrew quite a bit this past week or so."

"I've been very fortunate, I accept. I was trying to get hold of him up at the Hall but it just so happened I've bumped into him in the village instead. He's been very helpful, he's allowed me into your home, he's looking into Justin for us, he's been a good sounding-board as I've discussed your wrongful arrest with him. But I concede I've been fortunate to catch him when I have. Each time I've just bumped into him."

"But have you?" challenged Tom. "Have you bumped into him? Or has he 'bumped into you'? He seems to be popping through doors, there at telephone boxes or in pub gardens, just when you need him and, from how you've described him, he's been ever so friendly."

"Friendly, attentive, accommodating and patient – it's been good to have him around. I don't get your point Tom. Andrew has been a real asset, so what's your angle?"

"I'm just frightened for us, especially though, for you. As I remembered that deception by military intelligence, I suddenly saw all of your progress in a very different light. Put bluntly, I fear he's 'playing you' – he's using you to get what he wants."

"No," insisted Alba. "No, it's not like that, he's not like that. He's lovely and it's been lovely to spend time with him. It's been so lonely being by myself, so so lonely. Now, though, Andrew is, maybe just maybe, beginning to fill my emptiness. I can talk to him and we've shared our discoveries together of late. It's been lovely."

"Alba, we're friends," asserted Tom.

"Absolutely, for life," replied Alba.

"So, don't hate me for what I'm about to say and we remain friends, promise?"

"Promise," but Alba's voiced wavered as she said it.

"He is 'playing you'. I genuinely think there's a very real chance he's 'playing you'. He's after something or he's trying to hide something, I'm not sure which, but, it seems to me, he's using you to get what he really wants."

"No," said Alba. "He's not. He's been so sweet and helpful and, well, I've liked being around him. There's nothing underhand about him. He's been lovely to me."

"He's put a smoke screen around you, Alba. He's clouded you with attention, humour and the fact he's the heir to the Hall but..."

"No, Tom, there is no 'but'. So, drop it, do you hear me."

"I can't and I won't. I have to protect you, allow you to see through the smoke I think he's placed around you. He's using you. There, I've said it. He's using you. Remind me when you first came across him. I know, I might add, you've already told me but remind me. See if you suddenly see it as I now see things; because prior to my remand I doubt you'd ever spoken to him, you definitely weren't on first name terms and definitely weren't buying him cakes in the village café. When did it all change, Alba? When did Andrew enter your life?"

"He first spoke to me properly up at the Hall. It was the day after the funeral. I was running an errand for 'Bic', I got upset in the Orangery and Andrew came along and he comforted me. That's all. I still don't see what you're getting at."

"You've overlooked the key bit. You told me earlier what you were doing in the Orangery, which was?" prompted Tom.

"Collecting Vaughan's photograph. It was missing though."

"But you told Andrew what you were looking for?"

"Of course."

"Don't you think it a bit odd? He's never spoken to you before and all of a sudden, when you tell him you're looking for Vaughan's photograph, he's all interested in you – walks you around the grounds, comforts you, as you say, and then spends time looking for it with you back in the Orangery. Bit odd, don't you think? He keeps making out to you the Hall is financially broke and yet he spends his time walking a volunteer around the grounds and then helping her in an errand the Head Gardener has delegated all the way down, and no offence here Alba, to a volunteer. Bit odd don't you think?"

Alba said nothing.

"I remember," Tom continued, "the 'great unveiling' of all those photographs, I think it was a week you were visiting your mother. Andrew had even got a local reporter in to cover the event – he said, as a way to generate publicity for the Hall. He insisted all the heads of department were present one evening for the photo shoot. Trying to be accommodating, he'd given us a choice of evenings. No-one cared what evening it was but I was cheeky enough to say, everything else being equal, could it be the Wednesday and not the Tuesday, as I enjoyed my ritual of going to 'The Sun and Moon' on a Tuesday for pie-night. I remember the look on everyone's face; on Andrew's, Lord Hartfield's, the great-uncle's, Mrs Taylor's, on the other two heads, as I made my request in this 'heads of department' meeting. There I was, this scruffy gardener, covering for Mr Parker, who was off with appendicitis, telling all these big cheeses when I was available. Still can't believe I had the cheek! Several times, over the next few weeks,

I heard the great-uncle and Mrs Taylor talking, I think, from the few words I could make out, about the photographs but, whenever they saw me, they clammed up. Reckon they were still having a joke at my expense. Anyway, there we all were one Wednesday evening, in the Orangery, being photographed alongside the table with all those photographs on."

Tom paused, thinking Alba might say something, anything. She didn't, allowing Tom to fill the vacuum:

"Right, we've established Andrew spoke with you once he knew you were looking for Vaughan's photograph. When did you next see Andrew?"

"In the village the next morning, outside 'Stapleton's'," said Alba.

"That's where you spoke but where had he been, when you called after him?"

"Oh, in Vaughan's home. Nothing to that, though, he said he'd got a lift with his great-uncle, who was returning stuff from Vaughan's locker, as he needed to speak to Mrs Lyle."

"Is that the same Mrs Lyle who goes up to the Hall every day to deliver the papers for the café?"

"Yyy, err, esss," replied Alba hesitantly.

"But he didn't think to speak to her on any other day of the year? Rather, the day after he discovers someone is also looking for Vaughan's photograph, he has to go into the village to talk to Mrs Lyle – even though he doesn't speak to her at all that day. Probably he never intended to speak to her that day, he just had to lie on the spot to account for his presence, what with you having caught him in Vaughan's home."

"But he was only in Vaughan's home because he was accompanying his great-uncle," insisted Alba.

"The great-uncle told you that did he?" quizzed Tom.

"No, actually Andrew did. His great-uncle William just excused himself and went into the shop and then drove back to the Hall."

"Perhaps the great-uncle was under instruction from the heir to the manor to help him look for something or retrieve something or replace something in Vaughan's home and 'excused himself' because he knew they'd been compromised. When did you next see Andrew?"

"Again, at the village shop, about a week later. We bumped into each other."

"So once again, right by Vaughan's property. And you do know, like his grandfather, Andrew worked for military intelligence? Well, Andrew did until something happened whilst he was serving out in Kosovo in the nineties. If anyone could make a deliberate collision look like a casual bumping into someone, it would be Andrew Chapman, ex-intelligence officer, schooled in the dark arts developed out in the field during the break up of Yugoslavia."

"But he helped me find Vaughan's photograph, in your very own bedroom, Tom," insisted Alba.

"Did nothing about that visit strike you as odd? It did me, as you relayed it to me at the beginning of your visit today? How keen he was to dispose of some dead flowers from another room, whilst you were in the kitchen? Makes me wonder what he was putting back or moving before you noticed something out of place. How he said his focus was on sorting through Mrs Taylor's post whilst there but he never even picked it up off the door mat. How, on your walk away from Mrs Taylor's home, having initially failed to find the photograph, he was encouraging you to stop thinking about finding a photograph but on something else Mrs Taylor might have hidden in my room."

"But when I worked out it was a photograph that had been hidden, Andrew was as excited as me and we ran back to the cottage together."

"Did you? Might he not have been running after you, realising he had to keep tabs on you?"

"Tom, you're twisting things. It's all conjecture; you're making something out of nothing. He likes me. Plus, he's helping me, helping you in fact, I might point out. He's getting back to me on Justin's role in all this, after all."

"Alba, don't you think he could have spoken to the scorer by now and the auctioneer, Simon, and got back to you?" Does none of what I've said resonate with you and make you think we've been looking in the wrong direction? We've been focusing on village life, perhaps we should be focusing on life up at the Hall?"

Alba didn't know what to say. She scuffed her toes against the horrible wiry carpet tiles beneath her feet and felt her world was once again being torn away from her. Finally, unable to offer up anything else to say, Alba said:

"He's offered to take me riding, you know?"

"Has he? Well, I hope you're not found with a broken neck afterwards, with only Andrew for a witness, claiming your horse bolted or that it reared up unexpectedly and threw you."

A dejected, forlorn thirty-year-old woman sat opposite Tom and he was conscious of the bizarre role-reversal the pair of them now found themselves in – with Alba having come in so excited and energized by her progress and Tom dejected and alone, whereas now it was Alba who was being suffocated by a sense of loneliness and confusion whilst Tom was full of clarity and compassion for the person opposite him. Tom spoke once more:

"I hope I'm wrong. I so hope I am but I couldn't not say what has come into my mind this morning. We're a family and we look out for each other, even if in the short term it might hurt. You do understand, don't you?"

If one can nod quietly, Alba nodded quietly and then said:

"I guess I can see where you're coming from. I can't really say anything more about it now, it's too raw. I'll have to think about it when I get home. But I think you are wrong. You've just got to be wrong."

"Well, at least promise me you won't go horse-riding with him until the real murderer has been caught."

"Promise," replied a dejected Alba. She then added, "I wish they had a vending machine in here. I really could do with a cup of tea right now."

"You really don't get prison life, do you Alba? Inmates in here from all the different wings and you want to introduce boiling water. It's not just us versus the prison officers, you know. There's as many grudges between prisoners themselves, sometimes based purely on which wing they are on, as between prisoners and staff. So, boiling water, not a good idea."

"I just fancied a cup of tea, that's all. Which reminds me I left Mrs Taylor's teapot out in her back garden. I did find the TV remote, though. It was down the right-hand side of one of the armchairs."

"Oh, the remote. She was always losing it. I kept saying one day I'd Sellotape it to her right hand so she wouldn't lose it again. Bless her, she'd sit in her favourite chair, right-hand resting on the remote, channel-hoping, flicking between her soaps and her quiz shows. Why, by the way, did you decide to take her teapot out into the garden?" asked Tom.

"I emptied out the mouldy teabags; whoever had last tidied the kitchen and done the washing-up had forgotten to empty the pot. I guess police family liaison officers can't get everything right," replied Alba.

"I doubt the liaison bod did the washing-up. There was no immediate family returning to the home, meaning, from stories I've heard in here, the police would have left the place as the forensics team left it. She had a nephew. He was her closest family but was, from what I could make out, a 'black sheep'. Sadly, I think he'd got caught up with drugs as a teenager and could never break the habit. I think Mrs Taylor tried to help where she could, even paid off all his debts once. She spoke about it just once, she said to me that if she cleared all his debts it would give her nephew the chance of a clean start. Not sure where she raised the money from. It helped him for a while, a few months I reckon, but he relapsed and he quickly owed his dealers money once again. He stayed a couple of times, whilst I was lodging with her, but I fear both times were when he had to 'lie low', as people were looking for him, as opposed to a love for his aunt, despite what she had done for him. I reckon I last saw him in the spring – I recall he was talking about some yellow flowers in the garden and asking what they were called. I thought he was commenting upon the forsythia, which was in bloom, but it was daffodils he was referring to. It shocked me that someone didn't even know what a daffodil was but I guess, if you're brought up in a tower block in Portsmouth, horticulture probably isn't your thing."

So engrossed had Alba and Tom been in their conversations they hadn't heard the previous announcements from a prison officer as to ten and then two minutes of time left on the visit. This meant, when the officer called time on the visits it caught both of them off guard.

"Be careful out there," Tom said to Alba as she stood and picked up her cardigan.

"I will. And I'll think about what you've said but I still think you're wrong. I'm due back at the Hall tomorrow, for a day's volunteering."

"I hear Sally's formally covering for me up at the Hall," said Tom. Then, seeing Alba's awkward expression, he added:

"It's alright, she wrote to me at the end of last week to explain and to stress it was only whilst I was unavailable and she will be happy to drop back into the ranks upon my return. It was nice of her to write, not that she needed to. After all, someone had to cover my role – guess I'm just surprised, between you and me, that 'Bic' didn't ask you, Alba."

Not wanting to detract from Sally's moment, Alba simply replied:

"I think she'll do an excellent job until you get back."

Alba suddenly saw Jackie, six tables away, and she returned Alba's look. Keen to leave the prison with a friendly face, given the emotional turmoil Tom had left his companion with, Alba sought to wrap things up as quickly as possible:

"Being back up at the Hall tomorrow, I'll see what poking around

I can do and I'll see if I can chance across Philip, the scorer. If we can make some progress on the auctioneer's son Justin, I'll be happier. I know you didn't do it, Tom, and I'll keep digging until we get there."

"Thanks, Alba, but please stay safe."

"Will do and I'll be in touch."

Alba had got two tables away before Tom remembered something of importance and called out to her:

"Alba! Alba!"

Tom heard Alba say 'hold on Jackie' before turning back.

"Yes? Remembered something else of significance?" she asked.

"Kind of. You ought to do your trouser button up."

"I'd forgotten. Gosh, thanks, Tom," replied a relieved Alba.

As Tom watched her walk out of the visitors' hall, chatting to a younger woman as she did so, he thought to himself, as he put his hand to the photo in his trouser pocket, 'She's not Chloe but, I have to admit, she does look good in those jeans'.

CHAPTER 18

The Music Room

"Morning Alba," said Helen and Sally in unison as Alba entered the little gardeners' hut, tucked away as it was, beyond the rose garden.

"Morning," replied Alba as she placed her bunch of keys and rucksack in her locker and retrieved her volunteer's card, lanyard and day bag. She looked at Tom's locker, to the left of hers, and then Vaughan's, off several to the right. Both remained open and empty; both silent witnesses to absent friends.

As Helen passed Alba a hot drink, Alba filled her two friends in, following her visit to Tom the day before.

Concluding her summary, Alba asked whether either of them had seen Liz or her husband Philip this Tuesday morning, given they frequently turned up at the same time as them. Neither Helen nor Sally had, nor, they added, the tail-end of the previous week and wondered whether they were on holiday. Therefore, when Sally offered up the tasks for the early morning session, Alba didn't bother to ask for any in sight of the Hall itself, as a way of facilitating her happening across Liz or, more significantly, her husband. As a result, Alba ended up with the tasks of checking on the pheromone traps in the orchard and fruit thinning of the apple trees and Helen was given edging the grass in the sunken garden. David was already dead-heading in the rose garden, as Sally had also tasked him with a stint harvesting in the kitchen garden. Finally, Sally had reminded the others that today, according to a memo from the chef, it was Sam's birthday in case they bumped into her at any stage.

*

The orchard was the remotest corner of the gardens. Although Lord Hartfield owned the woodland beyond the orchard, the tenanted farmland beyond the woodland and part of the village itself, the orchard was, arguably, one of the loneliest parts of the actual gardens to work in. More so, when working by oneself; on a par only with tending the beds at the entrance gates on the main road, a mile and a half from the Hall itself. At this time of year, late July, the orchard felt remoter still; it was without the glorious blossom of spring or an abundance of apples waiting to be harvested, either of which enticed visitors to bother with this far-flung part of the garden. Even in the winter months, due to the trees being bare, and therefore the space being more open and airier, one felt less cut off, than Alba did today, from the rest of the grounds.

During the morning, one or two visitors did venture into where Alba was. They consisted of one anxious father looking for a lost four-year-old daughter, a solitary American tourist, well-spoken and polite, thrilled to be in the land of his fore-fathers, who asked after the age of the trees in the orchard, an elderly couple who were evidently intent on walking the orange route, as laid out on the visitors' map, and, lastly, a middle-aged man and a woman walking slowly hand-in-hand. Alba was convinced this couple were not husband and wife. She had seen them as part of a group of four on numerous other occasions throughout the year around the Hall; most recently a few weeks ago when she'd been working on the climbing hydrangeas by the tea shop and watched as the foursome had said their 'goodbyes' and parted as different couples, to the pairing she now saw, at the end of their visit. Here in the orchard, Alba couldn't help but observe the couple stop, turn and face one another. As the two kissed, Alba looked away but couldn't help but think how relaxed, happy and alive they looked compared to the other times Alba had observed them in the company of their legitimate spouses. The noise of Alba's ladder, as she readjusted its height, alerted the couple to her presence. Ending their moment of intimacy, they opted to return to the part of the gardens laid out as a wildflower meadow, leaving Alba once more alone.

*

"Sally said I'd find you here," said Andrew as he strode across the orchard towards Alba. "How did you get on yesterday? Did you get to see Tom and what did he think of our find?"

Alba said nothing initially, as she refilled a further trap that kills the male codling moth. She was several rungs up the ladder but as she came down, Andrew was at the ladder's side, a hand held out for Alba to take if she wanted it for balance. She didn't take it.

"What did he say? Bet it was a real encouragement for Tom," continued Andrew.

She relayed sections of her conversations with Tom. She said how Tom was not getting carried away with the progress she and Andrew had clearly made, how pleased he'd been to have a visit from the village's vicar and that they'd spoken of Mrs Taylor. Alba omitted Tom's concerns over Andrew's possible involvement. Then for the first time ever in her gardening life, Alba tapped the base of her spine to check that her red handled secateurs were still there in their holster, not out of a sense of 'oh, I hope they haven't unclipped themselves, I must go and find them', but out of a real sense of 'have I got any kind of weapon on me to protect myself?'

She found herself unable to move her left arm and her hand continued to rest on the red handles. She hoped it was a more natural look than it felt; it felt very defensive and unnatural.

"It was good to see him and he's bearing up," summarised Alba.

"But," suggested Andrew. "I sense there's something not quite right. You seem tense."

Finally, Alba moved her arm and put it to her neck and massaged the base of her skull. She sought to completely change the topic of the conversation:

"Just my neck, probably. Lots of looking up, craning my neck, funny angles you adopt when working off a ladder. I'll be fine in a few minutes. How are you, Andrew? Any progress on things here at the Hall since we spoke at the weekend?"

"Well, Simon is due here once again. He's getting one more sale out of us. We were hoping we wouldn't need to; you may even remember me saying a while back how we'd made some good prices and were hoping to hold onto the Italian carvings. However, after a further meeting with our bank last week, it now seems we didn't make enough. This is because our projected revenue has fallen. You see, visitor numbers have dropped off – we have a lack of volunteers to keep the Hall and gardens up to 'spec' and, perhaps more importantly, there's the loss of our 'good name'. That's due to these murders and all that comes with such acts – police cordons, helicopters, dogs and patrol cars – it's all been too much of a feature for too long. Not conducive to a 'happy visitor experience' would be a polite way of putting it. It seems people who were once our repeat visitors are prepared, at present, to travel further and go to Winston Churchill's home, Vita Sackville-West's gardens or Rudyard Kipling's place. And, before you say it," said Andrew, noticing a look he'd seen before in Alba's eyes, "I am not placing the financial viability of the Hall above the deaths of two people nor Tom's confinement to prison. But you did ask after things here at the Hall and everything that goes on up here has a monetary aspect to it."

"Yes, I did," conceded Alba. "Well, don't let me keep you, if you need to see him." With that, she relocated her ladder under the branches of another tree.

"Are you sure you're alright?" enquired Andrew. "You don't seem your normal self today. If your neck is troubling you, please stop. I can walk you back to the gardeners' restroom or I could even find you a quiet room in the Hall if you'd like. I'll ask one of our two maintenance men to come and put the ladder away."

"No, that's kind but I'm fine really and I don't want to let Sally down. She's trying her hardest to keep things on track in the garden. I guess I'm missing Vaughan and find this talk of money depressing," replied Alba.

"No, I insist," stated Andrew. "If you're not feeling quite right, the last thing I can allow, as your boss, is to leave you here climbing ladders all by yourself. Come on, I'm walking you to the Hall and will not take 'no' for an answer."

As Andrew radio-ed through to the duty maintenance man to come and collect the ladder and other bits, Alba found herself struck by a sadness, in that moment nibbling at her heart. A sadness which had been prompted by Andrew simply referring to himself as her 'boss'. Somewhere within herself she realised she had, in that moment, hoped he would have described himself in another way towards her – any other way, she didn't really know which, just some way that spoke of something between them that was 'other', other than boss and volunteer. In the next moment, though, she could hear all of Tom's concerns once again. She put her fingertips to her temples, in an attempt to calm her thoughts and suppress what felt like blood rushing round her brain at a million miles an hour.

"You're definitely coming with me," said Andrew as he watched Alba, fearing she was about to faint.

Collecting her bag, he led her out of the orchard, round the edge of the meadow area and back towards the main lawn as they headed towards the house.

*

"I find talking of money depressing, too," said Andrew *en route*. "Problem is, I can't afford not to at the present time. We have to sell some more artefacts but, in trying to do so, we've hit a further snag. You see, Hillstone Hall has featured in one too many sales of late. Simon really should have advised us on this point. Although we, and therefore Simon as well through his commission rates, have made good money from our earlier sales, we've lost our uniqueness. It wasn't that the lots in the earlier sales were any better than now, it was the fact that Hillstone Hall and the Chapman family were a 'new name' amongst the sellers and consequently a different piece of history for buyers to chase after. That newness and difference has ebbed away now. As I say, we've featured in one too many sales and all with the same auction house. We should have played 'a longer game', been less loyal to one auctioneer, even though the working relationship started so well and good money was raised. Separately, possibly we should have even spoken to another bank about re-structuring our debts as well. But time and tide wait for no-one and time is very much against us now; we're on a train and it's too late to change drivers. Nor can we get off until it either arrives safely at a station or crashes horribly down an embankment. It's proving to be a fraught journey. As I said on Sunday, we've got about three months to turn things around. Things are desperate up here, which has prompted one or two desperate actions by people. And to make matters worse, I've got to meet with Simon in half an hour. Even so, I can make you a cup of tea, get you settled and still get myself ready to meet with Simon."

Not getting a response from Alba, who remained lost in her thoughts, Andrew lapsed into similar silence.

*

As they walked across the lawn, Alba thought once more about what Tom had said yesterday. She then recalled she had spent all evening pacing up and down her hall, having hardly touched the salad she'd prepared herself for tea, and that she had lain awake half the night, partly due to the heat, but mostly because of what Tom had said. There was logic in what Tom had said, perhaps there was 'a case for Andrew to answer' and yet, and yet, mused Alba.

Then, as they progressed through the gardens, though maybe just maybe because she was able to look at Andrew as he walked her up to the Hall itself, her brain ceded her dilemma to her heart – or perhaps, more poetically, her knowledge gave way to wisdom. She challenged herself to remember that William Hazlitt quote. She did so and it scrolled through her mind:

"The seat of knowledge is in the head; of wisdom, in the heart. We are sure to judge wrong, if we do not feel right."

In that moment, as they approached the Orangery, Alba decided Tom was wrong. So certain was Alba that she virtually called out to Andrew, despite the fact that he was at her side:

"Sorry, Andrew. Lot going on, as usual, for both of us." She paused, having realised she couldn't tell him of Tom's worries, but was desperate to not lapse back into silence. She therefore asked:

"So, are the Italian carvings going this time, then?" as she gestured towards the Orangery, where the carvings were still housed.

"No, actually. As they were listed in a previous sale, we didn't want to create the impression we are desperate to sell them at any price, given they went unsold last time. This sale is more on family papers and books. Some of grandad's papers are being sold in fact. Some of his wartime correspondence speaks of the Dieppe raid and what with it being sixty years since the raid took place, Simon thought it would be a timely sale. Simon is really gearing his auction house up to these World War Two sixtieth anniversary events; Dieppe and El-Alamein this year, the raid on the Dams next year, for that he's very much after Bomber Command memorabilia, and then gearing up to the anniversary of the end of the war in Europe in three years' time."

"Are you seeing him by yourself?" queried Alba.

"Yes, grandad's not feeling too good this week. You don't need to worry, though, you won't have to come in and hold my hand. I can look after myself."

Alba remembered what Tom had told her about Andrew's time out in the Balkans but opted for a more innocent reply:

"That's good to hear. Plus, I really ought to be returning to your orchard for the rest of the morning and getting on with what Sally has asked me to do."

"Sally might be happy with that outcome," joked Andrew. "But not me," he added, more seriously, "I was worried for you. You're definitely coming in and sitting down for a bit."

"Whilst I've got you for a moment then, can I ask you something?" said Alba.

"Of course, you can."

They had, by now, stopped on the terrace, which was, as if to reinforce Andrew's earlier comments about reduced visitor numbers, devoid of anyone else.

"You've obviously been sharing a lot of your financial worries with me of late. I'm just intrigued about something you've referred to a couple of times."

"Really, what?" replied Andrew.

"On Sunday, when we were at Mrs Taylor's home, and again today, when summarising your financial situation, you've succinctly summarised it 'desperate'."

"It is."

"I don't doubt. Each time, though, you've then said it's prompted people to take desperate actions. I was just wondering what you mean."

"Have I? I hadn't really realised."

"You have," insisted Alba.

"Well, if you say so. I'm happy to tell you, since you've asked and there's no-one around. However, don't think it's got anything to do with Tom. Saying that, it has, but not in the way you might hope. Plus, to be clear, I'm not about to confess to a double murder.

Financially desperate things might be here at the Hall but I haven't been going around bumping people off to generate a bit of publicity in the belief it would bring the gawping masses in."

"I wasn't trying to accuse you of murder," pleaded Alba but somewhat weakly.

"I should hope not!" exclaimed Andrew. He then added, "Bit of a rash spot to challenge me if that's what you actually thought. Not another soul around. I mean, if I was the murderer, I could do you a real mischief this very instant and claim you tripped on the steps up to this terrace."

"Guess we just need a solitary black raven to land on one of the wooden benches here, an owl to hoot from its perch within the mighty yew tree or a church bell to strike to complete the mood of the moment," said Alba. She then ran her hand down the right lapel of his jacket, as she faced him, and patted her hand against his chest just once, before adding:

"But you're not. However, I am curious as to what you were referring to."

"Mostly, it was about staffing up here at the Hall as a way to reduce wage costs. My idea originally but grandad agreed. Unfortunately, I badly executed it and I fear we're now stuck with a recalcitrant Head Gardener." Responding to Alba's puzzled look, Andrew continued:

"I'd spoken to Mr Parker about his moving on, you see. I think it was mostly about reducing the wage bill and promoting youth but, I have to admit with hindsight, I don't really like him and was keen for him to go whether it affected the wage bill or not. You see, horticulturally, once Tom got the deputy's position, I knew he was our future. Not just his youth but his passion, his engagement with the team around him and his potential to be a gardener for modern times, through engaging with the community and local schools. All those things marked him out as our future. Keen to progress things along, I spoke with Mr Parker about moving on, making way for Tom and that, perhaps, Mr Parker needed a new challenge. As you might be able to guess, he didn't take very well to my suggestions, especially that I was inferring such a young lad could fill his shoes. In my defence, I would have put out feelers, written a good reference and helped him find a suitable garden to move on to. He wouldn't have any of it, though. So, now we're stuck with a demotivated incumbent Head, who's even more remote than previously – and I'm effectively his boss for goodness sake. Stuck with him: him and his burgundy coloured files that he always walks around with. Blast the man."

"Oh, yes, him and his coloured files. Every time I see that colour file in shops, like 'WH Smith's' or 'Ryman's', I immediately think of him. If one item defined a person, I'd say for him, it would be a burgundy coloured file," reflected Alba.

"Too true, too true. Could never buy a car or a tie in that colour, for the same reason in that it would always remind me of him. Not good. Come on then, Miss White, what would your item be?"

"Oh, I don't know."

"I'm not having that; you've got to try harder than that. It's like being asked to define yourself in terms of a single 'Lego' brick. A single item, but not 'Lego', if you'd be so kind; a single item that defines you and perhaps will allow me to always think of you when I see one," said Andrew.

"Let me think then," and Alba paused. They had by now walked the length of the terrace, away from the Orangery, and were by a door marked 'Private – family only'. Instinctively, Alba put her left hand round to the base of her spine and tapped her secateurs. She then unclipped them and presented them to Andrew.

"I'm tempted to say," she said, "my secateurs. But that seems a bit obvious and possibly captures Tom a fraction more than me."

Andrew passed them back to her without having even slid them out of the holster. As she clipped them back on, she continued:

"For David, a cricket ball or perhaps his bat. No definitely a cricket ball, for he's always regarded himself as a bowler more than a batsman, which made his innings on the day of Vaughan's murder all that more impressive. Forty-nine was a good score and he could have gone on if he hadn't tried to make that silly single right before lunch. Although, given the match was abandoned, perhaps it was a good thing he got himself out so he doesn't spend the rest of his life wondering what he might have scored. So, David, definitely a cricket ball. Vaughan, that's easy."

"Yes?" enquired Andrew.

"His journal," at which point Alba went and picked it out of her canvas bag, which Andrew was still then holding. The bag also contained her drinks bottle, her small first-aid kit and a bottle of sun-tan lotion. "This journal was truly Vaughan; I'll sit and look at it some more later today hopefully. Not sure about Sally, possibly a buckled golf club but you won't get my meaning there and don't tell her I said that. Helen a book of stamps, for she's always writing letters and sending birthday cards."

"You're good at this game for other people," commented Andrew, as he prodded her on the upper arm. "For yourself, though?"

"Hmmm, still thinking. Definitely easier to do for other people, I agree. Mrs Lyle, sadly, a five pound note or an unpaid newspaper bill, Sam, a cookbook, probably her new French one by all accounts, the Vicar, well, I don't know him very well, but perhaps a copy of his parish magazine, for he always seems to be trying to off-load them or hand delivering them whether you want one or not. And, as for me, before you give up on me, I'd say my teapot. My mustard yellow 'Denby' teapot and, if allowed to bend the rules already, my tea-strainer that I bought at the same time. Can't have a teapot without a tea-strainer," stated Alba adamantly.

"Wouldn't have guessed that for you and, alright, you can have both. I look forward to a cup of 'rosie lee' from it some time," said Andrew.

"You then, Mr Andrew Chapman? What would your single, all-defining, item be?" enquired Alba.

"Give me a moment. Grandma's is easy, a bottle of 'Chanel'

perfume. Grandad's would be his wristwatch, which his father gave him when grandad went off to war. Great-uncle's would be his silver cigarette case, with its motif, which he's had for simply ever. Similarly to grandad's, a reminder of his days in uniform; brought it back with him, so he once said. We've already done Mr Parker, Mrs Taylor hard to say, sadly. Perhaps that old vase she had in her living room, given we had a matching one in her office up at the Hall: it does seem we're allowed two items for some people," teased Andrew. He then added:

"She always seemed to justify filling the office-based one with flowers from the gardens here."

"And yours?" demanded Alba. "What would your item be?"

"I guess it would be…"

At that moment, though, Andrew was accosted by his great-uncle, who stepped out onto the terrace, through the door Andrew and Alba were right by.

"Ah, there you are Andrew. Was told you were out in the grounds. Thought I'd come looking for you."

"You alright, great-uncle? Something happened?"

"No, nothing to worry about. Barnes was looking for you about a couple of things. When he couldn't find you, I offered to hunt you down outside; I was coming out for a smoke in any case. There's something he wants you to sign and there's a message for you, from the auctioneer bloke."

"Simon, you mean?"

"Yes, him. Apparently, he's been delayed and will be at least half an hour late. Also asked if his wife could come too and amuse herself in the gardens whilst he's meeting with you."

"Blow me, he doesn't miss a trick, does he? I feel I can hardly say 'no' but, with all he's earnt out of us, you would think they'd be happy to pay," replied Andrew.

"Absolutely," agreed William. "Yet another person scrounging off us, if you want my opinion."

Given how vocal Andrew and his great-uncle were, in her presence, Alba felt empowered to offer her opinion, too:

"Sad, isn't it, how it so often seems to be the wealthiest people who are the tightest? How those with money in their pockets seem to think they have some kind of divine right not to have to pay their way. The more I hear about Simon and Anne, the less I like them."

"Too true, too true," agreed Andrew. "Thankfully, as you know Alba, we have precious little money left up here, so I know you're not talking about the Chapman family."

Having earnt a smile from Alba, that incorporated just a hint of sadness, in reply, Andrew addressed his great-uncle and added:

"Isn't that right, uncle? We're virtually broke. We'll be selling that silver cigarette case of yours next. It's probably the only bit of antique silver we'll have left in the family before too long. Actually, I was just talking to Alba here about it. Would you show it to her? You recognise Miss White from your previous encounters with her, don't you?"

"Do you smoke, Miss White?" enquired William.

"No," offered back Alba. "Never have."

"Well, then, I doubt you'll be interested in this case then, despite what Andrew might think. It's just something I keep my smokes in." With that, he inserted it in the internal left breast pocket of his jacket; Alba could just make out that there was engraving on one side as he did so. William's actions made it abundantly clear to both Alba and Andrew that he was not remotely interested in indulging a garden volunteer or even his great-nephew.

The awkwardness of the moment was broken as Barnes, Lord Hartfield's butler come secretary, came out of the door.

"Ah, there you both are. Good," stated Barnes. He registered Alba's presence but said nothing to her. He continued, speaking to the two men he had come in search of:

"Lord Hartfield has asked me to ask both of you to sign the card he told you about over breakfast as he would like it to get in the last post. So, if you could both spare a minute, could I ask you both to step inside and sign it now? I have it here," he added, gesturing to the envelope he was holding.

Barnes held the door open, in the full knowledge that his Lordship's orders would be adhered to by the men he had come in search of.

Andrew was about to follow his great-uncle through the door when he realised Alba hadn't moved. He turned to her and said:

"Come on, you're not standing out here all by yourself – and don't be put off by great-uncle's abruptness. He will warm to you."

Alba raised her eyebrows.

"Well, perhaps, maybe, who knows. Anyway, in you come. Don't feel awkward, you're not about to be a witness to my new will or anything like that. I think it's just a sympathy card about Mrs Taylor which grandad wants to get to 'Parks', the Funeral Directors, in good time. Come on, in you come."

*

It was a well-proportioned room, that Alba found herself stepping into. Large windows allowed the sunlight to fill the room. A high ceiling and wide, high doors, echoed the dimensions of the windows – windows which looked out towards the sunken garden and, beyond that, to a perfectly maintained yew hedge that hid the greenhouses beyond it from the house. The depth of the window recesses, plus a door, that was ajar and which led to a corridor, confirmed how thick the walls were throughout the house, which according to the guidebook, enabled the existence of two priest holes and three hidden rooms. Rumour had it that Liz, the room steward, had once, when the family had been abroad for a spell, gone round Hillstone Hall and hung ribbons from every window in every room – or, more accurately, every room she could find. For, despite her efforts, according to the same rumour, three small windows remained defiantly free of any such decoration.

However, the room Alba found herself within was in complete contrast to all the other rooms that she had previously seen in the Hall. It was unlike the rooms on public display, which the paying visitor got to walk through, dragging, as they did so, their normally bored children, save for the odd studious child passionately looking for the answers to each clue in their quiz, in the hope of earning a sticker – a sticker which normally would have got knocked off their T-shirt before they got back to the car park. For this room, was in desperate need of renovation; paint was peeling, several of the internal wooden window shutters were warped, and incapable of being completely folded away, the wooden floor was in desperate need of varnishing and an entire section of cornice was missing above one of the three windows. The room was spartanly furnished, with a bookcase, a large travelling chest, a wooden table and an eclectic mix of dining and occasional chairs. There was also a settee which, Alba thought, wouldn't have looked out of place in Mrs Taylor's living room, given its worn arms and sagging middle cushion.

Barnes removed the card from its envelope and placed it on the table for signing. Alba sat on a wooden dining chair, with its leather seat and high back, which she draped her sun hat from, at the far end of the table and, given she had nothing else to do, watched as first Andrew, who needed to borrow Barnes' pen, signed right-handed and then William, who had retrieved his own silver fountain pen from his internal right breast jacket pocket.

'Left-handed, like myself' reflected Alba, as William, pen in hand, quickly signed; enabling Alba to infer that, unlike Andrew, he hadn't bothered to put anything other than his name. Andrew, by comparison, had clearly written at least two sentences. In that moment, Alba realised that Andrew had been taught well by his grandfather and had learnt his grandfather's sense of duty and service towards the community in which he would one day be the next Lord Hartfield. A characteristic Alba realised was missing from William

Chapman; Alba sensed the only thing she and Andrew's great-uncle would ever have in common was the hand with which they signed their name.

Having signed, William immediately left the room, heading out onto the terrace once more, cigarette case in hand and jiggling a box of matches, which had been retrieved from another of his jacket pockets.

"I assume you'll be meeting the auctioneer in the library as usual?" enquired Barnes of Andrew.

"Yes, as before," confirmed Andrew.

"Very good, Mr Chapman. I'll have drinks brought in after forty-five minutes. You know he's running rather late?"

"Thank you, Barnes and, yes, great-uncle told me. In the meantime, two favours, if you would be so kind. I need to speak with Miss White here, for a few minutes, so please be kind enough to get my paperwork from my desk and have it ready for me in the library."

"Very good. And?" asked Barnes curious as to the other favour.

"Would you be kind enough to have a cup of tea and a biscuit or two brought in here? Alba, I mean Miss White, is not feeling quite herself and I think a drink would help."

"Of course." Then addressing Alba for the first time, Barnes asked:

"Definitely tea, madam? I can have coffee, herbal tea or a soft drink brought in if you'd prefer."

"Thank you but no. A cup of English breakfast tea would be just lovely."

"Very good. Anything else Mr Chapman?"

"No," replied Andrew. "Actually, I mean yes. Please ensure I have a pen with my papers; as I've just demonstrated I'm without one at the moment."

"Had already been noted, sir." With that Barnes, sympathy card in hand, left through the ajar door, into a corridor and was lost to the depths of the house, leaving just Alba and Andrew behind in what, though once upon a time was an elegant music room, was now a noticeable embarrassment to Andrew.

"Don't say I don't show you the hidden gems of Hillstone Hall," said Andrew as he drew up a chair next to Alba. "The Hall in all its glory!" he added. He spread out his arms to mirror the width of the room and, in so doing, giving the impression of a conductor gesticulating to an orchestra.

"I can see why it's not currently open to the public," offered back Alba.

"It's only just safe enough to open to the family and house staff."

It must have been a lovely room, once upon a time. What was it used for?" enquired Alba.

"A music room. Grandmother often says it was her favourite room of the house, especially when she was first engaged to grandfather. She said the room almost came alive on a summer evening as a pianist played the grand piano, the doors and windows were all flung open, the evening sun caught the strategically placed mirrors and the drinks were flowing."

"It would be lovely to see it restored," mused Alba.

"I've thought about it. Even spoken to the bank about financing its restoration, to be paid back by staging small concerts and performances by both established artists and up and coming new talent. But the bank and other possible investors were just not interested."

"Maybe one day," suggested Alba hopefully.

"Perhaps. For now, though, whilst I have you alone, I just wanted to update you quickly before the auctioneer arrives."

"But he's running late, isn't he?" queried Alba.

"That's what he's phoned up and said but I reckon he'll be here in just a few minutes. It's a ruse of his, apparently, so someone at his auction house let slip the last time I was up in town, to try and catch his needy clients out; getting us all flustered as we scramble around for our papers as he's sitting with us. And, before you say it, I won't be using him again. The trust in the relationship has just about gone on my part. So, quickly, I just wanted to update you with regards to Vaughan, specifically the auctioneer's son, Justin."

Alba looked expectantly at Andrew, relieved she hadn't had to pester him for an update. She bit her tongue, so she didn't say something along the lines of 'I was puzzled why it was taking you so long to get back to me on that and Tom was very suspicious on that point'. "Yes?" she simply said.

"Well, initially, sorry it's taken me a week to get back to you. Obviously, it should have been a simple thing to ask but Philip and Liz had a few days away last week. Anyway, I've spoken to him now and he said, for he and Justin were chatting together once the game had been abandoned, that Justin did indeed mention when he had moved to the village."

"Did he, when?" asked Alba.

"Guess what," said Andrew, "it was over the Easter weekend. Interesting, don't you think?"

"Very," replied Alba, somewhat unnecessarily.

"Philip also recalled Justin said he was surprised that Lord Hartfield knew he lived in the village and that it was rather short notice. However, before you get excited Alba, Philip also said that he, Philip, is one hundred per cent certain that Justin was on the field of play the whole time the game was being played. Apparently, Justin was one of the slip fielders, so there was absolutely no way he could have nipped off the field, even for a few minutes. Took an excellent catch by all accounts so wouldn't have been moved to one of the deep positions, where they tend to put the bowlers who need a rest. So, Justin couldn't have done it even though the broader timeline fits – that his move to the village was the thing which possibly unsettled Vaughan."

"Interesting," reflected Alba. "One step forward, one step back."

"Big step back. He couldn't be our murderer," stated Andrew.

Alba, finding herself just a little thrilled that Andrew was now talking about her mission to help Tom as a 'joint enterprise', corrected Andrew:

"Well, not Vaughan's murderer, assuming Philip is telling the truth."

"He is, I'm certain of it. So, we must rule Justin out."

"Of Vaughan's murder, yes. Not necessarily of Mrs Taylor's. Justin doesn't have an alibi for that, at least not that we know of. Perhaps he murdered her to protect an accomplice or, more loosely, to protect the person he realised did murder Vaughan."

"Like? For I'm not sure where you're going with this," said a confused Andrew.

"Like, his father or mother. Remember, when we saw Simon outside 'Stapleton's' the other week, after our drinks in the beer garden, Simon said they had watched their son play in the cricket match. He and Anne were standing with your grandfather and great-uncle, very close to where Vaughan was sitting. Very close."

"That's right, I remember. And he must have been close for he said he saw the war medals Vaughan had. But if he did it for the medals, why leave them in Tom's locker where they'd be found. He wasn't interviewed by the police on the day of Vaughan's murder, meaning he could have got them away. So why leave them to be discovered? Doesn't make sense."

"No. Unless, he was really after something else."

"Something else?" queried Andrew.

"Yes," replied Alba. "What if he was after something bigger. Perhaps he knew, through Anne, Vaughan had something else of greater value, of such a value that a few war medals would seem worth forgoing; use the medals to incriminate someone else and so allow yourself to walk away with the bigger prize. Whatever that might be."

"That's plausible. Plus, he was parked outside Vaughan's house that day we met him in the village, wasn't he? Furthermore, it's entirely possible I'd mentioned to Simon about our new deputy head gardener and how he was into his history and re-enactment and all that stuff."

"And perhaps Justin realised what his dad had done and killed Mrs Taylor when she somehow worked it out; maybe she'd heard them talking in the village," concluded Alba.

At that moment Barnes returned with a tea tray.

"Your tea Madam." As he placed the tray in front of Alba, Barnes continued, "Would you like me to pour?"

"Oh no, that's quite alright, I'll manage. Thank you anyway."

"If you're sure, madam." Then, addressing Andrew, Barnes added, "Sir, the auctioneer and his wife have turned up already. Apparently, the traffic was not as bad as they expected."

"You don't say," offered back Andrew, who turning to Alba said:

"What did I tell you, the man's trying to 'play us'."

"That was my impression, too, Sir, if I may be so forward. When he called earlier, his whole explanation didn't ring quite true."

"Happy for you to express your thoughts, Barnes. I want you to speak your mind and offer your opinions, I value your input."

"Just like your grandfather, Sir, if I may say. The staff value having a 'voice' here. Sorry, I digress. Your papers are all ready and in the library. Let me know when you want me to take him through."

"Now, if you'd be so kind, Barnes. I'm ready now and want him to know he hasn't caught me out."

"Did his wife come as well?" enquired Alba.

"She did, Madam."

"Why do you ask, Alba?" queried Andrew.

"Just an idea. Rather than allow her to roam the garden by herself, could you show her in here?"

"In here?" said Andrew.

"Yes, as I say an idea. Barnes, would you be so kind as to show Anne in here in five minutes, which will allow me, if I may be so bold, to drink my tea that you have so kindly brought me. Tell her Andrew has arranged for her to have an escorted tour of the garden by one of the long-standing and amazing garden volunteers. I think it's time I had a chat with Vaughan's former wife."

Barnes looked to Andrew for agreement and a simple nod from the heir to Hillstone Hall was all he needed.

Andrew paused before he followed Barnes out. He turned to Alba and said:

"Good idea, really good idea," said Andrew. "But don't expect Barnes to call you 'amazing'. That's not quite his style but don't take it personally. However, some of us think you are."

With that, Andrew bent down towards Alba. She thought he was about to kiss her on the cheek or forehead but, instead, he took one of the two biscuits from the plate in front of her.

"I'll come and find you later. Bring Anne back here when you've had enough of her and Barnes can guard her from then on. Good hunting," he enthused.

With that he was also through the door and lost to the inner core of the house. Alba took Vaughan's journal from her bag and placed it on the table. She then looked down at the tray in front of her and thought to herself, 'Oh, for goodness sake, he's left me the digestive'.

CHAPTER 19

Close, so close

Exactly five minutes later, Barnes brought Anne, the auctioneer's wife, into the old Music Room and said, in a voice, as was his way, devoid of all emotion:

"This is Miss White, who will be your guide around the garden."

"Thank you. Please convey to his Lordship what a nice gesture it is, for him to have laid on a guided tour for me and at such short notice."

"Of course, Madam," replied Barnes. As he turned to Alba to speak to her, he noticed a somewhat deflated look on her face.

"Miss White," he said. "If you would be so kind as to ring the bell just here," and he pointed to an internal doorbell, virtually hidden amongst the carvings around the white marble fireplace, "when you have finished your tour, I will return. So, unless there is anything else, I will take my leave."

Just as he was about to exit the room, he turned a final time and, speaking to Anne, said:

"Yes, his Lordship was very pleased his best gardener was available to show you around."

With that, having offered Alba the most discrete of nods, which earnt him a warm smile in return, Barnes left.

*

Alba stood.

She had already placed her tea tray away from her, on top of the large walnut brown travelling chest, deliberately leaving just Vaughan's journal in front of her, open on a page with his jottings on weather folklore; such as '*If Candlemas Day be cold and bright then winter will have another bite. But if Candlemas Day be all clouds and rain winter has gone and will not come again*'. Against this verse, in Vaughan's handwriting, was written February 2nd.

With energy in her voice, Alba spoke to the visitor:

"It's Anne, isn't it? I'm delighted to have been asked to show you the gardens here at Hillstone."

Anne stood there looking already bored; she had the air of a school pupil, now regretting having signed up to some obscure school trip simply to get themselves out of double PE. Anne watched Alba close the journal and place it in her bag, which was then slung over her shoulder. Having taken her sun hat in her left hand, Alba moved across the room to the door that led out onto the terrace. Despite opening the door virtually in the face of the same American tourist who had spoken to her in the orchard, it was he who apologised to Alba for being in the way. He then asked to be pointed in the direction of the shop and Alba obliged. As she watched him for a moment, as he turned and walked towards the Orangery and the mighty yew tree, which he needed to reach before looping round to the shop and tea room, Alba thought that as well as visitors having comments cards, which enabled them to give feedback on their experience, perhaps staff and volunteers should be allowed similar cards to offer feedback on the visitors themselves. This tourist, Alba decided, would score an easy ten out of ten.

Anne duly followed Alba out onto the terrace.

*

"So, is this your first visit to the Hall?" enquired Alba, as she led the other down from the terrace to the formal beds.

Anne acknowledged that it was but, beyond that, didn't offer Alba anything in conversation. She was disinterested in the formal beds, expressed a view that the long herbaceous borders must be too labour intensive as to be 'relevant to the modern urban garden' and that the formal rose garden was nothing more than a throw-back to a time of privilege and excess for the landed classes.

Alba was struck by the other's hypocrisy, given Anne had not even paid to get in, and, despite Alba's best efforts, could find nothing likeable in the other's character. Alba felt Anne was opinionated, without possessing underlying knowledge to inform those opinions. Also, that Anne was too quickly intolerant of young children, as they ran about the gardens, and that she dressed as if she was thirty years younger than she in fact was. Admittedly, Alba conceded to herself, that she, Alba, was hardly one for fashion, being as she was in her heavy gardening boots, pair of comfortable but worn jeans and a floral top from 'Laura Ashley', with both sleeves scrunched up to be above her elbows from her time in the orchard. However, Alba felt justified in regarding Anne as inappropriately dressed, in her tight white blouse, with its cropped sleeves, that was one if not two sizes too small for her, wearing an excess of silver bracelets, bangles and excessively chunky rings, and with dark trousers of a tightness that she, Alba, had painfully endured yesterday and which surely were uncomfortable from the moment Anne had put them on. The brash needless slither of a scarlet red belt, her handbag, with its clinking gold shoulder strap, and heel-less roman-esque leather sandals completed, in Alba's opinion, a somewhat sad sight but probably one straight out of some glossy fashion magazine.

Sensing the other would not be interested in the orchard, the kitchen garden or the greenhouses, given how the tour had so far gone, Alba led Anne to the small little dull-brown wooden pavilion which overlooked a single tennis court. Knowing where the door key was hidden, Alba went in and retrieved two cushions. She placed them on the steps and they sat down at Alba's suggestion.

"I sense," said Alba, "that an English country garden is not really your thing."

"Not really," replied Anne. "Thought I should come and see it once, given so much of Simon's work has come from this place but it's not really for me. I'd much rather be at our villa in Greece. We don't have a garden there, just a patio, a pool and a few citrus trees in large terracotta pots which Georgios, the local odd job man, comes and waters as necessary when he's there to check on things or to let the pool cleaners in."

"I can take you back to the Hall itself, if you'd like, but you won't be able to sit in one of the rooms open to the public and you've seen the state of the others, so probably here is as good as anywhere."

"We'll stay here – at least we're away from the noise all those children were making. Plus, Simon will be finished in an hour or so; he's got to be somewhere else at two o'clock."

"Will you have a chance to see your son, whilst you're passing through the village?" enquired Alba.

"Justin? How do you know about him?"

"I was in the village the other week, outside 'Stapleton's'," replied Alba. "I ended up speaking with your husband. He mentioned your son had recently moved here. Plus, I like watching the village cricket matches, so was there on the day of the Jubilee match. As you can imagine with a match such as that, we locals natter away on the boundary rope, trying to decipher the make-up of the Lord's team that he's put out."

Anne didn't respond and Alba, not having holidayed in Greece nor ever been to an auction, struggled to think of something else to say, by way of light conversation, but felt a desire to spare Barnes the tedium of sitting with this rather dull woman. All Alba could think to say was:

"Do you like cricket, then? You were at the Jubilee match too, weren't you?"

Anne stood up, faced Alba and, in quite hostile tones, said:

"What is this, an inquisition? You're just some scruffy garden bod here. You've got little leaves in your hair and one of your sleeves has a tear in it, sleeves which, I may point out you haven't even bothered to fold up neatly, you've just pushed them up beyond the elbow. And you've got dust and grime across one cheek. What business is it of yours whether I see my son or not? In fact, whether I have a son or not? Or whether I was at a cricket match? None of your damn business, miss. Who do you think you are?"

With that Anne took two strides towards the house. She then decided to vent her anger some more; she would claim that it stemmed from her perceived sense of personal intrusion from this scruffy garden volunteer. However, in fact it boiled out of a suppressed view of a day wasted, accompanying her husband to his business meetings. She confronted Alba once more and said, in decidedly unkind tones:

"I'm going back to the Hall. When I get there, I will say to his Lordship or his grandson that perhaps next time they select a garden tour guide who isn't a nosy person and who perhaps is slightly better attired. May I just say, also, your tours are really dull; I don't care for Latin names, the science behind crop rotations in the kitchen garden, which we didn't even get to I'm pleased to say, or why some previous Lord chose not to employ Humphry Repton to redesign the grounds at the end of the eighteenth century. I will make my own way back, thank you very much."

Alba was unfazed by the accusations as to her dress sense, her cleanliness, given she'd been working in the orchard earlier, or by how Andrew would hear Anne's complaint. Alba was stung, however, by the allegation that her tour had been boring; Helen had said it was good, when she had rehearsed it on her, and that young mother who had befriended Alba during the prison visits, said she had found, as they had exited the prison together yesterday, Alba's description of the Hall and gardens as like something from a fairy tale. It was the hurt from Anne's comment about Alba's garden tour that prompted

Alba's retort; Alba had been accused of giving Anne an inquisition, so by all the craft and guile Alba had within her, Anne would get one now. To the retreating figure of the significantly older woman, Alba defiantly called out:

"You do know you were standing right behind Vaughan at the cricket match, don't you?"

Alba paused for effect. She then added:

"And you do know that when your husband spoke to me in the village, when you were sitting in the car feeling unwell, he had parked right outside Vaughan's home? You know that as well, do you?"

Anne stopped. The look on her face, as she turned back to Alba, was one of shock and disbelief; Anne clearly didn't. Alba, however, didn't relent. Nor, in that moment, did she feel any sympathy for Anne. Alba added, figuratively going 'all guns blazing':

"Yes, you were right behind him. You were close, so close. And Simon knew the value of the items that Vaughan was holding, items that were, very shortly after, then taken from a dead man and hidden up here at the Hall; a place Simon knows his way around quite well and is frequently here by all accounts. Strange, your son moved to our village and now my beloved friend Vaughan is gone. So, excuse me but I think it is my damn business."

Anne took half a step away from Alba but stopped, trying to process everything Alba had said yet unaware that Alba had a final salvo to fire:

"Tell you what, let's go and speak to the 7th Lord Hartfield or his heir together, shall we? Perhaps they'd then like to ask Simon about the death of one of their volunteers, his interest in a pair of matching antique Chinese vases, with their lattice work and intricate gold handles, that the late housekeeper had. We could, whilst we're about it, reflect on an auctioneer's ability of not leaving fingerprints on items they've handled. What say you? Shall we go up to the Hall and get away from this dull garden and speak to the Lord or shall we sit a while and chat – just us two by ourselves?"

Alba repositioned her sunhat on her head and waited for the other's response. She hadn't stood at all during her 'verbal salvos' and, as she waited for Anne's response, realised that her seated position throughout had been wonderfully empowering; she hadn't needed wild hand or arm movements, getting into the other's personal space or wild bluster. What she had said had been wholly sufficient.

Alba waited.

*

Anne tentatively came and sat back down next to Alba. She said nothing for several minutes and, for all the make-up and gaudy jewellery that she wore, her age suddenly broke through the façade. She looked into the tennis court in front of her, with its faded white lines, sagging net and missing winding handle, but as she finally spoke, it was to Alba:

"That was Vaughan, was it?"

Alba said nothing but not now out of defiance or anger, rather because she knew Anne hadn't finished. It was simply a long pause.

"That was Vaughan, you say? I was right behind him and I never knew. We were close to him and that young woman he was talking to: guess she must have been his granddaughter. I remember I studied the back of his head, with his tidy grey hair and somewhat beaten up old leather hat – all the while not knowing it was him."

She lapsed back into silence but Alba was happy not to rush her. Anne then continued once more:

"Vaughan always had a thing for hats; Panama hats, Aussie hats, flat caps. Whatever the weather, location or company he always had a suitable hat with him. But I didn't know that was Vaughan at the cricket. How would I? I hadn't seen him for half a century and we hadn't exchanged photographs in all that time. We exchanged birthday cards and the like but that was Vaughan being the gentleman that he always was. Left to me, I guess, I'd have stopped writing soon after I divorced him but he was always good at remembering my birthday, so I always reciprocated. In all the years, I never sensed he was staying in touch out of malice or anything like that, he was just being nice. He didn't seem to mind when I told him I was getting remarried several years after we split but I'm surprised he never told me he had family."

"He didn't," interrupted Alba. "He never remarried."

"But the young woman he was with at the cricket match. She was so attentive and caring towards him as she sat there in her little white dress with its blue embroidered flowers. Who was she if not a granddaughter? She bumped into the Lord's brother I recall now, as she carried an old photograph."

"That was me," replied Alba.

Anne looked at her in disbelief.

"Yes, it was. I can scrub up pretty well you know." With that, Alba stood up and faced Anne. She wiped the grime from her cheek, untangled her sleeves, undid the next button of her top and then pulled it in at the sides, in order that it was tight around her mid-rift. She added:

"See. There is a figure under here somewhere. And, as for the old photograph, well that was a picture of Clive. Well, not just Clive. He was in the picture somewhere; it was a photograph of the whole RAF Squadron, but I never got to find out which one Clive was. Vaughan was murdered before he told me."

Alba then resumed her place on the cushion next to Anne, as Anne spoke again:

"Oh, Clive. Now that's a name I've not heard for a long long time. Dear Clive." With that Anne took out a hanky from her handbag and wiped tear-filled eyes.

"Sorry," Anne eventually said, having stemmed the flow of tears and rectified the worst of the damage to her make-up. "Dear Clive. He was so good looking and young – but we all were back then. So young. Him in his blue uniform. I met him first at a dance in Lincoln.

Despite there being so many RAF boys," at which point Anne gave a sad, poignant, smile as she said as an aside, "Yes, they used to say the city turned blue when the weather worsened and operations were cancelled and all these young men in their RAF uniforms descended on Lincoln, from the nearby airfields, to go to the cinema, to dance halls or to a pub. So many young men. Clive, though, stood out amongst them all – so handsome and dashing."

Alba sat and listened. She nodded to David, who was on his way to the kitchen garden, and had mouthed an 'are you OK?' to her.

Anne continued:

"We met lots of times after that, sometimes within larger groups, sometimes just the two of us. He took me to meet his parents when he had a few days leave, which was where I first met Vaughan. But Clive and I had fallen in love by then and would have got engaged soon after that I reckon. However, that love story never got told. The war took him, like it did so many. I stayed in touch with his family and ended up marrying Vaughan about a year later."

"Oh," said Alba.

"Please don't think I was deluding myself or trying to live a lie through Vaughan; I wasn't trying to pretend he was still Clive. They were brothers, yes, but different in looks and personality. As I'm sure you realised, Vaughan was so gentle and humble…"

"But strong when he hugged you," interjected Alba.

"Oh, yes, strong. Clive was the dashing war hero type whereas Vaughan was more the gentle giant."

Then, to answer the look in Alba's eyes, Anne added:

"I did love Vaughan originally. I assure you of that, though, with hindsight, I guess it was a different kind of love, not quite so passionate, not quite so intense. He'd gone through some horrors out in France. He told me about it once, just once mind you. Sadly, though, once the war had finished and the joy of having survived it had ebbed away, we realised we didn't have that much in common as husband and wife. The night times were lonely but, I think, it was the meal-times that were the worst, when we sat opposite each other and realised we had nothing to say that interested the other."

Anne sighed, a long heavy sigh, as if half a century of sadness had suddenly found an escape valve. Anne then continued:

"Yes, I loved him once but I had to divorce him. I felt I needed to live again and it was all too stale with Vaughan. He wanted to keep trying and, being the godly man that he was, didn't want to part but I had to get out and one Saturday morning I handed him back my wedding and engagement rings and moved back to my parents. He deserved someone else I thought but perhaps that was just my way of justifying leaving. But it seems he never found another."

"No," confirmed Alba.

"So, that was Vaughan I was standing behind. I still can't believe it and shortly after that he was dead – how shocking and how terrible," stated Anne.

Her sadness and emotion seemed genuine to Alba but, Alba felt, something was amiss.

"But surely you knew it was his house you were parked outside in the village the other week?" queried Alba.

"No, it just didn't connect. Obviously, I knew this was the village he'd moved to a couple of years ago but his new address was just something I'd written out not more than twice and some of these Sussex villages can be quite sprawling, as this one is; in fact some of the houses are tucked away all by themselves virtually in the woods. Recently, when Simon was driving around here, he took us down a farm track by mistake. There was farmland one side and woods the other and just this solitary cottage, all by itself, with its dark green shutters and little porch. Simon was not happy having to turn his new BMW car around there – scratched his front bumper having gone just a bit too far into the hedge at one point. Somehow, I imagined that was the type of place Vaughan lived in, not one right in the heart of the village next to the shop."

"So Simon hasn't mentioned to you, over the last couple of

weeks, that Vaughan had been right in front of you at the cricket or that it was his house you were parked outside. I did tell Simon," said a puzzled Alba, "when I spoke to him outside the village shop that Saturday morning. I'd have thought he'd have shared it with you."

"No," offered back Anne. "But he likes his secrets, does my husband. Never tells me when he has some high value items coming through his auction house. Plus, I'm often at our villa by myself and work is quite busy at the moment for him, especially with everything the Chapman family are selling, so maybe he forgot."

"Maybe," replied an unconvinced Alba.

"Poor Vaughan," said Anne. "It would have been nice to have said 'hello'. But now he's gone for good and there's nothing even tangible left to remember him by."

"Oh, I've got his gardening journal here, if you'd like to have a look for a few minutes," offered Alba; for even though she hadn't warmed to the other woman, she still felt compassion for her. "It's got some nice poems in, too."

Alba took it out of her bag and handed it to Anne.

"Oh, this battered old thing. Oh, it was you who got lumbered with it at the funeral, was it? All that tat that he wanted on his coffin. Strange how one man's treasure is another person's trash."

Anne turned it over in her hands. She thought about flicking through a few pages but, to Alba's surprise and hurt, Anne put it down beside her unopened.

"It's lasted pretty well, considering," said Anne, somewhat deadpan.

"Considering what?" asked Alba.

"Oh, considering he picked it out from amongst the long grass in a field next to the body of a dead German soldier."

"That would explain the faded German handwriting at the beginning, I guess," commented Alba.

"Guess so," agreed Anne. "But don't think Vaughan was one for looting. What happened that day was the only thing he ever told me about his time in the army."

"He never spoke to us about his time in uniform. Clive, yes, he always spoke about Clive but always seemed to clam up when we asked about his own experiences," contributed Alba.

"You'll understand why, when you hear. Don't think every German soldier was a bad person, nor every British one was a good one. Vaughan's story showed some of them were effectively in the wrong uniform. It was at a place called Tilly-sur-Seulles in late June '44, Vaughan said. The Germans had been shelling the company Vaughan was with and they'd lost radio communication with HQ; it and the radio operator had taken a direct hit. Despite Vaughan also being injured, his commanding Officer ordered him to go back and report on their situation and ask for orders."

"Poor Vaughan, he never said," said Alba but ever so softly, not wanting to break the flow of the other's recollection.

"On his way back, he wandered along thick hedgerows and through a wood, to the edge of a clearing. He said he saw a young German soldier trying to surrender to a British Officer and a Sergeant. Vaughan said the Officer just shot the German outright and, with the Sergeant, proceeded to loot the body. They took his watch, a ring and something that was bulky and shiny from a tunic pocket but discarded this book, which they'd removed from a breast pocket of this poor dead boy," said Anne tapping Vaughan's gardening journal with a ringed finger. "Vaughan reckoned the poor dead German could only have been eighteen, if that."

"Oh, my word," exclaimed Alba.

"They'd have shot Vaughan, too, he reckoned. For they then heard him, as he stumbled due to being already wounded. The Sergeant raised his gun but, fortunately, for Vaughan a stray German shell landed nearby at that moment. It killed the Sergeant and knocked the Officer out. Vaughan wasn't further wounded and, Vaughan being Vaughan, went and checked on everyone. As I say, the Sergeant was dead, the German was already dead and the Officer was unconscious and wounded in both legs. Bizarrely, the next thing Vaughan did was pick up this book; he said in that surreal moment it was as if all the horrors of war were being played out in terms of whether he allowed this notebook to also be lost, amongst the long grass, to the war or not. Then, for reasons I still can't fathom and I don't think Vaughan ever quite could, as the shelling started up once more, Vaughan carried this Officer back with him. Left him at a first aid post and then went to find his HQ. He never saw the Officer again and the Officer was hardly likely to search Vaughan out or recommend him for a medal."

"It's like a Hollywood film," said Alba but then regretted her apparent making light of the events. "Sorry, that sounded wrong. I wasn't trying to turn it into some 'John Wayne' film."

"I know what you're getting at but you could have worded it better; that's why Vaughan never wanted to talk about his experiences, save on that one occasion to me. I think, but this is stretching my memory to the limit, shortly after the war finished, I'd mentioned something about the horrors perpetrated by the German army and he corrected me. He wanted to distinguish between the Wehrmacht, which was the regular German army, and the Waffen-SS but then went on to tell me about this one experience to highlight that not all the evil people were wearing a German uniform."

"So, this journal is a real treasure" suggested Alba. "He'd meant it to go to someone else originally but then changed his mind; that person was left his secateurs and I was bequeathed this family heirloom."

"Oh no, it's no such thing," replied Anne and passed Vaughan's journal back to Alba. "It's always been just a scruffy notebook that he kept in our little garden shed. No, the real treasure was the engagement ring." At which point, Anne put her hands down to either side of her, with her palms against the wooden step she was sitting on, and then stretched out her legs and tilted her head back and laughed to herself. Having recomposed herself, she continued:

"Simon still tells me off now and again for handing it back. It was a family heirloom, given to Vaughan by his mother or grandmother, I forget which now, and had been given to her by some wealthy spinster she'd nursed, who's own father or grandfather or uncle or whatever had worked for the East India Company and made a sizeable fortune. It would have gone to Clive but with his death, Vaughan got it. Worth a small fortune but not that either of us knew it at the time. In any case, to Vaughan it was just a ring. He always said real beauty and value lay within a person, not what they wore, and that I could keep it. I gave it back though. I didn't know just how valuable it was until Simon showed me pictures of similar items many many years later when I was married to him. Poor Simon, for all his work as an auctioneer and for all the dreams he has of unearthing that one item which would make him, I had worn on my finger the type of thing he is searching for – and I had given it away. Poor Simon."

"Are you sure you don't want another look at Vaughan's book?" enquired Alba, as she held it above her open bag.

"No, not really but I don't suppose you've got a photo of him in your bag. It would be nice just to look at his face one last time, given they didn't put one on the order of service at his funeral."

"Sorry, no," replied Alba. "Probably the best person to ask would be the vicar. Vaughan was part of his congregation and probably featured in the parish magazine from time to time. He's the Reverend Quinn, in case you've forgotten his name. I'll call him, if you'd like, and ask him to have a look for you."

"Would you? It won't endear me to Simon but, if he can't be bothered to tell me I was standing behind my first husband on the day he died or that we had parked outside his house, then tough."

With that, Anne, having looked at her watch, stood up and added:

"I ought to be getting back to the house. Your garden tour was a bit lacking and you're quite a confrontational woman, Miss White, but it was interesting to talk. And, if you could speak to the vicar, that would be appreciated. He has my contact details, so perhaps you can ask him to post me something. No need for you to escort me back to the house, I can find my way easily enough."

Alba, nonplussed by the other's abruptness, just sat and watched the other woman as she walked away, back to the Hall, to Simon, her husband, to their big car and Greek villa and everything else that adorned her life, be it jewellery or expensive, but badly fitting, clothes. Alba thought to herself that Anne would have been far happier if she had bothered to work at her first marriage and stayed with Vaughan – a life, which Alba felt, would surely have been full of love and peace, compared to what Anne now had.

As she sat there, a couple of visitors asked her if she'd be willing to take their photograph as their children ran through the wild flower meadow in the background. As she heard the shutter click on their 'Canon' camera, as she successfully got all five people in the shot, an idea formed in her mind.

*

As Alba exited the tennis hut, having returned the cushions and locked up, David was returning from the kitchen garden with two wooden trays filled with pickings that were destined for the shop.

"Let me take one, if that would help," offered Alba. "These going to the shop or the tea room?"

"Thanks, to the shop. Who was that you were chatting to?"

"Vaughan's former wife, believe it or not."

"Really? Didn't know he'd been married. Are you sure?" asked David.

"Quite sure. I've hardly seen you since his funeral: you haven't been around as much recently. So, I've got quite a lot to fill you in on. Plus, there's a favour I suddenly want to ask you – it relates to the day Vaughan died."

*

Alba left David in the shop with the staff, as the punnets of soft fruit David had picked were priced up, and went into the tea room to see if Sam was there. She was and, with no customers to serve, was sitting at one of the tables with her mother, Mrs Rowan, who had popped in to surprise her on her birthday.

Sam instinctively got up, having heard the door go, to return to the serving isle. Alba gestured not to bother as she said:

"No, it's alright, Sam, just popped in to say 'hello' and to wish you a happy birthday. Morning Mrs Rowan," Alba added, "if you're here to try the cherry and almond slice I can assure you that yours is even better."

"Hello Alba. That's sweet of you to say. I'll drop you the recipe round, if you'd like. Anyway," she added, having turned to her daughter who was now standing behind the till, "I'd better be going, I've got a cake to decorate for someone. Pleased I was able to surprise you. Oh, what time did you say Chloe was popping round?"

"About 7pm, Mum. Thanks for coming, it was lovely to see you."

And then, as sometimes happens in life, fortune does indeed favour the good people. For had they come in just a minute earlier they'd have seen Sam sitting down with her mum at a table and not 'on duty' at all. However, by being that minute later, Lord Hartfield, his brother William, his grandson Andrew and the auctioneer and his wife, Simon and Anne, all entered and Lord Hartfield saw his employee standing exactly where he would expect her to be. Coincidentally, David, carrying two empty wooden trays, followed them in, looking for Alba, so they could walk back to the gardeners' hut together.

Lord Hartfield duly told Sam what he wanted for his group. As Alba, David and Mrs Rowan stood to one side, they heard Sam say:

"Very good your Lordship. That will all go through on code 085 and I'll bring it over to your table."

Then Alba heard Mrs Rowan say very softly:

"Oh yes, that's who else I saw that day."

But before Alba could ask her what she meant, Anne came over to speak to Alba. As she did so, Mrs Rowan said quickly to Alba:

"Must be going, the thing won't ice itself. I'll drop that recipe round."

With that she exited the shop and David, too, opted to wait outside, as Anne continued speaking to Alba:

"Ah, Miss White. It's fortuitous to bump into you again. I was thinking, as I walked back to the Hall after our little chat, of the photo you were carrying on the day of the cricket match."

"The day Vaughan was murdered, you mean?" still resenting the fact that so many seemed to pretend Vaughan hadn't been murdered.

"Well, yes, I guess so," replied Anne. "Anyway, it was a photo of Clive you said – him and the Squadron."

"Yes," offered back Alba.

"And you said you didn't know which one was Clive?"

"That's right, Vaughan was killed before he told me."

"Second row from the front, twelfth from the left. As I walked back to the Hall I remembered; Clive's birthday was the 2nd December, you see. Vaughan and I always found that a poignant coincidence and why, no doubt, even after all these years, Vaughan had never forgotten which one his brother was."

"Thank you for telling me. I will study it when I get home. It's sitting on my hall table at present as I don't know who to give it back to."

"You mean Vaughan didn't bequeath it to you as well as that tatty old book?"

"No. And it doesn't really suit my hall table," replied Alba, as she recollected the table's still cluttered appearance.

"Would I be allowed it, then, do you think?" asked Anne, with a level of passion that had been missing from her during their previous conversation when out in the gardens, save for when Clive's name had been first mentioned. "We're back in the village on Saturday, so I've just learnt. I could come and collect it then."

"I guess so," offered back Alba, "if I can ask you one question about Vaughan?"

"Yes," said a slightly nervous Anne.

"Why didn't he do something better with Clive's medals than keep them in a carrier bag? Why not frame them, donate them to the Hendon or Duxford Air Museums or even put them in cotton wool in a biscuit tin? Why just a plastic bag?"

"I asked him to do something better with them for all the short time we were married but he never would. Never would. Kept them in their original cardboard postage box, you know the little box with the letters 'OHMS' top left. No, probably you don't know. Anyway, he kept them in that until it wore out and after that it was a paper bag. It seems it became a plastic one once they'd been invented. As for why, I think he just never accepted his brother was gone. It wasn't helped by the fact there was no grave to visit, just his name on the town's memorial. We had nowhere personally to lay flowers or pay our respects. Clive and the rest of the crew were simply listed as missing, presumed killed. Vaughan found that difficult to accept. Therefore, keeping the medals loose, it was as if he expected Clive to walk in at any moment to finally collect them."

"Poor Vaughan," said Alba.

"Poor Clive," echoed Anne. "So young and handsome" and she wondered what it must have been like as he waited to board the plane, unbeknown to him, that last time.

CHAPTER 20

Bombers' Moon

As they stood waiting to board the lorry, which would take them to their aircraft, Pilot Officer Jim 'Scottie' McDowell, the crew's navigator, broke the silence:

"Actually, 'Skip', you probably don't need me on this trip. You must know the way to 'Happy Valley' by now. Mind if I have the night off?"

"If 'Scottie's' not going, can I stay behind too?" asked Flight Sergeant John Graham, the bomb aimer. "'Swanny' can leave his turret just before you start the bombing run and press the bomb release button for me. I could get to the flicks in Lincoln instead. When you get back I'll tell you whether the film was any good; it'll probably be rubbish mind you, so you might have a better evening than me."

"Sure, no problem," replied the crew's mid-upper gunner, Flight Sergeant Cyril 'Swanny' Williams in his rich Welsh accent. "Given you must have missed the Krupp factories, when we last bombed Essen, for we're going back tonight, I'll have a go at dropping our bomb load. How hard can it be?" There was, however, no sarcasm in Cyril's voice, it was purely said in dark humour amongst crew mates.

Flight Lieutenant Kenneth 'Aussie' Austell, Distinguished Flying Cross, the pilot of Lancaster 'O for Orange', was a tough no-nonsense New Zealander, who had volunteered to fight Nazi tyranny from his far away home town of Hamilton on the north island. He had a well drilled crew around him and he knew that his navigator, 'Scottie' McDowell, and bomb aimer, John Graham, were speaking in jest. They were all going tonight but, he conceded to himself, it was indeed true that he had flown to the Ruhr Valley several times before, both during his first tour of thirty bombing operations, and, more recently, just last month with his current crew. As he discarded a half-smoked cigarette, 'Aussie' spoke:

"Best we all go to 'Happy Valley' tonight. In any case, can't have 'Swanny' up front, we need him at the mid-turret to help keep 'Ginger' awake."

"Hey!" replied Flight Sergeant Stephen 'Ginger' Kent, Distinguished Flying Medal. "I've never fallen asleep on a mission yet. Two damaged night fighters are testimony to that."

The crew smiled as one, knowing 'Aussie' had been innocently pulling his rear-gunner's leg.

They lapsed back into silence. Their Lancaster was one of the furthest planes to reach from the Nissan huts they had just left, where they'd kitted up and checked their parachutes. Dispersed as the Squadron's planes were around the airfield, 'Aussie's' crew, as each crew going tonight, had to wait for a truck to take them out to their plane; they were not dressed for an evening stroll to it, in their heavy flying boots, thick woollen jumpers and jackets overlaid with their life jackets and parachutes. As for 'Scottie', there was no way he was walking with his burdensome navigator's bag.

They stood there, deep in their own thoughts.

'Aussie' lit another cigarette, which Flight Sergeant Ian Hutchinson, the wireless operator, who originated from Cape Town, South Africa, knew would not be more than half smoked before his skipper threw that one away too.

As he stood there, 'Aussie' thought again as to his decision to sign up to this, a second tour. As he stood waiting, he promised himself he wouldn't, if he survived tonight and the further eight operations they would be required to do after this one, sign up to a third tour. He would have done his duty and some and would be able to feel he had avenged the death of his best mate, Jack. He'd travelled half-way around the world with Jack, they'd gone through flight training school together and, as two pilots, had even been posted to the same Squadron, but Jack, flying a Manchester, had been shot down over the North Sea when he and his crew had been returning from a mine laying operation.

'Aussie's' last crew member, Flight Sergeant Clive Young, the flight engineer, who had recently been mentioned in a dispatch, and a born and bred Lancastrian, spoke:

"I'm pleased they were able to repair our crate after the damage she got last time out. Didn't fancy having to fly in the reserve aircraft over the Ruhr."

"Absolutely not," replied 'Ginger' on behalf of most of the rest of the crew. "The number of times it's come back on three engines scares me."

"But it keeps coming back," commented Ian reflectively. Clearly though, the wireless operator's thoughts were not shared by the rest of them.

"We need to come back as I've arranged to see Anne again tomorrow night," said Clive.

"Seeing her again, are we? Thought you'd have found someone else by now. You normally get through girlfriends as quickly as the moon changes," chided 'Swanny'.

Clive looked up in to the clear evening sky above them. 'Anne was different' he thought to himself and for a moment he found himself contemplating taking her for a moonlight stroll the following night. Quickly, though, he was back in the present; Bomber Command was not the place to be for day-dreamers – too many empty beds in the huts taught one not to be a day-dreamer or to plan for any kind of future. Nonetheless, Anne crept back into his thoughts once more before he reflected on the fact that the full moon would make target identification easier for John but, equally, the enemy's night fighters would have an easier job in seeing them, once the German radar had brought them in close.

Then, somewhat abstractedly, Clive said to his crew-mates, "You won't know this but my brother calculates his age by lunar cycles. According to him he's about 234. Eighteen to you or me. He's just been called up; gone into the Royal Engineers. When I took Anne to see mum and dad, he was on leave too. My parents were so thrilled to have both us boys home at the same time but it broke their hearts when they walked with us back to the station and said goodbye once again."

"Yeah," said 'Scottie' in his gruff Scottish voice, "reckon it's better not going home when you have leave. It's too painful."

"Probably no more leave until the tour's complete," said 'Aussie'. "Still, shorter trip tonight, that's something. Berlin is such a long way."

"'Happy Valley' or Berlin, some choice!" voiced Ian. "Less fuel, greater bomb load or max fuel and fewer bombs – take your pick."

"Either way, she'll be heavy to lift off. I'm sure our loads are in excess of what the designers ever calculated she could carry," said 'Aussie'.

They could hardly fail to hear the Merlin engines of some of the other crewed-up Lancasters burst into life as a solitary truck stopped in front of them, allowing the seven men to climb aboard. As they banged on the side, to tell the driver he was good to go, Clive said:

"Let's hope the Intelligence Officers are right about where they now think the heaviest flak concentrations will be. As I say, I've got a date tomorrow night."

As the truck pulled away to take them to their plane, 'O for Orange', a small group of WAAFs, colleagues of those women who would shortly be monitoring the Squadron's progress from the control rooms, waved them off – Flight Lieutenant Kenneth 'Aussie' Austell DFC, Pilot Officer Jim 'Scottie' McDowell, Flight Sergeant Ian Hutchinson, Flight Sergeant John Graham, Flight Sergeant Cyril 'Swanny' Williams, Flight Sergeant Stephen 'Ginger' Kent DFM and Flight Sergeant Clive Young.

"See you in the morning boys," called out one of those waving.

But 'O for Orange' did not come back.

CHAPTER 21

Table 7

"…and with new potatoes, please," said Alba.

Sam finished her scribbled notes and repeated their order:

"That's one steak and ale pie with chips and vegetables and one pan-fried salmon fillet – shame on you Alba, being it's a Tuesday – with salad and new potatoes. Nothing by way of starters. I'll bring your rolls and bar drinks over once I've handed your order into the kitchen."

"Thanks Sam. Oh, and may we have jug of tap water, too, please?" requested Alba.

"Course you can; I'll put some ice and lemon and lime slices in with it as it's a warm evening."

"Thank you," said the Reverend Quinn. "Not a lot of ice, mind you, don't want the water too diluted!" he added.

Sam and Alba looked at one another. Both had puzzled looks on their faces as they tried to work out whether there was any scientific basis to what the local vicar had just said.

*

TABLE 7

"Where was I?" asked Reverend Quinn, of Alba, once Sam had gone. "Oh, yes. I decided I couldn't keep disturbing you, be it in the tea shop up at the Hall, here, by turning up unannounced and invading your space, or at your own front door. Better, I thought, to tell you I'd be here and ask you to join me. Once I'd left you my message, I gambled and booked a table for two, hoping you might join me. Actually, I need to correct myself on that last point, so you don't get worried. What I did was, book for two individual diners but at the same table. The lunchtime barman was a bit confused as to my meaning."

"Nice of Sam to 'upgrade' us to Table 7 once she came on shift and had a look through the bookings and the proposed seating plan."

"Absolutely, the bloke who took my booking had placed us in the gang-way so Sam said, where we'd both been a fortnight ago. But I'm sure it was your name that earnt us the move from Sam."

To Alba's slight shame, she didn't disagree on the vicar's last point. Nonetheless, it was in good spirits that she sat here, opposite the Reverend Quinn. She'd listened to his message on her answerphone, once she'd got home from her day up at the Hall, and decided to take him up on his suggestion of a meal that evening. It would allow her to thank him personally for visiting Tom the previous week and also to allow her to pass on Anne's request for a photograph of Vaughan. A further thought had also trickled through her mind, in that she'd made a lot of progress towards helping Tom since she'd last met the vicar in 'The Sun and the Moon' and meeting him again might somehow help her keep that momentum going.

*

Here they then sat, at 'The Sun and Moon's' best table. It didn't overlook the beer garden, rather the front of the pub, where there was a wide pavement, a small number of pub-owned benches and, not that they could see them from where they sat inside, an array of well stocked and well-watered hanging baskets; baskets with their geraniums, both upright and trailing varieties, begonias, lobelia, fuchsias and lengths of variegated ivy dangling, giving depth to each basket in a way that the fuchsias gave height.

These tables, by being visible from the road and the pavement, were always made up, with the full array of cutlery, wine glasses and little tumblers for soft drinks or water and a condiments rack so fully stocked that a young child could happily count the sachets and reorder their arrangement for hours, so many sachets were there in their varying colours – the blues for tartar sauce, the red for ketchup, the brown for the predictable brown sauce and the yellow denoting mustard. In fact, the racks on these window tables were so well furnished, there were also the green sachets for salad cream, white for mayonnaise and ochre-coloured ones for the increasingly popular barbecue sauce.

The Reverend Quinn watched Alba as she re-arranged several, which to her mind were, misplaced sachets. He wondered whether, by way of making light conversation, to say that none of the sachets she was dutifully reordering matched her light plum colour top; a top with its 'crew' neck line, purely decorative buttons which went part-way down the front before they and the stitched pleats gave way to a looser lower half that fanned out ever so slightly. He opted to say nothing as a passing old vibrant red 'Land Rover Defender', towing an 'Ifor Williams' livestock trailer, caught his eye. 'Well, it would be a vibrant red', he thought, 'but for the fact it was heavily caked in mud – as such a vehicle should be'.

Sam brought their rolls and bar drinks over and assured them their food would be ready in about fifteen minutes. As she removed the oversized wine glasses, a size that Reverend Quinn thought would make a good communion goblet, Sam asked:

"May I take away the excess cutlery, too?"

"Perhaps just the ones for the starters, since we're not having any, but maybe leave the stuff for desserts," suggested the Reverend,

TABLE 7

which got an affirmative nod from Alba, who was already craving a portion of sticky toffee pudding and cream.

*

"It was a useful co-incidence," Alba started to say before correcting herself. "Or, as you'd prefer me to say, a 'God incidence'. See, I did listen to you the last time we were in here together, even if I don't quite get what you mean by that."

"I could explain, if you'd like?" offered Matthew.

"Depends," said Alba tentatively.

"It's to do with pre-determination, miracles and the purpose of prayer. I could continue," said Matthew, "but it might not be your thing for a Tuesday evening. Don't get me wrong, though, it's not beyond yours, or anyone's, understanding. For example, think of pre-determination as opting to walk through an arch. As you walk towards it, you see the words 'All are welcome' engraved on it."

"OK," said Alba, to indicate she had grasped the simple imagery.

"But then, having walked through it and beyond it, you look back and see the engraving on the other side. That though reads 'You have been chosen'. And as for miracles and praying, there are some wonderful books by CS Lewis, which I'd be happy to lend you."

"Didn't he write 'Narnia'?" suggested Alba.

"Yes, that's the guy. Very readable."

With that, however, Matthew went silent; he put his elbows on the table, put his hands together, inter-locking his fingers, and dipped his head so his lips pressed against some of the protruding knuckles. Alba initially thought he was praying or giving thanks but his wide open, unblinking eyes and fixed facial expression, suggested otherwise. He just sat there, his eyes boring into the table, unspeaking, as if he had stepped into a world all by himself and was there alone.

'Have I offended him?' thought Alba. She didn't think she had but was puzzled as to what he was doing or thinking. She sat there and sipped at her drink, unsure what to make of it all. Then, as she discretely buttered her brown roll, Matthew spoke:

"Sorry," he succinctly and quietly said.

"You alright?" queried Alba.

"Yes, just some painful memories that just got triggered."

"Oh, I'm sorry if I've just said something that's upset you," offered back Alba, struggling to think of anything it might have been.

"No, no, not at all. Believe me, nothing you said at all but you know how one thing someone says leads to another thing and then you find yourself thinking about something you weren't expecting to?"

"Yes. You can talk about it if you'd like," said Alba, unsure quite what she was letting herself in for.

"Thank you but I won't burden you."

"Sure?"

"Sure," replied Matthew but he then added:

"Have you seen the film 'Shadowlands' about CS Lewis' life?"

"No," replied Alba.

"Shame, you should. It's got Anthony Hopkins in." He paused and then simply repeated himself:

"You should."

However, before Alba could ask why, Matthew changed the subject completely, seeking to return the conversation to where he had interrupted Alba:

"You were saying 'It was a useful co-incidence'."

Alba took her dining companion's hint to move away from whatever painful conversation he didn't want to have. She therefore continued where she had left off:

"Yes, a useful co-incidence that you called and suggested meeting up tonight."

"Because?" enquired Matthew.

"Because I was talking to Vaughan's former wife earlier today." Alba went on to explain how Anne had accompanied her husband

TABLE 7

Simon to Hillstone Hall and how, she Alba, had offered to show Anne the garden.

With that, Alba asked Matthew if he could find a couple of nice pictures of Vaughan, to pass on to Anne when she was back in the village at the weekend. She also filled Matthew in on Anne's presence at the cricket match and her proximity to Vaughan throughout the morning.

"Blow!" exclaimed Matthew. "When I contacted her, to invite her to Vaughan's funeral, she mentioned she'd been at the match briefly. She didn't let on, though, she'd been there all morning watching her son play, had been part of Lord Hartfield's group or that she was so close to the crime scene. And, you say, she really didn't know she was literally right behind him at one stage?"

"That's what she said," offered back Alba. With that, Alba popped her final bit of bread in her mouth and thoughtfully chewed.

Sam passed their table at that point and mentioned their food would be about five minutes. Seeing Sam in that moment, got Alba thinking. It brought Sam's mum to Alba's mind. That in turn brought Neale's visit to Alba's home, with Mrs Rowan, to mind and that triggered a recollection of something Neale had said that afternoon. However, before she could in turn ask Matthew about something he had just said, he, having seen the Land Rover, now devoid of its trailer, pass the window in the opposite direction, said, with energy in his voice, to Alba:

"The park bench story. I feel I must tell you the park bench story."

"Really, what's brought that to mind, all of a sudden?" enquired Alba.

"You know, a bizarre little thing. A red Land Rover has just driven past, twice. A lovely vibrant red – 'Masai red' so Robin, a vicar friend of mine, told me once. He knows a thing or two about that make of car, even took me for a day's off-road driving to celebrate my ordination. He's a friend but also my mentor. Anyway, seeing this red car this evening reminded me of him and it was one of his sermons where he talked about park benches. God sometimes speaks in mysterious ways; it's as if I'm meant to share it with you this evening."

"Right," said Alba in unsure tones.

"Well, I'll try not to bore you. The gist of it though, is that we're all familiar with wooden park benches. Of course, they might not be in a park, they might be along a coastal walk, at a viewing point or outside a bowling club. But you know the type I mean, with their wooden slatted seat and backrest?"

"Yes, but I'm not sure where this is going," replied Alba.

"Bear with me. What do they almost always have on them, screwed into the middle of the backrest?"

"A metal memorial plaque?"

"Exactly," said Matthew. "A plaque placed there in memory of someone, with their name, perhaps their nickname, the date they were born and the date they died. But what's the most important thing on the plaque?" asked Matthew.

"Their name, I guess," offered Alba, who was by now a somewhat bemused dining companion.

"No, not that that is unimportant. The most important thing is the dash."

"The what?" said Alba. "The dash?"

"Yes, the dash. The little horizontal line between the date the person was born and the date they died. You see, the date you're born is somewhat arbitrary, and definitely beyond your control, whilst the date you die is also somewhat arbitrary and, usually, beyond your control. But what lies between those two dates, as represented by the dash on a park bench, is your life. All you do, your walk with God, the lives you touch, the parents you care for, the children you perhaps raise, the charities you help support, the neighbours you do the shopping for, the child in Africa who's education you fund, the prayers you offer up in life, the friend you hug when her marriage breaks down, all you do is captured, denoted, summarised, whatever,

TABLE 7

by the simple dash. That is what is key. We're given one life, just one, and we have to live the breadth of it, not just the length. The length is usually beyond our control but the breadth of it isn't. So, the dash on a park bench is the most important thing the engraver places on the metal plaque. And now, that's what captures my eye, each time I pass such a wooden bench, and I stop and I wonder what life the person lived and how sad it is that all that they were is hidden behind a single short straight line. As I think I said to you originally, a sermon I wished I'd written but it was very personal nonetheless."

"Very clever. I can see why it would work as an address during a funeral," said Alba. "But surely you can't remember every sermon you've ever heard at a funeral?"

"Oh goodness me, no," replied Matthew. "This one, however, was a bit different."

"How so?"

"It was the address Robin gave at my wife's funeral. She was twenty-seven when she died."

Not knowing what to say in response, Alba's embarrassment was masked by Sam's re-appearance with their food.

"Salmon, for you Alba, pie for you Reverend, extra jug of gravy just in case. Plates are hot so be careful. Anything else I can get you?"

"No, thank you," said Alba, still shocked by Matthew's revelation.

"This looks absolutely lovely and plentiful," added Matthew. "Thank you, Sam."

"Enjoy," Sam said and moved a couple of tables away to clear some empty glasses.

"May I say grace for us?" enquired Matthew. Getting a nod from a still stunned Alba, the Reverend Quinn gave thanks for the food, the kitchen staff, Sam who had served them and asked a blessing on Tom.

Alba was quite touched Matthew had remembered Tom in that way and, as Matthew tucked into his hearty steak pie, she said:

"I don't know what to say. Obviously, I'm so very sorry for you."

"Please don't worry or feel you have to ask me all about her. If our conversation encompasses her then I'll talk about her but, if not, that's OK. You didn't know her and I'm almost certainly not the only grieving person in this pub tonight. Plus, our food is here and it does look good."

Alba agreed that it did.

*

Only as they were half way through their food, could Alba, thinking again of how Matthew remembered Tom as he said grace, think of something to say:

"You visited Tom, he said when I saw him yesterday."

"Yes, last Friday," replied Matthew.

"And in the process, according to Tom, you've earnt yourself a bit of a reputation amongst the staff and the prisoners."

"Have I?" asked Matthew. "How so?"

"You getting through security apparently," replied Alba.

"Oh, the Bible business you mean?"

"Yes," offered back Alba. She then went on to relay Tom's understanding of what had happened and his puzzlement as to why the book Matthew did get in was, if anything, the one that shouldn't have been allowed through.

Matthew smiled at Alba and then said:

"You'd probably call it 'flying by the seat of my pants' but I'm minded to recall Proverbs 3: 5-6. But I won't give you yet another sermon. In earthly terms, I had a box of a dozen Bibles to be given out at the beginning of a Bible study course I was starting that evening – only Bible course now that's ever been started without a single Bible I reckon, given the prison confiscated them all!"

"But you got one in, Tom said you did."

"Yes. I was back in the prison car park, with that offish prison guard having confiscated all twelve, not knowing what to do. I said a little

TABLE 7

prayer and then I suddenly remembered in the glove compartment of my car was Vaughan's Bible. He'd left it there, the Sunday evening before he died, when I'd given him a lift home after Evensong. So, there it still was in my glove compartment, with all his scraps of paper and inserts and pencil jottings in the margins, and I knew, just knew, that that one I'd get through and be able to give to Tom. The offish guard, well, thankfully she gave up the fight when she saw me walk back in and didn't even look at it, just waved me through."

"Wow!" exclaimed Alba. "From how Tom described the reputation it's given you at HMP South Down, I reckon you could walk in with anything in your pocket and they'd let you through unsearched and unhindered."

As Matthew smiled, Alba detected a 'certain look' in his eyes.

"What's brought that look to your face? You're thinking about something, aren't you?" said Alba.

"I was just thinking of Vaughan's funeral. Not that that was making me smile, mind you. I was just suddenly remembering the things that were on his coffin; those five things."

"Sam said it was 'creepy' and Mrs Rowan that it was 'a weird end' to the service."

"And I said to you it was an unusual finale to a funeral service when we first spoke in the church hall after the funeral itself," contributed Matthew.

"Did you? You can remember what you said to me that day, can you?"

"Yes," Matthew replied almost inaudibly. "Yes, I can. But we didn't speak for long."

"No, sorry about that. I think you'd made a joke but I didn't take it very well and stormed off. Sorry," she added again, before adding, as she raised her half empty glass in her left hand and held it out into the middle of the table, in an act of reconciliation, in the hope that he would offer up his in return:

"Forgiven?" enquired Alba.

"You were that day, the moment you turned away from me."

As Matthew, with near-empty glass in his right hand, reciprocated Alba's gesture, and they 'chinked' together, Alba added:

"I went and picked up Vaughan's journal and the secateurs he'd bequeathed to Tom, when I went off in my strop."

"It was the secateurs I was just thinking of," interjected Matthew. "Perhaps I didn't need to entrust them to you after all. It would seem, with my new-found reputation at the prison, I could just take them in to Tom in person. What do you reckon?"

"Oh, yeah. Great idea!" joked Alba in reply, echoing Matthew's humorous interpretation of the situation. "Sure, a nice bladed article, nothing to worry about with that dangling from his right hip as he waited in the lunch queue or wandered the length of A-wing. What possible harm could come of that!"

"It would be fine," contributed Matthew. "I'd just put on my best dog collar and ask everyone to be nice to each other!"

Alba smiled a warm, warm smile and raised her glass once again as she said:

"To Tom. May he be safe whilst he's in there but back with us soon."

"Amen to that," said Matthew.

*

"All done, are we?" enquired Sam, somewhat unnecessarily, having seen their empty plates and knives and forks correctly placed together at an angle on their respective plates.

"Yes, thank you," Alba and Matthew replied in unison.

Having lifted the plates from the table, Sam continued:

"Would you like the bill or, as you hinted at earlier, to see the desserts board?"

"No to both, in one sense, since I already know what I'd like for dessert," replied Alba.

TABLE 7

"Ditto, for me," chimed Matthew.

"OK. What will it be?"

"Sticky toffee pudding and cream, for me, please," said Alba.

"Peach and apricot crumble, for me, if that's allowed" asked Matthew.

"Of course. With the crumble, do you want ice-cream, cream or custard?"

"Oh, custard please."

"So, that's one 'stp' with cream and one crumble with custard. Anything further to drink?"

"No thank you," replied Matthew on behalf of both of them, given Alba was still only halfway through her soft drink and they still had half a jug of tap water on the table too. Alba nodded her consent.

As Sam departed, having informed them it would just be a couple of minutes, Matthew said:

"Real chip off the old block, is Sam."

"Absolutely," confirmed Alba.

For a few minutes, as they waited, Alba asked Matthew about the age of the larger yew trees in the churchyard and what relatives were officially allowed to plant on a grave plot, until Matthew suddenly said, in a slightly embarrassed tone:

"Err, would you excuse me for a moment? Probably should only have ordered half a pint of 'Theakston's'."

"Of course. But I can't promise not to start on your pudding if it arrives before you return."

*

As she sat by herself, studying the less cluttered table in front of her, Alba instinctively turned her spoon, the pudding one that had been laid out above her placemat, when the table was originally set, around.

Having watched her do so, Sam, who had appeared with their puddings, asked:

"Why have you done that? You didn't pick it up and wipe it in your serviette or swop it with one from another table that's within reach. You've simply just turned it around. I mean, it's not important but, having just watched you do it, I'm suddenly curious as to why. Unless, you're not aware that you've just done it."

"Oh, people and their insignificant little details," commented Alba but as much to herself as in reply to Sam.

But still Sam looked expectantly, hoping Alba would explain.

"Well, simple really," said Alba. "I'm left-handed. Pudding spoons are always laid out for right-handed people – the handle is always to the right and the 'spoony' bit of the spoon is to the left. That's fine for the majority, such as Matthew who'll be back in a minute, but over my now thirty years, I can't think of one occasion in a pub or restaurant where I haven't needed to turn it around. As I was sitting here by myself, I noticed it was pointing the wrong way for me."

"Oh, I see," replied Sam. "Some people have such odd mannerisms. Take Mrs Lyle for instance, when she's in here meeting her accountant over morning coffee, she has a thing for the little flower vases we put out as part of our morning table arrangements. But each to their own, I guess."

But, as Sam spoke, Sam sensed Alba was suddenly deep in thought. Alba's eyes had narrowed perhaps fractionally and she was looking at neither Sam nor the food. Unbeknown to Sam, a barrage of images and sayings flashed through Alba's mind. Alba didn't notice Matthew's return, nor his 'thank you' to Sam as she placed the desserts down and moved away, nor care that he nicked a tiny corner of her pudding to taste it before starting on his own sizeable portion of butter-enriched fruit crumble.

Matthew could tell Alba was deep in thought and was happy just to enjoy his meal in someone else's company once again. Eventually, though, he felt he ought to say something, before other diners thought she was sulking or that they had fallen out.

TABLE 7

"You trying to work out the answer to life, the universe and everything?" he enquired as light-heartedly as he could.

"Not quite that," replied Alba.

"No need to. It's already been done."

"Are you being all theological again or referencing Douglas Adams?" queried Alba.

"Definitely Douglas Adams – I'm not being theological this time," said Matthew in reply. "You OK? You seemed deep in thought."

"Yes, just thinking about a few things," said Alba.

"Anything I can help with?" offered back Matthew.

"Yes, actually. A few minutes ago, we were making light of you smuggling Tom's secateurs into him in prison."

"And how it would be fine, so long as everyone was nice to each other."

"Sort of. But going back to the funeral," said Alba carefully, as if she were re-arranging pieces of a jigsaw puzzle in her mind as she did so, "and the five items on Vaughan's casket."

"The recipe, his hat, a red rose, his journal and the secateurs. Two of which you have, I might point out, and you've probably been given a copy of the recipe by now."

"I have, as a matter of fact. Ought to let Sam have a copy, too, now you mention it," commented Alba. "Anyway, that's not the point. Given you seem able to remember what you said that day."

"Well, what I said to you, not necessarily everything," said Matthew, offering up a pre-emptive self-defence in case he let Alba down on whatever she was about to ask.

"Can you remember what you said about Tom's secateurs?" As she asked, Matthew noticed Alba was twisting some of her hair around one of her fingers, as she waited for his recollection.

"Let me think," replied Matthew.

As she waited, she retracted her finger from her hair, ran her whole hand through it to untangle what she had just entwined and started the action all over again. She sat hoping. She thought she knew what he'd said about the items but didn't want to suggest it first and thereby lead him into a false recollection. She had to ask, not tell him why, not guide his answer nor 'put it out' as a statement. She had to ask and just wait for Matthew's reply.

It felt, she would concede later, the longest, most intense, twelve seconds of her life as she waited for his answer.

"I said, if memory serves me correctly," said Matthew, "'For Alba the journal and Tom is to have the secateurs'. Then I said something else, bear with me."

Alba twirled her hair once more and then Matthew spoke again:

"I think I said 'Vaughan had originally intended those to be the other way round, for Tom to get the journal' and so forth, but that 'he changed his notes and it was clear you, Alba, were to get the journal'. Do you want me to try and recall anything else? The service was probably recorded and put onto a cassette if you need a word for word transcript, for whatever reason has got your mind whirring this evening."

"No, no need to recall anything else tonight. That was my recollection, too, of what you said but I wanted your version as well. A copy of the cassette would be good mind you," replied Alba.

"Leave it with me – or more accurately, with the church office. Can I ask why?"

"There's a reason why Vaughan swopped those last two items around. And I think I now know. No, I do know, there's no 'think' about it. I will tell you, promise, but not tonight. I'm sorry to do this to you, for I have had a nice evening but," at which point Alba stood up, picked up her shoulder bag and light summer jacket. "But I have to go. There's someone I have to speak to. I simply have to go."

Matthew stood up in response to Alba's imminent departure but at a complete loss as to what was going on.

As she moved away from the table, Alba added:

"Be a sweetie and pay my bill. And thank Sam and leave her and the kitchen staff a tip on my behalf. Promise I'll pay you back, promise."

TABLE 7

The look on Matthew's bewildered face, prompted Alba to offer him just a little bit more by way of explanation:

"I've asked the right person, the right question but about the wrong person."

Matthew looked even more confused and unsure as to how to reply. Alba simply added:

"I think I can align the chess pieces. Don't forget to dig out the photographs of Vaughan for me."

With that, she was gone, leaving the parish vicar all alone. As he sat down, he said to himself:

"God speed your journey, Miss White, God speed whatever mission you are on."

After finishing his own, he duly finished Alba's sticky toffee pudding, which, he conceded, was the far better choice of the two and found himself thinking that he really must teach that woman how to play chess.

CHAPTER 22

Marks in the floor

She studied the floor, able to make out the areas of compression, where a grand piano had once been. Probably a double bass, some violins, even a harp had also divulged their notes, to the assembled guests on many an evening, as they drank their cocktails, in their dinner suits and evening gowns. They would have been in here, out on the terrace or perhaps further out into the formal gardens, enjoying themselves, carefree, perhaps, occasionally, falling in love, listening to a pianist or a band play, enjoying being waited upon, as drinks and canapés were offered around by waiters with an ability to be almost invisible amongst the guests.

The room itself would have felt alive. The candelabras and chandeliers would have cast their light upon the faces of those gathered. Whilst, although champagne glasses, mirrors and windows would each have tried to capture and hold the light that fell upon them, none of them would have been able to. Instead, the light would have worked its way through or off each of them and either back into the room itself, further illuminating the array of jewels which draped themselves from the necks and wrists of elegantly dressed ladies, or escaped out through the windows to land upon some young couple as they made their way into the sunken garden, in the silvery moonlight, hoping to have just a few minutes to talk about their future, away from her mother's prying ears.

Yes, thought Alba, as she studied the marks in the floor a final time, the music room would have been a beautiful and mesmerizing place to have experienced in its heyday – laughter, whispered conversations, fine perfumes, expensive clothes, sumptuous food and enchanting music. The light, the fragrances and music would have permeated everything they fell upon and together would have left those present spell-bound.

*

This Saturday afternoon, by comparison, was anything but enchanting. A grey damp day, as a cold front slowly made its way across this corner of the country, had kept the sun from both brightening up and warming up the music room. The constant fine rain reminded Alba of days exploring quaint little Cornish fishing villages under grey skies as a persistent 'mizzle' – where sea mist and fine drizzle combined – encouraged her to bury her chin in her coat's upturned collar and to keep her hands snug in her pockets. Today was the kind of day, she found herself thinking as she had on the morning itself, when Vaughan's, or indeed anyone's funeral, should have taken place.

The lights were on although three bulbs were in need of replacement and, had she not spent quite so much time studying the floor, would have looked to the ceiling and worried what damage the rain would eventually do to the room, as the water permeated its way down from a roof in desperate need of having its leadwork replaced.

She hadn't really chosen this room. However, the church hall was being used for a scouting event, 'The Sun and Moon' she wouldn't have sole use of and, whilst the cricket pavilion would have been ideal size wise, it would, even with the reason they were meeting together today, somehow still be inappropriate. So, when she had asked Andrew for somewhere to meet and he had suggested the old music room, she could find no reason to reject it, even though of all the rooms Hillstone Hall had, somewhere within herself she would have preferred the voluminous library.

*

Here they then were, Alba and thirteen other people. Barnes, given it was a cold, damp, albeit July, day, and they were in a cold damp room, had a small log fire going in the grand marble fireplace. He had also, at Alba's request, organised a couple of extra folding tables, with simple white sheets over them. Upon the tables were a coffee pot, an urn of tea, cups and saucers, three milk jugs and a couple of plates of biscuits. Some, like Mrs Rowan and Sally, had made themselves a hot drink and sat at the central wooden table but most stood unsure as to the reasoning of such an eclectic mix of people being gathered together on such a dreary weekend afternoon.

She had kept her reasoning from Edward Chapman, the 7th Lord Hartfield and Andrew, his heir, simply telling them who needed to be in attendance. At the time she'd made the telephone call to Andrew, even Alba had shocked herself when she had said to him 'I'm inviting three people, you just ensure all the people I've now told you to invite are equally there at four o'clock. No, I'm not telling you any more for now; a room big enough for seventeen people, that's all I'm saying'. She would have preferred it to have been the morning but, when she had spoken to the Reverend Quinn mid-week about his availability, he couldn't do the morning: as well as informing her the church hall would have fifty-plus scouts charging around from three different packs all day long, he said he was leading a marriage course from ten o'clock for a couple of hours and then was conducting a short home communion service, for a now house-bound parishioner at two. Given Alba needed the Reverend in attendance, the gathering was to be at four o'clock.

Helen brought Alba a cup of tea, accompanied by a couple of custard creams, and placed it at the end of the table near to where Alba was standing by herself. But sensing this was Alba's 'show', Helen then went and stood over with David by one of the large windows. As she did so, Helen reflected that Alba had been a bit of a mystery all day. She hadn't finished half the gardening tasks she'd been tasked with and each time Helen had seen her around the Hall during the day, Alba had been sitting, be it at the pavilion by the tennis court, on a bench on the terrace or on a fallen oak tree half way to the visitors' car park. The hand gestures and movement of her lips gave the impression, so it seemed to Helen, that Alba was having some animated conversations with herself. Had the day been ten degrees hotter, Helen would have worried that her friend was suffering from heatstroke. Even at a quarter to four, Helen, as she made her way back to the gardeners' bothy to offload her tools prior to attending this meeting in the music room, whatever it might be all about, had seen Alba virtually running down the main drive, back towards the visitors' carpark.

At a minute to four, Lord Hartfield, his brother and Andrew entered. Once Barnes, who had been standing as still as a sentry by the fireplace, as if he himself were part of the marble carvings, saw his Lordship enter, he went over and bowed ever so slightly and said:

"If that will be all, sir, then I will leave you and write up those letters you drafted earlier."

Despite his grandfather's nod of agreement in return, Andrew said:

"Actually, Barnes, if you could stay as well, then we will be complying with Miss White's wishes."

Barnes, a puzzled expression on his face, one Andrew conceded he'd never seen before on his grandfather's faithful and loyal employee, looked briefly over to Alba, then to Andrew and then to Lord Hartfield himself, who in turn looked to Andrew.

"Your presence has been requested, as has all of ours. I have asked Liz to be acting duty house manager for the remainder of the afternoon, so any crisis she will more than ably deal with. You are, therefore, to please remain," requested Andrew.

"If that is the case," added Lord Hartfield "and, though I am at a complete loss as to what this is all about, you are to stay but it would seem as an equal. Barnes, please, therefore, if you would like a drink have one. You are no more on duty than I am a Lord for the next half an hour or so. I am truly baffled as to what this is all about. Andrew," he continued as he turned to his heir, "any ideas?"

"Not completely. I'm surmising it's got something to do with Tom Wychfield but if Miss White is thinking of wanting to send him a 'thinking of you' card, she's got a slightly odd mix of people in here to sign it."

"Well, in that case," continued his Lordship and now once more to Barnes, "let's hope she tells us soon what it's all about. Come on, let me make you a coffee."

"Your Lordship," entreated Barnes, "you can't. It wouldn't be right."

"Look, I'm not going to make a habit of it but I'm not so aloof as to not make you a drink if I'm getting one for myself. Plus, those letters will still need to be written once we're out of here so I need to fill you up with coffee so you are awake later on."

As Andrew watched his grandfather and a rather embarrassed Barnes go and make themselves a drink, he cast his eye over those gathered. There was the full ensemble of garden volunteers, save for Tom for obvious reasons. The Reverend. Simon, his wife Anne and their son Justin. Then there was the village shopkeeper, Mrs Lyle. Sam and Chloe from the Hall's tea shop and, though he was not one hundred per cent sure but thought there was a family likeness, Sam's mother, Mrs Rowan. There was also a young man whom Andrew didn't recognise but who Alba had told him, when she had called him to arrange this gathering, would be Neale, a friend of hers and an author.

Andrew watched his grandfather take a seat whilst Barnes, with a reluctant cup in his hand went and adopted his more natural position by one of the internal doors. Andrew, sensing Alba was about to speak, beckoned his great-uncle in from the terrace. William Chapman, to the complete disgust of Sally, who watched him from where she was sitting, threw his cigarette under some of the box hedging around the sunken garden, and stepped back inside.

Alba unslung her day bag from her shoulder and placed it on the table in front of her, next to her half empty cup and one remaining biscuit and beside a biscuit tin, which had a picture of a Scottish stag on it – a tin she had already placed there. She glanced around the room one final time, reassuring herself everyone was here she'd requested, and that the extra item, which she had moved earlier, was still there on the mantlepiece and hadn't been noted by Barnes or one of the house staff during the afternoon and been moved back to the room it came from. Alba then looked at the Reverend, Neale and finally Andrew. She twisted her grandmother's ring, which she'd chosen to wear, took a final sip of tea and decided the time had come to establish the truth.

*

"My dear beloved friend Vaughan was murdered back at the beginning of June – sorry, our friend," and with that Alba looked to David, Helen and Sally. As Alba did so, she thought to herself 'blow I'm already bluffing what I rehearsed, come on girl, get a grip'. She continued:

"He wasn't young but he was definitely taken before his time. David and I had started to discuss what we'd do to mark his eightieth birthday but he was never allowed to reach that milestone. And that, though this is not why I have got you all here together this afternoon, really cut me up originally. He should have been allowed to reach it and many more years besides. But I take comfort from the knowledge that to Vaughan he had reached a more important milestone. He'd made a note of it in his battered old gardening journal but despite how many times I looked at the page I didn't understand its significance originally."

With that, Alba, having rummaged in her deep day bag in a way that one might have expected Mary Poppins to, brought out a tatty, mud-stained book and placed it on the table. Opening it at the page with the pink 'post-it' note, Alba read out:

"One thousand moons."

A room of blank expressions greeted those words, as she anticipated. She then continued:

"It was something I didn't understand to start with and to think I call myself a horticulturalist! Thankfully, it was something Vaughan's gardener, Jim, was able to explain. You see, to Vaughan, him reaching his thousandth lunar cycle was the milestone that mattered. He'd had his seventy-six-and-a-bit years and he found peace in that fact. So, I miss him terribly and he was murdered before his time but to me I am comforted, just a little, each time I look into his journal and see that he himself had circled around that phrase, a phrase he probably had written down decades before."

As she paused, Alba noticed an appreciative smile on David's face, as David too, found comfort in that small detail.

"However, I have not asked you all here for a horticultural talk." Alba made a point not to even look at Anne at that moment.

"What have you got us all here for?" asked an edgy Mrs Lyle. "I'm having to pay for Saturday cover and, given how miserable the weather is, I might well be making a loss as I speak. I haven't signed up for a tour of 'the unseen Hillstone Hall'."

"There's an idea," chipped in Andrew.

"Nor to spend an afternoon in sack cloth and ashes for my old neighbour."

"Mordecai might," and this time it was the Reverend Quinn who interrupted Mrs Lyle.

"Sorry but may I finish? So, Miss White why, may I ask, are we all here?" said an irritable and flustered Mrs Lyle.

"Simple really, Mrs Lyle," replied Alba. "I'd like to ask the person who murdered Vaughan and Mrs Taylor to confess. The rest of us, I thought, were entitled to hear the confession in person."

"What are you on about?" said Anne. "The police have arrested one of you do-gooding gardening people from up here at the Hall. What was his name? Come on Simon," she continued to her husband, "help me out with his name."

"Tom, I think," contributed Simon.

"That's right," said Anne. "Tom, the Head Gardener."

"Deputy Head," said Sally, the Acting Deputy Head, for no particular reason beyond a liking for people being factually correct.

"Whatever," replied Anne. "My first husband was stabbed by this person called Tom. Someone who pretended to be his friend but stabbed him for a set of war medals. Knew, as a set, they were worth a bit so stabbed him. Then he had to kill his landlady because she either found the medals or some blood-stained clothing or just suspected him for some other reason."

"That's right. We read it in the local paper. Justin showed it to us, didn't you?" Simon said in support of his wife but turning to Justin as he did so.

"That's right," replied Justin. "It was in all the local papers. Obviously, quiet little Sussex villages like ours don't get cold-hearted double murderers very often."

"But he didn't do it," exhorted Chloe, who, despite being the youngest person in the room and very much feeling the newcomer to life up at the Hall, was unable to hold her tongue any longer. "He didn't, I swear," she added.

"Oh, come now little thing," said Simon. "Course he did, the items taken were found amongst his possessions and he knew all about poisonous plants no doubt. Plus, so the papers said, he was with his landlady as she ate the poisonous plants."

"Actually," interjected Sam, "on that point the papers are wrong. I was serving him in 'The Sun and Moon' that evening."

"Really, sure on that are you, miss?" said Simon. "I reckon you've got your evenings mixed up."

"Don't patronise me, whoever you are. I might be many years your junior and you might be some bigwig up in the city or some friend of his Lordship," said an angry Sam in reply. She continued, to both her mother's pride and Andrew's encouragement, as he realised he had a potential new 'head of catering and events' before him:

"But I am correct. I served him that Tuesday evening. He was at table seven, it was pie night and he had shepherd's pie. He was talking a bit about Chloe here."

"Was he? Really?" asked Chloe.

"Yes, he was. So, he was definitely in the pub, talking about a girl he had a crush on, when the papers allegedly say he was poisoning his landlady." Sam paused but then felt compelled to add:

"Sorry, your Lordship, if I've spoken out of turn or have caused you offence."

"Thank you, Sam but no offence taken. I think Simon deserved your retort." With that, Lord Hartfield give a disappointed glance to the auctioneer, who was standing diagonally opposite to where his Lordship was sitting, much to Simon's embarrassment.

"See, I said he didn't do it," repeated Chloe.

"Well, even if not the second, he's still guilty of the first murder. He was the last person with him and had the missing items. The papers have also linked him to the knife," Simon responded.

"But he didn't, he didn't I told you," insisted Chloe.

"Really, eating steak pie in the pub on that occasion, was he?" said a still somewhat rattled Simon, feeling as if he had talked himself into a corner he now desperately was trying to get out of by bluster.

"No. But he wrote to me last week. The Reverend brought me his letter. Tom said he didn't do it, wouldn't have done it. Said that Vaughan was like a grandfather to him."

"Did he now? Well, that's alright then. Remind me to phone the prison and ask them to let him out," replied Simon with enough venom to reduce Chloe to tears. "Oh, for goodness sake pull yourself together; I'm afraid your *beau* is not what you first thought. I'm getting another coffee until someone can tell me what's really the point of us all being here."

As Helen and Sam consoled Chloe, Alba simply repeated herself:

"We are here to give the person the opportunity to do the first decent thing, I reckon, that they've done in a long long time and confess."

A silence fell across the room, interrupted only by the quiet broken sobs of Chloe and the sound of coffee being poured by Simon.

Yet, no-one left the room; for, whilst most had had plans they had cancelled to be here and thought this was a very odd kind of Saturday afternoon, such was the drama of the occasion, no-one present wanted to give everyone else the impression of a guilty conscience by being the first to leave.

*

It was roughly thirty seconds Alba waited before speaking again.

"To be fair, I didn't really expect a confession but I was just curious as to the level of remorse the person has. It would seem none."

"So, can we go now?" asked a frustrated Mrs Lyle. "You've had your little scene and I'll be amazed if you show your face around the Hall again after wasting his Lordship's time and taken advantage of his hospitality. But, if you do, I suggest you stick to weeding the gravel drive and raking up the autumn leaves."

With that Mrs Lyle took her cup over to the drinks table and started to put her coat on. Helen and Sally felt an awkwardness for Alba and feared for what their friend was indeed doing. Even Andrew, was puzzled as to what Alba was trying to achieve.

But just as a ripple of unease and movement started to take hold of the others, Alba, who had exchanged glances with David and received his 'nod of encouragement' to continue, said to everyone:

"If no confession is forthcoming, I guess I'll just have to prove it this afternoon. Here. Now."

"You can't!" announced Simon. "The police have got their man. You've got nothing. It seems to be this is all a fantasy you're living. You've got us all here to give substance to what is nothing more than fiction." Then, turning to Lord Hartfield, said:

"If you'll excuse us, we must be going. We've wasted enough of our afternoon with this woman's charade."

"But, Simon," replied Alba. "I can. I very much can prove who did it."

Simon stopped and turned around, unable to ignore the surety in Alba's voice.

As Alba took the lid off the biscuit tin in front of her, she said:

"In a way it starts with two pieces of millionaire's shortbread. Mrs Rowan's shortbread to be precise, which she made for the cricket match that took place on the Queen's Golden Jubilee day, the day Vaughan was murdered. These pieces in this tin are a new batch, that, at my request, Mrs Rowan kindly agreed to make yesterday for our gathering today."

Alba passed the tin to Mrs Rowan, who effortlessly moved around the room offering a piece to each of those present. She made a point of offering a piece to Neale first – a gesture of goodwill, instigated by Mrs Rowan, noticed only by Neale and Alba.

Once everyone who wanted a piece had a piece, Alba continued:

"Millionaire's shortbread was just one part of the lunch Mrs Rowan and Sam had worked so hard to put together for that day. It could have been a lovely day – the weather was kind, the cricket was good and, if I may say your Lordship," and here Alba addressed Lord Hartfield directly:

"You put a very good team together. The village team obviously play together throughout the season, so for your invitational eleven to put on such a contest, for the match was finely balanced when it had to be abandoned, says a lot about the effort you put in to put a serious side together."

"Thank you, Miss White. Kind of you to say so but the whole thing was in abeyance when one of my team dropped out at the last minute."

"Yes, a horse went lame as I understand. But you got someone else," said Alba, knowing but not saying who the last-minute replacement was – as if she wanted other people in the room to align the chess pieces themselves, to make the same links that she had made over the weeks.

"Yes," contributed Lord Hartfield, "Justin, here, Simon and Anne's son to those of you who don't know, was able to step in at the last minute."

"How convenient," commented Alba.

"Well," offered up Justin himself, "I was free and I had no distance to travel since I now live here in the village. If I may say, I recognise one or two of you here this afternoon, Mrs Lyle, obviously from our village shop. I've seen you," at which point Justin gestured to Sam, "in the village pub and," now referring to Reverend Quinn, "I'm guessing the dog collar denotes you're Father so and so. As for the rest of you, my apologies I have yet to come across you."

"Actually," said Matthew, keen to correct a misunderstanding, "I'm Reverend, not Father, Quinn; I feel it's more in keeping with my C of E calling. Been in the village long?"

"Getting on for six months, I guess. Moved here early March. Been an eventful few months; asked to play in the Lord's cricket team for starters."

"Played well, too. I recall. Took an excellent slip catch," said William Chapman, his Lordship's brother.

"Good of you to remember. Then what happened on the day itself, then the death of that lady who lived in an estate cottage, down the lane where I walk my dogs and now this somewhat bizarre village inquest that somehow we're all letting this woman 'chair' without seemingly getting anywhere, beyond offering out cakes. I don't think any of this," continued Justin but now with a smirk on his face, "was in the estate agent's particulars for the house I bought."

Alba, seeing Justin's parents, Mrs Lyle and Barnes smile at this last comment, felt she was losing the room. She sought to reassert herself:

"You may smirk Justin, but Vaughan was still alive when you took that catch. I was chatting to him at the time, on a wooden bench near the pavilion. But that was the last time I spoke to him or saw him alive. I went back to my spot near the beech trees, right round the boundary rope, opposite to the pavilion and where Vaughan was."

"That's right," contributed Neale, keen to help Alba make progress. "Alba and I were watching the game together. Vaughan could have sat with us, we asked him to but he wanted to be near the pavilion to watch the memorial flight for as long as possible. But a while before the flight came over, we saw, even from where we were sitting, a woman was standing right in front of him and talking to him."

"Arguing with him, it looked like to me," continued Alba. "Plus, the first time I visited Tom in prison, he recollected, right at the end of my visit, that Vaughan had said to him, when they were talking in the pavilion, that it was a desire to get away from this argumentative woman that drove him into the pavilion to simply get away from her."

"Really?" said Simon. "The person on remand, who was the last known person to be with the dead man, has now claimed a woman was arguing with Vaughan shortly before. Oh, that's alright then. Mystery solved. So, you've called us all here to help you find this mystery woman. Course. Happy to, we'll crack on with it straight away." He paused, before adding:

"This is getting ridiculous. Even if it's true, you've got no hope of tracing her."

"It is true but I don't need to trace her, for I already know who it was," said Alba.

"Do you now? Care to enlighten us, Miss White?" challenged Simon.

Alba could sense, in that split second before she spoke, that people were eyeing one another up, sensing the person was already present in the room.

"Mrs Lyle," said Alba softly. "Anything to say?"

Everyone looked to the owner of 'Stapleton's' and waited for a response but none was forthcoming. Mrs Lyle just stared ahead of her, silent and still.

"Nothing? You drove him inside, in one sense drove him to his death because someone followed him in shortly afterwards. He was an elderly man, trying to watch a game of cricket and waiting to watch some wartime planes fly overhead. You took all of that away from him. Have you nothing to say?" said an angry Alba.

Still Mrs Lyle said nothing. The silence prompted Lord Hartfield himself to speak:

"Mrs Lyle, I'm probably your biggest customer. More importantly, Vaughan was one of my faithful volunteers. Plus, I do now seem to remember seeing you at the match."

"Odd for someone who told me she hates cricket," added Alba.

"I would therefore be grateful if you answered Miss White here, even if it's to deny what she is alleging."

Yet still, Mrs Lyle remained silent.

CHAPTER 23

A negative ending

"Mrs Lyle," said Reverend Quinn. He could sense the internal battle, between pride, embarrassment and remorse she was now having with herself. He then simply said, as he took a couple of steps towards her:

"We are not here to judge you or what you may or may not have done but if there is a chance that the authorities have arrested an innocent man, then Miss White is right to bring us all here to draw out the truth. Therefore if, and I use that word deliberately for I am not assuming anything, you were there, arguing with Vaughan, then admitting it doesn't make you a bad person. It simply makes you human like the rest of us. Not one person here is perfect and definitely not me. Do you know," Reverend Quinn continued, as Mrs Lyle looked back at him through sad lonely eyes, "just four days before my wife died, I had a blazing row with her. I instigated it because I was having a bad day. Thankfully I apologised the next day but I have nonetheless regretted it every day of my life since. You can't ask for Vaughan's forgiveness, if it were you, but you can have ours and, knowing Vaughan as I did, I think he would have done so too, if you'd asked."

As Reverend Quinn fell silent, Mrs Lyle's head dropped and,

perhaps Neale, the author, would one day, in a future novel of his, be able to describe what it was like to watch a woman's pride and bitterness fall away and be left with, if not a newborn person, then at least someone with a softer side start to emerge – as if a butterfly was making its first tentative efforts to break away from its dark all-encompassing chrysalis.

A quiet voice could eventually be heard coming from Mrs Lyle:

"Alright, yes, it was me arguing with Vaughan that day. I'm not proud of it, at least not now. I guess at the time I didn't care. It's not easy running the village shop all by myself. I offer a service to the village and you'd all miss me if I sold up and let it be converted into a couple of maisonettes – yet more housing without shops to support them. Yes, you'd miss me if I went but so many of you take me for granted or just come in to moan about your newspaper delivery being an hour late. Or let your children come in and shoplift or expect me to forever put up your posters in my windows for free or complain I don't have a wide enough variety of produce and 'oh, Mrs Lyle, you really should stock larger boxes of cereals or a wider selection of greeting cards' or something else. Just occasionally, if the odd villager came in and said 'thank you' would that be so hard?"

Mrs Lyle paused, took a sip of her cold coffee, that was on one of the drinks tables beside her and then continued:

"And then I was promised the plot of land next to my shop by the people who were selling up. I had the chance to expand and turn a just above break-even business into something consistently profitable. However, I'd just lent what savings I had to a friend, probably my only friend in the village, because she was desperate to help her nephew clear his drug debts. When I lent it to her, given where the money was going, I didn't expect my friend to ever repay it but I lent it anyway. More fool me."

"That was a godly thing to do Mrs Lyle," said Helen. "Let me get you a fresh cup of coffee."

"Thank you," offered back Mrs Lyle.

"You're talking about Mrs Taylor, aren't you?" said Alba, as Barnes was already pouring a fresh cup making Helen's walk across the room redundant.

"Yes," replied Mrs Lyle. "It did clear her nephew's debts and Mrs Taylor was so grateful. But sadly, he's since relapsed but that's not relevant today. Going back to the plot of land, I still wanted it; the business needed it. But then Vaughan moved in and being the gardener that he was, he was never going to sell his side garden to me or to anyone. I think I always knew that but still I pestered him, badgered him, got in his face, all born out of my frustrations, with that sense of 'the thing that got away' – it was almost within my reach but then it eluded me. So, yes, I was arguing with Vaughan outside the pavilion, as he tried to watch the cricket. I wish I hadn't but I can't do anything about that now. The argument finished when Vaughan said he needed the toilet and made his way to the pavilion. But," and Mrs Lyle looked around the room, finally focusing on Alba herself, "I did not follow him in and I did not stab him out of anger or as a calculating act because somehow I had been able to previously break into his home and rewrite his will. I was angry with him but I left at that point and went back to my shop, since the only good thing about a silly game of cricket being played in the village is that it brings a few extra customers my way."

Mrs Lyle then fell silent once again, apart from a hesitant 'thank you', as she received a fresh cup of coffee.

"But I didn't follow him in," she suddenly repeated.

"I know you didn't," confirmed Alba. "And thank you for opening up about the pressures of running a small business in a village such as this – I think we can all understand some of the issues you face a little bit better now. I just wish, as I sense you now do, that your behaviour hadn't driven Vaughan inside a dark wooden pavilion on a warm summer's day, which gave someone the opportunity to strike."

"But," stated William, Lord Hartfield's brother, "aren't we now simply at the point which the police deduced weeks ago. It's all been very entertaining this gathering you've organised but you've simply proved who created the situation that Tom Wychfield took advantage of. I'm going for a cigarette."

"Could you hold on just a minute?" requested Alba.

"I'm sure you can hold out a little bit longer, great-uncle," said Andrew, in support of Alba.

William reluctantly heeded his great-nephew's request, shaking his box of matches one last vigorous time before dropping them back into his jacket pocket.

"Thank you for bearing with me," said Alba. "You see, everyone, I know Mrs Lyle didn't follow Vaughan into the pavilion. For there were two eyewitnesses, who between them, observed everyone who did enter the pavilion after Vaughan."

"Were there?" asked the Reverend Quinn.

"Yes, there were, in Mrs Rowan and Neale, my dear friend. Between them, not that they realised it originally, they saw everyone and, when the three of us met at my house a couple of weeks ago, I was able to compare their lists."

"Well, who did they see?" asked Chloe, sensing that there might now be something tangible to hold onto in her belief in Tom's innocence.

"To begin with, just to account for their presence, Mrs Rowan was, alongside Sam, working in the little kitchen area of the pavilion, as she put on the day's lunch, whilst Neale was in there as I'd asked him to check up on Vaughan as we could no longer see him from where we were sitting and we'd seen him already half stumble that day so were worried."

"Understandably," chipped in David.

"Exactly," continued Alba. "Needless to say, Neale located him in the pavilion, since, as we now know, he'd been driven in there for reasons we won't go over again. As for those Mrs Rowan and Neale saw between them and ignoring two young lads who snaffled a bowl of crisps…"

"Not my boys," stated David.

"Definitely not David's boys but we'll come back to them later," said Alba. "The first person of interest, as observed by Mrs Rowan, was an elderly gentleman."

"Oh, brilliant," said a defiant and resurgent Simon. "Just brilliant, Tom must be innocent and now all we have to do is find, no longer a mystery woman, but an elderly man who was at a cricket match. This is getting comical."

"I accept it was a bit of a vague description to begin with – all Mrs Rowan added to it was that he reminded her of someone. And, before you interrupt me again Simon, this unknown person was just an 'X' on my list of suspects until last Tuesday."

"That was my birthday," commented a puzzled Sam.

"Yes, it was," said Alba. "I had popped into the tea room here to wish you a happy day and your mum was visiting you as well and then," at which point Alba addressed Lord Hartfield directly, "your Lordship entered, with Andrew, Simon and Anne and William. David had also just entered as well. As Mrs Rowan stood next to me watching everyone come in, I heard her say, as much to herself as me, 'oh that's who else I saw that day'. Now she couldn't have been referring to David, not old enough and she'd have recognised him at Vaughan's funeral, plus he was out in the middle of the pitch when Vaughan was killed. She obviously would have known it was Lord Hartfield, who I might add, did go into the pavilion himself prior to ringing the bell to suspend play."

"Yes, I did," confirmed Lord Hartfield. "I used the toilet, spoke to Mrs Rowan, who'd come out of the kitchen, saw Vaughan asleep and then left to ring the bell to suspend play."

"Meaning," continued Alba, "the only other elderly person it could have been, because he 'reminded Mrs Rowan of someone', was William, given he's your Lordship's brother."

"I don't think so," replied William, suddenly uncomfortable at being the centre of the discussion.

"But you did," insisted Mrs Rowan. "As Alba says, I realised who you were when I was up here to surprise Sam on her birthday last week."

"Well, perhaps. Guess I went in to use the facilities, I'm an elderly man after all. But I didn't go in and kill Vaughan," said William.

"Vaughan was definitely still alive after you went in, William," agreed Alba. "For others entered the pavilion after you. Next it was a cricketer, but Mrs Rowan shooed him away and then Tom."

"And we're back to Tom," said Simon, receiving a nod of agreement from his wife. "Miss White, please just try and accept that the police have the right person."

"But it wasn't Tom. He went in and was chatting to Vaughan about his brother's wartime medals. Remember," and Alba addressed Simon directly on this point, "you, and the rest of His Lordship's group, were standing right behind me when I was with Vaughan on the bench outside the pavilion. You knew what he was carrying that day and how valuable they were. Didn't you?"

"Yes, I saw them. That's hardly a great revelation," Simon said in reply, "I admitted I knew what they were when I saw you and Andrew outside Mrs Lyle's village shop, weeks ago. Can we just be clear, for I feel you're trying to pin the crime on me, I didn't follow Tom in and murder Anne's ex-husband in a fit of jealously or to steal his brother's medals, as valuable as they are. I reckon I could get…"

"Clive's!" interjected Anne, her voice a mix of anger and passion. "His brother's name was Clive. Please can we at least honour him by using his name. Simon, I told you about him, as well as Vaughan, when you proposed to me. Please show your respect to Clive and call him by his name. Clive at least deserves that."

As Anne rummaged in her gaudy handbag, Alba retrieved from under the table the framed photograph of Clive, with all his Squadron comrades in front of, and on the wings of, a Lancaster bomber. Alba walked past Helen and David and stood in front of Anne and said:

"I think you ought to have this."

As Alba resumed her place at her end of the table, Anne, lost to the sands of time, carefully moved her finger along to the twelfth man from the left on the second row and stared at the young face looking out. She stared until finally she held the picture tight to her chest and fought back the emotions – and Simon suddenly saw, in his wife's tear-filled eyes, the depth and pain of love that he, Simon, had never been able to give her. In that moment, all he had the wherewithal to say was:

"I didn't kill Vaughan. I didn't follow Tom in."

"No, you didn't follow Tom in. That accolade falls to the minister here. Doesn't it, Reverend Quinn?"

Everyone turned to the minister.

"Me?" offered back Reverend Quinn.

"Yes," said Neale. "I was standing in the corridor to the toilets and the front doors – or are they the back doors? I still don't know, anyway the doors to the roadside of the building. You didn't see me as you came in but I saw you. Why did you come in? It wasn't for the toilets as everyone else seems to be claiming, for you'd have flushed me out – excuse the pun – or to take some food, for you didn't. So, why did you enter?"

"It's a bit awkward, really. I'd prefer not to say, if it's all the same to everyone."

"Oh, come now vicar," said William Chapman. "Mrs Lyle has shared things with us, I've allowed my memory to be restored for I've accepted I probably went in at some stage in the morning and Simon has been put in his place by most of the women in this room this afternoon. The least you can therefore do is admit you went in too."

"I'd rather not say," repeated Reverend Quinn.

"Interesting," said William. "I mean, my money was on Tom up until a few moments ago and, as my dear elder brother will tell you, I do like my bets, but it would seem that Miss White here and her friend Neale have, err how shall I describe it? Hmmm, how about a little parable for the godly man; something like Miss White and Neale have moved a log and found you creeping about in what was the dark and the dirt underneath it. And what is interesting, it would now seem that if you went in after Tom and didn't discover Vaughan with a knife in his back, given you didn't alert anyone, then that would very clearly indeed make you the last person to see him alive and, by definition, the person who stabbed him." William then looked past the Reverend, to Alba, and said:

"I salute you, my dear, you have done what none of us thought you would. You have exonerated Tom and found the real killer."

Then, turning to his right, William spoke to Barnes and said:

"Barnes, if you would be so good as to call the police; I think this church man has a few questions to answer."

With that William retrieved his box of matches, gave them a hearty shake, as if he were trying to get one to ignite without having to remove it from the box, and said to the room as a whole:

"Yes, well done Miss White. Not quite sure why he murdered him or, in fact, Mrs Taylor as well but I'm sure the police will establish that. And still not a word from you, vicar. Bit awkward, I guess, what with being a 'man of God' but also a double murderer."

Barnes, being Barnes, though, waited for his Lordship's instructions to call the police. Lord Hartfield, however, sensing further developments held back, which allowed the Reverend to speak and Barnes, instead, to add another log to the fire.

"First," said Reverend Quinn but William cut him short as he did so.

"Oh, found your tongue, have you? What will it be? A confession, claim you won't do it again and ask for us all to forgive you."

"First," repeated Reverend Quinn, "your log description wasn't a story with a meaning, which is what a parable is, it was nothing more than a comparison."

"Oh, don't get all theological with me as a way of deflecting your guilt."

"And second, it's a tad awkward explaining my presence because…"

"Because it makes you culpable, perhaps?" suggested Simon.

"No," replied Reverend Quinn. "Because Chloe is here." He looked to the young woman, with her back to one of the large windows, standing next to Sam, mouthed a 'sorry' and then continued:

"I had been trying to write my sermon for the original date of Chloe's confirmation service. But something had been troubling me about Chloe, or more specifically, a possible boyfriend of hers. You see, I'd been in the pub the night before and had heard Tom talk to a friend about a new girl called Chloe, who was working up at the Hall, and how he wanted to ask her out. I had nothing against Tom as such but, since I didn't know him, I was just a bit concerned whether a new boyfriend might distract her from the commitment she was about to make to the church family. I just felt I needed a bit more information about him and also a fresh take on Chloe herself. Oh dear, this sounds so 'big brotherly' but it never felt like that – I just wanted to make sure Chloe's decision to get confirmed – that is to give her voice, if you like, to the infant baptism she received sixteen years ago – was sound. Or, to put it another way, that, unlike the seed that fell on the rocky ground, her faith was deep rooted enough to withstand the thrill of a new boyfriend; in simple terms, was her faith strong enough to invite him to church on a Sunday evening or would she end up in a beer garden or a cinema at that time with him instead each week? So, I went to speak to Vaughan, who I knew knew Tom and also knew Chloe through church. I remembered Vaughan telling me he would be watching the cricket that day, so I went to find him there. I did but I found him in the pavilion talking to Tom. It wasn't right to disturb them, especially as it was, in part, Tom himself I wanted to talk about with Vaughan. So, I left and went back to the vicarage."

"I'd wondered why you turned up that day," commented Alba.

"I didn't murder Vaughan, I wish to add," said Reverend Quinn.

"Oh, I know," replied Alba. "No-one did."

*

"What?" said everyone in unison a moment later, save for David.

"At least," Alba added, "not until Lord Hartfield had wrung the bell to suspend play and everyone was watching the fly-past. You see, if Tom didn't do it, everyone who came in, before Tom left, couldn't have murdered Vaughan."

"Excuse me for asking," said a puzzled Lord Hartfield, "why then have we been going through everyone's movements that morning?"

"Twofold, if you like," replied Alba. "First, to demonstrate to everyone here, especially the guilty person, how important attention to detail is, for that was critical in my solving who had done it. Second, to establish who was in close proximity to the pavilion – for the murderer went in when everyone else was standing rooted to the spot, looking up, captivated by the sight and sound of those old aeroplanes as they dominated the clear, blue, June sky. That person realised they had an opportunity to act, not much more than a couple of minutes, they'd have guessed. I don't think they woke up that morning intending to kill but when they grasped that Vaughan was out of sight but in close proximity and everyone else around was fixated with something else unfolding, they seized their chance. Personally, I find that more chilling than if they had diligently planned it – that they took life so spontaneously is frightening to my mind."

"Someone went in, you say, when we were watching the planes?" said Lord Hartfield, as he processed what Alba had just said. "We've been discussing my movements, as well as William's, Neale's, the Reverend's, Simon's and Mrs Lyle's? You're inferring one of us did it, aren't you? My word, I don't believe it."

"Yes, I am – though it couldn't have been Neale for he was back with me on the far side of the pitch. He just couldn't have got there and back in the time. Not that I ever, ever, not for one moment, thought it was you, my dear dear friend," she said as she looked to where he was standing. As Neale smiled an understanding smile back, Alba added:

"But someone did go back in. They suddenly realised, having been in once and seen the layout, they had an opportunity when they realised everyone else was literally looking the other way."

Alba paused. She twisted her cup a full three hundred and sixty degrees on its saucer, took four deep breaths and then said:

"You went back in, didn't you William?"

*

Everyone looked to William to watch his reaction, everyone that is save for Lord Hartfield himself. He didn't turn to study his younger brother's face, rather he stood up, from where he was seated at the table and said, in no uncertain tones:

"Miss White. I understand your desire to help your friend Tom. We have accommodated your plea for a room to gather in, given you our time and, at your request, Barnes has laid out refreshments. However, what you have just inferred is wholly unacceptable."

"But…" attempted Alba in reply but his Lordship cut her short.

"No 'buts' Miss White. What you have just said is very offensive. You have abused our hospitality, you have offended the Hartfield family name and, more personally, you have insulted my dear brother. You are to apologise now and you are to surrender your volunteer's card on your way out for you are no longer welcome here. I am disappointed in you."

With that, and with having got the room's undivided attention, his Lordship sat down as he awaited an apology.

No apology came. However, as Alba slid her volunteer's card the length of the table to his Lordship, in a way that Sam Malone would have been proud of doing with a full beer glass in the 'Cheers' bar, she said:

"You are welcome to this card but I guarantee you will be offering it back to me before the hour is out."

"I don't think so," replied Edward Chapman.

"As for an apology," continued Alba, "I am afraid all I can say is that the truth sometimes does indeed hurt. I would have wished it to have been an 'outsider', some rogue person travelling through our village who murdered two people. For we, but especially you, would have then been spared the pain of it being 'one of our own'. But it was someone from within the village, more specifically someone from within your beautiful home, and that will be painful to confront. However, an innocent person is languishing in prison whilst the culprit has been free; free to pop down to the village shop, to drive his car, to wine and dine at Hillstone Hall every evening. I will tell you, tell everyone here in fact, how he did it, why he did it and how I came to find him out. I will begin."

"Miss White, I have never heard such claptrap in all my…"

Yet his Lordship was cut short as Andrew stepped towards his grandfather, placed a hand on the elderly man's shoulder and calmly said:

"Grandad, I sense we should hear Miss White out."

"Do you? Why?"

"Let's just hear what she has to say." Then, speaking to Alba directly, Andrew simply said:

"Miss White, would you please explain."

*

"The 'how' is pretty straight-forward. As we've already considered this afternoon, William was part of His Lordship's group standing right behind where I was sitting with Vaughan on the wooden bench. Anyone within that group was close enough to act. William, unlike Anne, would have known it was Vaughan they were right behind, having seen him around the Hall these past few months, coupled with the fact I was with him. William would have witnessed Mrs Lyle's histrionics and heard Vaughan's claim he was going off to the toilets. Having already been in to the pavilion once, undoubtedly to legitimately use the toilets himself on that first occasion, he would have grasped the layout of it, then with Vaughan not re-appearing coupled with the fly-past he gambled."

Alba paused momentarily – she would admit afterwards, purely for effect:

"Gambled that he wouldn't be noticed if he disappeared for two minutes. After all, everyone else was looking upwards and, given how exposed the cricket ground is, we were all studying the sky for several minutes. It doesn't take long to walk a few yards, nip in via the doors that open on to the parking area and stick a knife in the back of a sleeping man. He came away with the carrier bag with the medals in, realising there was a chance to plant them on someone else along with the knife he'd taken from the pavilion.

As for Mrs Taylor, I suspect William's plant knowledge is not so poor as I suspect he makes out – you can't run your own ranch in South America without a little horticultural knowledge. So, one Tuesday evening, when he knew Tom would be out, he went to Mrs Taylor's with some leaves from the aconite plant and mixed them into her salad."

As Alba paused, William clapped ever so slowly. He then spoke:

"Well done Miss White. Everything you have just said is entirely possible. But you could apply that same theory to Edward, Simon, Anne, anyone within reach of the pavilion. A nice theory but tenuous at the very best – almost anyone could have committed those two murders."

"Oh, I agree," said Alba. "But not the third murder – no-one else at the cricket match was present at the scene of the third murder unlike yourself."

"What the blazes," exclaimed Lord Hartfield. "You're alleging there's more? You've completely lost it."

Everyone else, save David, was equally stunned and at a complete loss, as they each, individually searched their short-term memories for someone else who had died since Mrs Taylor.

"Your Lordship and, I suspect, everyone else here save David, since he and I went through everything last night once the last piece of evidence was finally in our hands, your mental search for a third death will be futile. No-one has died since Mrs Taylor. You are all, as it were, looking the wrong way. There is a saying that *life is full of endings and partings but so few of us notice the beginnings and the arrivals*. It had been playing on my mind for some time that perhaps Vaughan's death was not the beginning of this tragedy. Whatever else I may now think about William, he is not detached from reality; there would have been reasons to his actions. Consequently, I realised I would have to look backwards, not forwards. It was when I was speaking to Anne, in the gardens here last week, just how far back I had to go; the 'beginning' of the story lies back almost in a different time and definitely in a different country; the time was June 1944 and the place was Tilly-sur-Seulles in France."

Alba then relayed, to those gathered in the music room, the wartime experience of Vaughan, as Anne had relayed it to her, when the two women had sat overlooking the Hall's solitary tennis court. Alba described how Vaughan, having been ordered back to seek out new orders, despite being injured himself, came upon a British Officer and a Sergeant who were with a young German soldier who was attempting to surrender. How Vaughan witnessed the Officer shoot dead the German and proceed to loot the body, taking a watch, a ring and something that was bulky and shiny – but discarding a notebook. That a stray shell exploding saved Vaughan's life; for it knocked out the Officer and killed the Sergeant, who had been about to shoot Vaughan, given Vaughan had seen what the other two had done. Finally, Alba relayed how Vaughan retrieved the book and, Vaughan being Vaughan, took the now injured and unconscious

Officer back to a first aid post, even though the Officer had moments before instructed his Sergeant to murder Vaughan.

"That's as you told it to me, isn't it, Anne?" concluded Alba.

"Yes," Anne replied. "And that's exactly as Vaughan relayed it to me all those years ago. Miss White has not exaggerated nor included any detail that didn't first come from Vaughan."

Then turning to William, Alba stated:

"You were that British Officer, weren't you William?"

"Even if I was in France in '44…" replied William but Alba interrupted him.

"Army records show you were in Normandy."

"Miss White, a lot of men were in Normandy. Don't forget we had literally just broken out of the beachhead. And yes, I have scars on my legs but a lot of us picked up injuries as we fought for King and country. I fear you have decided you want me to be the guilty party and are coming up with similarities in my life and Vaughan's and convincing yourself it's all linked."

"What was the connection to Mrs Taylor?" asked Sam.

"Blackmail, of sorts," replied Alba. "She'd made the connection between Vaughan and William's army days. I reckon from her photographic display in the Orangery. Some of you will remember there was a great unveiling, one Wednesday evening, when even the local press had sent someone along to report on this new display the Hall was putting on."

At which point Alba retrieved a copy of the 'East Sussex Gazette' from her bag and placed it on the table.

"Page five, if anyone wants a look later, has the article and a picture, showing the table with all the photographs and with his Lordship, his brother, Mrs Taylor and Tom all smiling back. Vaughan's photograph, the one he wanted on the table in the Orangery, not that you can make it out from this newspaper article, was of him as a soldier during his time in France." Alba paused and looked to David.

At the prompt, David retrieved a black and white photo from

the envelope he was holding and placed it on the table next to the newspaper.

"This is the photograph of Vaughan. Andrew and I found it in Tom's bedroom. It had been hidden in a picture frame to start with but then moved to be amongst Tom's army re-enactment gear under his bed." Alba looked directly at William as she added:

"It was in a bag under his bed. You'd been to the property once or twice previously to look for it, probably whilst Mrs Taylor was working up at the Hall and you used the estate keys to let yourself in. You were desperate to get it, for it links you to Vaughan. It was there all the time, hidden amongst a bundle of other black and white photographs of Tom and his re-enactment friends – it was there but you missed it. I didn't," stated Alba defiantly.

Alba thought she saw just a slight furrowing of William's eyebrows but it was a momentary change in his facial expression before he reverted to how he had been before.

Alba continued:

"Mrs Taylor having suspected William of Vaughan's murder, realised she had been given an opportunity to repay the debt, she would never have otherwise been able to clear, to Mrs Lyle. I wonder, but only William will be able to tell us, whether she was blunt and direct and asked for a lump sum to stay quiet or whether, which is my preferred idea, she was subtle and just hinted at what she knew and just hinted that she was in need of money to clear a debt she'd taken on for her nephew. Either way, William couldn't take the risk. He bought her silence once."

"Which allowed her to pay me back," added Mrs Lyle.

"Quite," concurred Alba. "Then, whether she hinted she might like some more or not, William decided to silence her and, in the bargain, further incriminate Tom. He selected a Tuesday when he knew Tom would be in the pub and put his plan into action, being very careful to tidy up after himself as Mrs Taylor lay poisoned in the other room. Unfortunately for him, he was a tad too tidy."

"If it is not too ridiculous a question, Miss White," said William. "How would I have known Tom would be out on a Tuesday?"

"Simple. There'd been a 'heads of department' meeting, which, amongst other things, had discussed the photographs in the Orangery and that Andrew wanted to invite a newspaper reporter along. Tom asked for it not to be on a Tuesday evening as he had a ritual of going to the pub that night of the week."

"Course, he did," said Sam. "As I said earlier, Tuesday is pie night."

Addressing Lord Hartfield, Alba said:

"I think, your Lordship, that if you ask Barnes here to retrieve the minutes he undoubtedly took during that meeting, you will find that not only did Tom make such an 'innocent' request but that William was present in that meeting."

"We will see, Miss White," replied Lord Hartfield. "May I point out you have given us an account of what was possible. Nothing you have said is impossible, no dinosaurs have had to step onto the page, if you like, to make your theory work. But it is only a theory. A creative one, I will grant you, but finding a missing photograph, searching for a six-month-old local newspaper article and a pink post-it note in Vaughan's old journal doesn't prove a thing. Conjecture is what you have given us, nothing more. I agree with my brother – you seem to have come up with a theory in your head and then fitted him into it."

The calmness of one brother was in contrast to the other as William suddenly said, as he stormed across the room:

"I've had enough of this claptrap and nonsense!"

With that he picked up the black and white photograph, of a man in uniform, which lay on the table in front of Alba and tore it in half. He then picked up the journal and, together with the torn photo, went to the fireplace and threw the items into the flames.

"Your theory," he said defiantly, as he threw in his entire box of matches which added, if not petrol to the fire, literally a box of matches to the fire, "has gone up in smoke."

For a moment everyone watched the fire, as it roared up and consumed the items William had just thrown onto it.

"I don't think so," stated Alba, as she recaptured everyone's attention. "And that is why Mrs Taylor's hiding place was just so absolutely amazingly perfect."

As Andrew realised what Alba had done, he said, to no-one else's understanding bar Alba's:

"The best place to hide a book is in a library."

She smiled back at him, as she remembered the disgruntled elderly women in the café, as she and Andrew swore their way through solving the puzzle, the thrill of the hunt and the sweat on their bodies, as they ran back to Mrs Taylor's home, on the day they found Vaughan's photo. She spoke to William, who had turned once more to watch the fire lick itself around the journal:

"All you've done is destroy a perfectly decent photograph of Tom in his re-enactment gear. Vaughan's photograph is here." With that, she removed a white envelope from between the pages of the 'East Sussex Gazette' and duly extracted the picture from within. "Very similar, you'll agree, especially when one is grabbed in haste to destroy in an open fire. And," even though everyone knew what she was about to say, "alongside the photo of Tom, you've just burnt my old diary, which I started to keep after I got engaged, thinking any children, I might have had, might want to read it one day. If anything, I'm quite grateful you've burnt it."

"It's amazing how weathered my boys got it to look," said David. "Just a few days with them – think they treated it a bit like a rugby ball – and it was roughed up quite well. What with some spilt coffee, in true "Blue Peter' make your own pirate's map' style, I think we got the look Alba asked for."

"And for those who are interested," said Alba, mentally letting go of the last painful memory of her failed romance, "the 'post-it' note marked the day when, so I later learnt, my fiancé first cheated on me."

After a further rummage in her bag, Alba, to no-one's surprise, not even Lord Hartfield's, brought out Vaughan's journal. This time, though, she didn't place it on the table, she held it ever so tightly. She also brought out a pair of holstered secateurs, which she effortlessly clipped to the base of her spine. She spoke once more – "The bag is almost empty."

As she instinctively tapped the holstered secateurs, she continued:

"I have, as I said I would do, explained how William did it and why he did it – to silence Vaughan and then Mrs Taylor in order that William's first murder remained secret. Maybe it was, in part, to spare his brother the shame, were the wartime truth ever to get out, but mostly, I reckon, it was his own self-interest. The only thing I will never know is whether Vaughan realised the significance of the photograph he had selected for the table in the Orangery. Did he use the one he did, having recognised William himself, as a 'shot across the bows', as it were, or was it just chance? What I must finally do – actually before that, Sam, would you be a dear and pour me a cup of tea? I'm just parched."

"Course," said Sam.

"Sorry, where was I? Oh, yes. What I must do is explain how I know; to turn theory and conjecture into fact and that begins with a 'why'. Why, of the things Vaughan bequeathed to the five of us, did he change his mind and swop two of them around? Tom was meant to have the journal and I was to get the secateurs. However, as Reverend Quinn, Matthew, said during the funeral, Vaughan changed his mind. Why? For weeks I mulled over why Vaughan didn't want Tom to have the journal. Why did I have to have it? But, not for the first time, I was looking at things in the wrong order, for the question should have been 'why couldn't I have the secateurs?'"

With that, Alba removed the secateurs from their holster with her left hand, tried to use them on an imaginary plant in front of her and declared:

"Bloody useless, excuse my French. I mean, Swiss made, top quality, but to me bloody useless. Why is that?"

As she slid them back in to their holster and mouthed a silent 'thank you' to Sam, on the arrival of a fresh cup of tea, she looked to Reverend Quinn and continued:

"I had a fine meal with Matthew last Tuesday in 'The Sun and Moon'. As Sam brought over our puddings, she caught me turning my pudding spoon around. She asked why I'd moved it – since I hadn't cleaned it in the process, I hadn't swopped it for another from a different table, I simply turned it around. As I explained to her then, and for the same reason why Vaughan's secateurs are useless to me, I'm left-handed. The spoon in the pub was laid out for a right-handed person to use, so instinctively I turned it around because I would naturally pick it up with my left. It's why Vaughan changed his original ideas around, for he knew I could never use what he wanted me to have. Tom, though, being right-handed, like Vaughan, would obviously be able to use then. I therefore got the journal. But as I was explaining to Sam about the spoon, a barrage of images came flooding into my mind. Snapshots of things that had happened over the weeks, all cascaded through my mind; a toddler pulling his mother across a prison courtyard by her left hand, Neale saluting Vaughan on the day of the fateful cricket match with his left hand and Vaughan saying *wrong hand, Neale, you've used the wrong hand, people salute with the right*, Tom's photo in the Orangery where you can see his holstered secateurs on his right hip, finding Mrs Taylor's TV remote control down the right-hand side of her armchair. All these images," repeated Alba.

She paused, took a sip of tea in the knowledge that she had the whole room's undivided attention, took another sip and delivered her *coup de grâce*:

"And yet the kettle in Mrs Taylor's kitchen, given it wasn't plugged in in some corner, rather it was in the middle of the counter, was pointing to the right, in that the handle was on the left. People always pick up kettles with their dominant hand, with the weight inwards, because that's the way you pour. Whoever was with Mrs Taylor on that fateful day, maybe as they lulled her into a false sense of security by offering to make a cup of tea as she counted some money, enabling them to be in the kitchen by themselves, or maybe afterwards, to pour boiling water over something they wanted to clean, was left-handed. Someone else had to be there, for Mrs Taylor was right-handed. I found the remote down the right-hand side of her favourite chair, plus Tom confirmed she was right-handed and also, as an aside, that she tended to leave washing up to the next morning. Tom also was right-handed. A left-handed person was present at the scene that evening. His Lordship, who I've been watching as he's drunk his coffee this afternoon, is right-handed, so too, Simon. Andrew, equally, is right-handed, for I watched him sign a sympathy card at this very table a few days ago. Whereas William is left-handed. I watched him sign the card too."

Alba unclipped Vaughan's secateurs and placed them on the table amongst everything else. From her bag she retrieved her final items – her own pair of left-handed red-handled secateurs, which she once again effortlessly clipped on as smoothly as doing up a zip, and a transparent plastic money bag, with its 'Midland Bank' griffin logo on, the type you used when handing in bundles of loose change to the bank. Within the clear plastic little bag were some oval discs. For now, though, she placed the bank bag and its contents in her pocket.

"Next, within this journal," said Alba, as she wiggled the book in her hand, "is a sketch. A very faded drawing but one sketched by a young man. Someone probably just in his twenties, if that, perhaps during a lull in a battle or in the back of an army truck, as Rommel moved this young man and his comrades around. A sketch maybe of his family crest, maybe of the town from which he came from or perhaps it has some regimental significance. And that drawing, within this journal, will match the engraving on William's silver cigarette case. I've only seen half of that engraving and this journal sketch is faded but I think you all will see they match. Useful you burnt the wrong book, isn't it William?"

William, indeed the whole room, remained in stunned silence, which, given they were in the old music room, seemed an insult to the room itself. As the chink of pottery echoed around, as Alba replaced her cup, she nodded, for what would be the final time that afternoon to David.

David, as before, stepped towards the table and took out a further two photographs and placed them before Alba.

"And finally," said Alba, "perhaps your Lordship would like photographic proof." And in the way she had slid her volunteer's card along the table to Lord Hartfield, she slid the two photographs.

"Two photos. Taken by David's boys on the day of the cricket match. This evidence has been in David's camera ever since and none of us knew. Just to be clear," said Alba directly to William, "the negatives are stored somewhere safely, out of your reach, so feel free to burn these too but further copies exist in David's home, my home and, as I say, the negatives are hidden elsewhere. It was when I was taking a photograph of some visitors here last week, and they were very precise that I had to capture their children in the background of the shot, that I wondered about any photographs people may have taken on the day Vaughan died and what they might have inadvertently captured."

As Lord Hartfield studied the pictures, others gathered around him to also look. They could make out, in one, an image of William walking towards the pavilion and, in the other, of him walking away from it.

"David's lads took a whole roll. These are just two and the numbering on the negatives prove, and David will agree with me here, that I haven't just selected two that 'fit a preconceived theory'. Images Tommy and Arthur captured before and after have the Lancaster, Spitfire and Hurricane in. These images could only have been taken during the fly-past."

"You see," said David, "I'd asked my boys to take some pictures of me playing cricket and some of the planes too, when they came over. But, boys being boys, they were in their own world and playing cricket in the practice nets most of the morning."

"That's right," added Neale, "I walked past them on my way to check up on Vaughan, remember."

"So," continued David, "only when they heard the planes did one of them remember to use my camera. They didn't get one of me but, thanks to the telephoto lens I'd put on, they got a few half decent ones of the planes and, not that I realised it at the time, given the place they were taking them from, on that side of the ground, some very useful ones of the pavilion and the people around it. In one of this sequence you can make out Mrs Rowan and Sam standing outside the pavilion next to his Lordship, in one you can make out some of the fielders including Justin, one is just grass and one is just sky…"

"They're better cricketers than photographers it would seem," said Neale.

"I think so, too," replied David. "Still, these two pictures we have here are very very interesting, don't you all think?"

"I thought," said Alba, "I was looking for a change in the village, in a relationship, in something around Easter time. That was when Vaughan was getting nervous, that was when he paid his gardener months up front, co-incidentally that was when Justin moved to the village, but it was back in December that I should have gone for the trigger."

"Why December?" enquired Mrs Lyle.

"Because," said Lord Hartfield, with his eyes closed and his voice heavy with sadness, "that was when William returned from Chile." Lord Hartfield opened his eyes and turned to his younger brother:

"You always joked the war had been good for you. Seems your looting in Europe set you up for life over there in the Americas. May I have a look at your silver cigarette case, the one that once belonged to a young German, so it would now seem?"

William Chapman walked from where he had been by the, now dying, fire to his brother. He placed the case down on the table. As he did so, Alba retrieved the little bank bag from her pocket and handed it to William.

"What's this?" William said with a kind of hollow, empty voice.

"Thirty seed heads from the *Lunaria* plant. Commonly referred to as honesty because, as you can see, the seed heads are translucent. Equally, the seed heads give it its Latin name, as they look like the full moon. In Denmark, which I know isn't Germany but I thought it was close enough, it is known as *judaspenge* – coins of Judas – which, to my mind, seems fitting."

At that point, Alba turned to Reverend Quinn and said:

"Matthew's Gospel, chapter 27 verses 3 to 10 but especially verse 4. But don't take my word for it."

"No, I'll re-read it myself later," replied Matthew.

As Lord Hartfield held his brother's silver cigarette case, William slowly walked out of the room onto the terrace and stood there. Had he gone out of sight half of the occupants of the room would have gone after him. But he just stood, staring at nothing in particular; just staring.

Lord Hartfield turned the case over in his hand one further time, he asked Alba to show him the faded drawing in Vaughan's journal, looked again at the two photographs and then said:

"Barnes, would you be so kind as to get the Chief Constable on the telephone in my study. Also, please ask Lady Hartfield to join me there."

As Barnes departed, Lord Hartfield said to Alba, as he handed her William's cigarette case:

"I'm not sure if I can say 'thank you' for what you have just done but you have my sincere apologies. Please also accept this back." With that, Lord Hartfield placed Alba's volunteer's card back in her left hand.

"It would be my pleasure," she replied.

As his Lordship exited the room, and as Neale helped himself to a further piece of Mrs Rowan's millionaire's shortbread, Andrew spoke:

"Got to hand it to you, that was remarkable. Truly remarkable. One question springs to mind."

"Just one?" mused Helen.

"Just one for now," continued Andrew. "Given I found Vaughan's wartime photograph with you, I'd like to know where you have hidden David's negatives?"

Alba smiled to herself. She gave a doe-eyed look to Sam, who got the hint and went and made a further, slightly stewed, cup of tea for her. As Sam did so, Alba moved to the fireplace and very gingerly lifted down the vase, the one she had placed there earlier and which had come from Mrs Taylor's office. Alba said:

"There's a matching one of these in Mrs Taylor's home."

"Is there?" commented Simon. "Oh, that changes its value altogether."

"Does it?" answered Alba.

"Absolutely. A matching pair, I reckon about £20. By itself, lucky to get a fiver but two would more than double the value."

"Twenty pounds," said Alba. "Really?"

"On a good day but then you've got to take off my commission, so probably best his Lordship just keeps them as flower vases."

"Right here," said Alba as she placed her hand inside and retrieved a strip of negatives. "David told me not to be so reckless as to hide them in here but, as with smuggling a picture of Chloe in to prison for Tom, the drama got to me."

With that she handed the negatives back to David and gratefully received the drink from Sam.

*

The following Tuesday, Alba was back in the gardeners' bothy getting ready for the day as Sally came in.

"Morning Sally," said Helen. "Kettle's just boiled. Drink?"

"Yes please, plus I just want to update you all on a couple of things."

With that David took off the battered old leather hat that he'd just placed on his head. As he sat down, he looked at it and conceded to himself, as he waited for Sally to speak, that it needed a bit of polish once again.

"Good news," said Sally as she appreciatively took a cup from Helen. "I've just had a meeting with his Lordship and his grandson and yes the rumour is indeed correct. Mr Parker has handed his resignation in and been allowed to leave with immediate effect; got a job at some large gardens over in Hampshire. I will continue to act up but now as acting head not acting deputy until Tom returns. The even better news, which came through at ten past eight this morning apparently, is that Tom is to be released later today once the prison have completed some paperwork their end. William Chapman was charged with two counts of murder last night. They are still investigating the third, I mean the first, but that's not for Tom to worry about. His Lordship will insist Tom takes a few weeks off but will return as Head Gardener when he is ready."

"That's brilliant news," said David.

"An answer to prayer," said Helen.

Alba, meanwhile, simply afforded herself the tiniest of smiles and reflected on a job well done.

"Oh, one other thing," added Sally. "The Hall has had someone make enquiries about becoming a garden volunteer. Says she knows very little about horticulture but is keen to learn and will be happy to do all the mundane tasks to begin with. Given we need all the help we can get, I left her a message to ask her to come in for a chat. Says she can't do many days as she has childcare issues and has to visit a family member every Monday but has heard all about the gardens here; she said the way someone described them to her, made them sound like 'something from a fairy tale'. So, she'll be enthusiastic if nothing else. Let's hope we can keep her. Her name is —"

"Jackie, short for Jacqueline, but I think Jacs suits her best," said Alba.

Acknowledgements

Lieutenant Colonel Gordon Chesney Wilson, Royal Horse Guards, Member of the Royal Victorian Order, Mentioned in Dispatches, does lie in the Zillebeke churchyard in Belgium. He, with the personal message on his headstone, can be found at plot B2. Aged 49, he died on 6th November 1914.

Glyndwr Michael served (in death) as Major William Martin, Royal Marines, as his part in Operation Mincemeat. He is buried in Nuestra Señora de la Soledad cemetery in Huelva, Spain, grave number 1886. In 2002, Isabel Naylor de Mendes was awarded the MBE for tending the grave for forty years.

All other military personnel written about within this book are fictitious.

WAAF stands for Women's Auxiliary Air Force.

*

'The Two Brewers' in Chipperfield, Hertfordshire is a real pub. It is a delightful country pub in a beautiful village. However, the last time I visited, when I asked for something from the local brewery, I was served a 'Doom Bar'. I remain puzzled. Not that any characters in this book are even remotely meant to be myself, I couldn't pass up the humour of that moment and not include it somewhere in this story. 'The Sun and Moon' public house is, by contrast, entirely fictitious.

*

I have used a quote by Pam Brown. I came across it in the book 'Seize the day! Enjoy the moment', published by Helen Exley (www. helenexley.com). Helen Exley, who hold the copyright, have kindly granted me permission to use the quote.

I have quoted the odd line from Douglas Adams' 'The Hitch-Hiker's Guide to the Galaxy'. The original radio scripts were published by Pan Books. As a novel it was published by Book Club Associates (hardback) and Pan Books (paperback). There were five books in the 'trilogy'. Douglas Adams was taken before his time. His writing remains brilliant.

I have used a saying of Catherine Douzel. I first came across this quote on my tea-tray at a café in Girona, Spain. I have been unable to trace anything else about her or who, if anyone, holds copyright to that quote.

I have made fleeting references to some of the classic TV programmes from years past – shows my characters would culturally identify with. I wish, here, to acknowledge the creative genius of the writers and the main actors who brought those shows about:

'Open all Hours' – written by Roy Clarke and featuring Ronnie Barker, David Jason and Lynda Baron.

'Only Fools and Horses' – written by John Sullivan and featuring David Jason, Nicholas Lyndhurst, Lennard Pearce and Buster Merryfield.

'Blackadder' – written by Rowan Atkinson, Ben Elton and Richard Curtis and featuring Rowan Atkinson, Tony Robinson, Hugh Laurie, Stephen Fry, Miranda Richardson and Tim McInnerny.

'The Two Ronnies' – many writers contributed to this show, including 'Gerald Wiley'. It, of course, starred Ronnie Barker and Ronnie Corbett.

'Mr Benn' – created by David McKee.

'Cheers' – produced by James Burrows, Glen and Les Charles and starred Ted Danson, Shelley Long, Nicholas Colasanto, Rhea Perlman and Woody Harrelson.

*

I would like to thank my brother-in-law, Nigel Head, for the original cover design that he created for this book and which forms the basis of the cover design which we now have.

I would like to thank Sybil Coombes, James Hogg and Sally Cassie, three fine teachers of English, for being points of contact at the proof-reading stage.

I would also like to thank Philip Panton, from the Lincolnshire Aviation Heritage Centre (www.lincsaviation.co.uk), for his advice on Chapter 20 of this book.

Finally, I would like to thank the team at Troubador Publishing Ltd. You've guided me through the post-writing stage expertly and are a pleasure to work with. Here's to working together again on the second book in the Alba White series:

Sandcastles by The Jupiter Hotel

To my darling Clare